This is a work of fiction. Names, characters, places, and incidents either are the product of the author's imagination or are used fictitiously. Any resemblance to actual persons, living or dead, events, or locales is entirely coincidental.

Copyright © 2022 by Lewis F. Clements

All rights reserved. No part of this book may be reproduced or used in any manner without written permission of the copyright owner except for the use of quotations in a book review. For more information, address: lewis.clements2@outlook.com

First paperback edition

Cover design by Simon Herman.
simonherman.co.uk

ISBN
ISBN (ebook)
www.lewisfclements.co.uk

This book is dedicated to my late wife Lesley and our four adult children, Zoe, Lucy, Jack and Christopher.

All of whom I am immensely proud.

One.

Professor Mary Elizabeth Kelso was a highly accomplished colorectal surgeon, who had worked for the NHS for several years until a dispute with a senior colleague had forced her to resign. The senior colleague had in fact made a mistake whilst operating on a woman and gone on holiday the next day. Mary had been brought in to remedy the error and had stated quite clearly that a mistake had been made in the original operation. The lady subsequently died.

The family sued the hospital and surgeon for clinical negligence and her colleague, the senior surgeon and head of the colorectal department had wanted her to give evidence to the court to say that it wasn't an error but 'adhesions' that had caused the problem.

Mary refused to tell a deliberate lie to the court. Her managers tried to put pressure on her to back up the lie that her colleague was going to tell the court, she refused point blank to commit perjury and was told in no uncertain terms, that, if she didn't back him up she would have to resign.

Which she duly did and looked for employment outside the NHS. Soon she found herself heading a cancer research team at MPharma in London where she had now worked for the best part of five years.

Now Mary and her team comprising four plus herself had made a startling discovery, they had just finished checking all the data from the exhaustive tests and trials that they had spent the last five years working on. They had verified their results for the umpteenth time and then copied all the data to two flash drives. Years of work, patience and perseverance had just paid off, big time. They had at last found a cure for all types of cancer.

Mary left her lab at around 19.00 hrs and went home. She, along with her colleagues were elated, they had achieved what they had set out to do. To cure cancer. Mary having seen once how all was not as it should be amongst the medical profession and the health service wanted to make sure that her team got full credit for this breakthrough. Arriving home she had a bite to eat and then, she waited until it was dark, left her mobile phone on the kitchen table and slipped out through the back door and across her large garden and exited onto the passage that ran the length of the road behind the houses, all the houses in her road are detached with large established gardens. Most were built at the beginning of the 20th century.

She reached the back of her friend's house, Robert Simpson a retired solicitor, his house is several doors down from her own. She crossed his garden and knocked on the back door, Robert opened it almost immediately, having watched her walk up the lawn towards the house. Mary left the flash drive with him, saying it is simply a precaution, but to keep it hidden and safe and not mention or part with it to anyone. Mary's main concern was that someone could steal her data. She wanted to make sure that it is in a safe place, after all the team's hard work, she wasn't about to let it fall into the wrong hands. She knew full well that should there be any problems later, Robert would confirm the date and time that she had given him the flash drive that contained all the details and test results for the cure.

The following day she had a meeting with her boss, the CEO of MPharma, Anthony Scarsdale and explained to him in great detail, what she and her team have developed.

She said. "To sum up, we have developed a cure for all known types of cancer – simple - 100% effective – few doses – and cheap to produce and administer. We have tested it to destruction, it works every time. With this cure cancer will become a thing of the past. It will be gone from our lives altogether."

Scarsdale rather than congratulating her said. "I see." His tone was worrying her as he seemed less than enthusiastic about a major breakthrough which had worldwide implications.

Prof Mary said to her boss. "I think that we should make an immediate announcement and let the world know that a cure, one that actually works, has been found."

Scarsdale said, "I think that we should hold back, for the time being. We don't want to be too hasty."

Prof Mary said "Whilst I agree with you that any announcement needs to be thought through, I think that we should make an announcement in 48 hrs, it should not be delayed longer as the NHS will take time over their approval process, and the sooner that is done, the sooner hope and relief can be brought to millions of people worldwide. Not to mention the ones that will die in the meantime."

Scarsdale said, "We have to take the time to consider the ramifications of such a discovery, particularly the effect that it would have on our business. I will need to talk with the board in the US as they would have to have the last word regarding any announcement."

Prof Mary is astonished with his reaction, but she is no fool, she understands the situation completely, and the financial loss to the company and the larger cancer industry would be astronomical.

Mary was angry and said, "If you aren't willing to make an announcement, then I will."

Scarsdale told her, "that would be a bad move, very bad indeed."

Leaving the meeting she thought. 'Have I just been threatened? It certainly sounded like it. A vast industry has been built up providing research, treatment, care, surgery, supply of the drugs and the equipment needed for all of this. Add to that the fact that, in recent years the number of people getting cancer has doubled, then you have a multi-billion-dollar industry growing at an alarming rate.

But what should take precedence? Money or lives? This not only stops cancer in its tracks but reverses the tumours back to healthy tissue, thus alleviating the need for surgery in all cases.

That would lead to cancer surgeons being redundant, amongst other things but wasn't that a small price to pay for such a massive breakthrough. They would simply have to retrain and find another speciality.

Other industries have had to change or stop altogether as a result of advances in science and technology. It's called progress. But she had often thought that some members of the medical profession and the drug companies would happily hold up progress so as not to damage their very nice financial positions or their bottom line.

Particularly the NHS. They were the most worrying because given the bad management that had taken place over the years the NHS were the biggest culprits and patient's lives came a distant second to maintaining the myth that they, the NHS were at the cutting edge of medical care, the sad truth was that they had been going backwards for decades and hiding the truth as they went, and whenever they were criticised, they simply blamed the government for not giving them more taxpayers money, which they steadfastly maintained was the reason for their ever worsening performance.

The fact of the matter was that the NHS was now run for the benefit of its staff and the major drug companies and equipment suppliers, patient care came a distant second.

They had also developed a world class system for covering up this state of affairs, particularly where medical errors were concerned. It was because of this that Mary and many other very talented people had chosen to leave the NHS and work in research for the private sector.

Over the years they had lost a lot of talented Doctors, Nurses and other health professionals due to this backward thinking mentality. Not to mention the number of unnecessary deaths that they were responsible for. Cover up after cover up had left them denuded of some of the best brains, but to the NHS it was a case of deny their failings, pretend that nothing is wrong and keep doing the same old things and consequently learn nothing, just blame a lack of resources.'

The NHS was losing medical staff at an alarming rate, due to an overbearing bureaucracy, and a system of cover ups that means nothing ever moves forward. They were acting like a mini-Communist/Marxist state. And had done so for years.

But why? Whose interests were being served by this. They couldn't be that stupid, so why weren't they learning from all the mistakes that were being made on a daily basis, again and again?

And what could be so important to override the chance to save the lives of millions of people and alleviate all the suffering that goes with these wicked diseases?

It would appear that money always takes precedence, the vested interests of shareholders and investors would be regarded as more important than the lives of millions of people worldwide who have cancer.

That is as ever was. Not just cancer, fossil fuels, unhealthy food, etc. Was the human race being turned into financial fodder for the benefit of the few? Or is it that this state of affairs already exists?

Two.

Professor Kelso is very angry that this discovery is being met with less than the enthusiasm that it should receive,

Mary returned to her lab/office. She is fuming, this should have been an historic day, and instead it has fallen flat. Her team have worked for years to find this cure, and it must be said that what they have now discovered, is better than any of them thought was possible. Certainly, in their lifetimes. The more that she thinks about Scarsdale's reaction the more concerned she is becoming.

She briefs the team on her meeting with Scarsdale and tells them that they may have to go public on their own with it, if the company won't make an announcement.

They all agree that they would give the board their 48hrs and if no progress has been made in that time then they would hold a press conference and make their own announcement.

She collected her briefcase and laptop, and left for the night to go home, Mary took a cab to Victoria and then the train to Haywards Heath. She got off the train at Haywards Heath but as she was going for a cab, and without understanding why, she decided not to take a cab home but walk up the hill into town and stretch her legs.

Something has spooked her. As she was walking up the hill, realisation dawns, the same guy? He had been opposite the office when she left work and then again in the tunnel coming down the steps from the platform at Haywards Heath station. Glad that she walked, she desperately has to stop herself from looking round.

Professor Kelso reached the top of the road and decided to stop and get a coffee in café rouge, she bought her coffee and sat at a table facing the door.
Sure enough 2 minutes, no more, and the same guy came walking past café rouge, a few seconds later he returned, entered, and bought a

coffee and a sandwich then he sat down a few tables away from Mary, eating his sandwich and drinking the coffee.

Prof Mary finished her coffee and left quickly having already paid. She walked slightly quicker and carried on into town, she needed to be sure. She crossed the road and went into the newsagents on the right side of the road and bought an evening paper, then leaving quickly, she nearly bumped into the same guy on exiting.

Now she is convinced, no way could he have eaten a sandwich and drunk his coffee, and then caught her up in the time. They exchange apologies for nearly knocking one another down and Mary continued on her way.

She marched the remainder of her way home. Why watch her? They know where she lives and in any event they can track her through her mobile. Maybe they are checking to make sure that she doesn't contact anyone. Being honest with herself, she had been expecting something like this. The CEO's reaction, he should have been getting out the champagne, not talking about ramifications. Ramifications! They'd cured cancer for Christ's sake, they should be celebrating. No his reaction was all wrong and Mary was worried.

Three.

She arrived back at her house, it is a fairly large 5-bedroom detached house that was built in the late eighteen hundred's, she lives there alone after her husband died a few years ago, they didn't have any children. They had lived there for nearly twenty-five years. She could see that her housekeeper had been in, the place was spotless, and there was a post it note on the fridge, to say that her supper is in the oven.

She went into the study and thought about what was happening. Yes, she is being followed, they can only be from work, no other rational explanation, they have moved fast. Concerned that she will pass the information to others maybe? Well, they are too late! But it just confirms what she originally thought about the people who are behind MPharma.

What is she going to do about it? The first thing to do, lock all windows and doors and make sure that she is secure. Then she disconnected her internet connection. Carefully she checked her paper files to make sure that nothing in the cabinet has been touched. She removed various critical papers relating to the cure and took them to the fireplace in the lounge where she very carefully burned them. Next she collected the ashes took them to the toilet and flushed them down. She has backup copies on her laptop and another flash drive just in case.

In case of what, she thinks? Her main concern is if someone breaks in and steals the laptop and her files from the filing cabinet. She has this flash drive and the one she gave to Robert for safekeeping.

Where to hide this one? She took it into her garage, through a connecting door, she has an old Snap-On 4 drawer tool chest which belonged to her late husband, pulls out the 2nd drawer down, and using gaffer tape she taped the flash drive to the underside of the drawer. Then she made sure that the drawer moved freely before returning into the house.

Mary went to the kitchen, heated up her supper, and poured herself a large whiskey, she sat down at the kitchen table to eat the food. All the time her mind was racing, what on earth is going on? She again checked the windows and doors, to make sure that they were all locked tight, and then she went to bed. Thinking about the day's events.

Was she being paranoid? Was the chap on the train a mere coincidence? No way, in any event, tomorrow morning's journey to work should be revealing. Now she needed to get some sleep.

Four.

06.00 next day, Mary got up, made coffee, showered, got dressed, packed her briefcase and left her house at 07.20 and walked to the station, taking her normal route. On reaching the station Mary, spotted the chap from the day before, ignoring him, she saw a notice in the entrance. "All services delayed due to an incident further up the line, more information will follow."

Mary knew what that meant, another poor devil had jumped in front of a train. Knowing also that it will be several hours before the line will open again, she returned home. Mary immediately sent an email to her colleagues, explaining what had happened, and then sat at her desk and attended to her incoming emails.

10.35 She decided to make a pot of coffee, switched on the television in the kitchen and watched the latest news, the breaking news item was of an explosion in one of the labs at MPharma, 4 people dead. As the bulletin goes on Mary gets the sickening realisation that the explosion has taken place in her lab and her whole team have been killed. And that, had the trains not been cancelled, she would be one of the dead. Suddenly she was very scared indeed.

Mary realised that they would know that she hadn't been there, the train guy would have reported in, she knew also that they would come after her very quickly. This was no accident. She needed to talk to Robert Simpson.

She couldn't risk the phone and how many were out there watching her house? Was the back route safe? She would have to chance it. She knows that there is only one way to find out, so she set off, watching carefully for any sign of movement or anyone watching. In the event it was ok all quiet, she got to Robert's house knocked on the back door and entered, her friend was there.

Five.

Mary told him what had happened, including her discovery, and what the flash drive contains. Robert felt that this was a very dangerous situation, and they have to move fast and get Mary somewhere safe. But where? It can't be anywhere that either of them has a connection with. As Robert believes that sooner or later they will discover the connection between the Prof and Robert.

They decide to talk to a friend of Robert's who owns a boat in the Solent. He also owns one of the local garages, who both Robert and Mary use. Gerry Dunbar, Robert feels that they need to get Prof Mary out of the country as fast as possible he also feels that she must not return to her house under any circumstances. Robert suggests that he goes back there and collects whatever she needs. He says that he will do this when he gets back from Gerry's.

But what after that? They would need to plan this carefully. At the moment no one knows where the Prof is, but they will soon start looking for her, if they haven't already.

Robert tells Prof Mary that it is better for her to stay put for the time being whilst he goes to see his friend, she must wait upstairs at his house and stay away from the windows until he gets back. She takes a bottle of water and some biscuits from the kitchen and goes upstairs to one of the back bedrooms.

Robert says, "It goes without saying that you must not answer the phone or the door, just ignore both. I will be back as soon as I can." With that he left the house got in his car and drove to his friend's garage.

Six.

Robert spoke with Gerry and explained the situation in detail, Gerry knows Robert well and has done so for many years. Thus he listens without question and realises that this is an urgent and potentially lethal situation. He also knows that Robert is not given to flights of fancy and that he is deadly serious.

They have already killed 4 people by the look of it. "Why not go to the police?"

"What chance would she stand" says Robert, "A. they wouldn't believe her and B. MPharma are a multi-billion pound worldwide conglomerate with connections to the top. Mary has a 0% chance of surviving. There is a fortune at stake not to mention the jobs, Cancer is a massive industry world-wide our dear old Prof has just wiped it out. No, given what they have already done, they have to stop her whatever the cost."

Gerry thinks for a bit and says, "OK first thing to do is move her from your place, without documentation it is no good trying to get her out of the country, getting her out is easy enough but what does she do then?"

Gerry continued, "My sister has a cottage on Anglesey, I could borrow it for enough time to get a proper escape plan together."

Robert says. "Sounds as though it could work"

Gerry says, "We'll book your car in for this afternoon, get the Prof in your car whilst it is in your garage get her to lie down in the foot-well in the back and come here. Park on the forecourt and then I will drive your car into the workshop. Prof Mary can then get out and get into my car which will be parked next to yours.

Someone will give you a lift home and then at lunch time I will go home, then on to Anglesey, settle our lady in to the cottage. Best if she avoids contact with any of the local people as far as is possible. My sisters' cottage is very remote, and well off the beaten track."

"She'll need her laptop and a new pay as you go phone for emergencies, but she mustn't call you under any circumstances. Can you go to her house and fetch her laptop before bringing her here. I can fully brief her on the way to Anglesey. I will get the phone in Bangor. That's another thing, money? She can't go anywhere near her own bank account."

Robert replies, "I will cover it all for the time being, just let me know what you need it's not a problem. No problem getting her laptop, I can slip in the back way when I go back to get her."

Gerry said, "It will all need to be cash and while we are about it, no calls, no smart phones, I will not be taking mine, the prof has left hers at home so, so far so good. Once I get her settled in, I will get her a phone. I will draw as much cash as I can for now"

Seven.

Meanwhile back at MPharma the boardroom was electric. The CEO plus three other directors were there, Harold Martin who was the head of security, and one of the main board, from the US, George Tobin. They were all aware that Professor Kelso was not in the lab when it blew up and worse still whilst they originally thought that she was in her house they had now realised that she was off on the loose somewhere and they didn't have a clue where.

They go over the potential losses that a cure would precipitate. They also discuss the coming pandemic and how this new situation could affect that plan.

Those losses would be astronomical, they are geared up for creating and selling treatments, not cures. Curing diseases is bad for business, treatments, preferably ones that patients have to take daily for the rest of their lives are much more lucrative. That is the basis for their business model going forward.

Treatments, not cures. Were they to cure all these diseases they would lose a huge amount of money. Particularly from the British National Health service, easily their biggest single source of funds. All compliments of the British taxpayer.

The American brings the meeting to a close "I need Mr Scarsdale and Harold Martin to stay behind".

When the others had left he said to them. "If any of this ever gets, out we are all in deep doo, doo, not only will it wipe out an industry that is worth 100's of billions annually, but half the drugs industry would also be gone overnight, and all our very lucrative jobs would go with it. Not to mention our very rich and powerful shareholders will be massively out of pocket. Consequently they won't like us anymore, and that would be very unhealthy, do I make myself clear." The other two nodded.
The head of security said. "The quickest way to dig her out of the woodwork is to blame her for the explosion, get the police involved and

then they can organise a manhunt with full media coverage. I have some good contacts in the Police force".

"Would that work?" said the CEO. "It has in the past" said the American. "But at the moment the police and everyone else think that this was a tragic accident, let's keep it that way for the time being. We can always put out a story later that Professor Kelso was becoming delusional and making wild claims about finding a cure for Cancer and that her behaviour was becoming more and more extreme. Then we would need something to link her to the explosion and the deaths of her four closest colleagues. But for the time being we need to leave things as they are, find Kelso and quietly make her disappear".

To the head of security the American said "Ok. in the meantime let's see if we can find anything to link her to the explosion."

Harold Martin said, "The police are still in the lab, the way it was rigged they will draw the conclusion that it was a gas leak set off by a spark from the electrical equipment".

"OK." said the American, "We'll leave it that way for now."

"Now to business, can we turn this drug into a treatment? One that the patients will have to keep taking daily for the rest of their lives. That way we can patent it and make a fortune out of it, our shares will go through the roof"

The CEO said. "According to Professor Kelso that can't be done. The only dosage that works is the one that wipes out the Cancer in its entirety, any less and it doesn't work at all. Anymore and you kill the patient. The dose has to be tailored to the individual. She's checked it all, over and over they've done exhaustive tests, she is very thorough and the best in her field. That's why we employ her. If we produce it and patent it in its present form what would we make from it annually?"

The American replied. "The market would be worth about a billion initially, but this would get diminished over time, remember it wipes out all cancers, so if someone is harbouring more than one type it all gets wiped out in one go. It would be a case of diminishing returns, we would be cutting our own throats, commercially that is."

"So we have to stop this whatever the cost. And bury the whole thing." Said George Tobin, "including Mary Kelso".

Eight.

Meanwhile, Gerry put his car in the workshop, checked the oil and the other levels and whilst no one was watching him, he removed the fuse for the GPS, thereby disabling it.

A short time later Robert pulled onto the forecourt. He parked and got out walked across the forecourt and talked to Gerry.

Gerry said, "All quiet at yours, Robert?" "Yeah but there is a BT van parked just down the road from the Prof's house, but my back is clear I think."

"Ok, but you can bet your neck that the BT van are the watchers" he took Robert's car keys and moved the car into the workshop, spoke briefly with Mary and then returned to the forecourt, joined Robert Simpson and they both walked into the showroom, through the back and into the workshop.

There were four mechanics working in the workshop. Gerry said, "Ok lads, you can take a tea break now," the mechanics all went to the tearoom, they didn't need telling twice.

Gerry and Robert then helped Prof Mary to change cars. Robert had collected the laptop and put it in the boot of Gerry's car. Mary is stiff and uncomfortable but relieved to be on the move. Once Mary had settled into the back of the car Gerry moved the car back to its normal parking space on the forecourt.

He didn't want to leave the Prof in the rear foot well too long so he said to Robert, "I will get one of the lads to run you home, but I am going to leave soon as I don't want to leave her in the back of the car for too long." With that he gave instructions to one of the lads to take Robert home, telling him that his car would be ready at lunchtime tomorrow. Robert left with the lad to go his house.
Gerry then told his secretary that he was leaving to go home. Went to his car and left for home, on arrival he opened the outer gate and garage

door with his remote control and drove in. Both doors closed behind him, once in the garage he let Mary out of the car, and they went into the house.

Mary needed to stretch out and drink a cup of tea, she was visibly shaken. A lot had happened in the last 48 hours, but she was a tough lady and bearing up well. Gerry poured her a large brandy.

He needed to get some things together for her as she had nothing with her at all. No clothes, toiletries etc. There would be some supplies at the cottage and anything else that she needed, Gerry could get at the supermarkets in Holyhead, he looked through his wife's wardrobe for stuff that would fit her, he rounded up what he had, packed it, went downstairs to find Mary fast asleep on the couch.

Gerry's wife Jenna was a schoolteacher, he wanted to get moving before she came home as he didn't want to have to explain all this to her yet, best she doesn't know for the time being. However he left her a note telling her that she must not reveal that he would be away for a day or so to anyone under any circumstances and that he would explain everything to her upon his return. He also told her to burn the note once she had read it.

He woke Mary and they packed the car. Gerry put a few cushions into the rear footwell, padding it out so that the cushions raised the level and covered the prop shaft tunnel as Mary would have to stay there until they reached the M25, he intended to head up through Lindfield then up to East Grinstead and on to Godstone before joining the M25 and heading west to the M40. The car had privacy glass in the rear so he figured that once they were on the M25, she would be able to sit up in the back and be more comfortable. They went back into the house made a quick flask of coffee and some sandwiches and set off for Anglesey. He also grabbed a few bits from the house that he thought they might need. He was hoping to make it well before midnight in which case he would drop Mary at the cottage and then go to Tesco in Holyhead in order to get the supplies that she would need. He had called his sister earlier to arrange using the cottage, she had confirmed where the key was hidden but she wasn't sure what supplies were in the cottage other than a few tins. He had also sworn her to secrecy, again saying that he would explain all later.

Nine.

The run up to the M25 was uneventful although slow going, once they got on to the M25 it was at a virtual standstill as usual.

On the way he talked with Mary, she explained what had happened in detail, she also told Gerry where she had hidden the flash drive. Gerry said that it will need to be collected and put somewhere safer. He will need Mary's key so that someone can retrieve it. They discuss the severity of the situation, and the obvious danger that they are all now in. And what their next move should be.

Gerry is also worried about Robert, he will be in the firing line once the people at MPharma realise that he is a close friend of Mary's, and she will most likely turn to him for help and that they will very quickly get her phone records and see that connection. Bearing in mind that it looks like they have already murdered 4 people, Robert is in a great deal of danger or soon will be.

They continue along the M25 and then M40, M6 and onto the M54 before joining the A5. He wanted to avoid the A55 because it is littered with cameras, so he remained on the A5 until Bangor and then headed to the cottage using only the Anglesey section of the A55 which has no cameras. The journey took a little over 5 hours.

The cottage was very remote and approached by a long dirt track. They arrived without incident, Gerry was happy that no one knew where they were at this stage. He went in, followed by Mary who was impressed with the cottage's location and its obvious comforts. They checked the kitchen which was well equipped but in terms of groceries had the basics but little else. They wrote a list and Gerry left her and set off to Tesco to get the supplies that were needed, they were open until midnight so he could get the groceries, but not the mobile phones as that part of the store would be closed due to the late hour.

This meant that he would have to wait until the morning, but he could go to Bangor, there was a mobile phone shop there that sold second-hand stuff and he felt that this would be better as it would be more anonymous. Returning to the cottage with the supplies. Mary had already checked the cottage over, disconnected the phone and internet connection, she had made a cup of tea without milk and was just starting to get her head around all that had occurred in the past few days. She felt safe, at least for the moment.

They unloaded the car and Mary started to get some food on the go as they were both hungry having only eaten the sandwiches in the car on the journey.

Gerry said "I will go to Bangor first thing in the morning and get two pay as you go mobiles. We will decide on pre-arranged times to switch them on for say 30 mins then if either needs to call the other they can do it at these times. Then switch off. You have got your laptop, but for now you can't go on the internet, it is just so that you can write everything down and keep a record."

"We have to decide what to do next" said Mary, "But by the look of it I should be OK here for a few days at least."

Gerry said "We need to decide what you are going to do in the longer term. You can't go home and for now you can't access your bank account. Between Robert and me we will keep you going with cash." Gerry then gave her £4000.00 which was most of what he had drawn from the safe in his office. "Just in case you need to make a move in a hurry".

Mary understood what he meant. Gerry said, "Keep as low a profile as possible, the postman doesn't come up here but leaves any mail at the local post office, so you don't have to worry about him".

The food was ready, so they ate, both caught up in their own thoughts and Gerry was particularly worried about Robert. They were both tired so turned in for the night. Both were exhausted as it had been a very long day indeed.

Gerry woke at around 06.00 hrs. He got the coffee on the go and very soon Mary was up as well. "Sleep ok?" said Gerry, "got off eventually but slept ok in the end. It is so lovely and quiet here and the air is very refreshing".

Gerry said, "I will go to Bangor and get the things we need then, I will go back home and see how the land lies. There is a friend who I need to talk to as well. Then the day after tomorrow I will come back up here, if I get the chance I will try and retrieve your flash drive before I come back."

Prof Mary said, "While you're out can you pick me up a pair of walking boots, as I might as well do some hiking while I am here. By the look of it there is plenty of foul weather clothing in the cottage."

"Will do," said Gerry, "What size are you?" "6" she replied". "Ok I'll go to Bangor now, I should be no longer than a couple of hours. Stay out of site for now, see you later." With that he set off for Bangor.

It was an easy run, and he was back at the cottage in under two hours, with boots, and two mobile phones, he had put £100.00 credit on each one, and some other bits & pieces that he thought Mary might need. Then they sat down and went over the plan for the next few days. Mary would keep a low profile at the cottage and would explore the surrounding area on foot, making sure to stay away from any populated areas. Gerry would return to Sussex, update Robert and see if he could access Prof Mary's house to retrieve the flash drive. Then he would return to Anglesey, hopefully by then they would have worked out what to do next.

He set off for the drive back to Sussex, again using the A5 and reversing his earlier route. Due to traffic conditions it took him just over 6 hours thus it was late afternoon when he got back to the garage. On his arrival he saw that Robert's car had not been collected, he got his workshop manager to call Robert to let him know that the car was ready for collection.

There was no reply on either his home or mobile phone numbers. Immediately Gerry was worried and told his secretary that he was going home and went straight to Roberts' house. When he turned into Robert's road his stomach turned, there were fire engines, police cars and an ambulance outside the house, which had been gutted by fire, somebody had got to Robert fast! Gerry stopped a short distance from the house. The ambulance pulled away, without using its blue lights or siren. Not a good sign.

He drove on past Mary's house, all looked quiet there, and headed home. He had to find out what had happened, he had the telephone number for Robert's son, who was captain of a frigate in the RN. He would call him. But first he had to consider what information they had extracted from Robert, if any? And what did he know? He knew about Gerry and the cottage in Anglesey, he didn't know the exact location though, but it would only be a matter of time before they did. He still had Roberts' car at the garage, what to do about that?

He went a long route home to check if he was being followed. It seemed clear enough, but if they knew where he lived they didn't need to follow him. He used the mobile that he had purchased in Wales to call Prof Mary, it was answered immediately, and he quickly updated her on the situation with Robert, Mary was very upset by the news, she felt responsible and a great sense of loss.

So far all was quiet at her end. Gerry told her to leave the cottage and find a vantage point, take binoculars from the cottage and watch the place to see if anyone was taking interest in it. He told her to be very careful and not show any signs of life in and around the cottage for now.

That done he switched the phone off and put it in a plastic sandwich bag that he had in the car, stopped in the lane and under the pretence of taking a pee dropped the phone on the ground and carefully stepped on it to press it into the soft ground. He looked round so that he would recognise the exact spot again and got back in the car and continued home. Carefully checking his mirrors to make sure that he wasn't being followed.

On arrival his wife Jenna was home she hadn't seen or noticed anything unusual but then she hadn't exactly been looking. He explained to her about all that had been happening and the danger that they were all in.

Ten.

Gerry put a call through to Robert Simpson's son who answered immediately, Gerry started to tell him about the fire, but he knew all about it, the police had already contacted him to tell him that his father had died in the fire. He, the son, was already on his way up from Portsmouth and reckoned that he was about 40 mins away. Gerry suggested that they meet at the garage. Gerry was visibly upset to hear that his friend had died. His upset quickly turned to anger.

He set off for the garage taking Jenna with him. Gerry was very careful to check his mirrors on the way, looking for any evidence of a tail or anyone paying interest in them. Jenna was being just as alert, she too understood the danger of their situation, and until this was resolved she knew that their lives were going to be upside down.

Jenna was thinking, who were these people who are so consumed by their greed that they are prepared to see people suffering in order to make even more money than they already have?

That they were prepared to kill innocent people to achieve this, was just incomprehensible. And they were getting away with it. How could that be happening?

When they got to the garage Robert's son Colin was just pulling in. Gerry opened the workshop door so that he could park out of sight. After introductions they went into Gerry's office, Colin asked what they knew so far.

Gerry told him the story from the time that he got involved and what Mary had filled him in on during the journey to Anglesey.

Initial thoughts from the police were that the fire had started in the kitchen and that Robert had been overcome by the smoke. After having heard from Gerry and his wife the son agreed that the fire had probably been deliberately set and that his father had most likely been tortured for information as to the Prof's whereabouts before they had killed him, and that it was also highly likely that he had eventually told them everything that he knew. The others agreed and realised that Gerry could now be the next target.

Gerry wanted to get up to Anglesey fast, just in case the Prof was in danger and that MPharma knew where she was. They decided that Gerry and Jenna would go back to their house collect some things and hot foot up to Anglesey. Colin would arrange the autopsy and set about the funeral arrangements and the business with the house, he would speak with his brother who is a solicitor working for his father's old firm.

Gerry gave him the number for the mobile stashed in the ground, Colin said he would buy a pay as you go first thing in the morning and call. With that Colin set off to go to his brother's house.

Gerry emptied the safe of cash which was about £9k they always kept a fair amount in the safe in case they had to pay cash for a car that they were going to buy. He went into the workshop and picked up a couple of large adjustable spanners, not much he thought, but it was all he had, for now. He put the adjustables in the front 2 door pockets. The rest of the stuff he had accumulated went in the boot, including a couple of spare fuel cans. The cash Jenna put in her handbag.

They locked up and drove back to their house, Gerry went via the lane where he had stashed the phone, stopped, collected the phone and continued to the house.

All was seemingly quiet, Jenna went upstairs and packed 2 large holdalls, she put in clothes for each of them, and their wash bags. Meanwhile Gerry sorted their passports, driving licences etc.

There was a knock at the front door, unusual, as they had an entry phone at the gate, he knew what it was and went to the door, opened it, there were two men on the doorstep, both looked fit and purposeful.

He took a step back as the first one drew a weapon, the man got the shock of his life, Gerry hit him with a straight right and he went down like a sack of potatoes, the second man was drawing his gun when Gerry's left hook caught him square in the side of his head, it nearly took his head off and the second guy went down like his friend. These guys were used to dealing with frightened people, neither expected what they got. Nor did they know that he had been middleweight boxing champion of the Royal Engineers two years in a row.

Gerry was pleased that his old skill was still there. He called to Jenna, "Quick go into the garage, on the shelves at the back are some large cable ties can you get them for me, please" she was back in a flash and Gerry used the cable ties to secure their arms and legs. He pulled them tight. These might be the men who had killed Robert. He wasn't worried about hurting them.

His immediate problem was what to do with them. They were starting to wake up, he went to the garage and got a roll of gaffer tape, returned and covered their mouths and eyes with the tape, his thinking was that whatever he did to them was justified as they would happily have tortured him and then killed both Jenna and him. Besides they would soon be missed and given the size and resources of the people that he was up against, there would certainly be more than these two.

He also wanted to question them on tape to see what they would reveal, if anything. He relieved them of their weapons, they had 2 spare magazines each and a few hundred pounds each in cash. Which he took. No identification though but the first guy had a note with a London number and a set of car keys with remote fob.

Neither had a mobile phone, maybe that was in the car, he said to Jenna, "I am going outside to check their car out, lock the door after me and don't open it unless you are certain that it is me and that I am alone."

Jenna said. "Take a torch and one of the guns with you."
"Ok no problem" and he picked up one of the guns, checked its load and got a torch from the kitchen.

Turning the hall light off, he slipped out through the front door. Jenna closed and locked it behind him and then picked up the other gun, she too checked the load and stuck it in the waist band of her jeans.

The two prisoners were wriggling on the floor, but they weren't going anywhere so she continued getting ready to leave.

Gerry was back in five minutes he said "It is all clear out there. They have a Focus parked in the lane, the remote opens it. I found a radio in it as well which makes me think that back up isn't very far away."

"All we can do for now is to put these two in their car and then park it up somewhere, we don't have time to question them so we will just leave them in a car park, perhaps Sainsbury's car park in Haywards Heath."

"Good idea" said Jenna. Gerry went out and drove the men's car as close to the front door as possible. They lugged their prisoners into the back of the Focus, Gerry said that he would drive the Focus and Jenna could follow in his car.

"I think we'll change cars, we took an Audi estate in the other day, I will get it taxed and as with all the sales cars it is the holding company that it is registered to. Might give us a little extra time before they are looking for it."

They loaded the car quickly and went to Sainsbury's in convoy, it wasn't far from their home, and they were there in a few minutes, Gerry parked the Focus well away from the main entrance to the supermarket. He got in with Jenna and she drove to the garage, they did a quick drive by, just to check all was clear.

Eleven.

Gerry went and opened the workshop, turned off the alarms and Jenna drove his car in. It was a simple matter to transfer what they had into the Audi as it was in the adjoining building which was the storage area for second-hand stock that wasn't ready for the forecourt or showroom.

Gerry checked oil, water etc. and saw that the tank was over 2/3rds full of diesel, which was plenty to get them to Anglesey. He disconnected the Multimedia Interface, thus rendering the GPS and any tracker unit inoperable as he had done before with his car. He figured that they could be using the latest technology to track them. If Gerry and Jenna didn't use any technological devices it would make them very hard to track. Both Gerry and Jenna had left their smart phones at the house.

He left a note for his secretary to tax the car as soon as she got to work the next day, once all was done they set off.

They chose the same route that Gerry had taken before and as the journey wore on, so traffic became lighter and progress was improved, they called Mary, all was quiet at her end she had done what Gerry suggested but all was clear so far, she had found a good vantage point and watched the cottage, but no one was paying any interest in it, yet.

Gerry was becoming worried that if Robert had told them about his sister, she was now in danger. Jenna called her and she was sure that no one was paying her any attention but would be vigilant.

He couldn't know that Robert Simpson had told them that it was Gerry's cottage, and that the cottage was in Scotland.

He called Mary when they got close to the cottage to confirm that they would arrive shortly. On arrival Mary was waiting for them, she hugged them both and they went into the cottage. She was visibly distressed about what had happened to Robert and felt that it was her fault. Jenny tried to console her saying that she couldn't have known that they would react in such a savage way, Mary said "I still feel responsible for what has happened to Robert."

Gerry said. "We have spoken with Robert's son Colin, he and his brother are dealing with Roberts' affairs and arranging an autopsy. Colin doesn't believe that this was an accident. We will know more when we have the results of the autopsy. In the meantime we have to decide on our next move. At this time of year there should be plenty of holiday lets available. I will get on to that straight away."

Then Mary said "If we can get this info into the public domain it may be that we can stop them in their tracks, particularly if we can show a link between the deaths of the four people at the lab and Robert, up till now the police are treating Robert's death as a tragic accident, but if we can prove a link to MPharma and get the details of the cure out in the open there would be no point in continuing to come after us. Because as things stand at the moment, none of us can go home."

Jenna said, "Maybe we should go after them instead of running?"

"What do you mean?" said Mary.

Jenna said. "First we find a credible source to get this cure out in the open, so that no one can deny its capabilities. Then we go after whoever is calling the shots, get some evidence against them and stop them somehow."

"They are still going to want to shut us up." Said Gerry. "We know that they are responsible for the deaths of five people, they still need to silence us, and what evidence is there that we could get?"

Mary said "The one to go after first, is Harold Martin, he is head of security and will be behind these guys who are doing the damage. I think that he should be top of the list along with Anthony Scarsdale the CEO, we need to find out who is pulling their strings. And go from there."

Gerry said, "Can we find out where he lives?"

Mary said, "There may be a way, but we would need to hack into their system to do it, you can bet your neck that my access will have been revoked."

"If you were to attempt it, they would have prior warning of the information that you were looking for, in any event" said Jenna.

Gerry said, "Ok let's all get some sleep, I will be speaking to Colin and Mike in the morning, so let's leave it there and start afresh tomorrow."

Jenna said. "Do you think someone should stand guard just in case, we could each do a three-hour shift? That way someone is awake at all times? The other two agreed and Mary volunteered to do the first shift, Gerry would do the second and then Jenna would do the third. "Ok that's settled" said Gerry.

Turning to Mary he said, "do you know how to use a handgun?"

"No" she said, "but if you go over the basics with me I'm sure that I will be able to manage it, if the need should arise."

Gerry went through the basics with her, made sure she knew how to load a round, take the safety off, and aim and fire whilst holding the firearm in one or two hands. She was a very practical lady and had the gist of it very quickly. Gerry was satisfied and went to bed leaving Mary on guard.

She in turn checked all the doors and windows, made sure both back and front doors were locked, removed the key from the back door and then settled down in the armchair facing the front door and the passage from the kitchen having switched of all the lights. Keeping the gun close to hand at all times.

She wondered if she could actually shoot someone, then thought, these people were totally ruthless, they gave no quarter and had no regard for human life, yes, someone like that didn't deserve her mercy. Especially after what they had done to Robert. Shoot them? She thought, yes, several times.

Before long Gerry returned, her three-hour shift had gone, with her lost in thought, still she was relieved to see Gerry.

"All quiet?" he asked.

"Not a sound, except nature." She replied. Gerry went and put the coffee on, Mary handed him the gun and said, "I am going to bed, take care".

"Sleep tight" Gerry said.

Twelve.

The rest of the night went without event and Jenna got up followed by Mary who decided that she would make breakfast for everyone. After eating Gerry went out and checked the surrounding area, all was quiet, he wondered how long that would last. The mobile rang, it was Colin, and his new number was now registered on Gerry's phone. Colin explained that he had arranged an autopsy on his father and that it would take place the following day, and he would be back in touch once he had some news.

Gerry explained to him that they had a plan, part of the plan was to move to a different location, in order to carry out their plan they would need somewhere closer to London, also that they needed someone who could hack into the MPharma system. Colin said that he would talk to his brother and see what they could do at their end.

They agreed to speak again later as soon as either of them had any further news.

Gerry thought about accommodation, they were planning to kidnap the head of security, thus needed somewhere out of the way where they could hold the guy while they questioned him. He had a pal, Sam Jarvis, he was an ex-car dealer turned property developer and had been in the army with Gerry. He knew him well, they had worked together in the army and Gerry trusted him with his life. Maybe he would have something.

Gerry called him, yes he had somewhere, he had recently purchased a disused farm, they hadn't started working on the farm yet, it was six hundred acres and one of the cottages on the farm was pretty remote, it had some furniture, it had three bedrooms and Sam remembered that the beds were still there. He gave Gerry the address and directions to get there and arranged to meet them there later, Gerry said that he would call Sam when he was about an hour away.
They tidied up the cottage packed the car and set off for Essex. Again the journey was uneventful, but it gave them a chance to discuss their

plan. They were going to capture Pharma's head of security, take him to a quiet location and then the women said that they would question him. Gerry almost felt sorry for him, but not quite.

These guys had murdered 5 innocent people without compunction, had smashed their lives to bits and would quite happily torture and kill the three of them. All for the greed of their paymasters, it was a sickening thought. But Gerry was also starting to wake up to the reality that the banks and multinationals were running things and if Pharma were happy to put millions of lives and suffering on the line for the sake of profit, were they the only ones or was it happening all over? The thought was chilling. But a distinct possibility given what they had seen so far.

They turned onto the M25 coming off the M1. He called Sam, who said that he would set off straight away, they were about an hour away given the traffic. All three of them kept a close eye for watchers. As they got closer they kept an eye for a meeting place with Colin and Mike, they saw several, but they wanted to get to the cottage and check it out before calling him.

They arrived at the farm soon enough and Sam was already there, it was pretty run down and no longer operating as a working farm and thankfully it was deserted. Sam said, "jump in your car and follow me."

Thirteen.

They followed Sam up the track.
Past the farm buildings and on along the track which twisted and turned.

They saw the cottage on the left side of the track, the track carried on past the cottage but there was a branch off that went to a parking area in front of the cottage, the parking area had thick hedgerow on two sides and the cottage making a third. It made a secluded area, but no garage. The cottage had three bedrooms and was sparsely furnished but it had beds.

It was a bit run down like the rest of the farm, but it would serve their purposes Gerry thought. Bedding was a bit sparse, but Sam said that he had some more at the main house which he would get for them. There was a useful looking shed to one side and a couple of other small outbuildings which Gerry would check out later. The first thing to do was make the place habitable. Fortunately both Jenna and Mary had spent plenty of time camping in remote places, so they weren't phased by the condition of the place.

Sam returned with bedding, towels and the like, meanwhile Mary had a meal going which smelled great. Gerry had checked the outbuildings and local area for vantage points etc. Jenna started to get the bedrooms sorted. There was a phone line and internet connection which were both working. Typical, thought Gerry, the place is falling down but the internet works.

Gerry gave Sam the mobile number and he set off home, leaving them alone. Meanwhile Mary had the computer up & running, she went straight to the MPharma website and pulled up a photo of the head of security, Harold Martin. She downloaded the photo and then did the same with Anthony Scarsdale, the CEO. She could put them on the flash drive and one of them could take them to the nearest town and get them printed. After doing this she disconnected the router.
Gerry reckoned that it wouldn't be hard to follow the CEO home, but the head of security would be a tougher bet. The others agreed. So for now

they would plan to follow the CEO home. Then decide when and where to grab him. They were all exhausted so decided to eat and get some rest, they would keep the same routine going with regard to keeping one of them armed and on watch at all times throughout the night.

Gerry asked Mary if she felt Ok having a loaded firearm. She said that she was fine with it and in fact, after what they had done to her team and Robert, it wouldn't worry her one iota if she had to shoot one of them.

Robert was a very close friend and a lovely person. His life was taken away from him because he had helped her. They had sent a very clear message that they were prepared to go to any lengths to preserve their already massive profits.

People have been turned into financial fodder, their only function is to keep big business making record profits year on year, and at the same time keeping the government's coffers topped up with money from the taxpayer. Which was then doled out to big business in ever growing amounts, the events of the past few days had given her time to think about all of this, she like most people had been too busy working and rushing about to see what had been creeping up on everybody.

She, like most people, probably, had been so wrapped up in her work so as not to notice the gradual progression of this nightmare scenario.

The more she thought about it the more she realised that the chances were that this wasn't the first time something like this had happened. Nor would it be the last. But what could they do about it, three people with limited resources against a huge multibillion dollar corporation.

Soon enough Gerry was up, he took over and Mary went to get some sleep. He checked over the doors and windows, all were well locked and secure. He settled down to his vigil. Thinking about their options, going to the press?

Waste of time, whilst we supposedly have a free press the media are complicit in this, they print what they are told to, and at the end of the day it is money that talks, the public are simply ignored, no one cares about people anymore, if they ever did. Only their wallets. And what they can get away with.

Anyway on to the matters in hand. He and Jenna should go to London and see if they could locate and follow the CEO, if they were lucky he would go straight home and then they would know where he lives. Once they have this info they would be able to plan how they would lift him. Mary would have to stay in Essex as she is far too recognisable, and it would put her in danger. They would need a van with a side door but given Gerry's contacts in the motor trade he should be able to borrow one without having to give much of an explanation.

He also needed to make a trip to his house to collect various items that he was going to need. Also he would try and get into Mary's house and retrieve the flash drive that she had hidden in the toolbox. Mary had told him about the rear entrance, but he would do a recce first in any event. He couldn't help thinking how tough Mary was. In a few short days her life had been shattered and her closest friend killed, yet she was maintaining a very stoic position. Jenna too was tough as nails, and he knew that already, all things considered, he had a pretty formidable team.

The other issue was the whereabouts of the flash drive that Mary had given to Robert, he would need to work on that one. It may be that it had been destroyed in the fire, but they needed to know. He would be meeting with Colin and Mike tomorrow, he could ask them if they had any ideas where their father would have hidden it.

Jenna appeared, the time had gone quickly, and all had remained quiet. Gerry wasn't surprised, they had been very careful to make sure that their location was secure, however once they grab the CEO the stakes would rise.

He made coffee for Jenna and went to get some sleep. It would soon be time to get on with talking to Colin & Mike and then down to Haywards Heath, collect the van, back to Essex, then the train to London to be outside the MPharma offices for 17.00 hrs, to wait until the CEO leaves. Hopefully follow him home then return to Essex. He didn't want to take the car into town because there would be a record when they pay the congestion charge, that was also going to be a problem if they had to lift him in London or if his home was in central London. Tomorrow will tell.

Mary was soon up as well, between them Jenna and Mary cooked breakfast, it was going to be a long day. Jenna said to Mary, "Be warned whatever you do don't let Gerry cook. He can ruin beans on toast". Mary laughed, Jenna said "I'm serious" laughing herself.

Mary reminded her to stock up on some essential supplies whilst they were out. Mary gave Jenna a list of items that she would need to assist in her interrogation of the CEO. Jenna looked at the list then said to Mary, "I don't know where I will get a scalpel?"

"A model or craft shop, it doesn't have to be best quality, just sharp." Said Mary.

"OK" said Jenna "I know where to get the rest of it"

Fourteen.

Gerry spoke with Colin on the phone. He wanted to meet them and bring his brother Mike. As Gerry and Jenna were going to be running around all day it was agreed that Colin and Mike would come to the cottage at the farm in the evening at around 20.00hrs. Gerry gave him the address and directions to the farm.

That done Gerry set about arranging to borrow a van, he figured that his garage would be being watched but he had a friend with premises in Burgess Hill, Josh Williams, ex RN. Again someone that had worked with Sam and him when they were in the services, he specialised in vans and other commercial vehicles. On calling him Josh said that he had a van they could use for a few days Gerry arranged to collect the van from his friend's premises later on in the day.

Gerry and Jenna set off, it took them nearly 2 hours to reach Burgess Hill, and they went straight to Gerry's friend's garage. He was waiting for them and had a pale blue transit ready for them. He had fuelled it up, and his mechanics had checked it over thoroughly. Gerry looked it over and felt that it would do the job admirably.

Jenna set off to do the shopping saying that once finished she would return to the farm. Gerry drove the van and went to Mary's house, he parked in the next road and following Mary's instructions went to the back of the house.

He used the code which she had given him to access the rear gate and keeping low he went to the back door, letting himself in with Mary's key, he listened carefully for any sign of life.

The house was quiet, Mary had called her housekeeper to say that she would be away for a couple of weeks and asked her to stay away for the time being. Mary had given Gerry a list of things she needed from her bedroom, it was clear to Gerry that the house had been searched, he collected the items from her bedroom and then went straight to the garage, saw the Snap-On box and opened the drawer, he felt underneath and quickly found the flash drive, with relief he put it in his pocket then he returned to the house, when he heard a noise he froze. The front door was opening, he ducked into the passageway leading to the kitchen.

He thought from the sound of it that there were two intruders, this was confirmed when one spoke. "We have to look everywhere again, they are convinced that she had left more than the files."

The paper files had been useless as Mary had removed and burned several pages that were critical for the cure without which anyone trying to discover her formula would be lost.

Gerry waited to see if anyone entered the kitchen, they were concentrating on the study which faced the front of the house, so he slipped out the back door and made his way to the rear gate, slipped through and was in the back passageway, then made his way to where he had parked the van. Got in and drove away slowly.

He had been seen, there had been a third watcher in a car at the end of Mary's Road. Gerry drove past him and was recognised by the watcher from a photograph that they had all been given. He noted the make, model and registration but didn't follow as he had been instructed not to as one follower was too easy to spot.

So far Mary and her friends had been one step ahead of them all the time, they weren't going to risk this breakthrough. It would be a simple matter to check the ownership of the van which would give them the beginning of a trail that would eventually lead them to Mary.

Mary was the cornerstone of all this, and they must find her before she managed to get this story out in the open and be believed. Their vigilance had paid off.

Fifteen.

Meanwhile Gerry headed for the farm. Again keeping a close watch on his mirrors. On arrival Jenna was already there with her shopping done. Mary had been busy cleaning up and sorting one of the outbuildings. It had a door and one window. No other means of entrance or light. With the cans of matt black paint that Jenna had bought for her, she sprayed the inside of the window making sure to cover all the glass. With Jenna's help they had strengthened the door and fitted a new hasp and padlock. The building had power going to it and they got a light working. "This is for our friend" said Mary, "we want him to be comfortable, don't we."

Gerry laughed he wouldn't want to be in this guy's shoes when these two got hold of him. Gerry and Jenna then drove in the Audi to the station and got the train to Liverpool Street station leaving the car in the station car park.

They got a cab into the West End, Gerry told the driver that they would need him to wait as they had more than one destination. The cabby said that was fine as long as they understood that he would keep the meter running. Gerry agreed and said. "I will give you an extra £200 on top of the metered fair. The cabby agreed to this, and they set off. On reaching the West end they got the cabby to park two streets away from MPharma's offices.

Having arrived with time to spare they went to a restaurant nearby and got something to eat, neither had eaten since breakfast and they were both hungry. They ate and left the restaurant.

Their plan was to do a walk past the main entrance and get an idea of the general terrain, there was a Costa coffee shop diagonally opposite the building, and worryingly there was another entrance to the side which led to an underground car park.

Gerry was angry with himself for not considering this eventuality, of course, the CEO would probably have a chauffeur driven car, never mind, they would be in a perfect position to see the CEO's car and get its registration number that might reveal his address, but more likely it would be registered to the company.

They went into Costa Coffee got a couple of drinks and sat down on stools at a raised table by the window. It was 17.25, they were expecting to see the CEO in the next 15 minutes. Mary had said that he had a reputation for leaving at 17.30 unless there was a good reason why not.

At 17.37 a silver Jaguar came out of the side vehicle entrance and headed north, as it passed their location they saw the CEO sitting in the back. They logged the number and got moving out of the coffee shop and round the corner to their waiting cab. Gerry told the driver which way they needed to go and asked him to try and catch up with the Silver Jaguar. With what Gerry was paying him he would have tried to win the Monte Carlo Rally in his cab.

They got moving and being in a black cab they caught up with the Silver Jaguar easily enough, traffic was heavy. In the event they didn't have to go far, they turned up the Finchley Road and passed the American school and took the next turning on the left. They continued down this road and took the 2nd on the right and the Jaguar pulled up on the left. Gerry told the cab driver to continue past and pull over just up the road. He saw the CEO get out of the car and go into a house on the left. The Jaguar drove away and passed them without a glance, it continued up the road and took the next right and was gone.

They waited for a few minutes and then Gerry got out of the cab and walked back down the road past the house and noted its number and layout at the front. It had a garage and space for 2 cars on the front. Not much, but in that part of town worth a pretty penny he thought. He had seen enough, he went back to the cab, and they headed back to Liverpool Street station.
They arrived at Liverpool Street station, Gerry paid the cabby, and they had a train within 10 minutes and then were on their way back to Essex. It took about 45 minutes, and they collected their car and were soon on the way back to the farm.

Jenna said. "Ok, do you think that we can pull this off?"

Gerry replied. "Yeah, we will have surprise on our side, I'll wait until he goes in, and the Jag has gone, knock on the door and as soon as he answers I'll grab him and put him in the van. You will have to park a little way down the road, then wait until I go in, count to ten and drive slowly up the road, Mary will have to be in the back, as you stop she will open the door, if we time it right I will push him into the van get in myself and close the door behind me. You drive away immediately keeping to the speed limit and we bring him to the farm. I will put a hood over his head and tie him with cable ties. The danger is, if we get stopped on the way back, and they look in the back, then we are in big trouble."

Jenna said "We're already in big trouble, this is our only way out of it. We didn't start this, they did."

Gerry knew what she meant. They reached the farm, all seemed quiet, and they drove past the entrance and continued up the road before Gerry pulled over. He turned off the engine and the lights, and waited, nothing, their back was clear. The farm was in a fairly remote area the land surrounding it was flat.

Sixteen.

The beauty of their new location was that being flat, you could see another vehicle coming a mile away. He turned the car around and headed back to the farm entrance. Once he turned in, he switched off the lights, and drove slowly along the lane to the cottage, he was careful to drive slowly enough not to have to use the brakes and on reaching the cottage, he could use the handbrake in order to stop.

They went in, Mary had prepared some food, they sat down at the table to eat but Gerry got up and looked out of the window, "just checking" he said. But something was making him feel uneasy. He couldn't put his finger on it, but something was troubling him. He joined the girls and they tucked into the meal that Mary had produced. Jenna filled Mary in on their trip to London while they ate. She told her the plan that they had discussed on the drive back from the station. Mary was impressed at what they had achieved, she couldn't wait to get her hands on Scarsdale.

Gerry heard a car, looked at his watch and saw that it was 19.55hrs he moved the curtain slightly to see who it was, a car pulled in slowly, it stopped, and Colin got out followed by his brother Mike.

Colin introduced Mike to the group, whilst Gerry had known Robert for several years he had never met Colin or Mike until the other day at his garage. They sat round the table and Mike explained that they had arranged an autopsy and had received a call from the doctor who had given them a run down on what he had found. Robert had been tortured, all his fingers had been broken, and there was no smoke in his lungs as he had died of a heart attack prior to the fire being lit. The police were viewing it as a burglary that had gone wrong.

Basically they had tortured him to death. Mary was visibly upset and had to leave the room for a few minutes. Jenna followed her to make sure that she was ok.

Mike said to Gerry "I believe that you have my dad's car at your garage?"

"Yes that's right" said Gerry. Mike went on "My dad called me the other day. He said the car was at your garage and that he had left something in the car which was very important and that I was to tell you and only you."

"Thanks" said Gerry "Did he tell you whereabouts in the car he left this item?" "No" said Mike

Gerry said, "I will get the car checked over, as you can see I am stuck here for the moment, but the first chance I get I will go over there."

Colin said. "Can you hang on to the car for the time being?"

"No problem we will keep it stored for as long as you need." Said Gerry.

A few minutes later the girls came back in. Colin was saying that they may have made some progress with a hacker, Mike has a client who may be able to help.

Mike said. "He is a lad who we defended a while back, he was accused of hacking into a banks system. He said that he had done it to show how easy it was as their systems aren't nearly as secure as they would have us believe. He had simply hacked into their system, he hadn't taken anything, nor had he intended to do so."

"What happened?" Gerry asked.

Mike said. "Once the bank realised that their system would be shown up in a public court, they dropped the case. It happens all the time. They don't want the public to know how bloody useless they are."

"Well let's hope that MPharma aren't any better" said Gerry. He didn't tell them about their planned kidnapping of the CEO tomorrow as he felt that it would be inappropriate as Colin was an officer in the Royal Navy and Mike being a solicitor, it could compromise both their positions.

Mike also said that he had spoken to an old school chum of his who is a senior copper, a DCS who told them that if they thought that their father had been murdered, they needed to get some evidence and he would get it to the right people and they would start an investigation, the brothers hadn't known about the autopsy result at this time, so he didn't know about this development.

Gerry said that they should keep it to themselves for the time being. They hadn't told the DCS that it was tied into what had happened at Mary's lab.

They discussed various matters relating to Robert's estate as he had left a small amount of money and some personal effects to Mary in his will. Mike went on. The personal effects were destroyed in the fire but if Mary gives me her bank details I will arrange to transfer the funds to her account.

Colin looking at his watch said. "We ought to get going, it's getting late."

Gerry said. "Ok, I will check the car the day after tomorrow and be in touch as soon as I've done it."

Before they drove away Gerry checked the surrounding area, looking for lights or sounds that were out of the ordinary. All seemed quiet and Colin and Mike set off. Gerry watched their lights as they drove along the lane and waited to see if any other lights showed, all ok he could see their lights as they joined the road at the entrance to the farm. He waited to see if any other lights joined them, but all was quiet, he kept watching for 5 minutes and then returned to the cottage, satisfied that they were not being followed.

He went back in and sat down with the girls. "Ok we now have to deal with tomorrow, are you both clear on what needs to be done?" They both nodded and Mary said. "Crystal, and I know exactly what I am going to do when we get him back here" Gerry shivered, he almost felt sorry for Scarsdale, almost.

"OK then let's eat something and get some sleep I'm starving, I'll do the first shift tonight" said Jenna. Gerry gave her the Glock he had already shown her how to use it, she checked it was loaded and put it in her waist band.

They cooked, ate and Gerry checked the outside, he went out and just stood in the shadows listening for any noises, and figuring all was quiet went back in, checked the doors and windows again and went to bed. They were all dog tired.

Seventeen.

The night passed quietly and then they were all up and making their preparations for the afternoon's endeavour.

Gerry sorted the van whilst Jenna checked the weapons, got the cable ties ready, gaffer tape et al. Mary prepped the outbuilding so that it was ready for their guest.

Gerry looked in, Mary had created a dungeon with two ropes hanging from the roof beams and a sheet of plastic on the floor under the ropes.

He said. "It's cold in here."

Mary replied, "Yeah, and it's going to get colder at night, should be nice for him. Look Gerry this man is probably responsible for the deaths of my whole team plus Robert who meant a lot to me. He will get no sympathy from me. These people have demonstrated clearly that they are totally ruthless. If you hadn't dealt with the two animals that came to your house, you and Jenna would most probably have gone the same way, they are not going to get any quarter from me."

Gerry said that he understood how she felt and with that he went to check on Jenna. She had all the kit that they would need organised and packed in a holdall. Gerry took it all to the van and also got some of the plastic sheeting that Jenna had purchased and laid it on the floor of the van securing it with gaffer tape.

With a final check they were good to go. Two and a half hours later they were parked in St. Johns Wood. They were in a road just off the high street the plan was to wait until a few minutes before he was due to get home, then move into his road and park up the road a little but facing his house with a view of the front door. As soon as the Jag drove away, Gerry would walk down to the house, knock on his door, as soon as Scarsdale opened it, Gerry would immobilise him, grab him and head for the pavement. Jenna would watch from where the van was parked and the moment she saw Gerry grab him she would drive quickly to the house, as soon as they stopped Mary would slide the side door open and Gerry would push him in and Jenna would set off and drive them to the farm, simple! Well that was the plan.

It was going dark so that would help. Gerry gave the signal for Jenna to drive to the road and park. She was nervous, they all were, and none of them had ever done anything like this before even Gerry with his army service hadn't done anything like this in the middle of a big city. Still they were committed now there was no turning back, and this was the only way that they could preserve their own lives.

The Jag turned into the road, stopped outside the house and Scarsdale got out. The Jag pulled away and Gerry got out of the van. He watched the Jag turn the corner and quickened his pace. Within seconds he reached the house and rang the doorbell. A few seconds and Scarsdale opened the door, without hesitation Gerry hit him in the solar plexus, not too hard just enough to wind him, Scarsdale looked totally shocked, and Gerry grabbed him, swung him round and with his arm around his torso lifted him bodily and went for the van. Jenna pulled up in the same instant and the door slid open. Gerry threw him in climbed in behind him and shouted go to Jenna as Mary slid the door shut.

Jenna drove away and headed for the farm. She knew her way out of London and headed for the north circular, whilst longer, this route wouldn't be near gridlock, whereas heading through London would be a nightmare and very slow going. The north circular and then M25 would be a bit quicker, not much but a bit.

Meanwhile Mary and Gerry had Scarsdale trussed up like a chicken, he was getting his breath back after Gerry's punch and tried to speak, Mary stuck a piece of gaffer tape across his mouth before any words came out, she wasn't exactly gentle either. Scarsdale looked terrified, and even more so when he recognised Mary. She searched him thoroughly, he only had a few coins and a handkerchief.

Then Mary taped up his eyes so that he couldn't see either. They had agreed beforehand that they wouldn't speak during the journey in order to unnerve him further.

Once they were on the M25 it took a further 1 hour 45 minutes to reach the farm. It went without a hitch, Jenna watched her mirrors closely, they weren't being followed and she was even more attentive once she got on the back lanes closer to the farm. Gerry had told her that as soon as she drove into the farm entrance, to stop, cut the engine and turn off the lights.

He got out and watched and listened, it was a remote spot, and the landscape was flat, he could see and hear if any other vehicles came along the lane. He stood there a few minutes, and satisfied that they weren't being tailed, got back in the van, told Jenna to drive up to the cottage slowly without lights or using her brakes.

They got to the cottage and again Gerry got out and 'sniffed the air' all seemed quiet. They moved the van close to the outbuilding, Mary unlocked it and Gerry lifted Scarsdale and carried him into the building and dumped him on the floor. Jenna came in as well and Gerry went to park the van.

He then went into the cottage and checked the place just to make sure. Went back to the outhouse, by which time they had Scarsdale standing up, tied with his hands above his head to the roof beams. His legs were spread apart and a washing up bowl was on the floor beneath him and between his legs.

Mary turned to Gerry and said. "We're all hungry so why don't you make something to eat? We are going to be busy for a while"
He said "Ok" and went to the kitchen, he knew when he wasn't wanted. Particularly as he was the world's worst cook.
As soon as he had gone Mary ripped the patches from Scarsdale's eyes. "Now" she said. "You are going to tell us every last detail about what happened in my lab and to my friend Robert Simpson."

Scarsdale having regained some of his composure said, "I'm not telling you a thing you bitch."

"I thought you would say that" said Mary with that she and Jenna donned surgical masks and gloves. They were both wearing scrubs.

Jenna picked up a pair of scissors and Mary said. "Cut his trousers off and whatever he has underneath" Jenna did just that, Mary went to a table at the side on which some other instruments were laid out.

"Don't worry" she said to Scarsdale, "They are all sterile."

Scarsdale was horrified, what are you doing he shrieked? Mary said. "You forget that I am a fully qualified and practiced surgeon. I am going to remove your private parts, surgically, and sew you up, so that you don't bleed to death, the bowl between your legs is to catch the blood because believe me you will bleed a lot so I will have to work quickly." She then gave Scarsdale a graphic description of how she would carry out this procedure. With that she picked up the scalpel and walked towards him.

Scarsdale was starting to panic but said. "You wouldn't dare."

Mary grabbed his privates and began to cut. Scarsdale screamed and said. "Ok I will tell you what you want to know, please just stop."

Mary said. "We want the truth, every last detail, if I suspect for one minute that you are lying to us, I will continue with what I was doing, is that clear?" Scarsdale nodded. Mary put a suture over the cut to stop the bleeding.

Jenna produced a tape recorder and positioned the microphone in order to pick up clearly what Scarsdale was going to say.

Mary started. "Ok we want to know who gave the order to murder my team and my friend Robert Simpson."

Scarsdale absolutely terrorised by Jenna and Mary's tactics was desperate to try and save his own skin he wasn't going to hold anything back.

"George Tobin, he is number two on the main board in the States."

"So MPharma is US owned?" Jenna said.

"No not exactly, whilst the head office is in the States the major shareholders are Chinese owned companies. Mostly registered in the Cayman Islands. The other big shareholder is Bob Towers the owner of Towersoft, the biggest software company in the world. He owns huge amounts of shares through supposedly charitable institutions and various trusts."

"Who calls the shots?" Mary asked, "Bob Towers through George Tobin." he replied. "Tobin runs the day-to-day affairs, but Towers has the final say, Tobin works for him."

"So George Tobin and Towers are the ones that we should be concentrating our efforts on." Mary said.

"Yes but it's not just MPharma who you should be concerned about."

"Who else?" asked Mary?

"The NHS, in some ways they could lose far more, their budget would be slashed, then there is the GMC many of their members would either be out of work or have to retrain, for the NHS the cost would be astronomical in terms of redundancy and early retirement. You could retrain the younger ones again but at a huge cost.

Everyone involved is making fortunes out of Cancer. It has become a huge industry. Specialist hospitals, providers of equipment the lot. Hundreds of thousands of jobs in the UK alone, millions worldwide." Scarsdale went on, "We had a meeting with George Tobin, Alex Williamson, who is the head of the NHS, Paul Grierson the head of the GMC, and an unnamed politician from the department of health. They all agreed that this cure had to be stopped and whatever tactics were necessary, had to be used in order to do so. None of the cancer causing, products have been banned' why do you think that is?"

Mary and Jenna were stunned.

Scarsdale continued, "You have to understand that global economics has led to extreme capitalism. People are simply a commodity in this scenario. Extreme capitalism has to be kept rolling, sucking as much money as possible out of every sphere of human life every minute of the day and night. A few million deaths per annum is acceptable to this way of thinking. As long as they are making money from it. What you have to remember is that death is a huge industry as well, all the big global insurance companies are making fortunes out of selling insurance policies to pay for funerals, at the same time they are buying up all the small funeral companies, again extreme capitalism, and nothing is excluded."

Jenna said, "It seems that any form of extremism is fatally flawed, as by its very nature it will destroy itself, but as usual as in with all types of extremism many lives are lost and huge suffering results, during its ascendency."

Mary said, "So the two people who are responsible for the killings of my team and Robert Simpson are, George Tobin and Harold Martin, with the backing of Bob Towers, the NHS, GMC and the government to name but a few."

"That's about the strength of it." replied Scarsdale.

Mary looked at her watch and said. "I think that is enough for today, we will continue this in the morning. We will bring you some food shortly, you've got a camp bed and blankets, so I suggest you make yourself comfortable."

Scarsdale was shocked by this "What you are going to just leave me in here?" he said.

Mary replied. "You guys have quite ruthlessly killed 5 good innocent people, had Gerry, not stopped your stooges you could add 2 more to that list, do you seriously think that we are going to give you any quarter? The best that you can hope for is that you come away from this alive with all your body parts intact."

Scarsdale just withered, his shoulders slumped, and his head drooped. With that Jenna attached a chain to his ankle that had been set into a beam against the wall at its other end. She padlocked the end round his ankle and released his hands.

She said, "That will give you some room to move, at least as far as the bucket in the corner, and you know what that is for."

Scarsdale said. "What about my clothes, can I at least get dressed?"

Jenna replied. "Just wrap the blanket around yourself for now. Don't bother trying to call out, we are miles from anywhere, so you won't be heard."

They left the outhouse, secured it, and then joined Gerry in the house.

Eighteen.

Gerry meanwhile had been gainfully employed and produced bowls of hot food for them. He put a bowlful and some bread on a tray with a 2-litre bottle of mineral water in a bag that he carried to the outhouse. Unlocking the door he carried it in. Scarsdale was sitting on the camp bed wrapped in a blanket.

He said. "Those two are going to kill me aren't they?"

Gerry said. "That's up to you mate, it depends on how you cooperate with us".

Without saying anymore he left the outhouse relocked the door and went back to join the girls in the house.

"So how did he respond to your questioning?"

Jenna replied with a smile. "Once he realised that we were serious, he was like putty, and it didn't take much to scare the living daylights out of him. When we finish eating we will play the tape for you."

After eating they played the tape for Gerry. "God help us," he said. "It is much worse than I thought, but do you believe him?"

Jenna said. "Yeah, everything except the bit where he says that he was bullied into it. He is as involved and as guilty as the rest of them. He was too scared to lie to us".

"Well if the government is involved there's not much point in going to the police as this will just get stamped on from high up. We need to think of another way that we can get details of the cure, and this information, out in the open where it can be acted upon before the authorities get a chance to squash it."

They spent the rest of the evening going over everything trying to find a solution. In the end Mary said. "Let's all sleep on it and see what we can come up with in the morning." Gerry and Jenna agreed.

Gerry went outside taking one of the guns with him, he said. "Just going to check our prisoner and I will have a general look around, then I will do the first shift on guard."

Again all was quiet, Gerry walked up the lane, cut back behind the house where there was a small mound which made a good vantage point he sat there for a few minutes allowing his eyes to adjust to the dark and listening. Once he was satisfied that all was quiet, and they were alone he went and checked on Scarsdale who was sound asleep.

He locked the outhouse and returned to the house where he went through his security checks on the doors and windows and then settled into the chair.

Again the night passed without incident, and they were all up early. Gerry had checked on Scarsdale before going off shift and Jenna did the same a few hours later.

Mary did the first check of the morning and Scarsdale was awake. She told him that he would be given breakfast shortly and then his questioning would continue, she had brought him water, soap and a towel so that he could wash.

His general demeanour was sullen, and he spoke little. She returned to the house, Gerry and Jenna were discussing taking the van back, Gerry didn't want to leave Mary on her own whilst they did that so he suggested that he would take the van back, get his friend to give him a lift to his garage and then he would use another of the firm's stock to drive back to Essex.

Mary protested that she could easily deal with Scarsdale on her own, but Jenna and Gerry insisted saying that should an emergency occur she would be on her own without transport and that it was only prudent to have some back up. Mary reluctantly agreed to this.

Gerry then checked the van thoroughly to make sure that nothing had been left in it. He cleaned the interior and once he returned the van he would get his friend to jet wash the wheel arches and the underside generally to clean off any mud that would lead back to the farm.

With that done he had a last conference with the girls before going to Burgess Hill. They discussed what they were going to do with Scarsdale and what their next move should be regarding Harold Martin the head of security, they decided to make a final decision once Gerry returned. He then set off for Burgess Hill.

Nineteen.

He went the long way around the M25 so as to avoid the ANPR cameras on the QE2 Bridge, these recorded every vehicle crossing in order to charge for the use of the bridge via the internet. Another con, he thought, as the bridge had been paid for with taxpayer's money, and now they were paying for it a second time in spite of the promise from the government that the crossing would be free after they had retrieved the initial cost. This had been achieved several years ago, yet they were still paying for it. He vowed that if he and Jenna were lucky enough to come out of all this alive then subject to her agreement they would sell up and make their lives in another part of the world. Somewhere that had a bit more respect for the people who lived there. Some chance, he thought. It started to rain, which would help clean the mud off the wheel arches, Gerry thought.

Soon enough he arrived at his friend's premises in Burgess Hill. It was on the industrial estate and was a fairly large site. As he drove toward it he noticed a car parked on the left with two occupants sitting in the front seats, he had seen this car before, cars being his business he had good awareness of vehicles that he knew. Then he remembered that this car had been parked at the end of Robert and Mary's Road when he had visited Mary's house just after he had picked the van up.

They were waiting for him to return in the van which would have been registered to the Burgess Hill address. So they were getting help from the authorities or someone at the DVLA. He would need to be careful. He saw Josh, he too being alert had noticed the car down the road.

"Been here all day that car." He said, Gerry decided to fill Josh in with the basic details of what had been happening.

Josh said. "Christ this country is turning into a mad house."

Gerry said. "It is not just here, it looks like it's a global thing, and now I have inadvertently involved you".

His mate said. "You know what, I don't give a flying fuck about them. All any of us do is graft and pay, pay, pay. I'm sick of it, we are almost 2nd class citizens in our own country, and a chance to have a go back would suit me down to the ground."

"Just be careful, this lot think they can do what they like and get away with it" said Gerry. "Our lives are being sacrificed on the altar of global economics, and they just don't care. As long as we all keep pouring money into it."

His mate said. "Seriously if there is any help that I can give to you and your friends don't hesitate. You know, I was in the Navy for nine years, I can look after myself. And look what they've done to that, the Navy that is."

"It's everything" Gerry said. "And everywhere, they have done it by stealth."

His friend said, "and the worst of it is we are bloody well paying them for doing it. Makes you wonder why any of us hang about here, emigrating certainly looks tempting".

Gerry replied, "I may have to, the way things are going, anyway back to the problem at hand, can you give me a lift to my garage."

"Sure no problem," he said. "Give me five minutes."

They were soon in Josh's car on the way to Haywards Heath. Gerry watched as the other car pulled out to follow them. They drove up past the station and on towards Ditchling Common the other car following.

Gerry said. "When you get to the end of the road go straight over the roundabout and onto the common."

"Ok." said Josh, "Once we are on the common I can easily put them off the road. If you're right, these guys are proper killers, so we need to deal with them and if they get hurt so much the better."

Gerry agreed, time to send a clear message. "Plus as long as we don't injure them too much the Police won't be called." Gerry said.

They got to the roundabout, slowed went straight over then Josh poodled for about 200 metres checking in his mirror to make sure there weren't any other cars following, he then signalled left and slowed so that the other car had to overtake him, he timed it just right as the other car came past he swerved hard right, he didn't hit the other car, but it was just enough to make the other driver swerve hard right and drive off the road, and into the ditch that ran alongside the road.

It ended up with 2 wheels in the ditch at an angle of about 45 degrees with its left-hand wheels in the air.

Josh laughed and said, "That's messed their day up, they will need a tow truck to get them out of there". He turned and winked at Gerry, "know any good garages locally?" they both laughed and carried on, shortly turning left and heading up to Haywards Heath.

The two occupants of the other car were shaken but not hurt, angrily they climbed out of the passenger door and tried to push their car out of the ditch. It was a complete waste of time as the car was very firmly stuck and was going to need a tow truck. They got on the phone to their base and arranged just that, meanwhile Gerry and Josh were well gone out of sight.

Gerry said. "You are going to have to watch your back for a bit after this."

Josh said. "They deserve all they get, and I would like to help in any way that I can."

"Ok, if you're sure about it, get yourself a non-registered mobile of the pre smart phone type, and take the number of mine, as soon as you have got it call mine, then we will be in communication and if I need anything I can call you".

"Ok." said Josh, they reached Gerry's garage and he said, "Drive past and we will just see if there are any others lurking about."

All seemed quiet but Gerry wasn't convinced, if I had their resources I would have both places covered he thought.

Then Josh said. "Have you spotted the BT van?

Gerry saw it. "Yeah got it, turn around and drop me outside the garage. Call me the moment you have a phone and watch your back." He got out of Josh's car and walked across his forecourt and into the showroom.

Brenda his PA was there talking to a customer. "Hi boss" she said, Gerry went straight to his office and Brenda finishing with the customer followed him in.

"All ok here?" He said, "No problems?"

She replied. "I have sold a couple of cars whilst you have been on holiday, if it keeps up this way you will be redundant." This made them both laugh.

He called in the workshop manager, Bob Coombes and sat them both down. Gerry then went through the broad outline of what had been happening. He said to them both. "For now you two are going to have to run the business for me, I will reflect your extra responsibilities in salary increases for both of you. Everything that I have told you is ultra-confidential so keep it to yourselves for your own safety and mine as well as Mary and Jenna. This situation will not last forever but whilst it is going on I need your complete cooperation and support, the question is, are you both OK with that?"

They both agreed, they had worked for him since he had bought the garage a few years ago, and he had always been a good boss, they were both happy to continue.

Turning to Bob he said, "I need to take a look at Robert's car, and I will need another car from stock."
Bob said. "We've got a Jag that has just come in. Brenda can tax it."
She interrupted, "Tax it in my name if it helps and use my address."
"Thanks" said Gerry, "But are you sure, things could get quite lively?"

"You know me boss, if I say it's ok, then it is."

"Ok, we need to shift it to a car park, as if it's being delivered to a customer, then one of you can give me a lift to it, that way with a bit of luck we will avoid the jokers in the BT van down the road."

Brenda said. "I will give you a lift in mine. My car is at the bottom of the yard, I can pull up next to the workshop and you can crawl into the back from there."

She then went to her office to tax the Jaguar. Gerry and Bob went into the workshop to search Robert's car. They very quickly found the flash drive, Robert had put it just under the driver's floor mat.

Bob then tasked one of the lads to take the Jag to the hotel car park, it was about a mile away. He then followed him to give him a lift back and at the same time check if they were being followed. They drove past the BT van and the occupants noted their exit from the garage but made no attempt to follow them. They were not the target, and it was a garage, cars went in and out all day.
They were looking for Gerry, their instructions were to take him alive and question him about Mary's whereabouts. Their mates had had a rough time of it when their car got pushed off the road. It had taken an hour for the tow truck to arrive and then a further hour and a half to get the car out of the ditch. They were on their way back to London on the train, they hadn't been injured in the crash, other than their pride and a few bruises after being knocked out at Gerry's house and then dumped, trussed up in their car and left in Sainsbury's car park. So the guys in the BT van were being very careful. They weren't about to make it 3–0. They had seen him arrive so far he hadn't left.

They had been fully briefed on Gerry's past, first in the Royal Engineers where he was the middleweight boxing champion 2 years running. He was also a very accomplished engineer but had eventually been part of a security division, his engineering skills being particularly useful. He had also been put on a counter surveillance initiative which had proved useful when overseas in places like Afghanistan and Iraq.

He would have stayed in the army but was finding it more and more difficult to carry out his duties with all the nonsense surrounding political correctness. A lot of people saw Political Correctness as creeping communism. The services were losing good people on a daily basis due to the ridiculous constraints that were being put on the serving men and women.

Still, since leaving the army he had worked hard on his business and had been successful, but now by the look of it he had become an enemy of the state by helping Mary try and save millions of lives worldwide.

They took the Jag via the filling station, whilst the lad was filling it Bob kept a close eye for any watchers. Satisfied, they then took the car to the nearby hotel car park, left it there and returned to the garage.

Bob gave the keys to Gerry saying. "We've filled her up, and left it parked on the left of the entrance where it can't be seen from the road. Gerry told Brenda to go a roundabout way to the hotel and look carefully for watchers. He said to Bob giving him some cash, buy a pay as you go mobile, but not a smart phone just an ordinary mobile, he wrote down his number and gave it to Bob. Call this number when you have it. "Will do," said Bob.

Gerry set off with Brenda, as planned she pulled up outside the workshop door and Gerry slid into the rear foot well. She turned out of the garage and headed for home which was the opposite direction to where the BT van was parked. Her thinking was that they had probably seen her leave to go home before, so keep it simple once down the road she could turn left and cut through the lanes to the hotel.

They soon arrived at the hotel, it occurred to her that they had the advantage in this area and knew all the back routes which the others did not.

She pulled up close to the Jag, Gerry was out in a flash and Brenda drove through the car park and headed home. Gerry sat in the car for two minutes before driving off.

Twenty.

He took his usual route through Lindfield, Forest Row, East Grinstead, Godstone, then joined the M25 and headed west again avoiding the Dartford crossing and its cameras. It would take him longer, but it was a necessary precaution. The journey gave him time to think, how had things got so bad in the world that any of this could even be happening?

Basically what the people were being told through the media and what was actually going on were two entirely different things. So was the media being complicit as well or were they simply being naïve? Good question he thought.

And, if the government was involved or government ministers, then their situation was about to get a lot more difficult. They had to have a plan. Did they dare involve the DCS that Robert's son knew? So far they'd been lucky with the people that they had involved. Give information to one wrong person and they would be in even deeper trouble.

What he didn't know was that MPharma's people knew where he was. They had another car further down the road when the Jag had been delivered which followed at a distance to the hotel and shortly after Bob had dropped the car off they had been able to fix a tracking device to the underside of the rear bumper this was held on with a sticky patch as the Jag like most modern cars had a plastic bumper not a metal one.

They followed him at a distance of around half a mile right round the M25 until he turned off onto the A127 and headed for Southend. They had been warned about his boxing skills after what had happened to the two guys who were supposed to grab him at his house, they also knew that he had two Glock automatics, so they planned to follow him to his destination and then call for reinforcements. No mistakes this time, also they figured, correctly, that he would lead them to Professor Kelso. So it would be game set and match.

Gerry continued his journey unaware that he was being tracked. But he started to feel uneasy, so far things had gone their way, but these were highly resourced and ruthless people, they had back up from the authorities, so they were bound to up the ante and so far they hadn't been too difficult to elude. There was a transport café on his left, so he decided to stop for a cuppa and called Jenna.

She reported that all had been quiet at the farm, Sam had called in to check that all was well and brought them some extra bedding, and he had also got a shopping list from them and was off doing a supermarket hit.

Gerry said. "I won't be long, so see if you can get him to wait until I get there if he gets back before me." Jenna said that she would, they finished the call and Gerry finished his tea.

He went back to the car checking around to see if anyone was paying attention to him. The car park was quiet only a handful of cars, all were without occupants which fitted with the number of customers in the café, but he still felt uneasy, he got in the car and continued up the A127.

About half a mile up the road he spotted a lay by, there was a black VW Golf GTI parked in it with what looked like two male occupants, he kept his eye on it as he went past, and both occupants were looking away from him. This stretch of the road was long and straight, there was a rise at the end and sure enough before he was out of sight the Golf pulled out of the layby.

He kept his speed constant and kept an eye out for another layby or somewhere that he could pull over for a bit. There was a garage on the left, he pulled up by the air and water, got out and made it look as if he was checking the offside front tyre. The Golf drove past, and Gerry put the air lead back in the machine, got in his car and then counted to thirty before moving off. About a mile up the road, sure enough there was the same black Golf, he thought if they were using a tracker, the only time that they had a chance to fit it was when the car was parked in the Hotel car park. He also figured that the range of the tracker was around one mile.

He could try and put some distance between them, but they would quickly know that he had put his foot down and he was never going to outrun the Golf GTI, especially once they got on to the smaller roads. His only real option was to find the tracker and put it on another car, again they would soon suss this, but he was running out of options.

He called Jenna to see if Sam had arrived yet, he had, he explained his dilemma to Sam. Sam suggested that he could drive towards Gerry with his tractor and trailer, park in one of the narrow lanes on Gerry's route, he would wait for Gerry to drive past and then pull across the road blocking it. He would choose a spot opposite a track going on to one of the other farms, the place he had in mind was about 6 miles from his own farm so they wouldn't be able to follow and locate the farm after Gerry had driven past and he had held up the Golf.

He would make it look as though he had broken down whilst turning into the farm and hold them up long enough for Gerry to get to the farm's entrance, stop, find the tracker and dispose of it.

Once he had found it he could smash it, then call Sam, Sam could then get the tractor going and clear the road letting the golf carry on, hopefully they would figure that they had lost him, not being able to find the signal again. And leave the area.

Gerry thought that it was a good plan and that it had every chance of succeeding. If he was wrong and there wasn't a tracker fitted to the Jag, well he would have lost them anyway. He told Sam that he would slow down to give him enough time to get in position.

Sam set off back to the farmyard where the tractor and trailer were parked, he coupled them up, checked the rear trailer lights were working and set off to intercept Gerry.

Meanwhile Gerry had slowed down, the guys in the Golf had slowed once they realised that they were catching up.

They saw that Gerry had turned off the A127 and followed, maintaining their distance at about half a mile. They thought that Gerry was having a problem with his car, having stopped at the garage and now slowing down.

Sam had briefed Jenna and Mary before he left, on his advice they had turned off the lights in the cottage in order that nothing could be seen should the MPharma people find their lair, Jenna checked both the Glocks and gave one to Mary, Scarsdale was still in his room where they had left him chained up, in between questioning him on and off all day. What he had said was very revealing and they had recorded the lot.

Gerry continued poodling through the lanes and shortly saw Sam's tractor parked on the verge up ahead, he flashed his lights and rolled down his window as he drove slowly past making sure that Sam saw him clearly. As he drove on he saw Sam drive across the road and block the road completely. He kept going albeit at the same slow pace and wanted to put as much distance as possible between the Golf and himself before putting his foot down as this would alert them that something was going on.

He gave it a mile and a half and then sprinted the last few miles to the farm. Meanwhile the Golf had reached the roadblock and the occupants were shouting at Sam to move as quickly as possible, Sam was giving a great impression of someone who was stuck, giving an apology and telling the two of them that they needed to calm down and that they would soon get home, they couldn't of course tell him that they were following someone and were about to lose their prey.
They said that they would help him push the tractor out of the way, Sam said. "Thank you, I would appreciate the help." knowing that it would take at least ten strong people to move the tractor. But let them waste time trying, he was laughing quietly as the three of them attempted to move it, and in spite of their efforts it didn't budge an inch.

Gerry had turned into the farm, he was out of the car with a torch and quickly checked all the places on the car where a tracker could be placed. His business was cars, he knew the few places that a tracker could be put. He very quickly found it under the rear bumper, peeled it off, laid it on a stone, and then smashed it to pieces using another stone. He picked up the pieces and dropped them down the nearest drain. He then drove quickly to the cottage, went in, grabbed one of the Glocks told Mary and Jenna that he would be back soon and was just going to check. He ran back down the track, watching out for headlights going along the lane. He waited behind the shrubbery that grew either side of the gate, positioning himself on the right-hand side facing the lane, this would give him a view of the rear of the car as it drove past the entrance without him being seen by the occupants.

The Golf soon drove past slowly, he saw the guy in the passenger side look up the track as they went past, it didn't stop but carried on down the lane. Gerry waited at the bottom of the lane for Sam's tractor to come into view.

After a few minutes he heard a buzzing sound, immediately he sensed something wrong, the sound was a drone, he looked up straining against the evening sky to see where it was, it was getting louder, and then he saw a shape and movement above the road and in the direction that the Golf had gone.

He quickly called Sam to see where he was and told him to find a layby and pull up for the moment. Sam was only about a mile from Gerry's position. Gerry said that he would call him again once it was safe to move. Gerry severed the connection, he was in a good position with plenty of cover above. But what if the drone had a heat sensor? It would see him for sure and it had nearly reached the farm entrance.

His only option was to stay where he was and get as close to the ground as possible and not to move. The drone stopped at the entrance and spun round slowly. It moved off, going up the track towards the cottage. It had gone straight past him and kept going. He realised that once it saw the Jag their location would be blown, even if he could shoot it down with a lucky shot they would know where they were. No this location was blown.

He called Sam quickly, filled him in and then did the same thing with Jenna and Mary. Sam said that he would be back at the farm, he reckoned he would be 3-4 minutes.

Gerry then ran up to the farm and went into the shed where the tractor etc. was normally kept along with all the other farm equipment. Gerry was figuring that having located them the two in the Golf would call for backup before making a move and depending on how close that was, dictated how much time they had. Sam arrived and drove up, reversed the trailer into its space and after uncoupling it did the same with the tractor.

Gerry said, "We need to cover the engine in case they have heat sensors on the drone." Sam had a pile of cardboard in the corner, that was waiting to be collected for recycling, they covered the engine with several layers to disguise the heat.

They heard the drone coming back down the track, but before reaching the buildings it veered to the side and cut diagonally across the fields in the direction that Gerry had seen the Golf go earlier. It was soon out of earshot.

Twenty-one.

Having covered the engine compartment of the tractor, they started to walk up the track towards the cottage. Listening all the time for anything out of the usual. It was inevitable that some kind of attack would come, they just didn't know when.

As they were halfway to the cottage they heard a shot, both started running towards the cottage, Gerry had the Glock in his hand and headed straight up the track, Sam who knew the lye of the land headed across the field on his left, he saw in the distance two shapes by the hedge that surrounded the cottage on two sides, they looked as though they were wearing battle fatigues and were clearly armed.

Sam slowed and headed for the hedge at the side, he was a bit exposed out in the field. He moved slowly and kept low, the guys that he could see were looking through the hedge in the direction of the cottage. They hadn't seen him as they were looking towards the cottage.

Gerry was moving up the track and had spotted another two who were kneeling on the ground tending to a third person who was lying in front of them. He moved into the hedge alongside the track. He called the girls, Jenna answered and told him that they had spotted these guys approaching, she had been walking back from the room housing Scarsdale, when they had made a move towards her, she had turned and shot the nearest one, she thought in the leg, but couldn't be sure.

Jenna had then got back into the house and now along with Mary they were watching the three on the track, and they in turn were in communication with others, but she didn't know where they were.

Sam did, they were in front of him, his phone vibrated, it was Gerry he filled him in on the whereabouts of the two that he had sight of. Gerry told him about the three in the lane. There were five in total that they were aware of, but they didn't know if that included the two from the Golf.

Gerry got closer to the ones in the track and could hear them speaking on the radio. They were telling the person on the other end that their friend needed medical attention quickly. Then he saw lights coming up the track he hid in the brush at the side. It was the Golf it went straight past him without seeing him and pulled up next to the wounded man. It had one occupant.

He got out, helped to pull the injured man into the back of the car, one of them got in the passenger seat with the driver and they headed off, leaving the other one behind. Who then turned his attention back to the cottage which was in total darkness. Jenna and Mary having turned off all the lights in the house.

They in turn were watching from an upstairs window and Jenna had him in her sights but felt that the range was too great for an accurate shot.

Then he turned and went to join his friends behind the hedge, watched by Sam & Gerry. Gerry went through a gap and caught up with Sam. He said, "They are together, probably deciding what to do next"

Gerry said. "Let's see if they split up again and then go for the nearest, if we can take them by surprise we stand a good chance".

They were about 50 metres from the three guys. They couldn't hear what was being said but after a few minutes two of them headed to the left and went along the hedge, turned the corner to their right and disappeared from view. Gerry reckoned they were headed to the back of the cottage, so he called Jenna. He told her what was happening and said to sit tight and be alert and that he and Sam were going to try and deal with the other one first.

He also asked her to drop some cable ties out of the window he figured that they were going to need them.

The other one still had all his attention on the cottage he hadn't looked behind which allowed Sam and Gerry to advance on him. Sam reached the guy and put his left hand around his face, covering his nose and mouth cutting off his air supply completely and lifted him bodily off the ground and at the same time grabbing his right wrist and forcing his arm around and up his back with such force that he tore all the ligaments in the guy's shoulder. He dropped his weapon.

Sam was massively strong, his father had owned a scrap yard and Sam had spent his time there from the time that he could walk. He had carried heavy loads around the yard from as far back as he could remember. When people remarked on his strength he would simply say that he had been born that way.

Sam put the guy down telling him that if he moved he would break his neck. Sam picked the weapon up and covered him whilst Gerry ran across the drive and collected the cable ties that Jenna had dropped out of the window.

She leant out of the window and said. "I can hear someone trying to break in the back door."

Gerry said. "Stay alert, as soon as we have this one tied up we will deal with them, in the meantime don't hesitate to shoot them."

"I won't." she said.

Sam searched him whilst Gerry trussed him up. He had nothing to gag him with so said. "If you make a sound I will let him loose on you, he will tear your arms off slowly." He nodded, he wasn't being paid enough to lose his life, so he just kept quiet.

Gerry and Sam headed around the cottage, both going different routes, they saw the two trying to break in, and Gerry advanced on them pointing his gun straight at them. "Freeze both of you, we have you well covered, and you don't stand a chance." They both swivelled in his direction not seeing Sam approaching them from what was now behind them, one started to raise his weapon Sam said "Don't, you will be dead before you can get a shot off. Drop your weapons now."

They did just that and put their hands up. Gerry tied their hands while Sam kept them covered, he called up to Jenna to bring the keys for the outbuilding that was holding Scarsdale, they then marched these two around to the front, Jenna was at the outbuilding unlocking the door, Gerry and Sam pushed them in and made them kneel down and tied their legs with the cable ties.

They went to collect the other one whilst Jenna covered the two in the room, they were soon back. This one was in a lot of pain due to the torn ligaments in his shoulder. No one was showing him any sympathy. Scarsdale had got a shock when they all came in.

"Some friends of yours" said Gerry. Scarsdale started to speak but no words came out.

Mary entered wearing her scrubs and mask carrying a stainless tray with her instruments on it. Tucked under her arm was a roll of plastic. It was getting a little crowded in there by this time, but she said, "Ok who is going to be first?"

Scarsdale groaned, and Gerry said "Gentlemen, I am going to ask you some questions, if you don't answer truthfully I am going to let this lady loose on you, she has a penchant for surgically removing certain vital parts of your anatomy. If you think that I am bluffing I suggest that you ask Mr. Scarsdale whether or not I am telling the truth."

Scarsdale terrified said. "She means it, and she is a fully trained surgeon, I suggest you tell them what they need to know."

"Where are the guys in the golf?" said Gerry.

One of them replied "They took our mate to get medical help, he had a bullet in his leg where one of you shot him."

"How long before they are back? And when did you last communicate with them?"

"We last spoke with them when they went to the clinic with our injured colleague, as to when they will be back I honestly don't know, they may carry on to London and are expecting us to call them when the job has been done."

"Which was?" said Gerry. "To capture you three and take you to a secure location" was the reply.

"And failing that what?" The guy looked down and didn't answer, "I think we know the answer to that" said Gerry.

"Who employed you." said Mary. When no one answered her she said "It is quite simple, you guys have killed five people already, my colleagues, who were also good friends of mine and a dear sweet old man who was my closest friend, if you don't cooperate with us without holding anything back then I will surgically remove a vital part of your anatomy and I assure you that I will enjoy every moment of it. You won't, I can guarantee that. And I don't have any anaesthetic so you will feel every cut, scrape and stitch. It won't be pleasant, and I will have to pour a strong disinfectant all over it to make sure you don't get an infection, which will sting like hell. Now for the last time, who employed you?"

The guy who had done all the talking so far said "Harold Martin, head of security for MPharma."
"I thought so" said Mary, "and where is he now?"

"I am not sure but until you grabbed us he was calling every couple of hours."

"And when did he call you last?"
"About an hour and twenty minutes ago" he said after consulting his watch.

"That gives us roughly 40 minutes" Gerry said turning to Mary and Jenna, "I think we need a chat".

Gerry checked that the prisoners were all tied securely, they went out to the cottage along with Sam.

"Ok so what next?" said Jenna.

"We need to find a new location fast. I need to talk to Robert's boys, we can't just keep running, we need to stop these people in their tracks. Also Sam is now in danger as they will soon find out that this is his land."

"Don't worry about me, I am starting to feel as you do that this has to be stopped. For this to be happening, guys running around armed to the teeth with absolute contempt for the law and people's lives, Gerry's right, we are just being treated as if our lives simply don't matter to these people and they have the full backing of the people in power, it has all gone too far, we either do something about it, or they win."

Mary said. "They have already won, we need to prise that victory from them, somehow."

"Well for now we have to get away from here a bit rapidly."

Sam said. "Look I have a friend in Colchester who runs a fairly upmarket estate agents, let me give him a call and see what he can do." With that he called the guy, yes he had somewhere suitable and after Sam explained how urgent it was agreed to meet Sam at the house in 30 minutes. Sam said that would be ok and after taking the address finished the call.

He told the others and gave them the address and directions saying that if they sorted this place and packed the car, he would check the new place out and call them, they could then travel directly to it. His friend had said that he wanted £1500.00 per week in cash which Gerry immediately agreed to.

"The next problem is, what do we do with our prisoners?" Gerry said.

Mary immediately said, "Kill them all slowly," she had a twinkle in her eye as she said it.

Jenna said. "As much as I would like to, it just isn't an option."

Mary said. "It's ok I was only joking, half that is."

Sam said. "They know where this place is, so just leave them here, their mates will be back soon, if they arrive after we have gone then that's fine, they will get rescued, leave Scarsdale as well if you have finished with him."

Gerry said to Sam, "This could come back and bite you."

Sam replied "No-one has had a good look at me I will say that you had rented the place and then left without a word. They will have to find me first and remember I live alone so there is nobody that I have to worry about, just me."

"Now we need to take their phone in to them, we just need to decide what we want them to say."

"Something like, they got away, come and get us because these people have captured us and left us trussed up in an outhouse. That should embarrass them sufficiently for now." Said Jenna, "let's get moving load the car and get away from here ASAP."

Gerry said "I will take the phone in there and watch over them when the call comes in."

"Ok we will get packed up." Said Jenna. Sam left to go and meet his estate agent friend.

Gerry said "We also need to decide what we are going to do with the small armoury that we have collected so far? Plus the radios and mobile phones."

He went to the outhouse and checked that they were all still tied up properly and that no-one was going anywhere, he told the guy who had done all the talking so far, what he was to say when his boss called and that the phone would be on speaker so that he could hear the whole conversation. A few minutes later the phone rang, Gerry checked and saw that the number calling was showing on the screen.

Twenty-Two.

He answered the call and held it in front of the guy. "Hello Harry, its Simon, we have a problem, and we have been captured by this lot and are now tied up and locked in an outhouse at the farm."

Martin exploded. "How the fuck did that happen? And where are they now?"

The one called Simon said "They have gone now, I heard them drive away a few minutes ago. We were outnumbered there are more of them than we were expecting, and they took us by surprise."

"Ok, the other two are still at the clinic as soon as they are finished there, I will get them to come back to you. We are still looking for that fool Scarsdale, he's disappeared." Said Harry.

Simon said. "He is here with us, he was already here when we were captured."

"This situation goes from bad to worse. He better have kept his mouth shut." Said Harold Martin, and he disconnected the call.

Gerry went out taking the phone with him and checked the Audi very carefully for tracking devices, he found none, he was going to leave the Jag at the farm as it was compromised, and they knew the registration number. He would get it recovered later. He also turned off the phone that he had taken from them and took the battery out of it.

They loaded the car and agreed that for the moment they would keep the armoury with them. Sam called to say that the house was adequate for their needs, and they set off.

He drove down the track without lights and they were all on the lookout for the Golf returning, once on the road he waited a little while, he turned the lights on. He saw, parked on the right, the car belonging to their prisoners, they left it alone as he didn't want to risk being seen by the occupants of the Golf if they came back whilst he was checking it.

The phone rang, it was Mike Simpson, he wanted to meet as soon as possible, Gerry told him that they were changing their location and that if he wanted to head towards the farm and that he, Gerry, would text him the address once he got to the new place which he figured would take him about 15 minutes. Long before Mike got to the A127.

They watched their backs carefully and made three stops to make sure no one was following them, and they reached the new address in good time. The house was fairly large, detached and had CCTV at the gate. This opened as they pulled up, they drove in, and the gate closed behind them. He immediately texted Mike Simpson with the address.

They drove up towards the house, adjoining it was a large double garage and as they approached, the door opened, the light came on inside and they drove in. As the main door closed Sam entered by way of the connecting door to the house.

Sam said. "All ok, you got away clean?"

"Yeah" Gerry said. "All is quiet".
Sam said. "The house has six bedrooms and fifteen acres of land, it has a good security system and is fully furnished and equipped."

"Any food in the cupboard? I for one am starving and I'm sure that the rest of you are as well."

Sam cut in. "There's a place down the road where we can get a decent meal then we can carry on into town it's about five miles, there is a 24 hr. Tesco where we can get some supplies."

"Sounds good." said Jenna, they all nodded approval. They locked the house got into Sam's car and went to the restaurant.
The food turned out well and they all tucked in.

Twenty-Three.

Mary said, "I have a friend who is a Professor at Sheffield university, I want to call him see what he thinks and try and get this into the open, he has a lot of media contacts."

Jenna said. "Do you trust him?"

"Yeah, I was one of his students, I know him well and he has a good sense of what is right and wrong, he will want to help us I am sure."

Gerry had just finished a call to Mike diverting him to the restaurant, he let the others go to the shop whilst he spoke with Mike. Mike who hadn't been far away when they had spoken arrived shortly after the others had left to go shopping.

Mike said, "I think that I have found our hacker, he is willing to help but being skint he wants wages". "That's ok, how much does he want?" Said Gerry.

Well that's the thing, he's really expensive" Mike smiled "£50 per day. He spends his life on a computer he thinks that's loads of money."

"Ok we'll look after him. What's his name and will he work from home, or would he like to work from the house?"

Mike said "His name is Norman, the house would probably be better, you could keep an eye on him there. There are items of equipment that he will probably need as well, you will have more room in the house than he has at home."

"Agreed." Said Gerry. "Best thing is if you give me a lift back to the house, then you will know where it is, and then get him over to us as quickly as possible, once he is here we can get him working on all of this. Get him to make a list of what he needs, and I will get it all tomorrow."
"Ok I will bring him to the house tomorrow first thing, I'll get him to make a list of what he is going to need."

They left the restaurant to go to the house, it only took a few minutes to get there, Gerry checking their back carefully. Gerry gave Mike the quick tour of the house and before long the others got back.

They had ransacked the supermarket by the look of it and were ready for any siege. Mike and Gerry brought them up to date on what they had discussed, and Mike got going home as he wanted to get Norman organised for tomorrow morning, when Mike would collect him and his kit and bring him to the house.

Sam said that he would get going as well, he wanted to return the next morning as he wanted to sit down and have a council of war with everyone sitting round a table to decide their next moves, he was keen to help and get this situation sorted once and for all, if they could? The others agreed and they left it like that.

Gerry made a quick call to Mike to see if he could get his brother to attend as well. Meanwhile Mary called her friend at Sheffield University. After hearing what she had to say, he also wanted to attend the following days meeting and said that he would set off early in order to be there in good time.

Twenty-Four.

The next morning, Sam and the Professor from Sheffield arrived within minutes of one another followed by Mike, his brother Colin, Norman the computer guy and one other who Colin introduced as DCS Richard Foley, who Mike explained, had come on the strict understanding that this whole scenario was off the record and that he had also agreed to keep anything discussed to himself until such time as the others were ready to go public about it.

Fortunately the house had a large dining room and a 12-seater table thus they were all able to sit round the table comfortably. Gerry had allocated a separate room for Norman to set up his equipment in and he was busily doing just that.

Mary started the meeting off, explaining who everyone was, what had happened so far and the various parts that they had all played up till now.

DCS Foley was the first to speak. "From what you are saying it is pretty clear that some serious crimes have taken place. Murder being on top of the list, not to mention kidnapping, possession of unlicensed firearms just for starters, so it must be clearly understood between all of you that I am simply not here and have not heard anything that you have been discussing."

There was general agreement to this, Gerry then said. "We cannot go public or report any of this officially to the authorities as our lives are very clearly at risk and given what has happened so far we don't trust anyone in authority."

Foley said "I understand that and that is why I am prepared to hear you guys out and see if I can help, if I can't do anything to help then as far as I am concerned this conversation never took place. Also, before you discuss any further kidnappings and the like you should ask me to leave the room. Apart from that I agree that something needs to be done, and that the larger picture stinks, due to the involvement of these elitist global businesses, members of the government, the courts, media etc. etc. These are conclusions that I and others on the force have drawn from what we have seen before I heard anything of what you have had to say today. The situation has been allowed to get completely out of control. Deliberately I might add."

Professor Grey from Sheffield cut in. "We have had instances where colleagues have spoken out about NHS failings and their cosy relationships with the drug companies and other suppliers, they have been told to shut up, if they wouldn't be silenced then they are sacked, ridiculed and had their otherwise good reputations destroyed. As for finding a cure for anything these days forget it. Cure cancer and you will shut down a huge multibillion-dollar industry.

A few years ago we were saying that 1 in 4 people would get cancer of some form in their lifetimes now it is 1 in 2. But given that cancer is massively on the rise no one wants to talk about the causes other than to blame smoking, which can't be good for you, but with fewer people smoking these days why is it still on the rise? The bottom line is that this rise is being caused by a compilation of many things, additives in food & drink, toxic air, mobile phones, the list just keeps getting bigger, the water you drink is full of carcinogens, but they all, including the government don't want it to stop. Why? Because the financial hit to all concerned would be devastating for all their businesses."

He went on. "In the upper echelons of the NHS you hear talk of P Day."

Jenna said. "What's that?" Professor Grey replied "Privatisation Day, I think. The guys at the top can't wait, they are all in for massive pay outs, share options, all sorts of payoffs and then their jobs back through the revolving door policy. They are running down front-line services so that the public get so pissed off that they won't care what or when it happens."

"The insurance companies are rubbing their hands together as after privatisation you will need insurance if you want medical care, anyone who can't afford it will have their premiums paid through the benefit system. You imagine what will happen when an insurance company can decide what treatment or surgery you can get? One thing is for sure, as far as the insurance companies are concerned this will become another very juicy income stream for them and massive profits for sure."

He went on, "The NHS is a failing monster, much of the cause for that is deliberate. That which is not deliberate sadly is down to an intrinsically bad and deep-rooted attitude, which seems to pervade the service, and sheer incompetence. If you just look at the medical accidents that come to light, then consider the ones that are covered up, you start to see the scale of the problem."

Foley said. "Sadly I have to agree with what Professor Grey is saying. We see it happening in front of our eyes on a daily basis. But take this to the people at the top and you will get short shrift, they know it is happening but are collectively turning a blind eye. Big money rules, it is quite simple. Gerry is quite correct when he says that the public have been turned into financial fodder. Everyone in authority knows it, but no one is prepared to risk their careers or their lives to speak up and try and do anything about it. They, like most of the population, have mortgages or rents to pay, plus cars on HP or leases, they can't afford to say anything, or they will be ridiculed and out on their ear."

Jenna said. "This comes back to what we were discussing the other night, extreme capitalism! The outcome of which could be a backlash that propels the left into power which in turn will cause massive nationalisation of major businesses and corporations which, as happened before are bound to fail with the government having to become ever more oppressive in order to keep control, leading to a complete loss of democracy and literally decades of chaos and oppression."

"So" Gerry said. "What can we do about it?"

Foley said. "Look we have the tape of Scarsdale and the others. That might be the beginnings of a case against them for conspiracy to murder, but the tapes were gained under duress so could be ruled as inadmissible, but it doesn't stop us looking into the backgrounds of all these guys, very discretely. I would like to think this through to see how we can proceed as we can't reveal our hand, these people are totally ruthless and wouldn't think twice about bumping us all off. We need to put a cast iron case together if we can, and then move against them fast. Even then we won't be safe. We are up against more than MPharma and their owners, much more."

Mary said. "We start with MPharma, get them behind bars and then go after the other big corporations one at a time, they will have left a trail. Maybe we should start with the ones who are ripping off the NHS. I bet that no one has ever done an in-depth investigation into NHS fraud and cover ups. To quote the US president. 'It is time to drain the swamp' before it is too late."

Gerry then said. "Ok let's just pause on that, get our thoughts and ideas together and then sit down again later in the day and see how we can take all this forward. That is of course subject to what other plans some of us might have for the rest of the day. We will organise lunch and I need to check and see how Norman is getting on." Everyone agreed that they should take a two-hour break.

Norman was busily setting up the new equipment that Gerry had purchased for him. He told Gerry that he would be ready to start working within the next hour. Gerry checked that Norman had everything he needed and left him to it.

Gerry then did a tour of the grounds to check for any weaknesses, he was quite impressed with the existing security measures, the owners obviously knew what they were doing.

Meanwhile Norman was busily hacking into Pharma's system. It didn't take him long. He was soon in and looking for staff addresses and quickly found the details for the head of security.

Gerry came in to see how he was getting on. Norman explained that he had developed a program that he called "intruder." It could enter any system and roam about undetected. It could copy everything in someone else's system, and they would never know that he had been there. He said to Gerry "If the powers that be knew that I have perfected my intruder, I would simply disappear. They couldn't take the chance that anyone else could get their hands on it. I can crack any system with this, and no-one will ever know."

"How can you do that?" said Gerry.

"Well, I'm not going to give you chapter and verse, but it waits for a user to log on and creeps in behind them. Once in it goes where it likes gathering all the data as it goes but leaving absolutely no trace. Because it leaves no trace at all it cannot be tracked back to me. Because it cannot be seen it passes through internal firewalls no problem at all. That's why the powers that be would love to get their hands on it. Next I am going to have a good look at the CEO's files oh and by the way there is the file on the head of security." He pointed to a file of papers on the table.

Gerry took it and left the room saying that he would look back in an hour or so. He went back and joined the others who had congregated back in the dining room.

The file was very interesting giving details of the HOS's address, phone numbers, bank account details etc. they were all impressed. He joined the others in the dining room to continue their discussions, he hadn't been there for more than 45 minutes when Norman came charging in saying, "You have got to come and see this".

"What do we need to see?" said Gerry.

"I will explain but you need to be looking at my computer screen to understand what I have found."

Twenty-Five.

With that they all trooped to Norman's room to see what the fuss was all about.

Norman said. "Whilst on the NHS private site I have discovered a file called K2, it is a very private file, but not just that, it links to several of the major NHS suppliers and shows what look like illicit payments to various offshore bank accounts which amount to over £2 billion in the last three months alone."

"It is a very secure site, better than I have seen before, but intruder still got in. The strange part is that it not only has links to the biggest pharmaceuticals but also to the biggest tech companies worldwide, arms companies, oil companies, media companies, billionaires, government ministers in the UK, US, Europe, China and Russia, you name it they are all here. I have only scratched the surface so far, but this is massive, and they have gone to a lot of trouble to keep it under the radar, give me few hours and I will know more."

The others were a little confused by this, but Norman went on "I have followed the payments to the offshore accounts, and they belong to the CEO's of NHS England and the top people at the various major drug companies that supply the NHS in the UK, plus big tech, big oil, big agriculture and more. It's a massive fraud. The file doesn't only relate to financial improprieties but much worse, it has a section that details all kinds of blatant medical mistakes that have been covered up. People killed, maimed and made very ill by botched operations, medical blunders and misdiagnosis. And that's just for starters. Basically the guys at the top of the NHS and the big drug companies are raping the NHS. It also catalogues drugs that have been put into general use that kill people but are not withdrawn because of the amount of money they are making from them."

He went on. "They are killing and maiming people wholesale and covering it all up. It's massive."

Gerry said. "Are you sure that no one knows that you have cracked their system?"

"Absolutely certain, my intruder cannot be seen and leaves no trace. The big problem we have is, that there are senior civil servants, politicians and senior police officers involved, there are also media Barons and editors, the lot. The scary part is that I have only scratched the surface, they are all at it and have been for years there are hundreds of people involved."

"Each of the major players has a spider's web of offshore account in various havens, the money comes in from various trusts in other parts of the world again offshore. All in turn are managed by firms of accountants in the jurisdictions where the accounts are held. It's a complex web but from what I can make out the beneficiaries are other trusts and some of the directors and shareholders of major pharmaceuticals, the biggest tech companies, big on-line retailers the lot. All the big boys. It is like they are just sucking huge amounts of money out of the economy, not just the NHS, which of course is all taxpayer's money and money that the government is borrowing at an alarming rate."

He went on "All I have done so far is scratch a tiny bit of the surface, I need some more time, and then I can give you far more info."
"OK," Gerry said. "We will leave you to it and we'll check back with you later. Just be ultra-careful."

With that they went back to the dining room. They were all buzzing, it was beginning to look like they had stumbled onto something much larger than any of them had even come close to thinking about. Add that to what they had all been witnessing with their own eyes, and the ramifications of the whole thing, were both staggering and frightening at the same time.

Mary was the first to speak. "We need to all take deep breath, and this is starting to look far more serious than we originally thought. Why are these people stealing all this money, why so much and how long has it been happening, what is it for? There must be a purpose as they are all mega rich anyway?"

Jenna said, "I think the best course of action, is to wait and give Norman more time to trawl through this information and see what else he comes up with."
The others agreed and decided that they should all eat and get some rest.
Three hours later they were all back, sitting round the table including Norman. He gave Gerry a folder and said, "This is much bigger and more terrifying than anything that I have read in my life." He continued, "P Day doesn't mean privatisation. It means Pandemic Day, or the day these people are going to release a virus throughout the world." Again he went on, the others were stunned. "Fact is, it looks like they started 3 months ago". "With China's compliance it has been released in a place called Wuhan, given all the international travel that the Chinese people do, it will steadily and quickly work its way around the world. Once it reaches a certain level of infection worldwide, a pandemic will be declared, and a second more deadly strain will be released.

This new strain will be more deadly, and start to kill people, mainly the old and infirm. It will then be announced as a Pandemic. It says that the aim will be to get the major countries to lock down, close businesses, schools etc. The only places that will be allowed to stay open are food shops, essential stuff like pharmacies and guess what, the big global online retailers, it is all in the file. And there is a lot more, this is the culmination of a plan started in the late 1990's. It's all there, emails, minutes of meetings, names, the lot!"

"The plan seems to be, to put all the smaller firms out of business and let the big guys swallow the trade that is left once they have gone, thereby increasing their profits and ultimately, control."

Prof. Grey put in "This has been talked about for a few years, the takeover, that is, but it was always dismissed as a conspiracy theory. If what Norman is saying is correct, and we have no reason to doubt him, then, it is already happening."

Jenna spoke, recovering from her initial stunned silence, "So basically, these people at the top are sucking up all the available money from the world's economy and using this pandemic to exert control over the rest of us whilst they carry out their plan."

She went on reading from the file that Norman had given to her. "One of their aims is to introduce a vaccine for the virus. Once people are vaccinated they will receive a health passport. With this health passport, which will initially be a paper document, certifying that you have been vaccinated, later, an app will be introduced that will be inserted into our smart phones, this will have all your health, financial and political details stored on it. Then anyone who doesn't have a smart phone with the correct information, will literally become a non-person, unable to get education, work, medical care and or travel."

Prof. Mary said "This will give them total control over our lives. Health, finance, employment everything. It will ultimately turn us all into their slaves. There must be something that we can do to stop this happening."

Norman spoke again, "Well there is something that I have been thinking about that might work, but it will take me months to set it up."

Gerry spoke next, "What are you thinking?"

Norman again. "Not sure at the moment exactly how it would work, and it will take me time to write and refine the programme, bearing in mind that it took the best part of a year to write "Intruder," the idea would be to transfer all these funds out of their accounts, and put them in various countries national banks, for instance for the UK, we would transfer their share to the bank of England, whatever they have taken from the US to the Federal reserve. We could also give some to the better charities, at the moment there are nearly 22 trillion US dollars spread throughout these accounts, all of it stolen from the taxpayers of various major countries worldwide."

Jenna said "I like the sound of that. It might just stop them and could weaken them so that hopefully they wouldn't be able to continue with their plans, especially if at the same time we made the information that we hold public. And as the money has been illegally gained, they wouldn't be in a hurry to admit to owning it or asking for it back."

"Short of bumping off all the major players it sounds like a solution that might work, if it can be done" said Gerry. "We also need to consider carefully what the ramifications of all this will be. At the moment we are a small group of people, with decent but finite resources, so we have to consider the costs. We need to keep it to the people present at the moment and keep this whole situation under total secrecy." He went on, "At the moment we don't know how safe this place is."

Jenna said. "We need to give Norman the time that he needs, all, except Sam, Mary, Gerry, Norman and myself, could return and carry on their normal lives, whilst we will watch over and help Norman and at the same time keep right out of the way in order to stay safe, as this lot aren't going to stop looking for us."

"Or how long we are safe here?" Mary interjected. "Given that it could take several months for Norman to write his program, maybe we should look at buying somewhere, that way we can fit it out with what we are going to need, also we will need to keep Norman with us, under our wing as it were."

They all agreed that this was the right way to go. They also agreed that Gerry, Jenna, Sam and Mary would stick together with Norman and in the meantime the others would sit tight and go about their lives and business as normal with no contact unless initiated by Gerry, Jenna or Mary. They also agreed that the only time the others would initiate contact would be in a dire emergency. Once they had a new base they would organise a meeting and at that meeting they would sort out further meeting places in advance, number each one and that a 14.00hrs meeting would mean 12.00 hrs i.e. always two hours before the agreed time on the phone.

Everyone also agreed that the others would get on with their lives and not have any communication with one another unless an emergency arose. No internet research into any of it, show zero interest in any of the subjects that have been discussed here, and that way they wouldn't draw attention to themselves. Just keep their heads down and act as if the subject didn't exist.

Twenty-Six.

After saying their goodbyes, Prof Grey, the brothers and Foley all left at seven-minute intervals, leaving Jenna, Mary, Sam, Norman and Gerry to get on with their planning.

Gerry was the first to speak, "I have got a plan forming in my head, I want to think it through before proposing it so will give it some thought overnight and reveal all in the morning. I suggest we all get some sleep and return to the subject fresh in the morning".

Mary said "OK, let's decide guard duties through the night and then get some sleep."

Sam agreed to do the first watch and with that the others retired to their respective rooms.

When Jenna and Gerry were alone in their room she asked him, "Ok what are you thinking?"

He said. "The boat, how do you fancy a nice cruise round the Med whilst Norman gets his act together? He says that he won't need internet access until he has written the programme, which makes us all much safer".

Jenna said, "It could work, tell me more."

"The boat is a safe bet, we are the only ones who know about it. The ownership is, as you know, through a private Guernsey trust. No correspondence of any kind has ever gone to the house or the business. It all goes to the administrators in Guernsey. They then post it on our private file on their server which only you or I can access. I am sure that MPharma or anyone else don't know that we own the boat."

"We would need to take Sam and Norman as well as Mary, but it would keep us all out of the way until this thing is dealt with, remember we are going up against some of the most powerful people in the world. They have already demonstrated that they will not hesitate to kill to keep their secrets relating to Cancer treatment safe.

This is much bigger with all the major tech companies involved as well, we might have to revert to posting letters in order to keep things safe. In any event everything that we do from now on has to be ultra-low tech."

"We could do all the organising from here, then when we have everything arranged and ready, we just go to the boat and then leave Lymington the next day, that way we are not hanging around, and no one gets to know the others too well, once we set sail we remain pretty anonymous, but the major drawback is of course, documents, there must be a way to get some false passports etc. but I wouldn't know where to start. On the plus side we can keep on the move which makes us harder to find."

Jenna said "Let's talk to Sam, Mary and Norman in the morning and see what they think? In the meantime we should get some sleep, you will be taking over from Sam in a few hours."

The night passed without incident. The morning found them all sitting around the dining room table eating breakfast and discussing their options. Gerry had outlined his plan to the others and so far all were in favour, but Norman, whose concern was that he had never been on a boat in his life and was worried about becoming seasick.

Sam was sure that he could get his Number two to look after his business while he was away and he was 100% behind Mary, Jenna and Gerry in their effort to derail this conspiracy, as to sit back and do nothing would be a moral failure on all their parts. Going to the authorities would be hazardous as they do not know who to trust. Everything to do with the government, press and police must be regarded as suspect for now.

Mary didn't see a problem as her father had owned boats all his life and Mary had spent many days sailing with him, she loved it and said that after what had happened in the last few days it would be a very welcome change.

Gerry explained to Norman that there were various remedies for sea sickness that actually worked and that, Francis Chichester was always seasick for the first few days of all his great voyages. It would take them all a few days to get their sea legs.

He said "Our biggest difficulty will be in sourcing documents as we will all need false passports and driving licenses. I for one don't have a clue how to go about getting them. Any ideas, anyone?"

Before anyone else had a chance to speak Norman smiling said. "Shouldn't be too difficult, I can access the Passport office system and issue them, then do the same thing with the DVLA. All I will need is, say, three addresses, one for Jenna and Gerry, another for Mary and Sam, best if we show them as married and another for myself. With those addresses I should be able to issue legitimate documents that stand up to any scrutiny. I will also need passport photos of each person, which I can scan in."

No one doubted Norman's abilities and Sam asked, "how long will it take you?" Norman replied, "About three working days depending on the post, maybe four, but no longer."

Mary said, "What about bank accounts and debit and credit cards, surely we will need them as how will we be able to pay for the things that we will need on the voyage?"

"I can set accounts up online, you will have to find a way of transferring your funds to those new accounts. The beauty of this is that as everything is so dependent on computers, as long as I have the correct info I can create all of this without leaving my desk."

Gerry said, "If I set up another account for my trust in Guernsey, could we transfer funds to that account and then transfer the funds onward to the new personal accounts?"

"Of course" said Norman. "As I said before, with everything computerised these days we can use the monster that the tech companies have created to do all of this for us. But I would recommend that you create another account on the Isle of Man, as it is more secure."

"We all need to write lists of what we are going to need to sort out before we go and what each of us will need for the journey. And spend some time looking for holes in the plan."

"Once I have a new identity and bank account I can get the lawyers in Guernsey who administer the trust to draw up a charter agreement in the new name to cover us for the duration of the voyage, I for one am looking forward to getting going." Gerry said.

Jenna said. "With all that has happened recently, I think we all are." There was a general consensus to this except for Norman, who was still concerned about seasickness, but Mary piped up, "Don't worry Norman, I am a medic so will make sure that we have the right medications etc. on board, you won't have a problem I promise."

This seemed to work as Norman visibly relaxed.

Gerry said to him "Just make a list of everything that you will need, I will get it for you."

"That won't be necessary, with the modifications that I have done to my laptop it will be more than adequate, a few extra flash drives wouldn't go amiss though."

"How many?"

"Four, each with 20 gigs of memory should be plenty."

"OK I will get it sorted, anything else you need?"

"No that should do it."

They all spent the next couple of hours sorting their lists out, Sam was trawling his contacts for three useable addresses, and when he was finished he told the others that he would have exactly what they needed for the next day.

He was joking with Mary about soon being man and wife, they were of similar ages so it would look right.

Mary said, "Just don't get any funny ideas," and then looking straight at him said "Mind you, I could do worse, you're not bad looking." At which point they all started laughing and Jenna said. "You see they are already acting like an old married couple."

It was the first time any of them had really laughed since this whole sorry affair had begun. It broke some of the tension that they had all felt since this had started.

Thirty minutes later they were watching the news on TV when the pandemic had just been announced and every news channel was covering the story. To Gerry and the others, it was a chilling sight to see the proof of what they had been reading from the info they had got from Norman's endeavours, and how easy it was to pull the wool over the eyes of the world's media and others.

Mary said, "And so it begins, I had been thinking that maybe there was someone in authority who was powerful enough that we could turn to but watching this start with what we already know and who is involved, we are all going to have to tread very carefully indeed."

Jenna said, "Given that they have killed five people and won't hesitate to kill us all, imagine how those efforts would be ramped up if they had the slightest inkling of what we know now."

Sam said "They will potentially kill millions worldwide, the perpetrators of this whole business are dangerously delusional and obsessive to a lethal degree. I agree that for now at least, we need to continue with the plan and keep the whole business to ourselves."

Gerry said, "I agree, approaching anyone in authority could get us killed, so for now we must not let anyone know that we are anywhere near this thing. It looks like the pandemic has started, the news is saying that it came from a lab in China. So all we can do is try and stop these guys from gaining the control that is their aim, and seizing all their funds might not be enough, as we don't know yet all the names of the people and organisations involved. We will have that info soon from Norman. Ok so let's all just crack on with our various tasks as I think the sooner we are out of the country and at sea the safer we will be."

Sam said, "I will need to collect some clothes and other stuff from my house, also we need to decide what we are going to do with the small arsenal that we have accumulated, and my vote is that we take it all with us, provided Gerry can find a safe place on the boat to hide these weapons?"

Gerry responded "I agree, we must have the ability to defend ourselves, the boat is just over 90 feet long, I will find somewhere, which is A. Well-hidden and B. Easily accessible when needs must. When you go to your place I can come with you, if you like and watch your back."

"Thanks." Said Sam. "You read my mind. I can't help but think that MPharma won't have stopped looking for us and by now they probably know where my house is."

Twenty-Seven.

Indeed, MPharma had identified Sam, they knew his address and were busily ransacking his house as they spoke.

Gerry and Sam, having set off almost immediately, armed with a loaded Glock pistol each, were soon close to Sam's house and did a tour of the local streets nearest to his house. They spotted a Mondeo parked nearby with one occupant, he was speaking on a radio as they passed him, they didn't slow down and weren't noticed by the occupant. There was plenty of traffic, so it was just another car passing by, it was a fairly busy road at that time of day as the local school was just up the road and it was chucking out time.

Gerry drove around the next corner, dropped Sam off, their plan was that Sam would walk up his driveway and go in through the front door, Gerry would park up close by and using the alleyways would go in through the back hopefully without being seen, Sam had given him a key to the back door and clear directions to reach the back of his house.

Sam opened his front door, he knew instinctively that someone was in there as he could smell tobacco smoke the moment the door was open. He walked in and was immediately confronted by a guy holding an Uzi and pointing it straight at Sam, he was sitting on the third step of the staircase which was almost opposite the front door and slightly to its left. He told Sam to freeze and that if he moved a muscle he would shoot him. Immediately next to the stairs was a corridor leading to the kitchen, the guy aiming the Uzi steadily at Sam, got up and walked towards him, never taking his eyes off Sam.

This was a mistake as his back was turned to the passageway coming from the kitchen, Gerry stepped out of the corridor and up behind the guy, the guy didn't hear a thing and Gerry hit him hard in the side of his head, he dropped the Uzi and toppled sideways almost unconscious but not quite. Sam went for him, grabbing his wrist and lifting his arm up whilst putting a foot on his chest. He wrenched the guy's arm sideways and there was a sickening crunch as ligaments and tendons were torn as his shoulder was dislocated, he screamed, and Sam let go of his arm and lifted him up bodily by his hair.

There was another one upstairs, who, on hearing the screams came running down the stairs gun in hand, Gerry shot him, he was aiming at his legs but hit him in the abdomen, he toppled forward and landed on the hall floor. Gerry moved fast and picked up both guns, put them out of reach and then went to check on the guy he had shot.

Meanwhile Sam was still holding the first guy by the hair, who had by now passed out, Sam dropped him and said to Gerry. "How is he?"

Gerry said. "Not good, I hit him in the stomach, he will die without immediate medical care."

Sam said, "Well we can't call an ambulance, but we will have to get the guy in the Mondeo to come round and he can take them both to hospital, they won't be able to explain that it happened during a break in, so they will have to make up a story, it's their problem."

The guy who had passed out was coming round, Gerry said to him, "You had better get on the radio really quick and get your mate round here to take you both to hospital, otherwise this guy will die, and we will dump you and the body in the woods, and then you can fend for yourselves."

Gerry went on. "You can give a message to your bosses, this is the third time that you have had a go at us. If you don't leave us alone, the next time you try something we will respond in kind, i.e. we will start killing you guys and then go after your bosses. It is quite simple, leave us alone and we will leave you alone. You must have realised by now that we are better at this than you are."

Sam said, "Forget the radio, I will go and get him." And taking one of the Glocks he set off round the corner to collect the guy in the Mondeo.

Sam walked round the corner and came up to the Mondeo from the rear, noting that the driver's window was open he quickly approached it, seeing the guy was looking at the screen of his mobile, Sam smashed him in the side of his head, whereupon he dropped his phone, Sam opened the driver's door, dragged him out and pushing him hard against the side of the car said. "You are going to drive with me to the house and pick up your mates, you will then take them to hospital, they are both hurt, one has a bullet in his gut, and the other one has a dislocated shoulder. If you try anything, or if I suspect that you are going to, I promise that I will break you in all sorts of places, do everything that we tell you and you will get out of this relatively unscathed."

Sam relieved him of his mobile phone, radio and the Glock that had been on the passenger seat. He pushed him back into the driver's seat and walked round the car and got in the passenger side, keeping his Glock trained on him at all times. They drove to the house entered the driveway and pulled up by the front door.

Gerry came out holding another of the guns and kept the driver covered whilst Sam went in and picked up the one who had been shot, carried him out to the car and laid him on the back seat, he quickly returned and got the other one putting him in the passenger seat next to the driver.

Gerry had put a pad of a folded towel over the wound and told the guy in the passenger seat to lean over to the back and keep pressure on the towel. He was complaining about his dislocated shoulder but complied.

Sam issued the same warning again and added. "Tell Tobin that we will come after him if this happens again. Now get moving."

The car moved off, as it did Gerry said just loud enough that the driver could hear, "We better get a move on as well if we are going to make it to Cornwall tonight."

Once the Mondeo was out of sight Gerry went to collect their car and Sam went into the house to collect what he had come for.

Gerry returned with the car, he drove into the driveway and pulled up by the front door. Sam came out and they loaded his gear into the car.

"They've trashed the place." Sam said.

"Don't worry, it will all be added to their bill, which we will collect by Direct Debit from them." They both started to laugh. "Is the house safe?"

"Yeah I will call my housekeeper, she will come in and clean up, I pay her well she will keep things to herself. I trust her, she has worked for me for years."

Twenty-Eight.

They set off to re-join the others, Gerry drove while Sam kept a good lookout for anyone showing an interest in them. They had also very carefully checked the car for any tracking devices, just in case. It was clean.

On the way they discussed what vehicle they would use to get to Lymington, deciding a people carrier would be best. Not wanting to leave a traceable vehicle in the marina car park, they decided that after dropping everyone at the boat, they could leave the vehicle in the car park at Southampton airport, get a cab to Southampton station then a cab to Lymington high street and walk from there to the marina. It wasn't perfect, so they would talk it over with Jenna and Mary when they got back.

After getting back to the house and discussing the plan with the girls the only modification would be to leave the vehicle in one of the supermarket car parks, but then Jenna said.

"Why not have a word with Josh, he might be able to help with a vehicle. If he doesn't have one, he will know how to get what we need, he said that he is keen to help so maybe he could hire a people carrier and drive us all to Lymington. That way we don't have to leave a vehicle anywhere at all?"

"Good thinking." Said Gerry. "He would be ideal as long as no-one is watching him. It would also solve the difficulty of getting the vehicle back without having to leave it somewhere and thus not leaving a trail to the boat." He went on "Josh has got an untraceable mobile which he bought after the last incident when we had to put them off the road, he sent me the number by text earlier so I will call him and see what he says."

Gerry did just that, Josh said. "It won't be a problem, I haven't got one but will hire a nine-seater, once you are ready just call me with the address and I will come straight there and pick you all up."

Gerry said. "Great, we will be ready to leave here in a few days and will call you then."

"I'll be there, no worries."

"I will call you when we are ready to move."

They finished the call, Gerry confirmed to the others what Josh had said and then they all carried on with getting ready to leave and working out what they would need.

Three days later they were all in the minibus on route to Lymington. Again they took the northern route round the M25 and then on to the M3, everyone was in high spirits, including Norman, as they were looking forward to getting out of the UK for a while with all the talk of lockdowns etc. All their new documents had arrived, and all were getting used to their new identities.

Given what they had learned and knowing what was really going on, they found the news bulletins somewhat amusing. The media had swallowed the story, hook line and sinker and were busily doing their best to scare the living daylights out of the entire population.

But as Gerry had pointed out, the perpetrators of all of this owned most of the mainstream media, so they were just writing what they had been told to write.

Gerry and Co had seen the plans, and they showed clearly that the first phase would try and overwhelm the various medical services as the pandemic grew, then once it started to come under control the various lockdowns would be eased and then a second wave would start.

It would be timed to coincide with the flu season, this would give the various health services the chance to list all the flu deaths amongst the elderly as Covid deaths, thus inflating the figures, as of course, every winter many older and frail people die from the flu. As well as other serious ailments. This in turn will ensure that people stay afraid of this virus and do as their governments tell them. The UK government would seek new powers, and, with their massive majority were assured of getting them through parliament. The key to it being, keeping everyone afraid of contracting this virus.

It was planned for the second wave to be worse than the first, and as soon as it looked like control was being achieved, then mutations of the original virus would be discovered which were more infectious, and this would then need further lockdowns.

Of course the great beneficiaries of this were the big tech companies coming up with systems like test and trace, big pharma who were grabbing billions to research a vaccine, which they would then sell to the various health organisations and grab even more billions. The online retailers who were enjoying the extra business with all the small retailers having been forced to close. Pubs bars and restaurants all closed meaning the big supermarkets would be doing extra business in food and alcohol sales, so basically a great big money grab for the big boys at the expense of the small businesses like retailers, and smaller firms like pubs and restaurants, who would be slowly driven out of business thus allowing the larger groups to swoop in and take over these companies on the cheap. And grow even larger than they were now. Growth increases their share value, so they will become even richer.

The aim, to push all this trade into the hands of the big supermarket groups and the online retailers. They also want to keep people locked in their houses with all the information that they were receiving coming from the media which they had control of, and via the internet, which again they had control of. The aim being to stop people talking face to face and passing info on this way.

The beauty of the internet is that anyone disputing the mainstream lies, could be censored as misinformation, fake news and conspiracy theories. Because the people who were behind this, ran the internet.

The US president was against all of this, but he was being ridiculed on a daily basis in the media, and part of the plan was to get rid of him at the next election which was only a few weeks away.

Norman had seen the outline of a plan to make sure that the incumbent would lose. The big tech boys were mounting their own misinformation campaign, and at the same time accessing electoral data bases throughout the US, adding hundreds of thousands of new voters, whose votes would be added to their candidates tally. At the same time censoring the president wherever and whenever they got the chance. With their control of the media and internet this was in their power to accomplish.

Between them they controlled what information could be put into the public domain and they were in a position to ridicule any detractors.

The incumbent US president was a flaw in their plan as he simply would not fall in with their proposals, so they would have to get rid of him at any cost. And putting their own man in, who would be nothing but a stooge, but would open the door for these perpetrators to get and maintain control.

According to the info that Norman had unearthed, they weren't worried about the British PM, James Blackford, as whilst he was against them initially, they had a plan to "convince" him of the benefits of their scheme.

They would give him a bad dose of the virus, which would do one of two things. Either the virus would kill him, in which case they could fiddle the election of his replacement, putting someone in his place who would be more compliant.

Or if by some miracle he survived, then they would have scared him into changing his view by letting him know that they could re-infect him any time they chose, with a dose that would kill him.

Mary said "A virus such as this is a very powerful weapon, we have to be careful that none of us gets it. Going off on the boat and keeping away from all the hot spots looks like being a very effective strategy at this time." The others wholeheartedly agreed with her.

At times on the journey they all fell silent, contemplating the absolute enormity of what they had discovered and the ramifications that were to follow. In reality they were all stunned with the realisation that they couldn't turn to the authorities as they, were all up to their necks in this.

Josh asked why the NHS were so involved, Mary answered, "£130 billion plus per annum, more than the annual turnover of some of the biggest companies, from what we have seen so far, they are stealing 10% plus of this money. That equates to £13 billion a year. That's why, they are major players in all of this."

"But how are they getting away with it?" he asked.
"With government connivance, the sums are so big. Just look at the current secretary of health, he's a spiv, a couple of million would buy him, no problem. This government and the ones before, going back to the 90's are all involved, no one will dare speak up because they are all up to their rotten seedy necks in it. And it has been going on in its present form for at least 20 years."

"Remember" Jenna said, "So far we have only had a chance to scratch the surface of the information that Norman has obtained, imagine what is to come?"

Gerry said, "Well we should have plenty of time to look through the cogent parts of it whilst we are on the boat."

Shortly after, they arrived at the marina in Lymington. They unloaded the vehicle and Gerry, and Sam took all their stuff to the boat whilst Josh took Jenna and Mary to the supermarket to get the supplies for the first leg of the journey.

Twenty-Nine.

Gerry went to the marina office to collect the charts that he had ordered from the Admiralty chart agents, and been delivered to the marina, he had purchased both paper and electronic charts, these would take them as far as the Greek Islands, which would be sufficient for their needs for now, he was planning to get any other charts that they would need for the ongoing trip once they were on their way.

The boat was in fine shape, having been looked after well by the marina people. On Gerry's instructions they had fuelled her up and topped up the water tanks. He felt good being back on board.

Forward of the main saloon was a dining area with a table for the use of the crew, he set Norman up in this area with his computers and ancillary equipment and told Norman to double check that everything was working ok and that he had everything he needed.

Gerry and Sam then set about getting the boat ready for tomorrows planned departure, the weather was set to be fair with a north/easterly, forecast to be force 4-5. Should be ideal conditions, but he also knew the sea and a 4-5 could quickly turn into a 5-6. But not a problem for them, the boat was Dutch built of aluminium to Lloyd's standard and was as sound as the day she had been built.

With a good deep keel and rod rigging. These conditions wouldn't worry her, but he was mindful that he wanted the start of the journey to be as easy as possible for Norman in particular, let him get used to the motion first he thought.

Gerry's plan for tomorrow was, to leave Lymington at first light and run down the coast towards Falmouth, if all was well then they would carry on and head south to Gibraltar. If they had any problems then they could head into Falmouth and deal with them there. He was looking forward to getting back to sea and at the same time a little nervous, a good thing.

The girls arrived back with Josh having emptied the local supermarket by the look of it.

They got everything loaded and stowed away on the boat whilst Sam cooked a meal for everyone.

With them all sitting down to eat, conversation quickly turned to the next days' departure. Gerry filled them in on his plan, there was a general air of excitement and even Norman was looking forward to getting going. They were all tired, so sorted out the night watch detail with Sam taking the first watch.

Josh decided to get going back home and told Gerry and the others that he wanted to help in any way that he could and that he could easily meet up with them, wherever they were.

Jenna said, "Why don't you come with us?"

He replied. "I would have to make some arrangements for the business and the house, but I would love to come. Maybe I could fly down to Gibraltar and meet you there?"

They all agreed that this was a good plan and Josh got going with Gerry telling him that he would call him once they knew an ETA for Gibraltar.

Thirty.

The next morning they were all up early and ready to get going, they cast off at 08.30 hrs. And motored down river towards the Solent. As they were leaving the marina Gerry spotted something that didn't look right. A solitary man had just turned and was walking away from the quayside, he was dressed in a suit and overcoat carrying a folded newspaper in his left hand. Dressed as he was, he looked out of place in a marina.

Gerry had spotted him in his periphery and as soon as he looked straight at him, the guy had turned and started to walk away.

Once out of the river they hoisted the main and genoa and set course for the Needles. Gerry then told the others what he had seen. "It could be nothing" he told them, "But I have learnt to trust my gut instinct, something just didn't look right with this guy, so we are going to have to watch things very carefully."

Sam said, "If you're right, then how did they find out about the boat?"
"I don't know yet, but we are going to have to search the boat with a fine-tooth comb to see if anyone has put a tracker on her."

"It is about 150 nm to Falmouth, which should take us around 17/18 hrs. I suggest we use that time to check the boat out, if all is well with the boat and we are all happy I suggest that we swerve Falmouth and head south, going straight to Gibraltar."

The boat was fitted with a device known as an AIS, (automatic identification system.) This gave a signal which identified the boat and gave its position on a continuous basis via satellite. Gerry's plan had been to deactivate it once they were past the needles, but first they had to see if any other tracking devices had been put on board.

Norman said, "I can very quickly make a basic radio receiver, if we switch off everything, like the radar, VHF, Sat Nav, etc. I will be able to quickly tell if anything on the boat is sending out a signal. Make sure all your phones are off as well and take the batteries out. It will take me no more than half an hour to make. I have all the components on board."

Gerry and Sam set about shutting everything down, Mary and Jenna started an external search for anything that was either out of place or looked like some sort of transmitting device.

Gerry was at the wheel, he was steering by compass alone, with a brisk north easterly, they were making good progress and he was enjoying himself, visibility was excellent, and it felt good to be at sea again.

Gerry's plan was, that once they reached the Needles, he would set a course for Cherbourg, then as long as they were certain that there wasn't a tracker on board, he would deactivate the AIS and then shortly after, would head west towards Falmouth.

Norman appeared with his receiver in his hand, he said to Gerry. "I will start at the stern, and work my way forward, if I don't find anything then I will start down below. But if something is transmitting even from below, I should pick it up from out here." With that he walked to the stern of the boat and immediately his device started giving off a signal which got louder as he reached the transom. There was a cap rail that went right round the boat. At the after end and on the centre line, this cap rail extended a few inches forward with a hole in the centre with a stainless lug to take the boarding passerelle. He looked beneath this and immediately found what he was looking for. It was a small device, about 1 inch by 2, and half an inch thick. It had what looked like a small aerial and was held onto the underside of the cap rail by a sticky pad.

The others all came to see what he had found, he said. "Well that was easy, maybe too easy? So I think I will keep looking just in case there is another one." Handing the device to Gerry he went off to search the rest of the boat.

Gerry said, "It could be that it was done in a hurry and that they probably didn't want to break into the boat just in case they were seen by the marina security people."

Their search revealed no more devices. They decided not to throw the tracker overboard but to attach it to one of the fenders with a weight on the other side of the fender in order to keep it upright and afloat. And then once they turned west again they would lower it carefully into the water and let it drift with the current. As it would keep moving, and with luck, it would be sometime before the enemy realised what had happened.

They passed the needles and 15 minutes later turned towards Cherbourg, Gerry gave it another hour and 20 minutes before lowering the fender with the tracker attached at the same time as turning the AIS off. They then turned west again and headed for a point 20 miles off Falmouth. They had decided not to go into Falmouth because of the tracker, but once they were abreast of the port they would turn southwest and head for Gibraltar. At all times staying at least 20 miles from the land.

They pushed on and passed Falmouth in the early hours and headed southwest to clear Isle de Ouessant by a good margin. The sailing was good so far and once they were passed Ouessant they started to encounter the long Atlantic swell, as the conditions were good this remained comfortable. They were now headed for a point 20nm off Cape Finisterre which by Gerry's reckoning should take them around 2 days. They weren't in a hurry, Norman was well settled in and beavering away, he hadn't had a problem with sea sickness yet and all the others were fine. All in all they were bowling along nicely. Gerry was still trying to fathom how they had found out about his boat.

Thirty-One.

Mary and Jenna, when not on watch were sifting through the stuff that Norman had stored on one of the flash drives, they were mightily impressed at how thorough he had been, the emails and various planning documents that the enemy had stored on what they thought was a totally secure system were terrifying, this was a huge plan to control the world's resources particularly the rare earth metals and along with the Chinese, once they had control of these resources, they would be in a position to control the underclass as they saw it, and literally turn them into slaves, at the same time making sure that this underclass had no cars or holidays, and were kept in lockdown when not at work thus reducing carbon emissions and congestion throughout the modern world.

Then the elite could do whatever they wanted and not be accused of causing global warming, as by keeping the masses under control, particularly where travel is concerned, no flights and no cars for the masses, thus they would reduce the majority of pollution in the sea, land and atmosphere. A system of credits would be introduced to replace money. These would be electronically generated, and ordinary people would be summarily fined if they didn't toe the line. These fines would be deducted from a person's credits electronically by the government. Travel would be regulated and a Covid passport would become compulsory, if you didn't have both of a Covid passport and sufficient credits you would not be given permission to travel from your home area.

The major baddy appeared to be the boss and owner of Towersoft, the biggest software company in the world. He was also buying up agricultural land in the US presumably in order to control food production. He has massive holdings in all the big pharmaceuticals, He is also majorly into Eugenics, (bump off the old and infirm).

Cash would be abolished, replaced by credits which could be taken away at the click of a mouse should the person or persons concerned step out of line.

Mary reading all this said. "Joe Stalin would be proud, none of this would happen overnight, it would be brought in a step at a time. First the lockdowns, then Covid passports to go to the pub or restaurant. Once established it will be necessary to have a C passport for kids to go to school or say, a football match or concert or the cinema. The aim again is control and reduction of the world's population and at the same time making fortunes from initially, the vaccine and later the technology and apps that everybody would need on their phones so that the perpetrators could keep control of these people. Communism on steroids. We have to stop these people one way or another."

Jenna said "Looking through some of these statements and emails, they already own the mainstream media, various governments and their law enforcement and security services. They have been quite clever in buying leading figures in all these organisations around the world to the point where we have nowhere to turn to without revealing ourselves. If we sent this lot to any of the authorities they would simply bury it all."

"And us." Mary said.

Thirty-Two.

Meanwhile, on the other side of the Atlantic a meeting was taking place at the offices of Towersoft Corp. the largest software company on the planet. The meeting was chaired by Bob Towers, owner and CEO of Towersoft. Attending were the heads of the major pharmaceutical companies, major oil, major power companies, Chung Lee Yong, multi billionaire and owner of some of the biggest companies in China, Trevor Barton, ex UK Labour prime minister, The CEO of the UK's NHS and a very senior member of the US Democrat party. Dr Fitzgerald head of US health. And the chief of the WHO. The president of IBM. And of course representatives of the major banking corporations. Also there was the speaker of the house of representatives in the US. She was also one of the richest women in America and a senior member of the Democrat party.

Bob Towers was the first to speak, he said, "Good morning everyone, glad you could all make it, first I would like to update the board on the ongoing Mary Kelso affair. So far she and her accomplices have managed to elude our people and done considerable damage to our operatives. They have sent a message to us, basically saying, leave us alone or we will start targeting your people.

So far Professor Kelso hasn't gone public with any of her findings, but we are ready with our friends in the media to discredit her should she do so. It is believed that Professor Kelso along with her friends left the UK in a boat a few days ago and were last tracked heading for France. However, these people have proven to be far more capable and resourceful than we originally expected, thus we have now engaged a team of ex special forces to track them down and deal with them once and for all. I will keep you updated on progress as and when. I will soon have extended background details of her accomplices in order that we may understand their capabilities better.

Now to the main business at hand Project C. We have all worked together on this project for the best part of 20 years. With this Covid virus we have unleashed on the world, we are now going to be able to carry out the next phases of our plan. I would like to complement our Chinese friends for their help in producing and spreading the virus to the rest of the world's populations. And more importantly providing the social experiment which is the blueprint for us to be able to control the world's population.

Critical to our plans is the so called Covid or health passport. As, once we have completed this phase we will, over time, be able to control most of the world's people and weed out the non-compliers in the first instance and then, reduce the planet's population by weeding out the weak, frail, and sub-classes.

I will now hand over the floor to our good friend Trevor Barton, who will update you on the UK situation."

Barton got up and spoke "As you know the UK has played a major part in the planning and execution of our project. I did many things during my time in power as Prime Minister of the UK, to facilitate all of this. One of the biggest successes was our drive to increase the British population by way of mass migration. We have an estimated 87million people in the UK today. We have also managed to persuade the British public that this figure is a little over 65 million.

This was meant to achieve two things, one, by increasing the population, you increase the size of the market, more people means more profit which is good for the global businesses who operate in the UK. It also puts more upward pressure on the housing market. Higher property values means that the banks can lend ever more money to house owners who in turn spend the extra borrowings on cars, holidays, furniture etc. This keeps the economy buoyant.

And with people owing huge sums of money to the banks etc. those people have got to stay in work and are kept in check by their fear of losing their jobs and subsequently their houses and other possessions like cars. So far this has worked very well for us.

Second. Our aim was to dilute the essentially British sense of fair play and their insistence on democracy, in order to facilitate the erosion of freedoms and increase our control over the people. The UK is important in this respect as traditionally they have stood out against oppression and basically are a troublesome lot. This so far has been only partially successful, but the Brexit vote has shown us that the people of the UK are still as difficult as ever. For this to succeed we need to make them more compliant. This pandemic and the fear factor will help us, but we must always bear in mind that the fearmongering re. Brexit that we produced along with our friends in the mainstream media had the opposite effect and led to a Tory government with a huge majority, with James Blackford as prime minister. He is an out and out Brexiteer who will oppose that which we are trying to achieve. We were hoping for another hung parliament.

One way to get him on board will be to give him a heavy dose of Covid, this will do one of two things. One it may kill him, which for us would be the best outcome, as we could then get our own man in the job.

Second, if he survives we can use his infection as leverage against him by telling him quietly that he won't be so lucky next time. Knowing him as I do, he will roll over, no problem. He's not noted for his bravery.

Another reason why the UK is of major importance to our scheme is the National Health Service. Over recent years we have creamed off close to £500 billion from this organisation, we expect to get an extra £60 billion during this pandemic, thanks in no small part to the help and cooperation of the current health secretary, he is to all intents and purposes a useful idiot. And is helping us with our scheme in return for a financial reward. £10 million is a huge amount for him, but we may have to dispose of him afterwards, should he turn out to be a security risk, given that he is so untrustworthy. But that's a situation we can deal with later."

Chung Lee Yong was next to speak, "As you all know, with the help of our friend Trevor Barton, we have been able to infiltrate all the British universities with Chinese students, most are members of the CCP. During the last 30 years those students have slowly but surely changed the way British students think. We have been slowly able to denigrate UK history, which the British people hold dear to their hearts and is a huge part of the British culture, strength, and sense of fair play. We have always known that key to achieving our aim of world domination, it will be necessary to change the British mentality, who were always very proud of their history and achievements in the past. Slowly we have changed their thinking and have been able to start rewriting their history, and at the same time convincing them to be ashamed of that history.

As time goes by this is becoming easier for us, as the older generation who are eyewitnesses to some of the more recent history are dying off. This, we are now able to accelerate with our virus, which is killing off large numbers of this older generation. At the same time the CCP is investing large amounts into buying up UK companies which increases our ability to control that which happens in the UK."

Thirty-Three.

Meanwhile back in the Bay of Biscay two days of good sailing later.

Wind Charmer was approaching the northwest tip of Spain, Sam who was on watch could see what looked like a patrol boat steaming towards them, he wasn't concerned as they were well out in international waters and were on course to pass the NW coast of Spain by at least 20 NM. He alerted the rest of the crew and Gerry, Jenna and Mary all came up to the cockpit to take a look. During their crossing they had seen several cargo ships but no fishing boats and this was the first patrol vessel they had seen. It was heading straight for them and Gerry looking through binoculars saw that she was flying the Spanish flag.

He kept her under observation as she drew nearer heading straight for them. At the same time the wind had come round to the southwest and they were pushing into it. They set about making a sail change as up until now they had been lucky with the wind at their stern. They altered course to the west slightly to give them a better aspect to this changing wind. The sea was becoming rougher which was normal for this area of the Bay.

The patrol boat altered her course soon after, still heading directly towards Wind Charmer. They held their new course, and the patrol boat was soon passing them on their port side, the patrol boat slowed and called them on the radio. "What ship where from?" they asked. Gerry replied. "Wind Charmer, Lymington UK." The patrol boat acknowledged their communication and asked. "Where are you bound?" Gerry replied. "Gibraltar." The patrol boat acknowledged and wishing them "Bon Voyage" moved away and continued on its course.

Sam said. "I wonder what that was all about." Gerry replied. "Pretty standard enquiry, unless they have been told to watch for us, in which case they will be busy reporting our position, speed, course etc."

Jenna said, "We should be in Gib. in a couple of days it will be interesting to see what sort of reception we receive when we get there."

They pressed on although things were getting a bit lumpy, soon they had reached a waypoint 20 odd miles west from the NW tip of Spain and soon thereafter altered course to a more southerly heading which made things more comfortable as they no longer had the wind on their nose.

Sam said, "Just to be on the safe side, let's have the Uzis up here just in case" Gerry said. "Good thinking" and went below to retrieve them from the compartment where they had been hidden.
Returning to the cockpit he checked they were both loaded and ready to fire when and if they were needed.

Jenna appeared to take her watch, and Sam went below. Gerry stayed in the cockpit as it was the second part of his watch. The sun was going down, and it would soon be dark. They were well out to sea and there were no other ships in their vicinity.

The wind was holding, and they were making good progress averaging 9 knots over the ground. It was a clear night with only a new moon, and with no ambient light the night sky was a mass of stars which was like being in a dome.

Gerry was standing against the stern rail, he thought that he could detect a sound and immediately looked to port. Concentrating his gaze in that direction he heard it again this time slightly louder but could see nothing in the darkness.

He told Jenna. "Not sure, but I think I heard something, could be a fast-moving boat with an outboard."

Jenna listened intently, then heard it as well, Gerry said. "It is getting louder" and went and called Sam to come up.

Gerry was scanning to port with the binoculars and could make out a dark shape approaching he could just make out the foam from a bow wave, as it got closer he could see the dark shapes of 5 or 6 occupants and could see that one of them was aiming what looked like a rocket launcher at Wind Charmer. The inflatable was bouncing about as the sea at this point was quite choppy.

Sam arrived in the cockpit, quickly looking to starboard he made out a second inflatable coming from ahead of them aiming for their starboard side, one of the occupants was also carrying a rocket launcher and trying to aim at them whilst the inflatable bounced on the waves.

Gerry saw that the occupants were wearing night vision goggles, he quickly grabbed a handheld searchlight and aiming it directly at the men in the inflatable switched it on. Its powerful beam blinded them temporarily, the one with the rocket launcher fired, but a combination of being blinded and the inflatable bouncing on the waves meant that the rocket went well over their heads.

Sam having grabbed one of the Uzis opened fire on the inflatable on their Starboard side, he emptied a whole clip into it taking out 2 of the occupants and shredding the bow tube. The inflatable losing its buoyancy, ploughed bow first into the next wave, stopping dead, upending the boat and throwing all the occupants forward into the water.

Gerry grabbing the other Uzi fired at the other boat which had more or less the same effect, killing instantly 3 of the men aboard, one of them got a shot off which caught Gerry in his right shoulder. He felt the sting as the bullet passed through his shoulder. He put another mag in the Uzi and by this time the remaining occupants were in the water, he shot each one, making sure that they were all dead.

At the same time Jenna had turned Wind Charmer into the wind which had stopped the boat. Both inflatables and the remaining four survivors were now on the port side. Sam reloaded and they filled both inflatables with holes, the weight of their outboard motors taking them to the bottom as the air from their tubes escaped.

Three of the bodies were still afloat, the bullets that had killed them had somehow missed their lifejackets which had inflated once they were in the water. Mary who was now on deck holding one of the Glocks took careful aim at the lifejackets and put two bullets in each one, they too sank to the bottom.

The four survivors were left bobbing about in the water, Gerry and Co. had absolutely no intention of picking them up, and they had lost their weapons and were no longer a threat. One called out. "Help us, you can't just leave us here."

Gerry said. "We are going to leave you to your fate, you would have happily killed us all."

Mary said. "With luck the sharks in this area will make short work of their bodies and the prevailing currents will take what's left deep into the Atlantic."

Gerry said, "We did warn them, they should have listened to us."

Jenna said "They would have killed us all without any compunction or remorse.
They got what they deserved, we just need to make sure there are no traces of this that can lead back to us. I suggest we sail out to sea for a couple of hours, then ditch all the weapons overboard. We will be meeting up with Josh in Gib and he being ex RN, and having spent a lot of time there, he might be able to help us re-stock our armoury, these people have declared war on us and sure as hell they won't stop now."

With that they turned the boat and headed west. Leaving the 4 survivors to their fate. With only their combat gear and life jackets, their chances of survival were very slim. Unless they were picked up by another vessel soon, hypothermia would set in after a few hours, and that would be the end for them.

Mary tended to Gerry's wounded shoulder and expertly patched him up. The bullet had grazed him and left a nasty gash. She said to Gerry, "Before we get to Gib throw away any blood-stained clothing, you will need to keep the wound covered whilst we are in port in case anyone sees it and starts asking questions, but with luck the bleeding will have stopped by then. Just wear a dark coloured long-sleeved shirt for now."

Jenna said. "Once the sun comes up in the morning we must carefully check the boat for blood stains and make sure there are no traces of bullets or holes.

With luck the one that hit Gerry carried on over the side, but we need to check carefully to make sure. We also need to try and do something with the GPS, its memory will show that we were on the spot where all this took place and that we were stopped for more or less 30 minutes."

Norman who had come up to the cockpit spoke up. "Erasing the GPS's memory won't be hard, I can also get it to show that we were nowhere near this area if you like."

Norman was as good as his word, he sanitised the memory on the GPS and loaded a new route which took them more than 25 NM from the point of the incident. By the time he had finished they were at a good point to turn southeast and resume their course towards Gibraltar.

They all felt that the patrol boat had had something to do with these attackers knowing where they were.

Mary said. "This gives us a clear idea of how powerful our enemies are, and that is why we are correct in keeping all this to ourselves until we know the full story and able to work out who, if anyone, we can trust.

Sam said. "What we have to be on the lookout for is, if they came from a larger vessel they could still be a threat."

Thirty-Four.

The sun came up and it was a fine clear day. They set about ditching the weapons having cleaned them all carefully, they were in very deep water so there was no danger of a fishing boat trawling them up, and then they checked the boat thoroughly for damage, bullet holes or marks and cleaned all traces of Gerry's blood from the cockpit and surrounding area, finishing off using the deck wash that pumped sea water through a hose at a good pressure, which cleaned the decks beautifully.

It turned out that Wind Charmer had not sustained any damage at all.

The rest of the day went without incident, the sea was reasonable, and Wind Charmer barrelled along comfortably at a steady 9 knots over the ground. Gerry felt that at this rate they should reach Gib by teatime the following day. They needed to be careful around the approaches to Gib as the Spanish patrol boats in the area were well known for interfering with British registered vessels.

The evening was clear once the sun went down, and apart from seeing a few vessels in the distance on both sides, nothing came close in either direction. Gerry had put the radar on once it was dark, whilst it wouldn't pick up any inflatables, they would be able to see any larger vessels paying an interest in them.

Being 30 odd NM off the Portuguese coast they could just make out the occasional flash of light from the East of their position. The night passed without any further incidents, and they all felt that whoever had sent the 2 boats after them was probably wondering where they were or what had happened to their men.

"Let them wonder" Sam said, "If that missile had hit us we would be vapour. The only way we are going to survive this is to be as ruthless and cold blooded as they are. Also they can't exactly go public and ask for a full air and sea search, as that would mean explaining what these guys were doing out there."

No one argued with him, all were feeling the same way.

The closer they got to the Strait of Gibraltar the more vessels they could see around them and on radar. It was a very busy part of the world for shipping so other than those asleep, everyone else was keeping a good lookout.

Their first sight of land came in the form of mountains just vaguely in the far distance. Judging by their bearing the mountains were on the African side of the Straits.

They arrived in the marina in Gibraltar just as the sun was going down, they had spotted many vessels throughout the day, but none had paid them any attention. They went first to the fuel berth and topped up the fuel and water tanks, they had hardly used the main engine since leaving the UK, so they only had to top up what the main generator had used. From there they shifted the boat to a visitor's birth.

As they were tying up Josh appeared. He had been careful, he had flown from Luton to Madrid, hired a car and driven to La Linea, parked the car there and walked across the border, then got a cab to the marina. Once they were ready to leave he would call the hire company and tell them where the car was, saying that he had a family emergency and would have to fly home from Gibraltar.

Gerry reckoned that it would be better to move the car to Malaga airport and tell them that he was flying from there. He could get the train from Malaga to La Linea. They were planning on a two-day stopover in Gib so he would have plenty of time to do this.

Sam filled him in on the incident that had taken place with the inflatables and explained that they were now unarmed.

They were hoping that due to Josh's time in the Navy that perhaps there was someone he knew from his navy days who could help. It was a long shot but worth a try.

Josh said. "There is someone who might be able to help, I will have to visit a couple of pubs this evening and see if he is still around."

Sam said. "Maybe I should go with you and watch your back, just in case."

Josh said. "Why not, it will look better two guys out for a drink but if he is there let me talk to him on his own, he might start to worry if there is someone there that he doesn't know."

"Suits me" Sam replied.

Gerry said. "Best if you go for a walk around town first, just to make sure that no one is following. From our last known position, it won't take a genius to figure that we have stopped here for a restock, so be very vigilant at all times, I will feel much happier once we are out of here. We may have bought a little time as the other side will still be trying to find out where their men have got to."

Thirty-Five.

Which they were, Towers was expecting a report by now to say that the matter had been dealt with, but he had heard nothing, which made him feel uneasy to say the least. He had taken control of the situation since the previous failures and was not a happy man.

He decided to wait 24 hours before making his next move.

Sam and Josh set off into town and did some sightseeing taking in Government house, various monuments and made their way to the Angry Friar pub, all the time keeping a good eye for anyone paying the slightest interest in them. So far so good, no-one stood out and they both knew what to look for due to their training in the services. Josh knew Gib well having been stationed there for over a year.

So they were able to use back streets and alleys to reach the pub. Anyone following them would stand out, they hoped, but they generally felt that their presence in Gib was still unknown to the other side.

They figured as well, and rightly so, that this state of affairs would not last, they needed to move fast to stay one step ahead of this enemy.

They got to the pub, Josh's friend Jorge Ruiz was nowhere to be seen, the barman confirmed that he was a regular visitor but usually came in later. They had a beer and moved on up the hill to the next pub on Josh's list of possibilities, this was a dead end as well. The barman here said that he hadn't seen Jorge for a while, but he used to come in regularly. They had another drink and continued to the third on Josh's list. As they walked up the hill they got lucky, Josh spotted his friend on the other side of the road walking down the road towards them.

Jorge spotted them and gave a flick of his head to the left and turned and walked into an Italian restaurant on his left. They crossed the road and entered the restaurant, Jorge was sitting at a table in the back right hand corner, and he waved them over. They sat down and Jorge shook hands with both of them and said. "Well my friend it has been a long time, how is life treating you and who is your friend?"

"Life isn't bad, this is Sam a good friend who I would trust with my life, you don't seem surprised to see me?"

"I'm not, the barman from the Angry Friar called me and described you both, rather well, I might add. Gibraltar is a village, not much happens here without me getting to know about it. So I figure that this isn't a social visit."

"No not exactly" said Josh, "we are looking for some equipment."

Jorge gave an enquiring look towards Sam who said. "It's ok I need to stretch my legs so will leave you two to conduct your business. Josh said. "Ok I will meet you back at the Angry Friar, give us 30 minutes."

With that Sam went for a walk whilst watching carefully for anything that he didn't like the look of. As they entered the restaurant, he had seen a pair of guys that he thought he had seen earlier when walking around with Josh.

He wandered up the hill looking in shop windows and generally just looking about, there was a town map on a display at the next intersection. He stopped looked at it for a few seconds tracing a route with his finger, then abruptly stopped, turned and walked quickly back the way he had just come. Sure enough, there were the same two guys that he had seen earlier loitering, about thirty metres away down the hill.

He walked briskly towards them and then past, ignoring them as if he was in a hurry. He turned up the first passageway he came to and walked quickly to a recess, the passageway had several doors leading off it that were the entrances to various flats that ran behind the shops and offices on the main street.

He ducked into the recess and was completely hidden from view, as they walked up the passageway towards him he could hear them discussing where they thought he had gone. As they got to the recess where Sam was hiding he emerged into the passageway, grabbing each of them by the throat he bodily lifted them off the ground and held them against the wall. They were terrified, he had lifted them with ease, and both were unable to move, Sam was frighteningly strong, and neither could speak or move.

Sam spoke. "Why are you following me and who put you up to it? If you don't answer quickly and truthfully I will snap both your necks in an instant."

They were both terrified, this guy had lifted them both off their feet without difficulty, neither wanted to argue with him.

Sam released his grip enough for them to talk. One of them spoke. "We work for Jorge Ruiz, we were just supposed to keep an eye out for anyone following you and your friend."

Sam said. "Call him on your mobile, I want him to confirm that." He released them and they called Jorge who was still in the restaurant with Josh.

Jorge confirmed to Sam that they were in fact working for him. He gave them the phone back and said. "Come into the pub with me, I will buy you both a drink."

With that they walked out of the passage and into the adjacent pub. Sam bought them a large whisky each, they were both still shaking but slowly relaxed once they realised that Sam was not going to kill them.
Once they had finished their drinks Sam said. "Give me 30 seconds and then follow me at a distance to the Angry Friar just to make sure that my back is clear, OK."

They both nodded in agreement, they were so scared of him that had he told them to jump off the top of the rock, they would have done so without arguing.

Sam made his way back to the Angry Friar. Followed at a distance by the other two.

Meanwhile Josh had explained to Jorge that he needed 3 x M16s or equivalent and a pair of 9mm Glocks Plus plenty of ammo for both. Jorge said that he could manage that, and the cost would be £15k delivered.

Josh explained to Jorge that they were on a boat, Jorge said "I can get them delivered to you by boat. If you leave a couple of hours before sunset the day after tomorrow my friends will follow you in a fishing boat, keep to 6 knots and once you are in international waters they will come close alongside. The goods will be in a cheap inflatable, they will throw you a line attached to it and continue without stopping, you can haul it in and be on your way. I take it that you are going east. Josh confirmed that this was correct.

Josh gave him details of Wind Charmer and where she was berthed in the Marina.

Jorge said. "That's good, they will follow you until it goes dark and that you are both in international waters, when you can do the pickup. Then just continue on your way, all you will need to do is bring me the money in the morning."

Josh said. "That's fine but Sam will bring you the money as I have to go up the coast tomorrow, say same place 11.30 in the morning." Jorge agreed and they parted company. Josh made his way back to the Angry Friar and Jorge waited 10 minutes and made his way back home.

Josh met up with Sam, they had a quick beer while Sam filled him in on the incident with Jorge's minders and then made their way back to the boat, again checking that they weren't being followed. Josh had checked with Jorge's two lads that no one had been following them and sent them on their way back to their boss.

They got back to the boat and explained to Gerry and the Girls what had been arranged with Jorge, Gerry was a bit reticent at first regarding delaying their departure until the evening on the day after tomorrow but acquiesced once he had given it some thought and felt it was a better plan.

Sam filled them in on the incident with Jorge's minders, Mary said. "Poor devils it will take them a while to get over that."

Sam said. "We can't take any chances at all, the people that we are up against won't give us a glimmer of a chance. We literally can't take our eye off the ball for a second."

They ate in the cockpit, decided on watch details for the night and then those that weren't on watch got some sleep.

The night went without incident, the following morning Josh set off for Malaga, Sam went with Jenna and Mary to meet up with Jorge with the money, and then to the shops, to re-stock supplies for the boat while Gerry and Norman stayed on board. Gerry's arm was healing well, and he felt that the more he rested it the quicker it would heal. Norman was working on his algorithm to steal all the money that this cabal of billionaires had stolen from the various country's taxpayers.

At the same time he was working on a virus that would crash Towersoft's systems, he wanted to give them a virus of their own to deal with.

The news was that Britain, the US and most of mainland Europe were being panicked into nationwide lockdowns and bringing in legislation to remove various freedoms, which is exactly what the Cabal had planned. He couldn't help thinking how naïve these politicians were and how easily they were being hoodwinked. No common sense at all, and the media were just as bad, they just went along with it.

He had the evidence in front of him. He knew that it was all a put-up job, but it was scary how easily led the politicians were, and as for the NHS, well, from what he had seen they are up to their necks in it and were regarded by the Cabal as the world's biggest authority on cover ups. They were also the Cabal's largest contributor, they were in fact, a major player in all of this.

From what he had seen, they had developed a system that went into play the moment a mistake by one of their staff occurred. The priority is making sure that the truth and blame remained hidden. The mantra being, it is cheaper to kill than to maim. If the truth ever came out some individuals would be prosecuted for murder. Small wonder medical care in the UK was becoming some of the worst in the world. And the worst part was that the British taxpayer was paying through the nose for this abject failure.

Mistake after mistake was being made, and because none of it was ever admitted, nothing was ever learned or improved on. It was probably the biggest scandal in the world, but due to their refined systems of cover ups and their close relationship with the big pharmaceutical companies, and mainstream media nothing has ever been done about it. The big pharmaceutical companies were making billions out of the NHS. The British public on the other hand were being fleeced in order to keep this state of affairs going.

Their advice on cover ups and disinformation had been invaluable to the Cabal in carrying out their plans. They, the NHS, were the experts. They had been getting away with it for decades. And, again the hard-working British public were paying for it, as usual. Add to that the billions of British taxpayer's money that they were wasting or just paying out to their suppliers including the big pharmaceuticals, it just got worse year after year.

Up on deck Gerry was giving the cockpit and surrounding areas a good clean, he was taking it slowly in order not to make his shoulder worse and also that way he could keep a weather eye out for anyone taking an interest in them or the boat.

So far apart from a few obvious tourists and boat owners no one had stood out. He was looking forward to getting back on the move, his feeling was that the more that they kept moving the safer they were. They had to give Norman the time that he needed to perfect his algorithm. Once that was done they could decide how to put their plan into action, and where to do this from.

Soon Jenna, Sam and Mary were back with all their supplies, once everything was loaded on the boat and whilst Sam and Mary were below.

Jenna said to Gerry. "You must have noticed that those two are getting on rather well."

Gerry said. "Yeah I had noticed, and it can only be a good thing, they are both single and I think that Sam is only three years older than Mary so that seems as though it could work out for them."

Jenna said. "They are in the galley cooking up the evening meal. Chatting away like they have been married for years. I think it's great."

"It would be nice for something good to come out of all this. They do get on very well."

A couple of hours later Josh got back, having returned the hire car, he had got the train from Malaga to a place called Bobadilla, and then on down to La Linea. A cab to the border and then he had walked to the marina.

They all, apart from Norman, spent the rest of the day getting Wind Charmer ready for sea the following evening. Carefully loading and stashing the supplies for the next part of the journey.

Keeping up their system of watches, one of them at all times was up topsides keeping an eye out. Gerry was convinced that the Cabal knew where they were and as the marina was overlooked by several buildings, it would be easy to keep an eye on them.

He figured that they wouldn't try anything whilst they were still in port as it was too public a place. Any danger would come after they had left and were well on their way in international waters. They would be ready for them. So long as nothing happened before receiving their weapons.

Again the night passed without incident, all were up early and looking forward to being at sea again. They spent the day finishing off their preparations, Gerry's plan was to head straight for Naples, but he told the marina people that their next stop would be the Balearic Islands.

He calculated that the distance was 980 nm and would take them, 4.5 to 5 days to get there, all being well and with a favourable wind.

It was soon time to leave port. Gerry had been to the marina office settled up and dealt with the formalities. He was informed by customs that lockdowns were starting all over Europe and that Italy was likely to lockdown soon as it looked like they had the worst outbreak in Europe so far.

Gerry told them that their next destination was Palma in Mallorca, and they weren't scheduled to go anywhere near Italy.
With all the formalities taken care of he returned to the boat, they cast off, and made their way out of the harbour, and more or less immediately turned due south and headed towards Europa Point staying as close as they dared to the Rock. Once clear of Europa Point they would turn East and head towards the Balearics.

Thirty-Six.

Josh was detailed with keeping a good eye astern, looking for the fishing boat that was to rendezvous with them and hand over their cargo of munitions.

Sure enough just as they were about to go round Europa point, he saw a small fishing vessel clear the port entrance and turn south following their course. The sun was setting so the timing should be just right. They had shortened sail. The wind was southerly, and they were making about 5 knots. Which should be slow enough for the other vessel to catch them by the time full darkness came.

Josh was also keeping a good watch to make sure no one else was showing any interest in them. The further east they went on their present course, the further the land, which was on both sides of them, receded. They were keeping a close watch for anything appearing from the Spanish side, after the incident with the two inflatables, Gerry was convinced that it was the Spanish patrol boat, which had alerted the Cabal of their whereabouts and position.

He wasn't wrong.

The Cabal had very easily put an alert on the Spanish system to report any sightings of Wind Charmer and report their position but take no action. They had to be careful with doing this as the Spanish were well known for interfering with other countries investigations, if they thought they could gain from it. But they had routed the enquiry through the CIA, so were prepared to take the chance.

Wind Charmer had been watched from the Rock as she left Gib and rounded Europa point. They knew the direction the boat was taking.

Towers had by now been informed that their crack team had disappeared without trace and was now working out his next move. He had lost 12 supposedly experienced troops and he was guessing that to have lost them all, they must have been accidentally run down by a passing ship. It was a mystery that he was never going to solve.

Losing 12 operatives didn't faze him one bit, he was planning to kill millions of what he regarded as worthless individuals. He had felt for years that the world was overcrowded, and the only solution was to kill off the old, the infirm and the crippled who could no longer work and according to his way of thinking, were a drain on the world's dwindling resources.

Which, when his plans eventually worked out he, and the other members of his Cabal would end up controlling those resources. Once they had achieved this they would control the remaining populations, get rid of the politicians and rule the world with a system similar to that used in China.

He was in fact quite mad and completely delusional. So were most of his Cabal. Most were billionaires and all felt that, as a result of their success, they had divine rights and that, they, and only they, knew how to sort out the world's problems.

They were no different than the likes of Hitler, Stalin and Mau Tse Tung. All felt they had the right to rule the world and as a result killed and maimed millions of ordinary people, causing hardship and grief to millions more. This lot were no different and had to be stopped, quickly.

Next time would be different he thought. Also he had the pandemic to think about, he had no idea that the same people that he was trying to kill off over a cure for cancer, knew every last detail of his plan for the human race.

Gerry had slowed Wind Charmer reducing sail to do so, the sun had gone down, and it was getting darker by the minute, Josh was watching the fishing boat as it closed the gap between them. Shortly it had caught up and was passing them on their starboard side. Leaving a gap of around 20 feet and slowing to match Wind Charmer's speed.

A guy on the port side hurled a coiled line to them which Josh caught, connected to it as promised by Jorge, was a small inflatable loaded to the gunnels with several holdalls. Josh carefully hauled the inflatable towards Wind Charmer and secured it on the starboard side. By now Gerry had stopped the boat and Jenna being the lightest went over the side into the inflatable and started to pass the bags up to Sam and Josh whilst Gerry kept the boat steady.

Once all was loaded Gerry got the boat underway again but keeping to 5/6 knots for the moment. Sam hauled the small inflatable aboard, and with a sharp knife slashed the inflatable's tubes. He then threw it back into the sea and watched it sink below.

The others including Mary and Norman helped check the arms and then stashed them below. Being 90 feet overall there was plenty of room to hide them away so that if they got boarded, there was a good chance that the guns wouldn't be found.

Sam kept one of the M16's out plus a couple of spare mags, just in case. If they were boarded by the Spanish he could very easily drop them overboard.

Slowly over the next two hours Gerry brought Wind Charmer up to speed. The wind was coming from the southwest, a steady force 6, and as they bore deeper into the med and further from land on both sides, the effect of the mountains on the African side was diminishing.

As usual for the Med the sea was being whipped up into a short sharp chop as a result of the increase in wind, but it was steady. Being on their starboard aft quarter, Wind Charmer was handling it well and making a good 9/10 knots over the ground.

By dawn the next day they were flying along making good progress and the night had not revealed any problems from passing vessels or patrol craft. They discussed this state of affairs and felt that the Cabal might be trying to lull them into a false sense of security. They all felt uneasy as no one knew what would happen next. The Cabal was not going to give up, that was for sure, they, the Cabal had too much at stake.

They were regularly listening to the world service. Italy had been hit badly by the pandemic and was under lockdown refusing to let any foreign vessels enter their ports. Mary pointed out that this was probably a good thing and that they had enough supplies for two weeks and Wind Charmer could easily stay at sea for this amount of time. Wind Charmer had crossed the Atlantic twice and was a very capable vessel.

Gerry's worry was still the same, how had they found out about Wind Charmer? He was sitting in the cockpit with the others, Wind Charmer was on auto pilot, the wind had eased, and she was bowling along nicely at 7 knots.

Norman asked Josh if he had hired the minibus in his own name. Josh told him that yes he had.

Norman said. "That's more than likely the answer, all the major hire companies and some of the smaller ones are all connected to a central database. Worldwide, guess who runs it for the hire companies. Towersoft that's who. All they would have needed to do is put an alert on the system with all your names and addresses, then hey presto as soon as one of you hires a vehicle an alert goes straight through to the Cabal, with full details of you, your names addresses, DVLA number. Full details of the vehicle hired etc. That's how they found out. They could have easily followed Josh to Essex and then all of us to Lymington. Gerry you said that you didn't like the look of that bloke in the marina as we were leaving?"

Gerry said, "That's right."

"He had probably been watching us since the moment we arrived there. Somehow we had been followed to Lymington. They, the Cabal, as soon as they knew where we were and what boat we were on could have easily accessed the marina's system and got full details from it. The rest we know."

Josh was really upset about this as he felt that he had let the others down. Mary tried to console him. "Josh forget it you weren't to know, and we should have all been more careful, what's done is done and we need to decide on our next move."

Gerry said. "If anyone is to blame it was me for being naïve and thinking that the boat was secure, when it was too easy for them to watch us once they knew about it."

Jenna said. "Ok, recriminations apart, we need to decide what to do about it. Because we need more time for Norman to finish his algorithm and then proceed with our plan. For that we need a safe haven."

Sam cut in. "Presently we are on course for Naples, Italy is shut to visiting yachts due to their lockdown in response to the pandemic. But Gerry, do you remember the Sicilian guy we worked with in Bosnia?"

"Sure he was a Captain with the Italian special forces, Piero Cantolini, good soldier and trustworthy. Why what are you thinking?"
"If my memory is correct, his family own a vineyard on Sicily. Maybe we could speak with him and see if there is a place we can rent for a while on Sicily. Somewhere fairly remote where we won't stand out and is very definitely low tech. The lower the better, but also easily defended."

Sam said. "I still have his contact details, if we keep going to Naples we will be able to anchor in the bay outside the port, they won't let us enter but will let us order ship's supplies by phone and have them delivered out to the boat. I can then try and contact him and see if I can arrange a meeting. We may have to sail down to Sicily in order to do that."

Jenna said. "Sicily sounds like a plan that could work. But where do we park Wind Charmer whilst we are there?"

"Let's wait until I have spoken with Cantolini and see what he thinks. He knows the local area."

Later in the day they passed well to the South of the Balearics and a few hours later Gerry was about to alter course for Naples.

Looking at the chart he saw that it made more sense just to head straight for Palermo. It would take a couple of days to get there then Sam could call their friend. They could get supplies delivered out to them there, just as they could with Naples.

He spoke to the others, and they agreed that it would be much simpler and easier to head straight for Palermo. With that Gerry plotted a course to take them 2 miles North of Cabo San Vito, which was on the Northwest tip of Sicily.

The run from there would be easy into Palermo.

Gerry altered course accordingly and Wind Charmer settled into the 2-day run to Palermo. With the brisk South Westerly wind more or less behind them, they were making good time.

Thirty-Seven.

The following 2 days were delightful sailing and as they approached Cabo San Vito they started to pick up the Italian mobile phone system which allowed Sam to start trying to contact their friend.

He first tried the mobile number that he had for Piero, the number was either out of service or he had changed it. He then tried the number for the vineyard which was answered immediately. He spoke to the receptionist in English, and she replied in heavily accented English. She told him that Sr. Cantolini was out checking the vines and that mobile reception was patchy out there.

Sam said that he would keep trying his mobile but left his name and number in case he had not managed to contact Sr. Cantolini in the meantime and perhaps she would be so kind as to ask Sr. Cantolini to call Sam once he returned. The receptionist confirmed that she would do this and Sam, thanking her, severed the connection.

Sam and the others were all relieved that contact had been made and they didn't have long to wait. 40 minutes later Piero was calling Sam. He was delighted to hear from Sam and his first question was to enquire about Gerry.

Sam explained that he was with Gerry, his wife and friends on Gerry's boat. That they were on route to Palermo and that they were close to Cabo San Vito and intended to go to Palermo to restock their supplies.

Piero said. "Why go to Palermo? It is on lock down. You will be better off going to Trapani, it is closer and if you go to the yacht marina, I can arrange for you to berth there whilst you take on supplies. I will meet you there, what is your ETA?"

Gerry interrupted "About three hours, give or take."

Piero said. "Good that's settled give me the name of your boat and I will make all the arrangements. I will ensure that there will not be any formalities. I am only 1 hour's drive away so will be there to greet you."

Sam confirmed they would be there and switched off his phone. Gerry set Wind Charmer on a course that would take them directly to Trapani.

In the event it took them just over 2 hours to arrive at the harbour, on entering they received a radio call from the berthing master who directed them to a suitable berth. Piero was waiting with the port captain as they berthed.

Once tied up alongside Piero came aboard with the port captain, who welcomed them and explained that as they were guests of Sr. Cantolini there would be no need for formalities as everything had been taken care of by their friend. He went on to explain that to all intents and purposes, they weren't there.

The port captain then left, all the others sat in the cockpit and after hugs and some back slapping Sam introduced Piero to Jenna, Mary, Josh and Norman.

Piero had brought a case of red wine as a gift for them, once opened they saw that it was a 1964 vintage from the Cantolini vineyard and there was only one thing to do and that was open a bottle and toast one another.

Piero then said. "Ok my friends in what way can I help you, and what brings you to my pretty island?"

Before they arrived they had decided to take Piero into their confidence and so Gerry explained what had happened from the beginning and what had brought them to Sicily. He also explained Norman's part in it and that they were looking for a base where Norman could finish his work.

Piero explained. "Due to my family's friendship with the Port Captain your details will not be entered on the computer system thus no one from outside would know of your presence in the marina for now."

He went on. "When I leave, I will give instructions that if anyone shows any interest at all in you or your boat they will need to report it directly to me. My family's vineyard is no more than 1 hour's drive from here, we have nearly 700 hectares and there are many houses and cottages on the estate, there is one that has 6 bedrooms which has been refurbished recently and is empty at the moment, that would be ideal for your purposes, we would just need to get internet facilities installed but I can arrange this today and you will have full service in a few days."

Norman said. "For now it would be better not to have an internet connection, as I don't need it at the moment and if we don't go online we can't be traced. The way to beat these people is to keep everything as low tech as possible until we are ready to make our move. Once we make our move it will be too late for them. With luck."

Piero said. "I will have it all ready for you to move in tomorrow if that suits you. I can send a car to pick you up at around 12.00hrs."

Gerry said, "It will need to be a big car, there are six of us."

"Of course. I will send 2 cars, it is a pleasure to be able to help you. We all have a responsibility to thwart these people if we can."

The others all thanked him, and he left. They then set about cleaning Wind Charmer and preparing her for the stopover in the marina. They then took the boat to the fuel birth and topped up her fuel and water tanks so that she was ready in case they needed to make a hasty exit from Sicily.

Thirty-Eight.

Once back on the berth. Mary said to Gerry. "I need to look at your shoulder and change the dressing, how does it feel?"

"Not bad if anything it is just a bit sore, the stitches pull a bit when I move it, but apart from that all seems well."

Mary removed the bandage and had a good look saying. "It is healing nicely and looks lovely and clean. Give it a couple more days and I will take the stitches out."

She cleaned the wound and redressed it. Gerry couldn't help thinking that, it was very useful to have their own qualified surgeon on board.

Towers was again chairing a meeting only this time there were a reduced number of attendees. Amongst them was a new face, Major Albright Brand, an ex-US navy seal and a very ruthless individual.

The representative from China was also there. He and Brand had had an earlier meeting.

Brand got up to speak. "Gentlemen, so far every time that we have gone after these people, we have come off worst. They have run rings around us, every single time. The reason being that we have been under estimating, their capabilities, courage, and devotion to staying alive and they have been one step ahead of us all the time as a result. My first question to you is why? Why not just let them publish their findings and be done with it."

Bob Towers got up and spoke. "Should this cure be developed it will wipe out a trade that runs to hundreds of billions a year, for us in the tech industry and our friends in the big pharmaceutical businesses, of which we are major investors and shareholders as well. This cure would wipe out the Cancer business overnight. And believe me, from our point of view, it is a business nothing more. We need Cancer and other illnesses to get worse not better. We are in the business of making treatments not cures, curing an illness is bad for business. If this cheap and simple cure gets out into the public domain others will follow.

Another major example is the common cold. There are many cures for this but so far collectively we have kept them hidden. Again, cure the common cold and we lose $100's of billions annually. Go into any drugstore or pharmacy and you will see hundreds of products to relieve the common cold or flu symptoms. And guess what? We either make those products or own large amounts of the companies that make them.

Cure these things and all that business goes. No, we have to stop these people and we have to do it quickly.

Similarly with our pandemic project we stand to make billions on Personal Protection equipment and the vaccine, plus of course all the tech they will need for track & trace systems that we have persuaded the various governments are vital. Added to that, the amount of data we will acquire from all of these various things will make us the most powerful people on the planet. We will know everything about everybody. Then, we will be able to achieve absolute control worldwide.

The Chinese got up to speak. "Having spoken to Major Brand earlier we have agreed to lend you a four-man detachment from our special forces. They will have forged South Korean papers and each man is a highly trained assassin. They will be given the task of eliminating these people once and for all. Believe me gentlemen when I say, they will carry out this task with deadly devotion. And they are very good at what they do. Let me assure you, they will not fail."

Thirty-Nine.

Back in Trapani, the night passed without incident. They kept up their watch routine. All were agreed that they were not out of the woods yet, and with all the facilities that were available to the Cabal, it was just a matter of time before they caught up with Gerry and Co again. The Cabal had too much at stake, and so far were clueless as to the amount of information that Norman had extracted from their systems.

Gerry checked the boat thoroughly before leaving her. She was too big to hide, and he had to rely on the Port Captain and his staff to keep a watch over her. Soon enough Piero arrived driving a Range Rover followed by two Alfa Romeo SUV's.

They had packed the clothes and gear that they needed, including their laptops and Norman's memory sticks and locked up the boat. They put their gear in the Range Rover, then Gerry, Jenna and Norman got in the first Alpha, Sam and Mary, whose romance was blossoming, they had spent the last two nights sharing a cabin, got in the second Alfa with Josh and the convoy set off with Piero in the lead.

Gerry left a key with the port captain in case of emergencies.

Leaving the Marina they drove around Trapani and took the road heading south towards Fontanasalsa. Once on the open road Gerry spotted a crew bus full of what looked like farm labourers in a lay by at the side of the road. He kept an eye on the crew bus and shortly after the second Alfa passed it, the crew bus pulled onto the road keeping a good distance behind them.

Gerry spoke to the driver. "There's a crew bus back there that may be following us." The driver replied in heavily accented English. "It is following us, they are our back up." Gerry smiled with the knowledge that Piero was taking things very seriously. "Don't worry Signor, Piero has made careful arrangements, there will be others on the route, just sit back and relax, this is our island."

Forty.

Meanwhile.... Four supposed South Korean's were disembarking a flight from Hong Kong into London Heathrow airport. They were straight through immigration as each was carrying a diplomatic passport. They were met by a guy who was posing as an attaché at the South Korean embassy, he was in fact one of the many Chinese agents who had been infiltrated into the UK and EU, and most major cities were full of them.

He explained to the four that thanks to the US Central Intelligence Agency, again using Chinese agents, they had been able to ascertain that Wind Charmer was in fact in Sicily in a port known as Trapani and had been there for two days. They, the four were to proceed to Naples on the next flight and thereafter by car to Reggio Calabria and then by ferry on foot to Messina. They would be met there and provided with all the armaments and surveillance equipment that they would need to carry out their task.

They expected to be in Sicily by the following morning, due to flight times and ferry schedules. Once there, they would head for Trapani, confirm that the boat was still there and carry out their mission using their own initiative. They had been given free reign, the only instruction they had received was that these people were to be eliminated in whatever way they felt was expedient. They were also instructed to take possession of any scientific information relating to this cure for cancer.

Reaching the small town of Niuri the convoy turned inland onto a small country lane. About a kilometre up this lane the convoy passed a large farm truck parked in a layby, once the convoy had passed this truck, it pulled out and blocked the road so that no other vehicles could get through. It was a quiet road, but Piero wasn't taking any chances.

Two kilometres further on and the convoy turned left onto a rarely used farm track and headed up into a forest on the side of the hill. The two Alfa's continued to follow the Range Rover, but the crew bus made several stops dropping off two armed men at each stop. Their job was to plot themselves up where they couldn't be seen and observe the road to make sure that the convoy was not being followed.

After another kilometre or so Gerry spoke to the driver. "How far are we from the Cantolini estate?" The driver replied. "We have been on the estate since we turned off the main road, this is all Cantolini land from now on. We came in by the back door."

The driver's name was Federico, he was a very competent and smooth driver, he went on to say "The Cantolini family own all the land that you can see around and more, they have grown wine here for several generations. They are a well-respected and liked family on Sicily and have a lot of very good and powerful friends. It would be a mistake for the people chasing you to mess with them."

Gerry said. "These people don't care, they are delusional and think that they have divine rights. They must be stopped."

Shortly after, they arrived at a very secluded stone-built cottage, as Piero had told them, it had been recently restored, and the roof and windows were obviously new.

Once inside they could see that the Cantolini's had spent quite a lot of money on the restoration, the cottage was well equipped and was fully furnished and looked as though the work had been done to a high standard. It was tastefully furnished throughout.

They unloaded the cars and the Range Rover, they had brought what fresh food they had on the boat and Piero said. "Anything you need just give Federico a list and he will get it for you. There is a small supermarket in the village which stocks most things."

Gerry said, "We left our arms on the boat, we will need to collect them at some stage preferably sooner rather than later."

"Are they in a safe place on board?" Piero asked.

"Yeah, they are well hidden."

"In that case, why don't you leave them where they are, to save transporting them and I will send one of the lads back with everything that you will need and ammunition as well."

He went on to say. "I have posted guards around the cottage, they are all well-hidden and understand that anyone approaching the cottage must not be able to see them, in that regard they are all non-smokers as anyone approaching could not only smell the smoke but would be able to see them after dark due to the glow of the cigarettes. Remember it gets very dark at night here as there are no streetlights, so the slightest glow from a cigarette or torch can be seen easily. I have also left instructions that any non-native arrivals at the airport and ferry ports should be reported to me at once."

Gerry gave him an enquiring look and said. "How did you manage that? I'm impressed."

"Easily done, the Chief of the Island's police force is my uncle."

With that he left them to get on with moving in. Jenna and Mary gave Federico a list of items they would need from the shop, and he left to do just that.

Mary and Jenna helped Norman get set up with his equipment in the smallest bedroom and he got to work creating his programme. Norman, although he had enjoyed the sailing, was glad to be back on dry land.

A short time later whilst they were getting organised a vehicle pulled up, it was one of Piero's men, and he had brought with him a small armoury. 3 x Uzis, 4 x Glock 9mm machine pistols, and a couple of sawn-off shotguns. Plenty of spare mags and boxes of ammunition and a box of hand grenades.

His name was Alfredo, he checked everything with Sam and Gerry remarking that they probably had enough to hold off a small army. He confirmed that Piero had posted guards in the forest and hills behind the cottage, so to be careful not to shoot any of them. He had also brought them a couple of handheld radios set to the same channel as the guards in order that should there be any problems, the guards would be able to warn them.

Also he said. "If any of you go for a walk or leave the cottage for any reason take one of the radios with you. Also I would recommend that you go in pairs and not alone, just as a precaution. And take a weapon."

"Will do" Gerry said. "It looks like there are some spectacular walks around here. Having been on the boat for the last couple of weeks, we could all do with the exercise."

Jenna said to him. "Your English is very good and so are the others that we have spoken to. Where did you learn to speak it so well?"

"All employees of the estate have to learn English and be able to speak it well. It is a condition of our employment, I was sent to the UK to learn mine, and spent 6 months with a family in Wiltshire. They are Sicilian, but for six months I had to speak English and nothing else. You soon pick it up that way."

With that he took his leave of them, and they carried on getting settled in.
Gerry said. "Is anyone hungry, I can cook something up if you like?"
Jenna and Mary looked at one another and Jenna said. "No it's OK, Mary and I have a plan for today's meal. We will do it."

Mary said. "I will take a look at your arm after we have eaten. The stitches should be ready to come out now. How is it feeling?"

"Fine." He said. "I had almost forgotten about it."

"Good." Mary said and went off to join Jenna in the kitchen.

Sam, Gerry and Josh all went outside to check on the lye of the land, the cottage was well placed on a small plateau, the surrounding area was fairly rocky, and the cottage was secluded by the terrain.

The cottage and plateau faced west and in the far distance they had an uninterrupted view of the sea. It was a warm fine day and with the mountains behind them this place felt secure and with Piero's guards dotted around they were confident that should anyone come after them, they would at least get some prior warning.

The girls called them for food, they went back in, and a fine meal had been prepared and laid out on the table. They ate and once finished Mary sat Gerry down and attended to his wounded shoulder.

Looking at it she remarked. "It has healed beautifully, so I will take the stitches out, just go easy on it for a few days to give it a chance to heal properly."

"What no gunfights or punch ups." He said with a smile.

"Gunfights are allowed but no fisticuffs." Mary said laughing.

The others watched on making all sorts of wisecracks, as Mary removed his stitches. Everyone seemed to be a little more relaxed after the events of the last few weeks, feeling a little safer knowing that they now had friends watching their backs. They knew that they weren't safe yet, but it was a start. They also enjoyed one another's company, which helped enormously but no one was going to let their guard down, just yet.

Federico returned with their supplies, he had got them plenty of fresh food which they all thought was a class above that which they had seen in the British supermarkets for some time.

Federico took his leave from them, they got the bedrooms sorted out and soon it was time to turn in.

They sorted the watches out and Jenna took the first stint armed to the teeth with a Glock and one of the sawn-off shotguns, which Sam had told her was probably the best close-range weapon of the lot.

He said to Jenna. "You just have to point that in the general direction of any intruders and fire both barrels, even if they are wearing a vest, you will stop them in their tracks."

Forty-One.

He then went to join Mary in bed. Gerry was still up and came and sat with Jenna. They talked for a while about how their lives had changed in the last few weeks and what the future might hold for them once this was all over. It had certainly changed their lives as neither saw going back to the UK and resuming their previous lives as a viable option.

They also discussed what Mary and Jenna had been reading, about the way these billionaires were planning to get control of the world's population and its resources. By way of taking control of Money, and abolishing cash completely, control of Agriculture, Energy, Education, and Employment, Healthcare, and Food production.

They want to introduce a system similar to China, whereby, if you toe the party line, you can earn credits, live in a decent area, and get a good education and healthcare for your kids. And travel.

Don't toe the line and you become a non-person, no job, a very small hand out from the authorities and you would be living in a camp somewhere. Your children wouldn't get a decent education or healthcare.

They want to control all the world's resources and keep them for their own benefit only.

Jenna said "It's the same old story. It's the rich what gets the pleasure and the poor what gets the blame. Trevor Barton and his chums just refined it, again it comes down to Extreme Capitalism. Which is the same as Fascism, Nazism, Communism, and all the other oppressive systems perpetrated by delusional people who think that they have the divine right to tell everyone else how to lead their lives. And history shows us that whenever this happens, it is the everyday people who suffer and pay the cost."

The following morning was fine and dry. The first ferry arriving at Messina brought the 4 Chinese posing as South Korean diplomats, in spite of their looks, they looked like soldiers in suits, and they were fast tracked through customs and were met by a chauffeur driving a VW crew bus.

A list of their needs had been sent in advance of their arrival and the driver informed them that all the stuff that they had requested was waiting for them at the villa that had been rented for them. There was also a Fiat saloon waiting for them at the villa, the leader of the four, Wen Lee, told the driver to head for the marina in Trapani before going to the villa.

The driver said. "No problem, we go almost past it on the way."
"How long will it take?" asked Wen.
"About 3.5 hours, give or take, it depends on the traffic."

In the end it took them just over 3 hours to reach the marina, traffic was light, and they were able to make good time.

The driver pulled into the main car park. Wen and one of the others got out and walked to the marina office.

They explained that their boss was thinking of bringing his boat there and that they were looking to see if the marina could accommodate a boat that was 30 metres o/all length and 7metres wide.

The girl at the desk confirmed that they could accommodate vessels of up to fifty metres.

Wen asked her if it was OK to have a look round, she told them that it would be ok, and that the berthing master was not around but would be back in 30 minutes, so that if they had a look round and came back afterwards, he would be back and able to answer all their questions.

They thanked her and went to wander around, she noted that they made a beeline for Wind Charmer and showed no interest in any of the other beautiful yachts that were berthed nearby.

She had been instructed by her boss to immediately report anyone showing interest in Wind Charmer and picked up the phone, called the port captain and reported what she had seen to him.

He in turn, called Piero and passed the information and description of the two Chinese looking men to him. Also that they had shown a great deal of interest in Wind Charmer and nothing else.

That was the second call that Piero had received about this matter, the first being a call from one of his uncle's colleagues earlier to say that four supposed diplomats from South Korea had disembarked the morning ferry and had been picked up by a grey VW crew bus, he had further told him that they looked more like soldiers than diplomats.

The girl had also remarked to her boss at the marina that they looked more like thugs than boating people. Piero thanked him and asked him, that if they came back to talk to the berthing master, could he try and keep them there until his people arrived so that they could get a good look at these Chinese looking guys. He then sent two of his people to the marina to check them out.

Piero then got in his car and drove to the cottage to talk to Gerry.

The Koreans spent some time wandering around the marina feigning interest in various parts, but it was obvious that their main interest had been Wind Charmer.

They returned to the office a while later and were met by the port captain whose name was Massimo Fellini, he offered to take them on a guided tour of all the marina's facilities. They welcomed this and went with him on the tour. He showed them the boatyard, and chandlery and explained to them the various facilities that the marina had including fuel and fresh water.

He also showed them a potential berth for their employer's yacht and then asked them whether it was a power or sailboat? And of course what make it was?

Wen, after a little hesitation answered that it was a sailboat similar to the one that they had seen earlier and pointing out Wind Charmer, he said. "That one, I think her name is Wind Charmer."

Fellini explained to them that Wind Charmer was just under thirty metres in overall length and that the berth he had offered them would accommodate a vessel of comparable size. He asked them more questions about their boss's boat but, Wen explained that they had been sent to look at potential marinas for the boat but had not actually seen it and therefore only had scant details.

Fellini thought that this was odd, as a phone call to the marina would have provided them with all the information that they required. He said nothing but invited them to one of the bars in the marina for a coffee. They agreed to this, and Fellini led them to the nearest bar, he was trying to hang on to them until Piero's people arrived, the problem being that most boaters would sit and chat about boats and sailing, for hours but these two did not have a clue, so he asked the usual questions like how they were enjoying their stay in Sicily and telling them about the wonderful beaches nearby.
Wen said. "That boat we saw earlier, Wind Charmer, is she for sale? And does the owner get much use of her?"

Fellini replied. "He is in the UK at the moment and will probably be back in a month or so. Unfortunately, I cannot give you any further info regarding her, other than to say that I don't think she is for sale. We are not allowed to provide information to third parties about any of the boats here as it is confidential information."

Wen thanked him saying that he understood, they finished their coffees and talked some more about the various places of interest in the local area. The Koreans then took their leave of him. Fortunately as they were walking from the bar still with Fellini, Piero's two men arrived and walking past them, got a good look at the Koreans. They showed no interest in either Fellini, who they both knew well, or the two Koreans. Instead they continued to the marina office and waited for Fellini to return.

Fellini walked Wen and his friend to their car noting that there were three others waiting in the VW, he wasn't worried about getting their vehicle's registration number as they had this on CCTV.

He gave Wen his card and a brochure and said. "If you get your boss to email me with details of his boat I will send him a quote for berthing and full details of the marina's facilities."

With that Wen thanked him, got in the VW and they drove off. Fellini returned to the marina office, thankful that they had gone as he hadn't felt relaxed talking to them, and he doubted that their enquiry was genuine.

He immediately spoke with the two guys that Piero had sent. "They were definitely not interested in bringing a boat here. They didn't ask any of the right questions and were more interested in talking about Wind Charmer than anything else. Also they were not diplomats or office workers, one look at their hands told a story, bashed up knuckles and bruises. They looked like a couple of thugs."

"Have you got them on CCTV?"

"Yes, I will get my receptionist to make you a copy of today's disk." With that he spoke with the receptionist, and she very quickly copied the disk.

"My friend will stay here and keep an eye on the boat I will take the disk to Sr. Cantolini and then return here. We are under orders to keep an eye on the boat at all times."

He took the disk and set off to go back to the vineyard. The other one remained, and Fellini checked that he had what he needed and left him to it.

His name was Miguel, he headed straight for the boat and had a good look round her to see if anything had been damaged or interfered with in any way.

All looked Ok he went on board checked the deck and had a careful look at the rigging and anywhere something could be hidden. All looked good and he went below, checked the bilges and again all looked ok. The two Chinese had not been on board according to the CCTV, they hadn't had a key, and Miguel had been given one by Fellini.

Satisfied that all was well he called Cantolini and reported to him.

Forty-Two.

Cantolini was with Gerry and Sam and had given them a rundown of the day's events so far. He passed on Miguel's report to Gerry and told him that a copy of the CCTV disk was on its way to them.

"That will be very interesting to see." Said Gerry.

Piero said. "My uncle is checking the registration of the vehicle they were in, I should have that information within the next hour. He is also making enquiries with the various letting agents in the area, to see if there is any connection with properties that have been rented recently. We might get lucky and then we will have a probable location for them."

Gerry said. "Thanks for what you are doing for us, I am just concerned that we are putting you and your people in great danger. These people are very ruthless and won't hesitate to kill."

Piero said. "Don't worry, we understand the risks, but our futures are at stake as well. From what you have shown me, these guys are a danger to all of us, so I am just glad to be in a position to help stop them. If we can?"

Sam said. "We just need to stay out of their way until Norman has finished his work, then we just might have to go after the people in California."

Gerry said. "Yeah one thing at a time, first we have to deal with these 'Diplomats.'"

Piero said. "Let's wait and see if we get a location for them, and also some idea of what their next move will be."

The Koreans were now ensconced in their rented villa. They had underestimated the capabilities of the Sicilian people and the close-knit community therein. They were planning to kidnap the port captain, torture him and find the location of Mary and her friends.

As Wen believed that he knew more than he had divulged to them. Depending on their location they would then set about killing them all. That was something that they had been ordered to carry out, that was their mission. They weren't supposed to kidnap them for any reason. They were simply ordered to kill them all and retrieve any scientific information that they were in possession of. Which is exactly what they planned to do.

Thus their first move was to find them, and they thought that the quickest way to achieve that, was to kidnap the port captain and get him to talk. Wen was convinced that he knew where Gerry and his friends had gone.

In the villa there was all the equipment that they had ordered including, machine pistols, explosives, a rocket launcher, radios, and night vision goggles.

Wen felt that a daylight operation would be best as their targets would be more relaxed during daylight. But before they could mount an offensive they needed to know the location.

Their plan therefore was to try and capture the port captain at his home that evening.

Wen despatched two of his people to the marina in order to watch and see when the port captain left work and then follow him home.

They weren't far from the marina which made things easier. So Wen's plan was, once they knew where the port captain lived, the two who had followed him home would return to the villa, collect the other two and then take the port captain from his home.

Piero was with Gerry and Sam when he received a call from his uncle who told him that they had traced the VW crew bus to a Chinese national who it was thought worked for the Yong corporation who had an office facility in Palermo. He would have confirmation of this later, and that the same individual had recently rented a large villa situated overlooking the coast about eight kilometres from the marina. He gave Piero the address and also told him that the same person had rented a Fiat saloon which had been delivered by the hire company to the very same villa.

Piero thanked him and said. "Ok we will take it from here." He finished the call turned to Gerry and Sam and said. "We have their location, and make, model and registration of their car. I am going to send some of my people to do a drive by on this location, they can photograph it as they drive by. I will tell them not to stop but to come straight back here and report."

He called one of his people, gave him all the information that he had just received and gave instructions of what he needed them to do.

Forty-Three.

The CCTV disk arrived, and they went into the cottage to look at it. Watching the 'Diplomats' move around the marina Sam remarked. "No way are these guys office workers, they are 100% military. You only have to see the way they move, they are soldiers and look pretty dangerous to me."

Gerry said. "Absolutely spot on. Let's decide what we do about them once Piero's people come back after their drive past."

The next call came from the two Sicilians at the marina, they reported that two of the Koreans had returned to the marina and were sitting in their car at the marina car park. Piero told them to just watch, and report back when they made their next move.

Piero then called Fellini to bring him up to date on what was happening. Fellini said that he would be going home soon but would alert his staff to be vigilant.

Fifteen minutes later the two Sicilians called Piero again to say that Fellini had left to go home, and the Koreans had followed him. Piero said. "Follow them from a distance, I will tell Fellini not to go home but to go to the old farmhouse on the edge of the estate, you guys stay well back and follow them there, it will take you about 40 minutes to get there and I will send some more guys to wait in the farmhouse for Fellini. We will see what happens."

"Ok boss, we will keep you posted." With that they drove off and followed in the direction that Fellini and the Koreans had taken.

He then phoned Fellini. Told him that he was being followed and not to go home but to go straight to the old farmhouse. Fellini said that he would do this.

Piero then sent 4 of his people to the old farmhouse telling them to keep out of sight but to turn on some lights in the old house to make it look lived in. Also to drive up and down the driveway a few times to make it look as though it had been used recently. They had roughly 30 minutes to do this, so they got moving straight away. Piero had also told them to leave the front door unlocked so that Fellini could walk straight in as if he lived there and park their own car out of site in the adjacent barn. Two were to hide outside and make sure that they weren't seen and the other two were to wait in the house for Fellini to arrive, again to make sure that they weren't seen.

Piero, Gerry and Sam then left on foot, armed to the teeth to go to the old farmhouse. It was a 15-minute walk. It was along a downhill path as the land dropped away to the road. They stopped before reaching the farmhouse where they had plenty of cover but could see the house and the road going past. And waited.

It wasn't long before Fellini pulled into the driveway and got out of his car, he went straight into the house without looking back. The Koreans saw him drive in, noted where the house was situated, and kept going down the road. They went about half a kilometre and turned around and headed back the way they had come passing Piero's two men coming the other way. The Koreans didn't give them a second glance but as a precaution they kept going, passed the house and stopped about a kilometre up the road and called Piero.

Piero told them to find a place where the car could not be seen and await further instructions. All the land surrounding this area belonged to the Cantolini family and these guys having worked for them since they were kids knew the local area like the backs of their hands.

Piero told them all to sit tight, stay out of sight and wait to see what happens next. He told the guys in the house to stay put. And the ones who had followed Fellini to make their way to the house, not on the road but overland parallel to it, and then hide somewhere with a good view of the road and the entrance to the farmhouse. "Then we wait." he told them.

In the event, they waited nearly two hours. Then the guys down by the road reported that the car had returned and now there were 4 Koreans, they said that the Fiat had gone past and stopped a short distance up the road and one of them had got out and walked back past the house and carried on. The car drove up the road turned around and made its way slowly back. They passed the house and drove on collecting their friend as they went. The car returned a few moments later and parked about 50 metres from the driveway where it could not be seen from the house.

"Ok." Said Wen. "This is what we are going to do. Two of you can go around the back and I will approach the front door. If you can get in through a back door or window without making a lot of noise and alerting the occupants then quickly call me on the radio. I will then knock on the front door which should do two things. A. It will divert their attention enabling you to enter without being heard. B. It will give me access to the interior of the house without having to break the door down. Once there are three of us in the house, all armed then I am sure that the occupant or occupants will be very compliant. We will then be able to take this Fellini guy with us and dispose of anyone else in the house. We will then take Fellini to our base where we will be able to extract from him the information that we require. Is everyone clear on that?"

They all nodded their assent.

He went on. "The last member of our team will remain with the car and once we have Fellini under our control he will drive up to the house and we can then put him in the boot and leave the area and return to our base."

With that he despatched two of his guys to go to the back of the house, he then waited a full minute, walked up the road, entered the driveway and walked to the front door.

He had no idea that he was being watched by several of Piero's men and so was the car and the guys that had gone to the back of the house. The back door had been deliberately left unlocked as four of Piero's men were already in the house with Fellini.

Once Wen was out of sight two Sicilians approached the Korean's car from its rear. The driver was smoking a cigarette and had his window open. One went to the open window and putting a silenced automatic to the driver's head, ordered him out of the car. The Sicilians walked him down the road and onto the land next to the road, they tied his hands and feet tightly so that he couldn't move a muscle and gagged him. They then laid him on the ground so that he was well concealed and then they returned to the car, took out the keys and then punctured all four tyres.

Meanwhile Wen had received his message to say that the other two were in the kitchen at the back of the house. He waited a few seconds and then knocked on the door. It wasn't opened immediately but he could hear movement inside.

Piero and his men meanwhile were closing in on the back of the house having seen the Korean guys go inside.

As these guys crept down the passage to the living area, one of the Sicilians had crept up behind them and garrotted the first one, the second came face to face with a sawn-off shotgun. He stopped dead in his tracks and dropped his gun and raised his hands. They made him kneel down and tied his hands and feet very tightly. Then they searched him thoroughly and took his gun, knife, radio and mobile phone.

The two outside who had dealt with the driver came up the drive behind Wen just as Fellini opened the door, suddenly he was aware of movement behind him, he spun round and was confronted by one Guy with an Uzi, the other with a sawn-off shotgun.

He was fast, kicking the shotgun from the man's hand and pushing the other one over ran down the driveway and turned towards his car. They knew that the car was disabled and without keys, so he wasn't going very far. They also knew where his base was so they just let him go with the knowledge that they would catch up with him later.

Wen had reached the car seeing that it was empty, the tyres were flat, and his man had gone, cursed and then continued running down the road back towards his base.

He called his original driver and told him where he was and to come and collect him immediately. The driver said that it would take him nearly an hour to reach him and would leave at once. Wen said. "I will keep heading in your direction so keep an eye out for me." He kept running for a couple of kilometres and then slowed to a fast walk. He could have run the whole way but needed to conserve his energy and strength.

Piero, Gerry and Sam, entered by the back door. By the time they got there all was under control. One of the Koreans was dead, having been garrotted, one was well and truly tied up and two of Piero's men had gone to collect the third guy who they had left near the road, gagged, with his hands and feet tied.

Piero called one of his friends who ran a motor business and asked him to come with a trailer to collect the Korean's car. Being a hire car, it would be fitted with a tracker as standard equipment. Piero's plan was to get the car moved to another location and leave it there. Eventually the hire company would find the car and collect it. There was nothing they could do with it as the hire company would already know its location, but by moving it they stood a chance of muddying the waters. Coupled with the fact that the Korean who had escaped knew the location in any event.

They had a body to dispose of and the other 2 Koreans needed to be moved to another location on the estate, where they could be kept secure and questioned. He had such a place. It was on the far side of the estate, a controlled atmosphere store that was used during the harvest period. At the moment it was empty but as it was a cool store the building was lined with panels which made it more or less soundproof. It was a stand-alone unit and well away from other buildings on the estate so Piero was figuring that they could torture the Koreans without being seen or heard.

He had the two prisoners, stripped, thoroughly searched for electronic bugs etc. The Sicilians gave them a set of overalls each and some ill-fitting work boots and then took them to the storage unit, leaving their clothes and possessions behind.

Piero then instructed another of his men to smash the phones and radios and take them up to the boiler room near the main house and burn everything including their clothes, but before he took the clothes double check for trackers or bugs.

He got the remaining lads to clean up the farmhouse and leave it as it was, before they had used it to lure the Koreans to the trap. It had previously been empty as it was next on the list to be refurbished and modernised for staff use.

Forty-Four.

The body of the dead Korean guy was wrapped in plastic sheeting, having been stripped of all its clothes they too went to the boiler room. The body would soon be "sleeping with the fishes."

The body was then taken to the nearby fishing harbour, put on board a fishing boat owned by friends of the Cantolini's, taken several miles out to sea. It was then hung by its ankles over the side, one of the fishermen then opened the abdomen with a very sharp knife, from the sternum to the pelvis. The body was then released into the water where it sank immediately.

Having opened the abdomen there was no danger that gasses would build up inside and bring it to the surface. It was just food for the fish and other marine life. The boat then continued its night's fishing as if nothing had happened.

Gerry, Sam and Piero then went to the storage unit, the prisoners were tied by their ankles hanging from a roof beam.

Piero said to Gerry, aloud so that the Koreans could hear him. "I will get my people to interrogate them, they know how to inflict pain." He knew they spoke English and could understand him.

Gerry said. "There is no need. We have something infinitely worse planned for them. Mary is a fully trained and experienced surgeon. She will remove various parts of their anatomy and keep them alive and awake while she does it."

Piero said, smiling, "This I have got to see."

The two Koreans were terrified, understanding every word.

Gerry called Jenna on the radio and told her that they had two guests who needed interviewing. He asked Jenna to bring Mary to the storage unit with her tools.

Piero interrupting said. "It's a long walk, tell her I will send Federico to collect them in the car."

Gerry passed this on to Jenna, Piero despatched Federico to the cottage to collect the girls.

When they arrived at the storage unit, Federico got some plastic sheeting and a couple of large bowls.

She said. "I will need them the other way around, with their arms tied and their legs spread apart." She put the plastic sheeting on the floor beneath them and a bowl under each one.

Federico brought her a small table, and she laid her instruments on it so that the two Koreans could see them clearly.

One of them spoke. "You can't touch us, we are Chinese citizens and there will be repercussions if you harm us."

"Ah, you are Chinese not Korean diplomats."

The guy said. "Yes and now you must release us straight away otherwise you will be in serious trouble."

Mary said. "Thanks for that info, you have just made my job a whole lot easier. You are the people that kill, maim, and torture Uighur Muslims. My conscience will be much clearer for knowing that. I don't have any anaesthetic with me, so this is going to be very uncomfortable for you, and I guarantee that you won't enjoy the experience."

He spat in her face and called her an English whore.

She then began to cut away the lower half of the man's overalls. Then she explained to him in graphic detail what she was going to do to him.

Mary said. "You have the choice, you can tell us what we want to know, or I will literally cut your balls off. Which is it to be?"

He spat at her again and said. "I am going to enjoy killing you slowly."

Mary looked at him and said. "So be it." With that she lifted his scrotum and starting at the back began to make an incision, from the back towards the front. He started screaming at once. The Chinese started cursing her in his native language, Mary ignored him completely, finishing the incision, she said. "Now that's finished, a little more work and your testicles will drop. Then I can snip them off. Once I have done that, the operation is irreversible. So if you don't want to be a eunuch, you better start talking now. Who are you working for?"

The Chinese was screaming expletives at Mary and then said. "If I talk, my life will be over, whatever I do now, I lose, so keep going and kill me because I am dead anyway."

Mary said. "Ok I will just leave you there and work on your friend. You will slowly bleed to death, it may take a few hours, so if you change your mind tell me."

Mary turned her attention to the other one, he was terrified. "Ok now it is your turn, you heard what your friend has said. I am going to give you the same chance that I gave him. Do you want to tell me who you are working for, or shall I start working on you?"

He said. "No I will talk if you promise to let us go."

"Of course." Said Mary, "I will have to stitch your friend up first, he will have difficulty walking for a few days, but if you tell me what you know, you can both go."

"We work for the Chinese government, but we were sent on this mission by Mr. Chung Lee Yong. Wen is our leader, he is the one who has escaped, but Chung Lee Yong is one of China's richest and most powerful men. He works closely with the CCP.

"What were your orders?"

"To kill you all, but first we were to torture you for the scientific information that you have. Then kill you and dispose of your bodies."

Mary turned to the others and speaking quietly, she said. "Chung Lee Yong is one of the top guys working with Towers. We can't let them go, as they know where we are and Sr. Cantolini's involvement. We need to find and capture this Wen guy and then dispose of all three, what do you all think?"

Piero was first to speak. "I think that it is our only option. What else can we do? These are very dangerous people, and we have to be totally ruthless in order to survive. There is simply too much at stake. We know where Wen is, so we need to take him before he gets a chance to do anything else, then dispose of all three."

The others agreed that sadly, it was their only option.

Piero went on. "I have despatched four of my people to their villa. I have told them to keep an eye out to see if this guy Wen returns, if and when he does they will report to me."

In fact Wen had been collected by his comrade in the VW, he was back at the villa, gathering the equipment that he was going to need. He had instructed his driver to find out who owned the farmhouse that they had attacked, and to return to him once he had the information.

Once he knew who owned the farmhouse and land he planned to scour the area to see where his original targets were. He was a soldier and was happy to remain outside in the hills behind the farmhouse, once he knew where his targets were based, he could finalise his plan.

He then sat back to wait, it was dark, so he turned all the lights in the villa off and waited for his driver to return. With no car in the driveway the place looked empty. There had been a lot of Sicilians guarding his targets and he needed to know who they worked for, before proceeding with his plan.

Piero's men had reached the villa, they had driven past and noted that the place looked empty. So they drove further along the road before stopping and two of them got out and staying on the land on the opposite side of the road went back to the villa. The other two carried on until they found a secluded place to park and waited. The two who had gone back to the villa had done the same, found places to hide but with a good view of the villa, they too waited and watched.

It wasn't long before the VW returned followed by another Fiat saloon. The Sicilians waited in their hiding places and watched the VW and the Fiat turn into the driveway of the villa and drive up to the front door.

No lights were on, but the door opened letting the two drivers in. The Sicilians realised that Wen had been inside the villa the whole time and relayed this info to the other two. They decided to just keep watching to see what happened next.

Shortly afterwards the VW driver came out, he opened the rear door of the VW and started carrying stuff inside. He did this 3 times and then went in speaking to Wen he said. "All the land around that farmhouse belongs to the Cantolini family. They are very rich, powerful and well connected on this Island and throughout Italy. They are also very well liked, and we must be careful how we deal with them.

They employ about 300 people of whom 50 are hard core, local people most of whom have served with the eldest son Piero in the Italian special forces, these guys are very well trained, experienced in combat and fiercely loyal to the Cantolini's. They have killed one of our men and I don't know what has happened to the others, they may also be dead or worse, have been taken prisoner."

Wen said. "I don't care who they are, I was sent here to do a job and I intend to carry it out. If these Sicilians get in my way I will kill them all if necessary. I am sure that they are harbouring these British people. That is my next task, to find out where on this estate they are hiding."

The driver said. "The estate is over 400 hectares, it will take you a long time to find them, if they are still there?"

Wen said "I will find them you can be sure of that. Did you bring the map I asked for?"

"I brought everything that was on your list including a large-scale map of the area which shows the extent of the Cantolini estate."

Wen took the map and examined the lye of the land surrounding the Cantolini estate, he was looking for a back way onto the land and very quickly found what he was looking for. A trail that led over the mountains backing onto the land. It would be a long hike but nothing that would worry him. The driver had brought him a large rucksack, into which he put a small gas burner, small groundsheet, food, water and a waterproof jacket.

He had a small hand bearing compass with a lanyard for hanging round his neck. He put this in one of the side pockets of his rucksack. He also had a billy can which hooked onto the side and a bed roll that would sit on top, making him look like a tourist hiking in the mountains.

He also had a Chinese made QBZ-95 assault rifle, which he broke down, wrapped the parts in one of the t-shirts that had been left behind by one of his comrades, who was either dead by now but certainly captured. He was sure he wouldn't need it again whatever had happened. He put rubber bands around the package and carefully inserted it in the rucksack.

Next came one of the QSZ-92-9mm handguns, he had asked for a Glock 9mm, which was a superior weapon but had to make do with what was available.

He put in spare mags and several boxes of ammunition for the assault rifle.

Then came the two blocks of Semtex which he wrapped, again in clothes left by his comrades, he had no respect for them, as in his mind they had failed in their task and deserved all that happened to them, he was however confident that they would not talk. He was wrong about that.

Next he put a box of pencil timers into a side pocket. He hefted the rucksack to feel the weight, he had carried heavier loads before so felt that this was easily within his capabilities.

Next in was a small but powerful torch then, a couple of towels on top, then he strapped a 3-litre empty water bottle to the side, there was no point filling it just yet as he had noted that there were several mountain streams on his route. Then strapping the bed roll to the top he felt that the bag was ready. The other handgun he checked and put in his waistband, in the small of his back.

The map went into his pocket along with a spare magazine for the QSZ.

Having got everything ready, he told the VW driver that he could go, and the Fiat driver to stay, as Wen needed him to drive to a spot in the mountains where he would start his trek. The driver could then take the Fiat back to his base, which would mean that Wen didn't have to leave a car in the mountains which could be a problem later.

Forty-Five.

Back at the storage facility, Piero was having a change of heart. Mary had sewn up the Chinese guy's nether region but left them both tied up. They all went outside for a chat. Piero said. "There might be another way of dealing with these two. I will speak with my uncle, these guys have entered the country on false passports, and we caught them in possession of unlicensed firearms. Not to mention attempted murder and kidnapping He may be able to hold them incognito on remand somewhere. Let me call him and see what he thinks?"

All thought that this was worth a shot as no-one was happy about disposing of them in cold blood in spite of the fact that these guys would have killed them all without a second thought.

He called his uncle who confirmed that he could have them held under anti- terrorism laws, they could be held in solitary confinement for the time being and he agreed to send a vehicle with a police escort, they would first be taken before a judge, who would order that they be held in solitary confinement in the local prison. They could be held on remand for a year before appearing before a judge again.

He would also speak with the director of the prison and make sure that these guys were to be held without any contact with the outside world, which meant no visitors or lawyers and absolutely no-one was to know that they were there.

With that done, Gerry and co went back to the cottage and Piero and his men waited for the police to arrive and take the Chinese guys away.

Wen was ready to leave, the VW driver had loaded up with the others' belongings and drove off. Wen got in the Fiat and put his rucksack in the foot well behind the driver so that he could access it easily on the journey. They then left with Wen in the passenger seat.

The Sicilians called their friends in the car to say that Wen was mobile, they immediately drove to where the others were. They decided that they would follow Wen and the others would remain outside the villa.

They called to Piero and told him what they were doing, he said that he would send another car to them for back up. Which he did straight away.

Wen had gone in the direction of the estate with the Sicilians following, they didn't switch on their lights and kept a good distance behind, just making out the taillights of the Fiat.

The guys going to collect their friends at the villa were expecting to pass the Fiat and the following car on the road going the other way. They had been told to keep an eye out for it but to drive on past if they saw it. They had a description of the Fiat and its registration number.

In the event they got lucky, 30 minutes later they spotted the Fiat as it turned left on to a narrow road that led up to the Eastern side of the mountain.

A short while later they saw their friends following without lights, they pulled up and told them that the Fiat had turned left onto the mountain road, they said that they would continue for a half kilometre and then turn and follow at a safe distance again without lights.

The lead car set off in pursuit of the Fiat. Knowing that it had turned onto the mountain road they were easy to follow as, as the road climbed into the mountains there were very few turn offs from this road. They could follow at a safe distance, and as the road twisted and turned they would be able to see the Fiat as it climbed up the mountain.

The second car carried on down the road and after a good distance, turned and followed the lead car at a safe distance.

The lead car reached the mountain road turnoff and turned to follow the Fiat. It was a narrow and twisting road as it wound its way up the side of the mountain, with sheer drops on the left-hand side.

As the Fiat climbed Wen was looking carefully for any sign of a vehicle following them. He couldn't see any lights, but it was patchy cloud with a bright full moon which meant that he could occasionally see the road below as it climbed.

Forty-Six.

Wen caught a glimpse of a reflection on the road below during a break in the clouds. He told his driver to slow down and kept watching, during the next cloud break, sure enough he saw the reflection again and it was moving in the same direction as they were. He was sure now that, they were being followed.
He told his driver once they had gone round the next right-hand bend to slow right down and as they were going uphill slowly anyway, to let the car almost come to a halt, before applying the handbrake to stop the car, and at no time to use the footbrake as the brake lights would be seen by the following vehicle which was travelling without lights. As far as Wen was concerned this car was following them. Otherwise why was it driving up a dangerous mountain road without lights?

He reached into his rucksack and took out the assault rifle, unwrapped and assembled the weapon, after they went round the next right hander, the driver brought the car to a standstill, Wen got out and told the driver to carry on and get round the next right hander and to pull up and wait for him out of sight.

The Fiat pulled away and Wen, carrying the assault rifle found a large rock on the mountain side of the road. He got behind it and waited. Sure enough he started to hear the other vehicle coming up the road.

As the car came round the right hander towards his position he quickly stepped into the road, took aim at the windscreen of the car and fired emptying a full clip directly into the car's windscreen, moving the barrel slowly from left to right.

The two occupants never stood a chance, both were hit in the head and died instantly. The car carried on towards him and slowly came to a halt. It then rolled slowly backwards gathering momentum, until it went straight off the road and rolled down the mountainside.

He didn't need to check, he knew that he had killed both the occupants. He then sprinted up the road and very quickly reached the Fiat. Getting in he told the driver to get going and to turn off his lights.

The car had rolled about 200 metres down the mountain and came to a stop against a large boulder with a sickening crunch. A small flame was streaking out from under the bonnet which soon engulfed the whole car.

Their friends in the other car saw the flash as the fire got going, the driver accelerated and soon reached the spot where the first car had gone off the road. The car was burning strongly now with a thick plume of black smoke rising from it.

They ran down the mountain and stopped short of the car, when with sickening disbelief, recognised it as the Alfa Romeo of their compatriots, they could see their friends were dead in the car with the car ablaze.

They quickly called Piero and explained what they had seen. Piero was mortified and very upset to have lost two good friends. He told them to go down to the car and see if they could ascertain what had caused them to go off the side of the mountain.

They went the last fifty yards, the majority of the fire had burned out. The interior was still smouldering, and they could see their two friends clearly. Their bodies were charred black, but what was clear was that their heads were smashed and there were holes in them. The bonnet and front end of the car were riddled with bullet holes as well.

They called Piero and described the scene to him. He said. "So they were ambushed, most certainly by this Wen guy. We will make him pay for this."

He went on. "I will notify the police, continue slowly up the mountain and see if you can see where they stopped, he obviously had a reason for going up there. I suspect that he is trying to come down the mountain on foot and get on to the estate without being seen. He will part company with the Fiat at some time and then move on foot. He will probably tell the Fiat driver to continue on past the mountain and make his way north where he can join the main road between Trapani and Palermo. We will make sure those exits are covered, I will speak with my uncle. We need to know where he stopped, you two know those mountains well, see if you can spot a place where there is a trail that leads down to the estate."

"Will do boss, they said."

He then filled Gerry and co. in on what had happened, they were both sad and furious about the two men who had been killed. Piero said. "I will make sure that their deaths will be avenged, you can count on that. In the meantime we have this guy Wen to deal with. How is Norman getting on with his algorithm?"

Gerry said. "He is making good progress, but we should get back there and make sure all is well."

With that they returned quickly to the cottage, all was well, and Norman was working on his algorithm, Josh had been on watch and reported that all was quiet.

They filled him in on the night's events so far.

Josh said. "So this fella Wen is somewhere on the estate with murder and mayhem in mind, it's a big estate so he has a lot of ground to cover."

Piero said. "I have told all my people to be extra vigilant where this guy is concerned and that if they come across him, shoot first and ask questions later. From what we understand from the other two he is a very dangerous man indeed."

Gerry said, "I think we all need to eat and get some sleep, we will take turns to keep watch through the night as usual."

Piero said. "I have posted guards around the cottage, we have the advantage as my guys know the lye of the land, Wen doesn't, and we will soon run him to ground."

Josh volunteered to cook up some food, Sam said that he was starving, so were the others, so he got on with making a meal, refusing Gerry's offer to help. He had been forewarned by Jenna and Mary.

Piero left to return home, Federico was with him, they had sorted out the guards around the cottage and instigated a search of the estate. They knew roughly where Wen's starting point would be and thus they were concentrating the search in the north-eastern part of the estate.

Forty-Seven.

Back at the cottage after the meal, they were all sitting round the table discussing how Norman was getting on. He was explaining to the others that he was well ahead of his original schedule. He estimated that another two weeks should see him ready to go. The others were well pleased with this state of affairs.

In the interim, Mary, Jenna and Josh had been trawling through all the information that Norman had downloaded from originally the NHS and then from Towersoft's secret files. The consensus of opinion was that this was a very real conspiracy and an extremely dangerous one. As things were progressing they were very likely to pull it off successfully.

The list of people involved was frightening. It included several high-ranking members of the Democrat party in the US. Also Trevor Barton, ex-prime minister of the UK, and by the look of it the sitting prime minister and his family were sympathetic to this world take over. Anyone standing against these guys was literally being silenced. It was clear that the big social media companies were censoring doctors, scientists and politicians, in fact anyone who was speaking out against the misinformation and propaganda that these people were putting out. The owners of the big social media companies were up to their collective necks in it as well.

In fact one of the few voices speaking out was the incumbent US president. Who, as far as anyone could see, was being criticised in the mainstream media on a daily basis. The mainstream media too were involved heavily in all of this. All were expecting to gain considerably during this pandemic. Particularly the big Tech companies and big pharmaceuticals who were grabbing billions from in particular, the US and the UK.

As far as the incumbent US president was concerned, they had a plan to replace him with a week kneed Democrat, who was very friendly with China and extremely pliable, the Chinese Communist Party were up to their necks in it as well. It was their political model that would be used once the takeover was complete. The British NHS and the BBC were involved and actively working to help achieve this aim.

Jenna's question was. "Once we have relieved them of their funds how do we stop them and make sure that they can't come back at us. Hopefully once this is all over we will be able to get back to some sort of normal life."

Mary said. "The only way I can see that is, at some time we have to engage with the authorities and get these people locked up or dealt with. The problem we have, looking at this list of names is that most of the people that one would instinctively go to, are on the list."

Gerry said. "I don't see any top officers from the armed forces, on either side of the Atlantic or the head of the UK's or the US intelligence services on these lists."

Sam said. "Maybe we should talk to DCS Foley he may be able to get us an audience with Sir Malcolm Villiers, the UK chief of intelligence. If he is not involved and it certainly looks that way, and given the clear evidence that we have, it shouldn't be too difficult to get him on side."

Norman said. "Once I release my algorithm, I could hack all their systems and literally lock them out of their own systems, including the Chinese, which would throw them all into chaos. By the time they get back in we will have moved all their money from the various accounts."

Gerry said. "Ok it is getting late, let's sort out guard duties and then get some sleep. We can then return to this in the morning and decide on our next move. Also we need to get up to date on the latest developments regarding the pandemic."

Forty-Eight.

Meanwhile the two Sicilians who had gone up the mountain, had found the spot where the Fiat had stopped, they had found a parking area where they could see the tyre tracks of a vehicle that had stopped, it looked like the passenger had got out and walked off in the direction of a trail leading down the mountain towards the Cantolini estate. The tracks showed that the car had then continued up the road just as Piero had predicted.

They called Piero and reported what they had found. He told them to wait there, and he would send back up, then and only then, they were to follow the tracks down the mountain very carefully. He wasn't going to lose any more men to these people.

Piero then called his uncle, gave him the registration number, colour, and make of the Fiat. Also he told him the road that the car was on and where it would most likely re-join the road from Trapani to Palermo.

His uncle told him that an unmarked van and escort would soon be arriving at the storage facility to collect the two Chinese that they were holding. He asked Piero. "Do you want the car and driver to disappear as well?"

"That will be the best thing for now."

"No problem, it will be done."

Piero thanked him and finished the call. He then arranged for his people to keep an eye out for Wen in the hills behind the estate, with instructions to take him alive if at all possible and then he sent four guys to meet with the two on the mountain. Two for back up and the other two were to drive both vehicles back to the main house.

With all that done he too got some sleep. He figured that tomorrow was going to be a big day. The guys that he had left at the storage facility could deal with the handover of the two prisoners.

Forty-Nine.

Wen was slowly making his way down the trail which would lead him to the estate. Once there, he would check as many houses as he could until he found the one with the English in it. He kept to the path but occasionally would deviate either side if the going was good, he was looking for a place to cook some food and rest before continuing to the estate. This was a big mistake.

Whilst waiting for the backup to arrive, the two guys found a vantage point where they could observe the trail as far as possible, being so high up gave them the advantage, they had both grown up in this area, and knew the terrain like the proverbial back of their hands.

Both had binoculars and concentrated on where the trail wound its way down. It wasn't long before one of them saw a momentary flash of light. Wen had used his torch for a few seconds to check out the ground, they had seen this and were able to confirm his rough position. They kept up their vigil until the others arrived.

They had heard the car coming, the driver had not used his lights as just as Wen stood out when he used his torch, Wen would easily see them if they had their lights on. Using the handbrake to stop the car as well meant that Wen had no idea that he was being followed. In fact he thought that he was safe having murdered the two who had followed him earlier.

Once they had their backup the original two started down the mountain slowly, the other two followed three minutes later. Having seen his light they knew the trail that he was taking and more importantly knew where he was headed.

They called Federico, who was standing in whilst Piero got some sleep. Reporting to him Wen's rough position and direction of travel. He then despatched four more guys who did the same as the ones above, two then a three-minute gap and then two more. Again these guys were intimate with the mountain and its various trails, this enabled them to cut across the rough ground so that they could intersect Wen's path.

Wen had stopped and using his gas burner started to cook himself some hot food which would sustain him through the night. Unlucky for him, the slight breeze that night took the cooking smell towards his pursuers. This told them that he had stopped. They continued for a short while and then stopped themselves, not wanting Wen to hear them moving and not wanting to get too close just yet.

They wanted to follow him at a safe distance until morning. Their plan was to keep him under surveillance until their friends were closer at which time they could surround him and take him alive.

They reported to the guys coming towards them, they in turn confirmed that they were still a few hours away. The other two caught them up, and all except one got some sleep whilst they waited for Wen to get on the move again.

Fifty.

The Pandemic raged on, with the NHS manipulating the death toll by counting every death that occurred where the victim had tested positive for Corona virus 28 days prior to their death, being counted as a death due to the virus, regardless of the actual cause of death. This was being done throughout Europe and the US and was going exactly as had been planned. Once again the NHS was the major player in this deception. They were the experts.

The aim being to frighten the living daylights out of the world's population and scare them into taking the dodgy vaccination that big pharma were in the process of producing. By using fear and moral blackmail they were confident that they could coerce the majority into taking the vaccine when it was offered to them. Of course it was the big pharmaceuticals that were going to make extra billions from this pandemic, but that had been part of the plan all along. Bob Towers and the other Tech giants all held huge shareholdings in the big pharmaceuticals through offshore companies and were sure to make billions for themselves. Not to mention the billions that they were making from things like track and trace. The fact that this money was being taken from the taxpayers of the various countries mattered to them not one bit.

The mainstream media on both sides of the Atlantic also owned by the same people were simply trotting out exactly what this Cabal wanted them to. Anyone trying to put an opposing view was either de-platformed or censored. Well known scientists who raised any objections or opposing views were ridiculed by the social media companies and censored. Bob Towers and his cronies were delighted at the way it was all working out. The only fly in the ointment was this bloody woman Mary Kelso, thank God she knew nothing of their plan for world domination he thought.

He couldn't have been more mistaken. Still he thought, Wen and his boys may have already dealt with that situation. Again he was mistaken, and although he was convinced his plans were coming to fruition others had vastly different ideas.

Fifty-One.

The sun was coming up and Wen was getting ready to move on. He had to use his torch to check that he had not dropped anything, this was seen by the watchers which had the effect of confirming his position. They actually managed to spot him moving from his concealed location on to the trail. They were a good half a kilometre away from him but saw him clearly, carrying his rucksack as he moved off. They waited a few minutes before moving off themselves at a few minutes interval each.

They also reported to the others who were coming up the mountain giving them his starting point and direction of travel. Again they reported their position and Wen's approximate to Piero, who was now up and making his way to the cottage to see Gerry and the others.

Wen was still a long way from the cottage and thus they had plenty of time to plan their next move. Piero was considering moving them to a holiday villa which he owned through an offshore fund. The villa was located on the south side of the island and his ownership, and its location was known only to him and his immediate family.

If he could move them without being noticed it would be ideal and make a sensible plan. With his small army he could easily deal with Wen, of that he was confident.

Wen was now moving at quite a fast pace, being daylight he could move faster, and he was keen to get on to the Cantolini estate which by his reckoning was only a couple of kilometres ahead. So far he hadn't seen anyone else on the trail. He was also confident that no one knew where he was but was wondering if anybody had come across the burnt-out car yet. He hadn't heard any other vehicles during the night, so he was happy to keep going at a good pace.

The guys coming up towards him were on the trail on the northeast corner of the estate. With the information that they had, they figured that within the next hour they would bump into him, so they looked for a good place to stop and conceal themselves, somewhere they could lie in wait for him. Knowing the area well, this didn't take long and within five minutes they were safely concealed in a place where they could monitor the trail but were out of sight.

They called the others to tell them where they had stopped, which they considered as good a place for an ambush as any.

Fifty-Two.

At the cottage Piero arrived, the gang had just finished eating and Norman was talking about Wind Charmer asking Gerry what the rules were, regarding British registration.

Norman asked him, "Presumably this is all done on a computer system and consequently the Cabal had traced them through the name of the vessel and its registered number, which would be recorded on the systems that marinas use."

Gerry confirmed this and also said. "It is all done on the vessel's name and official number which is carved into the main cross beam in the vessel's interior. Why what are you thinking?"

Norman said "I could change the entry on the British registry's data base. That would be easy. In fact easier still would be to create a new entry. You have your new identity, so I could do it all in your new name. We would need an address for them to send the documents to. I am figuring that it is all done electronically, so once I have put the new details into their data base, the only human intervention will probably be, someone checking the documents are correct and putting them in an envelope. We would also need to change the boat's name."

Gerry said. "So creating a different vessel completely, we would need to do a few things physically, 1. Get a good carpenter to carve a new piece of timber with the new official number on. Then bond this to the main beam so that it looks genuine, that shouldn't be difficult as the boat yard in Trapani has some excellent craftsmen, 2. Change the name on the stern of the vessel, again by either screwing or bonding a new name board over the old name. 3. There are manuals and documents on board that carry the name Wind Charmer, we can change these with sticky labels. And anything that we cannot change can just be destroyed. Or left for safekeeping with Piero."

Jenna said. "We would have to go through the boat with a fine toothcomb in order to make sure that we haven't missed something with the old name on it."

Piero then said. "That all sounds great. I can talk to the yard and get them to quietly change the official number and to make it look absolutely original. And make a new name board for the transom. But you would have to put that in place whilst at sea, so that you leave Trapani as Wind Charmer and arrive at the next destination with the new name."

Sam said, "I can sort a new address for the new documents and get them posted on to an address here that we can easily access."

Piero said. "I have a solution for that. I was thinking that as these people think that you are somewhere on the estate, it may be a good time to move location. And in that regard I have an anonymous holiday place on the south coast. I can move you there later today or in the morning. Soon Norman will need internet access and you can have that at the villa. Should any enquiries be made at a later date, I can explain that you were just renting it for a holiday and were introduced by a business acquaintance."

Gerry said. "What about dealing with this guy, Wen?

"Trust me, he will soon be wishing that he had never been born. He killed two of my men. We don't forgive or forget that."

They decided that this would be a good move, Norman could change the boat's registration and launch his algorithm from this villa and maybe they could arrange a meeting with Sir Malcolm Villiers at the same time. Gerry had already messaged Mike to get him to speak to Foley and see if he could set up a meeting with Villiers. He was waiting for an answer.

Piero said. "I will make the arrangements with the boatyard for the work on Wind Charmer, I will need to know the new name before I can get it all done. Meanwhile I will arrange transport to the villa. Maybe a crew bus with escort and we will look to moving you tomorrow, if that works for you?"

Gerry said. "The new name will be JENMA. Named after Jenna and Mary."

Piero said. "I like it, very apt." and wrote the name down on a piece of paper, saying, "I will pass this on to the yard manager along with the new registered number.

They were all happy with this arrangement. Gerry's idea was that once the algorithm had been released they could move back on to the boat, set sail, once out at sea they could change the name. The official number would be changed before they left the marina and then the name on the stern could be changed once they were well on their way.

Piero then received a call from his uncle to say that the Fiat and its driver had been detained and the car was on its way to the pound and the driver was on his way to the prison. He would be kept in isolation and the other two would not know that he had been captured as well.

Fifty-Three.

Up on the mountain, Wen was moving closer to the four Sicilians who were lying in wait for him, the others were still following Wen, they were keeping a good distance so as to remain unseen. They figured that he was at least an hour away from the guys waiting below and would use that hour to simply move closer to him so that by the time he reached the ambush they would be close enough to stop him should he try and escape.

The advantage that they had was twofold, one they outnumbered him and two, they knew the terrain well. This part of the trail was surrounded either side by huge boulders that were the result of an avalanche over a hundred years ago. Some were the size of houses. The trail had evolved through animals and people picking their way through these boulders over the years and creating the trail that existed today.

It was a perfect place for the ambush as they could hide amongst the boulders close to the trail, Wen had to stick to the path as he didn't have any other option. He didn't know the area, but the Sicilians did.

Soon enough Wen entered the ambush area, realising that it was a good place for an ambush stopped and listened carefully. Hearing nothing unusual he continued albeit at a slower pace.

He passed the position of Marco, the biggest Sicilian of the lot, who was armed with a sawn-off shotgun, Marco had moved about 10 metres up the trail from the others.

Once Wen had passed him, he waited a few seconds and then moved onto the trail. Without any warning, he fired both barrels into the lower half of Wen's legs, which took him of his feet, and he landed on his back, blood pouring from his calves and ankles. He rolled over onto his front and taking his assault rifle fired at the area behind him. It was a waste of time because as soon as Marco had shot him he had stepped back behind the boulder.

Wen very quickly saw that he was firing at thin air. The pain in his legs was starting with a vengeance. He rolled back and immediately saw that he has surrounded by men with a mixture of sawn-off shotguns and small sub machine guns. He knew when he was beaten and that he could maybe hit one of them before he was blasted to bits, literally.

Marco then appeared from behind him and relieved him of all his weapons. Wen was really starting to feel the pain now but raised his hands. They took his rucksack and searched it carefully. One of the Sicilians applied tourniquets to his thighs and bandaged his lower legs. This was done without any consideration for Wen, as one of them said to him. "We can't have you dying on us yet, our boss wants to talk to you first."

They searched Wen carefully and tied his wrists behind his back with rough rope.

They called Piero and told him that they had him prisoner, Piero said that there was another track about half a kilometre from their position and that he would send a vehicle to collect them. So to head for the point where the path they were on intersected, this track.

So far in spite of the pain that he was obviously feeling, Wen had not uttered a sound.

Without further ado, Marco lifted him up over his shoulder and they all set off down the path to rendezvous with the vehicle that Piero was sending for them.

Piero let the others know that they had taken Wen. And that Marco had shot him in both lower legs.

He said to Mary. "We might need your help as he is bleeding quite a lot, they will take him to the storage facility."

"Ok, let me collect my stuff and I will come with you."

Sam said. "I will come as well."
Jenna said. "Whilst you guys do that. We will start packing this place up. That way we can make the move today."

Mary gathered her things and she and Sam joined Piero in his Range Rover and they set off to go to the storage facility.

Fifty-Four.

Piero had despatched a long wheelbase land rover, which reached the rendezvous a few minutes before Marco and the others arrived. On arrival they put Wen on the floor in the back, the Land Rover had two bench seats in the back running down each side, all except Marco climbed in and he got in next to the driver. The guys in the back put their feet on Wen, with his legs badly damaged and his hands tied behind his back, he wasn't going anywhere in a hurry.

By the time Piero, Mary and Sam arrived they had Wen tied face down to a table in the storage facility.

When Mary approached him he started talking. "You are the bitch that I came here to kill. I will kill you, I am a Chinese citizen, and you have to hand me over to the authorities and my country will put your people under so much pressure that they will have to release me. Then I will come back and kill you. I demand that you call the police now and hand me over to them. If you don't, you will be in a lot of trouble."

Mary in spite of Wen's protestations set about trying to deal with his wounds and not being too gentle about it.

Wen was screaming all sorts of abuse at Mary.

Sam walked over to him and whispered in his ear. "If you don't shut up, I will tear your head off and give it to these guys to use as a football."

He shut up straight away.

Mary did what she could with his legs, but they were a mess. Piero whispered in her ear. "Don't worry too much, he won't be around for much longer."

Mary finished up, bandaged his legs and put her equipment away.

Then Wen said. "Now hand me over to the police, you won't get me to talk so don't waste your time.

"We don't need you to talk, we know all about you. We know who you work for, and what your mission was? You have failed and you killed two of my close friends, I intend to make you regret that."

Piero turned to Federico and said quietly. "Take him to the port and get the lads down there to take him shark fishing tonight."

"Will do boss."

"Make sure we don't see him again, dead or alive."

Piero then left to take Mary and Sam back.

His phone rang, it was his uncle. "We have detained the VW driver, he says he works for a Chinese infrastructure company in Palermo called Yong Corp. I've checked, and it is owned by Chung Lee Yong. What do you want us to do with him?"

"Can you hold him incognito, like the others?"

"Of course."

"Ok, do that for the time being, and we will decide what to do with him later."

"Consider it done."

Arriving at the cottage he saw that Gerry and the others were ready to make the move.

He told them that it was a 4/5-hour drive, so we can set off today or leave in the morning.

They elected to get going right away, Piero called the main house and told them to send a minibus and an escort car. With a driver and guard in the escort car.

Gerry then asked him "What is happening with Wen?"

He said. "Don't worry about him. You won't be seeing him again." And left it there.

The vehicles arrived and they set about loading them. Half an hour later they were on their way to Pozzallo.

Fifty-Five.

Federico meanwhile had taken Wen to the fishing port. They carried him to the boat, mysteriously, no one was on duty in the office, so they weren't seen taking Wen to the same fishing boat that had taken the body of his compatriot out to sea.

The boat set off and headed for deep water, Wen who was in a lot of pain kept demanding that he should be handed over to the authorities and that when the Chinese found out that he was being held by these people there would be severe retribution.

The Sicilian fishermen all claimed not to speak any English and just ignored him. He was starting to get worried. They had him trussed up below and his injuries were making life uncomfortable. He spoke to Federico and said that if he was released his country would pay him a huge sum of money. Federico ignored him.

After a couple of hours they were well out of sight of land, the boat came to a halt. It was a calm, still day very hot without a ripple on the water.

The fishermen came for him and manhandled him up to the deck, they tied his arms in front, very tightly. Stripped him naked and put a life jacket on him.

Wen was starting to get the picture. He said to Federico. "Ok stop this now and I will tell you what I know."

Federico said. "We are not interested in what you have to say. You killed two of our friends, this little boat trip comes with the compliments of the Cantolini family." And spat in his face.

Then one of the crewmen put a hook through the rope binding his arms the hook was connected to a long coil of rope which was sitting on the aft deck.

The same guy then pulled out a fish gutting knife, he cut off the bandages covering his wounds and made 2 deep cuts on the back of his legs, then 2 crew lifted him up bodily and threw him over the stern into the water.

Wen was screaming at them in Chinese, no one took any notice and the boat moved on slowly taking up the slack. They then towed him further out to sea. With his legs bleeding and his kicking in the water he soon attracted the interest of some tiger sharks, they moved in slowly and then attacked in a frenzy, and Wen's screams were soon silenced as the sharks fed on his body. He died fairly quickly but the sharks kept feeding.

They stopped the boat, hauled what was left of Wen alongside, they cut off the remains of the lifejacket, and the ropes binding his arms and let what was left of him sink into the deep waters, as he went down the sharks renewed their interest in him and started feeding again. What was left of him would not be seen again.

The fishing boat continued on its way and started fishing after an hour. They remained at sea for the rest of the day and then returned to port with their catch.

Federico called his boss to say that they had had, a great day's fishing.

Fifty-Six.

The journey to Pozzallo was very enjoyable with variously spectacular views of the coast on one side and mountains on the other. They stopped to eat at a small, picturesque village on the coast. The food was local, fresh and beautifully cooked. Everyone thought that it was delicious. It was the first meal that they had eaten in a restaurant since arriving in Sicily.

They continued their journey enjoying the countryside and sea views, arriving at the villa in the late afternoon.

The villa was impressive, situated high on a hill overlooking the sea, panoramic views all round. Being recently built it was very well equipped. There was a large swimming pool and delightful grounds. There were five good sized bedrooms. It was also very private.

Piero was obviously very proud of the villa. He explained that it had been built to his own design.

They moved their stuff in and set Norman up in the fifth bedroom with his equipment. He turned the internet off and disconnected the router. He said. "We don't need that yet and it is best to keep it disconnected for the time being." He then set about putting the final touches to his algorithm.

Piero said. "I have put things in motion for the work on Wind Charmer, and that should be done within a week. Then you can move the boat to the local marina here, and of course do the name change on the way. By the way, there is an Alfa Romeo saloon in the garage, feel free to use it, you will need a car for getting into town and collecting supplies."

Piero then got ready to leave, after showing them how the various systems in the house worked.

He said. "I will come back in a couple of days, some of my guys will be arriving later, they will stay in a villa close by. Their job is to watch your backs locally and will come and introduce themselves to you once they are here."

They all thanked him for what he had been doing for them so far.

He said. "Really you don't have to thank me. I am just happy to be able to help with this and it is an honour to be able to help stop these delusional maniacs. Someone has to and it is obvious that the authorities who should be stopping them are, by and large either too frightened, incredibly stupid or complicit in some way. You have my full support, and I will help you in any way that I can."

With that he left them to continue getting themselves organised.

Once organised they all sat round the large teak table on the patio overlooking the pool and the sea.

Gerry said, "We need to decide on our next move. I am waiting to hear back from Foley and in the meantime it is a case of, once Norman has launched his algorithm, what do we do next?

Fifty-Seven.

In California, Bob Towers was chairing a meeting of the main protagonists of the Cabal. He was starting to get worried about the Mary Kelso situation. The elite soldiers that they had sent to intercept these people at sea, had disappeared off the face of the earth, and Wen and his people plus two others had similarly disappeared. He turned to Chung Lee Yong and said, "Do you have any further news?

Chung replied. "Other than what you already know. There has been no word from Wen or any of his group. Two of my employees from the office in Sicily are out of contact. One was liaison with Wen, the other a driver. None have been in contact and my attempts to contact them have not been successful. I cannot add anything further other than to say, that I have people making enquiries. I will report back when I have further news."

Towers said. "Okay we will have to park that situation for the time being and move on. To all intents and purposes, our pandemic is going well and better than we originally thought. The British PM is 100% on board along with the Chancellor of the Exchequer and the Health Secretary. I can't emphasise the importance of the British people in all of this. As you know, and with the help of Trevor, when he was prime minister, we have slowly over the past 30 years been able to swell the population of the UK by about 20 million. With luck we have achieved our aim of diluting the Battle of Britain spirit, which ultimately led to the defeat of Adolf Hitler and the Nazis.

This has been important as the British would have caused us a lot of problems with their rebellious sense of fair play, and insistence on keeping trial by jury and their obsession with democracy, trial by jury will be one of the first things that we will abolish.

Keeping people locked down, is helping to make them compliant and afraid, at the same time when we give them some of their freedoms back, they will become grateful to the authorities. It then becomes easier to lock them down again by introducing a supposed more virulent and deadlier strain.

The fear factor is huge, and again is having the desired effect, in the end the people will just about accept anything, to make that fear stop.

The track and trace system which the UK and US governments have paid us billions for, is doing exactly what we wanted, causing absolute chaos!

It is decimating the working population and thus, things like the post, food deliveries and of course the NHS, are being brought to their knees by staff members being pinged, and then having to self-isolate. Which means that they cannot go to work. Which in turn is causing the kind of chaos that we were hoping for."

Chung spoke again. "Our plan to infiltrate the British and US universities is also going well. Our people are slowly turning the other student's thinking in order to eliminate freedom of speech both here in the US, and in the UK. We are slowly destroying that Great British history that they have used for centuries to give them a sense of wellbeing and achievement. It has been the backbone of their society for hundreds of years. Coupled with convincing them that they are not only racist but have been practicing something that we invented called white privilege, we are slowly making the younger ones feel guilty about the British Empire's past achievements and at the same time castigating anyone who speaks out against what we are doing. Basically it amounts to a concerted attack on the way of life in the West, which in the main allows freedom of speech and expression. By eroding these basic tenets, the people will be much easier to control.

It will not be long now, whereby we will have achieved our aim of total control."

Towers spoke again. "By the beginning of next year we will have our own man in the Whitehouse. Thereby making our ultimate objective of world domination a reality. We will own everything, if you want a house you will have to rent it from us, same with cars and anything else that people want. We will own everything, and the people will own nothing. That way, if they step out of line, we just take their home, vehicle, and furniture, and everything else they possess from them and put them in a re-education camp.

If you can't own anything, you won't be able to accumulate wealth. That way no one can become rich and powerful. By doing this we secure our position so that we cannot be challenged by anyone, ever."

Fifty-Eight.

Back in Sicily, Gerry and Co. had concluded that their best bet, once Norman had launched his algorithm was that they should get back on the boat and set sail for the Greek islands.

Foley had called Gerry and he was going to, very discretely, speak with Villiers with a view to arranging a meeting with them. They were thus waiting to hear what the outcome of that conversation would be.

Before deploying his algorithm, Norman wanted to have another look inside Towersoft's system, just to get up to date with any changes that might have taken place in the meantime. Between them they had started printing and collating a dossier that could be given to Villiers should he come to meet with them.

Fortunately the villa was equipped with a commercial printer as Piero used it as his office when staying there. They decided to wait until the following morning before switching on the router and for Norman to do his checking.

The following morning Gerry heard from Foley that on his, (Foley's) word Villiers would attend a meeting in Sicily along with his number two Morgan Jones, and he had asked Foley to attend as well. He would be back in touch as soon as he knew when they would be arriving in Palermo.

Foley said that they would call Gerry once they arrived in Palermo. In the meantime Gerry would arrange a venue for the meeting.

He spoke with Piero, who recommended the hotel Politeama near the centre of Palermo as a good place to stay and the food had a good reputation. They could use it for their meeting and stay the night if necessary.

Piero also said that he could arrange an escort for them who would double as bodyguards. Gerry was pleased to have this help, as he would take Norman with him and leave the others at the villa. It was a drive of about 315 kilometres, with which he had no problem, driving there and back in a day.

He passed this information on to Foley who told him that they should be there no later than 12.00 hrs the day after tomorrow. But would call him on arrival in any event.

They spent the rest of the day preparing a dossier for Villiers. This was the safest way for them to give him what he needed, as they didn't want to use email. Keeping it low tech was the best way for the information to stay secure. With Towersofts reach and near monopoly of operating systems and the internet, they weren't taking any chances.

Gerry also checked the car over thoroughly to make sure it was ready to go.

Norman had found more evidence of the conspiracy. It was in the form of an agreement between China and the Cabal. Basically it said that once they had their man safely ensconced in the Whitehouse. He, the new President would order US forces to leave Afghanistan. The Brits would have to follow suit as their situation in the country would become untenable.

Once they had both left Afghanistan, China would then move in, unopposed and swallow up the whole country and making it part of China. Afghanistan had huge mineral deposits, including Lithium, and China would immediately set about exploiting these deposits and increasing the size of their empire at the same time.

Once they held Afghanistan it would be easy for them to invade Iran and Pakistan. Once they held Iran and Pakistan as well, they would easily take Iraq which would give them a border with their main aim, Saudi Arabia.

The Cabal would ensure that the West would not oppose them. Their man in the Whitehouse would do exactly as he was told.

Without the Americans, Britain and the EU would be powerless to stop them.

This latest information was included in the dossier for Villiers.

In return the Chinese would help the Cabal take over the US, UK, and the EU. They had already infiltrated hundreds of thousands of Chinese into the UK and the EU. They weren't in a hurry, if it took another 30 years to accomplish, they were willing to wait.

It was a terrifying prospect and a very real one.

36 hours later, Gerry and Norman were on their way to Palermo. Gerry was enjoying himself, the Alfa that Piero had lent to them was a 3.0 turbocharged V6, petrol. It went like a rocket and was very well adapted to the Sicilian roads. Norman was also enjoying the ride, being driven faster than he had ever been in his life.

The escort car was doing a good job of keeping up with Gerry. The driver of this vehicle was not only quick but knew the roads well. He was however impressed with Gerry's performance.

Fifty-Nine.

They were soon in Palermo and heading for the hotel. Foley had been in touch, and they had agreed to meet in the coffee bar at the hotel.

When they entered the coffee bar Gerry spotted Foley and the other two sitting at a table near the back, facing the entrance.

Foley made the introductions and after ordering coffee, they got straight down to business.

Gerry said. "I am assuming that DCS Foley has filled you in with the outline of what has and is happening."

Villiers replied "Yes, he has brought us up to date on what he knows so far. It all looks pretty bad to me if you are only half accurate."

Gerry said. "It is much worse than we originally thought." Passing them a copy of the dossier each. He then set out to explain the situation as they saw it. Referring to the document he pointed out the unequivocal case that they had produced against the parties concerned. Including transcripts of the tape recordings that they had made of the various confessions of, first the people sent by MPharma and later the Chinese.

Villiers asked. "Where are these people now and what has happened to them?"

"I'm not sure, once we finished with them we let them go." Gerry lied.

"It is going to take me a while to go through this dossier. Looks like you have done a very thorough job. How did you get all this info?"

"I can only answer that if it remains off the record. For now at least, as, if this lot find out what we know, they will probably send the Chinese army after us."

Villiers replied. "That's a given, yours and your friend's involvement will be kept absolutely confidential. The only people who will know your names are Morgan Jones and myself."

"Ok, my friend Norman here has hacked all their systems, including Towersoft and the NHS. We have loads more evidence, which once you have had a chance to go through the dossier, we can supply to you. There are literally thousands of pages. It will scare the living daylights out of you. Our own Prime Minister is up to his neck in it. The Chancellor of the Exchequer is another one. You will see."

Villiers said. "We will have to set up a secure way of getting the rest of the evidence to us. In the meantime we are mightily impressed with what Norman has done so far and would love to know how he has done it. Particularly to have done it without any of them knowing about it."

"Again that is something that must be kept 100% secret. If the US authorities knew about him, they would literally kidnap him and hide him away somewhere, where they could steal his system, pick his brains clean and when they were finished, would simply and quietly dispose of him."
Morgan said, "It looks like you don't trust anyone in authority?"

"Nor will you, once you have read the evidence." Said Norman.

Villiers said. "We have been hearing mutterings of this, but until now nothing concrete. This changes everything, but we already have a shortlist of people who we believe are 100% trustworthy. We have based them in a newly purchased safe house in Hampshire. They will be working from there."

Norman said. "It will only be safe as long as you don't use the internet or smart phones, don't even have them there, turned off. Disconnect any landlines and only communicate using couriers. Any computers that you use, get your tech boys to completely disable any internet capabilities. Not just switching it off but take out the hardware that the machine uses to access the internet."

Gerry asked. "Who purchased the safe house?"

"A solicitor who I use sometimes, he doesn't have any links to our organisation other than through me. The funds to buy the house have been channelled through a Swiss based trust, it is totally secret."

Norman said. "Sounds ok, just don't use any smart phones, not even if they are encrypted. Get a couple of the old type of phones. The way to beat these people is to keep everything low tech."

"Ok, understood, said Villiers. "We will set up a courier who can collect documents from you and deliver them to the safe house. Now gentlemen, I think that is enough for now. We will stay here for the next two days and look in depth through what you have given us, so may I suggest that we meet again the day after tomorrow."

Gerry said. "That's fine but we will need to choose another location. Decide on that now and a time, that way we won't need to make any phone calls."

Foley looking at his guidebook said. "What about the Museo delle Maioliche, it is on the Via Giuseppe Garibaldi 11. At 12.00 hrs the day after tomorrow."

"Sounds good we will be there."
With that they parted company. Gerry and Norman went back to their car, Villiers, Foley and Jones set off to find a restaurant.

Sixty.

Chung had despatched two of his people to investigate what had happened in Palermo. They had only been in the city for an hour and were walking towards Chung's office in the centre of Palermo they just happened to walk past the hotel as Gerry and Norman walked out and crossed the road. Neither recognised the other, the two Chinese operatives walked on, blissfully unaware that they had just walked past one of their targets.

Likewise, Gerry and Norman were completely unaware that these two had been sent to investigate the situation in Sicily and find out what had happened to Wen and his compatriots.

After going to the offices, they had planned to go to Trapani and check on the boat and make sure that she was still there. They were picking up a car at Chung's offices and then they would make their way to Trapani. They also had decided that they would use a different hotel each night.

Their next port of call would be to the Cantolini estate, and after that they would make enquiries with the Island's police force.

They didn't have much to go on, all they really knew was that the four operatives sent by Chung had disappeared off the face of the earth. Likewise the driver and the liaison with these men had both disappeared along with their respective vehicles. That was all they knew so far.

Gerry and Norman reached their car. Parked a few spaces behind the car was the vehicle with their two guards inside. They gave a wave and thumbs up to Gerry, who got into his car with Norman, and they drove off, they had told the guards earlier that they would go back to Pozzallo via Trapani, as they too wanted to check on Wind Charmer.

They set off with the guard vehicle roughly a half kilometre behind. Again the driver had to keep his foot down in order to keep up with Gerry. He was enjoying himself as he enjoyed driving fast and keeping up with Gerry gave him the excuse to do so. Both Gerry and Norman were hungry, so they decided to stop at the next suitable place and get something to eat. Gerry called the guards on the radio to let them know that he would be stopping at the next available place to eat. A few minutes later they found such a place, it was a general services but had what looked like a decent restaurant. They went in and were directed to a table by the window. The guards waited ten minutes and then entered and sat at a different table without acknowledging Gerry and Norman.

They enjoyed a delicious lunch and were in the restaurant for just over an hour. Whilst they were eating the two Chinese drove past on their way to Trapani.

They then carried on with the journey, again the escort waited a few minutes and took up station about 500 metres behind them with Gerry doing his usual and driving flat out.

Soon catching up with the two Chinese, Gerry quickly overtook them, but as they passed Norman glanced to his right and looked straight at the driver, who in turn was looking at him. The driver said to his passenger. "These Italians are mad drivers."

Shortly after the escort car passed them as well. Norman turned to Gerry a little further down the road and said. "Those guys in the car we just passed were Chinese, I'm sure that I have seen the driver before."

"When?"

"Not sure, but I'm certain that I recognise him from somewhere."

Gerry kept up the pace and called their escort and told them what Norman had said.

They said that they would pull up at the next service station. Let them pass and then follow them at a safe distance just to see where they are going.

Gerry carried on and was certain that whatever they were doing, they weren't following him as they were going so slowly that they had now disappeared from his rear-view mirror.

They were soon at the marina and pulled into the car park. Gerry and Norman waited in their car for the escort to catch up. Ten minutes later the car with the Chinese guys pulled in, the men got out and wondered off in the direction of the marina office and shortly after, the escort vehicle pulled in.
Norman suddenly said. "I remember now, we saw them in Palermo just after we left the hotel."

Gerry said. "Are you sure? Because if they were in Palermo that wasn't a coincidence."

"I am dead certain, after everything that has happened, I notice Chinese people. They were there."

Gerry got out and went and spoke with the Sicilians. "We may have a problem, the two Chinese were in Palermo, and Norman recognised them."

One of the Sicilians said. "Wait here boss, I will go to the office and see what they are up to."

He got out and went straight to the office, they were in there talking to the receptionist, showing her some photographs and asking if she had seen any of the men in the photos.

The Sicilian was looking over their shoulder and spotted the photo of Wen. He winked at the receptionist who was telling them that she was sure that she hadn't seen them, but she would ask the port Captain if they wanted. They nodded and she took the photos into the back office closing the door behind her.

She spoke quickly to him and explained that they were looking for the men in the pictures. And that she had told the Chinese that she hadn't seen them. The port captain said. "I will come and talk to them."

Fellini came out and spoke with them. Tapping the picture of Wen, he said. "I think this guy came in a few days ago with another man. They were enquiring about a mooring for their boss's boat. I haven't seen them since."

They thanked him and left.

Gerry and Norman saw them walk back to the car park, get in their car and instead of heading back towards Palermo, headed the other way towards the South. The Sicilian who had gone into the office returned and spoke with Gerry.

He said. "They were looking for Wen and his boys."

Gerry said. "Ok, why don't you follow them, they were driving slowly earlier, you should catch them easily. Let Piero know what's happening. I will check on the boat and catch you up, let's see what they do next."

"Ok." he said and set off in pursuit of the Chinese guys.

Gerry and Norman went to check the boat out. They went on board and as everything looked as they had left her, went quickly back to the car stopping to have a quick word with Fellini on the way.

Fellini explained that the work to change the boats name had been done. The official number had been changed on the main beam and the new name board had been left in one of the lockers in the forward cabin.

Gerry was impressed as he had not noticed that the official number had been changed.

Thanking Fellini, they returned to their car and headed south as well.

Driving at his usual pace it took Gerry 25 minutes to catch the escort car.

Gerry called them on the radio. "I think it is best if you continue to follow them as you are, we will drop back but stay in radio range. That way we can see what they are up to."

"Roger that." Came the reply.

Gerry dropped back and then maintained the same pace as the escort car.

He spoke with Piero, as these guys were now headed in the direction of the Cantolini estate, they agreed that the best course of action would be to see what they did next. Piero would have his people on alert. If they tried to enter the estate, they would be intercepted and questioned as to why they were there? If they carried on past, then Piero would send further vehicles to keep up the surveillance leaving Gerry and his escort to continue on to Pozzallo, in either case it was important for Gerry and Norman not to be seen by these Chinese guys, so once past the entrance to the estate they were to continue their journey and not get involved.

Gerry relayed these instructions to the escort car. They were not far now from the western boundary of the estate.

The two Chinese arrived at the main gate and pulled in, stopping at the entrance gate which was situated 20 metres from the road. There was a guardhouse and a guard standing in front of the gate and to one side.

He approached the car and spoke to the driver in English. "Can I help you?"
"We would like to speak with the owner Sr. Piero Cantolini." Said the driver.

"I will call the house and see if he is available, please wait."

He went into the guardhouse called Piero and told him what they had said.
Piero said, "Ask them why they want to see me, and take your time." The guard waited a full five minutes before returning to the car.

"Sr. Cantolini would like to know why you want to speak with him."

"We are trying to locate our colleague who was hiking in the mountains behind this estate, but who hasn't been seen or heard from for a few days. And we were wondering if we could have permission to execute a search on your land to see if we can find him."

"Ok wait there, I will see what he says."

He walked back, slowly into the guardhouse and called Piero again.

"They say that they are looking for a colleague who was hiking in the mountain but has disappeared and they would like permission to conduct a search of the estate."

"Ok, tell them this, as it is a working estate with machinery in use at all times that would be too dangerous and therefore would be out of the question. However, as their friend is missing, they should alert the local police force who will engage the mountain rescue people to make a proper search of the mountain for their colleague. Parts of the mountain are quite dangerous due to rock falls and the like and it would not be sensible for them to go on their own. I will instruct all estate staff to keep an eye out for their man. Give them directions to the local police station and send them on their way."

The guard waited another five minutes before returning to the car and relaying the message in its entirety. And gave them directions to the police station.

The driver thanked him very politely, he turned around and headed for the main road. He turned back towards the north in line with the directions that he had been given.

The passenger spoke. "I don't believe a word of it and as for the police and mountain rescue, they are the last people that we need getting involved with all of this."

Sixty-One.

Very shortly they had a tail, consisting of an Iveco van and an Alfa Romeo. They were both keeping well back and as there was plenty of traffic at that time of day, they were pretty certain that they wouldn't be noticed.

Gerry and Norman with their escort in tow were well on their way in the opposite direction.

The two Chinese carried on towards Palermo, making a detour to the villa where Wen and his people had stayed.

The watchers couldn't see what they were doing in the villa as they had to position themselves where they couldn't be seen by the Chinese guys.

They were in there for about 30 minutes, after which they left and continued on towards Palermo. With the watchers following at their usual distance.

They went straight to the Grand Hotel Piazza Borsa, parked their car and went in. One of the Sicilians followed and saw them get in the lift and go up to the top floor. He went back to the car, and they called Piero. He told them to return to base.

Next he called his uncle and asked him to check them out. He didn't know their names, all he knew was that they were Chinese and probably staying at the Grand Hotel.

Sixty-Two.

Gerry and Norman had just reached the villa. They reported to the others about their meeting with Villiers and the events on the journey back relating to the two Chinese guys.

Jenna said. "It may be a good idea once we have launched Norman's algorithm to get back on the boat and get clear of Sicily.

Sam said. "I was thinking the same thing. But where do we go?

Josh said. "I fancy the Greek Islands, there are loads of good anchorages, it would mean that we can stay away from marinas and hot spots. Just go in when we need supplies."

Norman said. "The algorithm is ready to go. We just have to decide when we are going to launch it. Because when we do, I am pretty sure that all hell is going to break loose. When we go ahead with this, I will crash their various systems, and that will give us a few days grace. Initially they won't know who has done it. But if they do find out, they are going to come after us with a vengeance."

"Alright, we will wait until we have seen Villiers again, hear what he has to say and then make our decision as to timing."

The two Chinese in Palermo were pouring over the map. They had the printout from the Fiat's tracker. The car had disappeared, but the tracker's data had been uploaded to the office in Palermo. However it had stopped feeding data to their office when the vehicle had returned to the main road West of Palermo.

What they didn't know was, that when the police had intercepted the car and taken the driver into custody. They had also disconnected the tracker before taking the car to the pound.

They had done the same with the VW and driver.

The two Chinese could see that the car had stopped twice on the mountain road. They decided that the following day they would take a trip along the mountain road and check out the two places where the car had stopped. They marked both places on the map. And called it a night.

In Pozzallo the others were going through all the paperwork again and started compiling the second dossier for Villiers. This included an exhaustive list of all the major players in the Cabal.

Mary said. "It will be interesting to see Villiers' reaction to the names of the present Prime Minister and our friend Trevor Barton, amongst others, like the Chancellor of the Exchequer, and the health secretary, not to mention the boss of the NHS, to name but a few of the high-profile people involved in this. And that just covers the English. Added to that it appears that the Scottish and Welsh first ministers, are up to their respective necks with the CCP, doing a deal that means if they can achieve independence from the UK, then the CCP will step in with funding to bridge the gap left by the lack of the billions that the Westminster government gives them each year. They would in the event of independence from the UK, become satellite states of China. A terrifying prospect."

Sam said. "With all these people involved, we are going to have to be very careful indeed. At least Villiers' name is not on the list."

"He is going to have to be very careful himself. We need to get this list to him fast, just in case he is thinking of talking to any of the people on the list. Some who are quite close to him?" Said Gerry.

They too called it a night.

Sixty-Three.

The next day.

The two Chinamen set off to investigate the mountain road.
Piero who had anticipated, their next move, sent his people to the mountain to keep an eye out for them.

Gerry and the others carried on preparing the second dossier for Villiers.

Piero's uncle had despatched a team to follow the Chinese guys and they would be reporting back during the day. Their instructions were to follow only, but not interfere.

The next thing Piero heard was that the Chinese guys had turned off the main road and headed up the mountain following the route that Wen had taken previously. He passed this info on to the watchers. They were plotted up in various positions on the mountain and had a clear view of the road.

Their first stop was at the place where the Fiat had stopped and Wen had killed the two Sicilians, they spent about 15 minutes looking around and noticing a burnt area some 300 metres from the road, they walked down to investigate.

The wreck of the Alfa had been removed but it was still clear that a car had gone over the edge and caught fire. They knew that it wasn't Wen's car as according to the tracker info, the Fiat had continued up the road and stopped again.

On coming back up they saw the exact spot where this car had gone over the edge. They also found, broken glass and some pieces of plastic that looked like it had come from a vehicle of some sort.

Looking around a little further up the road they spotted some shell casings on the ground at the edge of the road. The markings on these shells showed they were of Chinese origin. They gathered them up and put them in a plastic bag so that they could be examined later.

They continued on their journey and stopped at the next spot where the Fiat had stopped. This had a small parking area and looking around saw that there was a path leading down the mountain.

They decided to follow this trail down the hill to see where it went. What they weren't aware of was the fact that, their progress was being monitored at all times by Piero's people who were continually reporting back to their boss.

Continuing down this path for some time one of them spotted a change in colour on the ground. There was a reddish-brown patch on the floor in the middle of the path. On closer inspection they thought that it was blood, maybe from an animal that had been attacked by another animal or shot by a hunter.

They took samples anyway. Then one of them noticed the shell casings, they had been kicked to the side of the path. On examination they saw that these casings were the same as the ones that they had picked up earlier. They figured that had they come from Wen's gun, that there was every likelihood that the blood was from Wen or one of his people.

Then they continued on down the path, eventually coming to a fence with a gate that said that it was private land and not to enter. This was the boundary of the Cantolini estate. Deciding not to enter the estate for now and as the main trail that they were on went off to their right. They continued along it, and after about twenty minutes, found themselves back at the road.

They walked back up the road and after another hour and thirty minutes, arrived at their car. Both were feeling the effects of the heat on the mountainside. They decided to drive on up the road in the direction that the Fiat had gone previously. They could see that this road eventually intersected the main road between Trapani and Palermo and that it was on this main road that the tracker had stopped sending its signal. On reaching the main road they turned right and after about five kilometres came to the position where the signal had stopped, it was a large lay-by where a couple of HGVs were parked with the drivers taking a rest break.

Sixty-Four.

Gerry and Co had spent the day finalising the documents for Villiers. Their time was taken up with doing this, whilst enjoying the swimming pool and idyllic location where the villa was situated.

They also discussed the next phase of their enterprise. They could lose themselves in and around the Greek Islands, for a time, and afterwards explore the coast of Croatia, which has some beautiful places well worth visiting. But hopefully at some time they would get their lives back to normal. Although Gerry reckoned that he would be quite happy just to keep sailing around the world.

The following morning, Gerry set off to meet with Villiers, Morgan Jones and DCs Foley at the Museo delle Maioliche. He took Jenna with him and left Norman behind.

They arrived early, Foley and the others were already there. They went to a very nice-looking café which was just inside the main entrance.

After an initial chat about the journey and the two Chinese who had been lurking on the mountain behind the estate.

Gerry gave Villiers the latest dossier. Villiers said. "I have been looking through the information that you gave me the day before yesterday, to be frank with you, it is the most frightening thing that I have read in my whole life. If the perpetrators of this scheme pull it off, we will end up being ruled by a consortium made up of the CCP and these various billionaires. It will be the end of any sort of democracy, and we will finish up with a modern form of slavery, but on a much grander scale than the world has ever seen in the past.

I agree with you that this has to be stopped, whatever the cost. The big question is, how do we stop them?"

"We are part of the way there, we have discovered that they are sitting on over twenty trillion dollars. This money has been stolen over the years from the taxpayers of the western world. Their plan involved using this money to buy up small businesses, agricultural land and housing for the moment and some has already been used to buy up and control the mainstream media.

They want to create a system of credits where everything will be rented, from them. Norman has been working on an algorithm that will basically steal it back and reimburse the countries that it has been stolen from."

Jones said. "That will slow them down, but it won't stop them, not if they are being backed by China. On top of that the PM is working to help them along with others in the government, and the opposition are doing the same. Add to that, Trevor Barton, a man who should be in prison anyway, is coordinating this scheme and is openly helping to pull it off. This is huge and just about the most dangerous set of circumstances to confront the free world since Adolf Hitler. It may turn out to be worse."

Villiers said. "Having looked through the list of people involved, that you have just given me. I am going to have to be very careful with whom I reveal this information to. Because this probably isn't an exhaustive list. There will be others who are close to the people on the list and are working towards the same aim. They are just too far down the food chain to be included on the main list."

Gerry said. "Just be sure that whoever you talk to isn't involved in this as the perpetrators have shown that they are more than willing to kill anyone who gets in their way. So be very, very careful."

Villiers said. "There are people that I can talk to, they aren't in the security services or part of the government, but they are 100% loyal to the country and what it has always stood for, I will also have to speak with the minister of defence. He is not on the list, and I feel that he is suitably senior that were he to be involved, he would be on the list. However since DCS Foley is our link to you, his name will only be known to Morgan Jones and myself. Your names will be kept secret as well, under the same terms."

"Foley has our contact number, it is an older type of mobile and not a smart phone, we check it for messages every day at 14.00 hrs local time. If you call it and either leave a message or send a text do not use a land line or smart phone of any description. In fact it would be better to use DCS Foley's phone to contact us." Said Jenna.

"Ok we will get one as well, an anonymous pay as you go and give the number to Foley, he can then pass that number on to you guys, that way if you need to contact us in an emergency you will be able to use that number."

Villiers went on. "We will be returning to the UK tonight, once I am back I will be going down to Hampshire in order to bring the team down there up to date with all the information that you have given me. Once we have had a chance for an in depth look at all of this, we will then be able to decide on our next move. And we will be back in touch as soon as this is done. In the meantime I hope that you can keep digging into this conspiracy against the human race."

Gerry said. "Ok that's fine we will make our way back and wait to hear from you."

With that the meeting broke up and Gerry and Jenna went back to their car and headed back to Pozzallo.

Sixty-Five.

The two Chinamen meanwhile had got back to the Yong Corp office in Palermo. They handed over the samples to the scientific department and one of them called Yong to bring him up to date on what they had found. He also confirmed that as of yesterday, Wind Charmer was still at her berth in Trapani.

Yong went on to say. "For the moment we have decided not to waste any more resources on this, so for the time being, just keep an eye on their boat and then if there is any movement there let me know. I will also send two more people from the States to assist you in this mission. So for the time being just take up a watching brief."

"We collected various shell casings and some soil samples which may contain blood, we can check this against Wen's DNA and his people to see if we get a match, the lab here is checking these out and I will notify you once I have the results."

"Ok, call me when you have the results to hand. In the meantime just keep a watch on their boat and also there must be someone there on the island who is in the know, who can be persuaded to help us. Either by paying them or some other form of coercion. You know what I mean?"

"Yes boss, it will be done. Leave it to me."

Gerry and Jenna arrived back at the villa. They sat on the terrace with the others and gave them an update on their meeting with Villiers.

Gerry then said. "What I think that we should do next, is launch the algorithm.

Norman said, "I would like to trawl their system for a few days first, that way I can get all the up-to-date info from them before I shut their system down. Also the US presidential elections start in a couple of weeks, I can get their plans for that, from what I have seen so far, as soon as they have their man in place, they will start to take control."

Mary said "From what we now know so far, they are pushing this vaccination like mad, and their intention is, to start telling people that they need one dose, then they are going to push for a second booster jab. Once that is rolled out they will then push for a third. By doing this out three or four times a year to most of the population on the planet, imagine how much money they will make. The Big Pharmaceuticals aren't going to give it away for free. I also need to talk with Professor Grey because from what I have seen so far, this vaccination is unlike any we have seen in the past. It is a Gene altering drug, and as such it won't achieve their aim with a single dose. It has to be administered over a period of time for it to have the desired effect."

"Which is?" Jenna said.

"As far as I can tell, with the info that I have seen, primarily it will hasten the deaths of the old and infirm. Then this Covid passport will be used to control movement so that the poorer people will no longer be able to afford to travel further than a few miles from their homes. Once it all goes electronic, as it were, it will become compulsory to have a smart phone. All a person's private, medical and political affiliations will be stored on the phone and then, by setting up electronic readers all around, they will be able to download any info once a person passes one of these readers. This means that they will be able to keep tabs on everyone. Just like the CCP is already doing in China. Throw facial recognition into the mix and you won't even be able to give your phone to another person whilst you move about freely.

I need to speak with Professor Grey, to find out the actual chemical makeup of this drug, because as from what I have seen so far, it is not like any other vaccine that has ever been produced. Also they would have us believe that this drug has been researched and produced in record time. That is virtually impossible in the time that they have had, and I suspect that it has been worked on in absolute secrecy for a number of years."

"Do you think that the various health services have known about this state of affairs?" asked Josh.

"Certainly the US and UK services are right up to their necks in it. I don't know about the others yet but given the way the medical profession closes ranks and sticks together, it wouldn't surprise me. They couldn't have got it this far without help from some of the medics and scientists around the globe. Where the scientists are concerned you have to bear in mind that big Pharma fund most of their research in the universities and within some private companies. Meaning that if they don't comply, or they speak out against it, their funding is stopped.

You must also remember that in the UK particularly, the NHS has an almost total monopoly where health care is concerned. Any medics that speak out are sacked and they find that they cannot get a job elsewhere. They then ridicule those medics, using the mainstream media, who are in turn controlled by the Cabal. Remember they have been working on this and refining it for the last thirty years. At least"

"So this goes back to when Trevor Barton took over the Labour Party." Sam said.

"Probably," replied Gerry. "It would also go a long way in explaining why they had to get rid of Margaret Thatcher, she would have seen through this in a flash. Her getting Alzheimer's was very convenient in the light of what has happened since."

"That's the Chinese for you. Lots of patience, they look at the long game, as opposed to the West where everything has to be done at once. Short termism, no patience at all." Said Josh.

Jenna said, "The beauty of all this technology is, they have recorded just about everything that they have been doing on what they thought was a totally secure system. Without Norman and his 'Intruder' no one would ever have been the wiser."

Norman smiling said, "That's ok, just call me Mr Wonderful."

Everyone laughed.

Gerry got a call from Piero, "Just heard from my uncle, his people report that these two Chinese guys have changed locations and have moved to a hotel in Trapani. It overlooks the marina, presumably they have chosen this location to keep an eye on Wind Charmer. I have told him not to do anything for now other than to keep them under observation."

"Yeah that sounds like the best plan. We are thinking of moving the boat soon, but the jury is still out on that one. We will decide on that tomorrow."

"Ok, I will have a run down to you tomorrow, that way we can catch up and discuss our next steps. Better not to talk on the phone."

They ended the call.

Sixty-Six.

By the next morning, Villiers, Jones and Foley were back in London. Villiers set up an urgent meeting with the defence minister, he had arranged to meet him at his club for lunch. He was going to brief the minister and then spend the rest of the day checking through the information that he had received from Foley, and cross reference this with that which they already knew, which wasn't much.

But what he had received from Foley was very detailed and they had obviously done a very thorough job. He was mightily impressed. The following day he and Morgan Jones were due to go to the safe house in Hampshire and appraise the team down there on the events happening at the moment. But before that he and Jones needed to go through everything once more.

Along with Morgan Jones he set off in his chauffeur driven Jaguar to meet with the minister, as they went through Belgravia the car stopped at a building, this building had no identification on the outside, carrying his briefcase Villiers went in and was met in reception by a man called Anthony Carmichael, they had a brief conversation and Villiers handed him a file that contained copies of the two dossiers that he had been given by Gerry and his friends. He also gave him the address of the safe house.

He then returned to the car and continued on to the club where he and Morgan joined the minister for lunch.

He briefed the minister on the rough outline on the information they had received but stopped short of explaining who or where he had received the information. Also he made no mention of DCS Foley.

He also told him about the safe house, that it was in Hampshire but again, stopped short of giving him the exact details of its location. He did explain however what its general purpose was.

The minister took it all on board and agreed with Villiers that he, the minister, should keep all this information under wraps for the time being.

With that, they finished their lunch and parted company. As soon as Villiers had left, the minister made a frantic call with his mobile. He spoke for about five minutes and by the end of the call he was starting to sweat profusely. He went to the bathroom and washed his face before returning to the restaurant where he ordered a large brandy, his hands were shaking and his head was spinning, he had never been so frightened in his life.

Villiers and Jones went back to their office and continued going through and checking as much as they could. This took up the rest of the day and most of that evening.

The following day they set off in the chauffeur driven Jaguar for the journey down to Hampshire. They went via a mobile phone shop and purchased with cash, four pay as you go phones of the pre smart phone variety.

Taking the M3 out of London they carried on down to junction 8 where they turned off the motorway and headed in the direction of Axford, reaching the village of Axford they turned right onto the B3046. Shortly after, Villiers told his driver to pull up at the next lay by. Once the car had stopped, Villiers got out, opened the bonnet and removed the fuse for the GPS and the tracker that was fitted to all ministry cars. They then continued on the B3046 until they came to the village of Cheriton. Where they turned left, the safe house was about a mile along this road on the left.

It was a fairly large place in 4 acres of grounds. The car turned in to the driveway which led to the house that could not be seen from the road.

He and Jones got out and entered the house. Their car had been seen on CCTV, and they had been identified by the in-house security guards, had this not been the case the car would have been stopped by two-armed security guards who would have stopped them before they reached the house, questioned the occupants and not allowed them to proceed further.

Jones and Villiers went directly to the dining room. The other members of Villiers' team were already assembled around a large, polished mahogany table.

There was no need for introductions as both Villiers and Jones were well known to the team which consisted of six well-chosen and trusted operatives. Three women and three men. As they all worked for Villiers and were his most trusted people, he had absolute confidence in each and every one of them.

When they were all seated, Villiers spoke. "Ladies and Gentlemen, this group was put together to look into rumours that some sort of conspiracy was in progress, which had the ultimate aim of taking control of the free world for the benefit of the perpetrators.

Up until a few days ago this was nothing more than a rumour, but as you know, we felt that due to its severity and possible ramifications we could not ignore it and thus set up this team to see if there was any validity to these rumours. It would appear that we were absolutely right to do so."

He produced the dossier and laid it out on the table. Then continued speaking.
"The contents of this dossier prove beyond any reasonable doubt that the rumours are not only true, but this conspiracy is well under way. And far worse than we originally thought. I will pass this copy to you so that you can copy it, and all look through it at your leisure. It is a very comprehensive report, I won't reveal its origins but suffice to say that it comes from a trusted and competent source. Furthermore from this minute onwards, I would request that you all hand over your smartphones, whilst they are encrypted, they cannot be trusted to be 100% secure. But before doing so please switch them off and remove the batteries, they will be kept in the lead lined security safe in the basement."

The six others around the table duly took out their batteries and handed them to Jones who took them down to the basement and put them in the safe. He was back at the table 5 minutes later.

Villiers continued, "I have brought with me two old type non smart phones, these are the only form of communication that you will be allowed to use until this thing is over. Am I absolutely clear on that? No smart phones, no emails and certainly no use of the internet or the land line. This whole business must be kept absolutely low tech. Disconnect all the internet routers and put them in the basement safe as well. Only call me or Jones in emergencies.

I want you all to go through this dossier and come up with an action plan to stop these people. We will return in a couple of days to give you all a chance to read and assimilate this evidence and discuss our next moves.

This matter must not be discussed with anyone who is not in this room at the moment. Once you have read the dossiers you will understand why these precautions are an absolute must."

"I want to reiterate that the information I have given you is absolutely 100% sound. The source is impeccable, and the perpetrators do not know that it is in our possession. It is vital that we keep it that way. Everything that you need for now is in the dossier. Any questions?" there were none. Each of the individuals knew exactly what was expected of them.

"Very well I will return the day after tomorrow at which time we will formulate a plan and decide on our next moves."

And with that he and Jones left the house got back in their car and headed home. When they got on the B3046 Villiers told the driver to stop at the same lay by where they had stopped on the way down. He wanted to reconnect the tracker and GPS.

Sixty-Seven.

As they approached the lay by, the road was straight for about half a mile, Villiers saw that the lay by was occupied by a large truck, it was a huge recovery vehicle of the type used for towing HGV's Villiers didn't want an audience when he was replacing the fuse for the tracker and GPS. But the truck moved onto the road and drove towards them. Villiers was relieved with this and watched the truck accelerate towards them.

As it got closer he noticed that the driver was wearing a crash helmet, he thought this was strange, he was too late, the truck reached them and then swerved into their path. They never stood a chance, the truck hit them head on, their combined speed must have been close to 90 MPH. It destroyed the Jaguar and knocked it spinning backwards and flying off the road into the trees. Villiers and his driver were killed instantly, Morgan Jones being in the back survived but was badly injured.

The truck carried on down the road hardly damaged, the Jaguar was smashed to pieces.

Another car, a Ford Mondeo which had been parked up the road and must have alerted the truck that they were coming. The Ford pulled up, the driver looked across at the smashed Jaguar, and then accelerated away.

Two minutes later another car came down the road, the driver spotted the Jaguar and seeing that there were people in the car called for an ambulance, by the time it arrived Morgan Jones had died as well.

The police arrived shortly after the ambulance followed by the fire brigade. The police closed the road due to the severity of the accident and ran the car's registration number through their computer. On seeing that the car belonged to the MOD a call was immediately put through to them.

Once it was known whose car it was, the police were told that the bodies could be removed from the car by the ambulance service, but that the road was to remain closed, and the car was not to be touched until people from the security services arrived. They also told the police that there must be no press release and they must guard the car until their people arrived.

The Intelligence service guys arrived by helicopter some twenty minutes later. They identified the bodies and told the police that a recovery vehicle was on its way to collect what was left of the car. The fire brigade had to cut the roof off the vehicle in order to get the bodies out. The bodies were taken to the mortuary at the local hospital. Later, they would be taken to London.

The security people along with the police accident investigation officers examined the car. It quickly became apparent that the Jaguar had been hit on its front right-hand corner by a much larger and heavier vehicle before being knocked off the road and into the trees.

It had been a massive impact and judging by the damage to the car and the trajectory it had taken afterwards, the accident investigators and the security men agreed that it had most probably been done deliberately.

They could see that whatever had hit the Jaguar was red, there were clear traces of red paint on the Jag.

The whole area was searched meticulously, and all pieces of both vehicles spread around the scene were collected and bagged.

The recovery vehicle arrived, and the Jaguar was loaded on the back and was taken away to be examined in a clean environment.

Sixty-Eight.

Foley was in his office at Scotland Yard, on hearing the news about Villiers and Jones he realised two things. One, that this had been a deliberate act carried out with ruthless efficiency. Two that he knew exactly who was behind it. There had been a security leak and it had to have come from someone who could access information from the Jaguar's tracker, as how else would they have known where the vehicle would be?

He needed to watch his back carefully, very carefully. He also needed to contact Gerry to let him know what had happened to Villiers and Jones. Above all he needed to decide who he could turn to next?

He left the office crossing the road and walked towards a nearby coffee shop where he could call Gerry using the safe mobile.

Walking along towards the coffee shop, he saw two men walking towards him, they were both dressed in dark suits, as he reached them a black Range Rover pulled up alongside. One of the men produced his ID and showed it to Foley. He knew about people with this kind of identification but had never seen one in the flesh.

The one with the ID said, "DCS Foley, would you come with us, please get in the car."

He complied and got into the Range Rover and the vehicle went straight to the building in Belgravia that Villiers had visited the day before.

The Range Rover drove around the back of the building and turned into an open door which had a roller shutter, this closed as soon as they drove through it. Foley was escorted into the building, they walked straight to the lift which took them to the top floor.

On exiting the lift he was taken to a room that was bare except for a board table with about a dozen chairs around it. The table had a glass top which entirely covered the mahogany top. He was told to sit down, his escort remained standing, a door on his left opened and a man walked in. As soon as he was seated the men who had brought Foley to the building left the room.

The man spoke "Good afternoon Mr Foley, my name is Anthony Carmichael. You won't have heard of me, and you are strictly forbidden to mention my name, nor can you do a background check on me or this building or anyone in it to anyone. Is that absolutely clear?"

Foley said that it was, he had a rough idea who these people were and felt it best to say as little as possible until he knew more about what this was all about.

"As far as you are concerned, I don't exist nor does this building. In short the conversation that we are about to have never took place. You have no doubt heard what has happened to Malcolm Villiers and his number two, Morgan Jones.

I will tell you that Malcom Villiers was a very dear and close friend. We are very sad about his murder and the loss of a truly good man someone who has always put our country's best interests first.

For your information and only yours, my colleagues in this building and I are charged with one mission. For want of a better description that mission is to 'Defend the Realm'. This organisation has existed in the background in our country for centuries. Our respective families have done this for the same amount of time. We are charged with defending our country and our Royal Family against all and any serious threats. We have the Royal warrant and enormous powers.

I would point out that Her Majesty the Queen knows about us but no one else in the royal family does. The information will be passed to the heir to the throne when his mother passes away and not before. This is how it is done and has been for hundreds of years.

The reason we have become involved is because Malcolm Villiers saw in the dossier that you had provided him with, a quote by Bob Towers which said.

'Once we take over the UK it is going to give me great pleasure to evict the Queen from Buckingham Palace and use it as my London home and headquarters. The Royal family will be taken away and quietly disposed of.' That is a direct and credible threat to the realm, which my colleagues and I are charged with defending. By any means that we see fit to employ."

Foley was somewhat taken aback by this statement but not entirely surprised. He said. "I have heard vague mutterings regarding the existence of an organisation such as yours, but put them down to just that, rumours. I never actually believed that your organisation existed. I now know otherwise."

"Well now you do know, as I say this conversation never took place and I must inform you that should you ever repeat any of it, your life will be forfeit and that of anyone you have told. We are made up of some of the most powerful British families in the world. People who rarely appear in the public domain. We are privately funded, and we have billions at our disposal, none of which I might add is taxpayer money. For that matter, not the Prime Minister nor any member of the House of Commons knows of our existence. We have always kept it that way and will continue to do so."

Foley said. "Very well, you can be assured of my discretion in this matter at all times. I, like you want to stop these people and am prepared to do anything that is necessary to achieve that aim. I will give you all the help and cooperation that I can"

"Now, I will need to meet with the people who provided you with this information, as I will need to talk to them first-hand before we can act on it. Thus I need you to arrange such a meeting as soon as is practically possible and it goes without saying that everything you have told us will be treated with the utmost discretion and secrecy. Villiers has provided us with a copy of the dossier that you gave him. This is a very dangerous situation but believe me when I say that in due course the people involved in this will be dealt with in the severest manner. They have absolutely no idea what they are up against."

Carmichael went on. "Villiers spoke with one other person after speaking with me yesterday. That was our current Minister of Defence, it is he who we believe notified the 'Cabal' of Villiers's findings which led to his and Jones's deaths. They moved very fast indeed. He too will be dealt with. In due course. As will all the people on your list."

"Very well I will contact my people and set up a meeting."

"Good, I will give you a mobile number that I can be contacted on. And don't worry we are ahead of you there. None of us uses or possesses a smart phone.

Very well, I look forward to hearing from you later in the day. When you speak with your people, could you ask them to delay releasing their algorithm until after our meeting? I don't want the other side to realise what we are capable of doing just yet."

"I will call you once I have arranged the meeting, I take it you can move at short notice?"

"Be assured our company jet, shall we call it, is already on standby."

With that Foley left and was driven back to Scotland Yard, they dropped him off about 200 yards from the building.

Sixty-Nine.

Foley then walked to the coffee house and made his call to Gerry. What he didn't know was that he now had a couple of ex SAS minders who were experts at remaining in the shadows. Compliments of Carmichael, who was making sure that nothing untoward was going to happen to him.

Speaking to Gerry, he filled him in on what had happened to Villiers and Jones, he arranged a meeting with him and the others for the following day.

Gerry said, "How did they find out that Villiers was on the case?"

"I will answer that question tomorrow."

"Ok, I will choose a venue and call you back with its location. Who are we going to meet?"

"I can't tell you that, suffice to say that you now have some very powerful friends. More powerful than you could ever imagine. All will be revealed tomorrow."

"Will you have a vehicle at your disposal? Because I am thinking that it might be best if you fly into Catania airport."

"That won't be a problem. We will be coming by way of a private jet."

"Very well, and most intriguing, I will call you later."

With that they finished the call and Gerry went to tell the others about his conversation with Foley and the sad news about Villiers and Jones.

Jenna said. "These people are serious bad guys. They don't care who they hurt."

Mary said, "Considering what they are going to do with this vaccine, this is minor stuff."

"What do you mean?" said Josh.

Mary explained. "With the latest information that Norman has accessed, this is not a vaccine in the normal sense of the word. It is a gene altering drug. But it does minimise the effects of the virus. It won't stop you getting it or passing it on. It will only work for a short time they will tell us. So every three months or so you will need a booster shot. This will go on for a year or more, people will get fed up with this and then they will be offered a drug eluting implant that will last for five years after which it will be replaced with a new one. This won't be just a drug eluting implant but will be able to be programmed with all your financial, health and personal details, in fact your life history. There will be receivers installed throughout the world. As you pass one of these the receivers will pass the information via satellite to their main server in California thus the Cabal will be able to know who you are what you are doing and where. But the cleverest part is that by altering a person's genes over time it will make people more compliant and happy to be, what amounts to slaves.

Part of their ultimate aim is to reduce the world's population. The big worry is Africa. At its present rate the population in Africa will mushroom to several billion in the next three decades. This will lead to famine and disease. Again the main concern is that as the population soars millions will head north to Europe the UK and Scandinavia. Others will head across the Atlantic to the States. The sheer numbers will make it impossible to control. Add to this the population explosion in South America and you will have a perfect storm.

They will literally murder millions in order to control this situation and the best way to do this will be another Pandemic. It looks like the present pandemic is a trial run. Another part of the plan is to introduce this Pandemic into Africa, the vaccine for that will be aimed at sterilising the greater part of the African population and thereby keeping the numbers under control it will also kill off the old and infirm. They are not there yet but soon will be. That is their long-term plan."

Sam said, "I can see that this solution would appeal to a lot of people, particularly those who are sitting pretty."

Mary said. "Judging by what I have read. The goal is to reduce the world's population down to around two billion. That way the world's diminishing resources will last a lot longer. Especially when you factor in, that, by reducing the large proportion of the remainder to slaves, they won't have cars or be able to travel or any of the other things that they enjoy now but use up those diminishing resources, they, the elite shall we call them, will be able to go on leading the privileged lifestyles that they enjoy at the moment.

"God help us all." Said Jenna.

Gerry said. "OK I will call Foley back. Plan for them to fly into Catania, and then it is probably best if we meet here. It will be more private, and we won't be out in the open."

He made the call, told Foley to go to Catania, he, Gerry would get Piero to leave a car in the airport car park there, and they were to drive to Pozzallo, and then call. Gerry would then meet them and lead them to the Villa.

He then called Piero who immediately agreed to do just that. He told Gerry the registration number of the car, another Alfa Romeo, and told him that the keys would be left on the inside wheel rim of the left rear wheel.

Gerry thanked him and then immediately called Foley and passed on the arrangements to him.

Foley said, "We should be with you by 10.30 hrs in the morning and will call you once we get to Pozzallo."

Gerry repeated that they were to call on arrival at Pozzallo and he would drive down and lead them to the villa.

Seventy.

The two Chinese guys were safely ensconced in the hotel overlooking the marina they couldn't see the boat from their balcony, but they could see the car park and the marina entrance. They were also expecting their reinforcements to arrive at any minute.

Piero was on his way to Palermo for a business meeting, he decided to check on the boat on his way past.

The Chinese reinforcements had arrived, they were discussing their plans and the new instructions that had arrived from Yong. Those instructions were to find these people and eliminate them at all costs, word had come from England that the British security services had somehow become involved and that the head of the UK's security force had been eliminated along with his deputy. They were now tasked with clearing up the loose end, which was Professor Kelso and her accomplices.

The Chinese guys had also received the lab reports on the casings and the blood. The lab had confirmed that the DNA from the blood and the fingerprints on the casings belonged to Wen. They drew the conclusion that he was most probably dead along with his three compatriots as nothing had been heard from any of them. Were they still alive and able to, they would have reported in by now.

They agreed that they needed to find some local help, someone who worked for Cantolini who could be either bribed or blackmailed somehow into helping them to find the English people.

Whilst they were discussing this Piero arrived at the marina. One of them who was sitting on the hotel room balcony recognised Piero from the photo in the file that they had been given.

They decided to go down to the carpark and try to fix a tracking device to Cantolini's Range Rover in the hope that he might lead them to the English. Two of them went down to do just that. They reached the

Range Rover and quickly attached a tracker to the underside of the rear bumper. They couldn't use a magnetic device as the Range Rover's rear bumper was plastic, so they used a sticky pad to fix it and quickly returned to the hotel room and waited for Cantolini to return to his car.

Piero spoke briefly with Fellini and they both walked down to Wind Charmer, they didn't go on board but checked the mooring lines and made sure that all looked OK. Satisfied that all was well Piero returned to his vehicle and continued to his business meeting in the centre of Palermo. Two of the Chinese followed at a distance.

They in turn were followed by two plainclothes cops in an unmarked car.

Piero reaching the centre of town parked his car and walked across the road and went into a building that was occupied by his lawyers. The Chinese parked nearby and waited for him to come out, they immediately called the two guys at the hotel and proposed that should Cantolini return via the same route to his estate this would involve him taking the coast road and that there were several quiet places on that road where, if they could stop him, they would be able to overpower him and take him somewhere, where they could extract the information that they needed.

It was a question of where could they take him? The villa that Wen had used was out of the question as its location was known to the other side.

The plain clothed cops reported in that it looked like these guys were following Piero. His uncle was informed immediately and he in turn called Piero, told him what they had seen and despatched two more vehicles with two cops in each car, Piero had told his uncle that he would be returning via the coast road and would be setting off in about thirty minutes.

The cops went ahead and chose a service area where they could watch the road and follow once Piero and the Chinese had passed them. It was turning into quite a convoy, but they wanted to make sure that Piero's back was well and truly covered.

Piero in turn called the estate and instructed Federico and Marco to head up the coast road and to wait in a place where they could cover the road. Piero would call them when he got close, and they could then move out in front of him. His plan was to turn off the main road onto a quiet lane where they could box the Chinese in and deal with them.

Piero waited and then left the lawyers office thirty minutes later. He went straight to his car and set off for the estate. The cops watching the Chinese were surprised that they didn't move straight away but followed after Piero was out of sight and didn't seem to be in a hurry yet took the same route.

They continued out of Trapani still taking the same route as Piero had done. They quickly figured that they must be using some sort of tracking device as the Chinese weren't keeping the Range Rover in sight and reported this to Piero.

He changed his plan. Twenty kilometres further down the coast road was an old track that led to a disused quarry with several old derelict sheds that were on the point of falling down. He called Federico and told him to divert to the old quarry conceal their car in one of the old sheds and wait. He would lead the Chinese to the quarry, and they could ambush them there. It was a quiet area where they wouldn't be disturbed. He was starting to get angry that the Chinese could come to Sicily, his home, and behave as though they owned the place.

The fact that Yong Corp had offices in Palermo meant that they must have some investments on the island, and he was going to find out what these were.

He had already seen from the information that Gerry and Co had shown him that various Chinese companies which are controlled by the CCP, were infiltrating Europe, the US, and just about anywhere else in the world and that they had now gained a foothold in universities and schools as well. This had been going on for the last thirty years. Seemingly the various country's governments were turning a blind eye to this. The big question is why?

With the uncontrolled greed, that has followed the extreme Capitalism brought on by Globalism. The giant corporations that had grown throughout this time weren't far away from achieving the aim of controlling the world without firing a shot.

This uncontrolled greed was ultimately leading to the destruction of the Atmosphere, the Oceans, the Rain Forests and the Arctic and Antarctic and it would be this state of affairs that they would ultimately use to reduce the planet's population and simply take control of the remainder. A clever plan that the way things were going had every chance of succeeding.

It also occurred to him that throughout history, governments had always watered down the truth about matters like these. Populations were, as far as possible kept in the dark. It followed therefore that if they were stating that these various things were actually happening, then it was a good bet that the situation was in fact, much worse.

The daily briefings by the UK government which were being rolled out to the public had the smell of an agenda that wasn't being talked about. Politicians almost always lie. It was their modus operando, they learned to behave this way at university. Always keep the public in the dark. Because if they ever knew the true story about what was actually happening, there would be riots in the streets and an uprising fuelled by anger, the like of which had never been encountered before. So many lies were being told by those in power that they had lost sight of what was good for the world and were so trapped by their own lies that they had reached the point of no return a long time ago.

He thought that Gerry and Co were correct in stating that these people must be stopped and soon. They were becoming ever more powerful by the day. The problem was that as soon as you got rid of one lot, others would take their place and things would just keep on going down the same path. What to do about it was the biggest question of all. How do you turn the world back from the present dire situation?

Seventy-One.

His thoughts were interrupted as he had reached the turn off for the old quarry. He slowed down to give the Chinese followers a chance to close the gap. He reached the corner and turned left, the road started to climb immediately, the disused quarry was about three kilometres along this road on the right.

Federico and Marco had confirmed that they were in position, he continued up the road and reached the quarry in a few minutes, parked his Range Rover and got out carrying a clip board. He started looking around giving the impression that he was looking at the site with a view to possibly buying it.

He worked his way slowly towards the shed which Marco and Federico were hiding in.

The Chinese meanwhile had pulled up short, noting from the tracker that Piero had stopped. They were in two cars, one of the guys from the first car got out carrying a radio and made his way towards where Piero had parked.

He could see the Range Rover and could see Piero wandering about on his own. Perfect, he thought, we can take him here and as the place was probably deserted they could use it to extract the information that they wanted from him.

He called the others on the radio and told them to move in. The two cars roared up the road, the occupants jumped out quickly and surrounded Piero, they were all holding guns and were pointing them at him.

Then, all hell broke loose, two cop cars came flying in and Federico and Marco emerged from the shed, both armed. One of the Chinese immediately tried to grab Piero, Marco shot him in the head, he died instantly. By this time the cops were out of their cars and pointing guns at the other three Chinese, and Piero had moved towards Marco and Federico and well out of the line of fire.

The Chinese quickly realising that they were outnumbered and outgunned dropped their weapons and raised their hands. They were used to bullying unarmed peasant farmers in their homeland, not people like these Sicilians who were obviously well trained, professional and could fight. They had seriously underestimated the opposition.

Piero spoke quietly to the cops whilst Federico and Marco trussed the Chinese with plasticuffs that had been given to them by the cops. They then led them into the shed.

After speaking with Piero, the cops left. Piero then went into the shed and joined the others. The three Chinese were on their knees with their hands bound behind their backs.

Piero first checked that they all spoke and understood English. They all nodded.

He spoke directly to them. "I will give you a message to give to your boss Yong. This is the one and only time that your boss will get this warning. We have far more friends in the United States than he does. So here's the deal. He has 48 hours to close down his offices in Palermo and any others that he has on the Island of Sicily and leave. If not, we will burn down his offices and destroy any and all assets that he holds on the Island.

Furthermore, in the United States, we will do the same thing and Yong will be assassinated. Wherever he chooses to hide. With the help of our friends in the US, we will come after him in a big way. Nothing he owns or cares about will be safe. Do you understand?"

Again they all nodded.

Piero went on. "You three have exactly twelve hours to leave Sicily and the Italian mainland as well. Should you not do so, you too will be killed. Is that clear?"

Again they nodded.

Piero turned to Federico and said. "Did you search them thoroughly?

"Yeah boss all their stuff is on the floor over there."

Piero went over and checked. There were keys, wallets, spare ammo, their guns, some money and their mobile phones. Marco came over and collected up the guns and ammo.

Federico cut their cuffs off and Piero spoke again. "Ok take your keys, wallets, and money. Then go. Remember you have 12 hours and Yong has 48 hours to clear all his affairs and staff from Sicily. If you think that I won't do what I say, just have a look at your friend as you walk out and take his body with you. That's exactly what will happen to you should you not comply with what I have said."

With that he allowed them to go back to their cars and he heard them drive off back the way that they had come. He called the cops, who were waiting back on the main road and said, "Ok they are on their way. If they are not out of Italy inside of 12 hours notify me immediately."

"Will do" was the reply.

Piero then turned his attention to the Range Rover, but Marco was already underneath it looking for the tracking device. It didn't take him long to find, he removed it, got up from the floor and handed it to Piero.

He looked the device over, then placed it on the top of a boulder, picked up a rock and smashed it to pieces.

"Ok gents let's go home. He got into his car and the other two followed him home.

Back on the main road he called Gerry and brought him up to date on the day's events. Gerry told him that they were having a meeting tomorrow with the guys from London, and the following day, they were going to move Wind Charmer nearer to their present location. And then in the next few days they would provision her and continue their Mediterranean cruise. But would meet up with Piero before they left.

Piero said, "Why not take her to Marina di Ragusa, it is about 30 kilometres West of Pozzallo. I will come with you and smooth the way with the port authorities down there. It is has a very nice new 750 berth marina, which would be ideal whilst you prepare the boat for the next part of your cruise."

"Sounds great," said Gerry. "We will change her name on the way. We have all the new documents, and the new name board is on the boat.

They agreed to speak after tomorrow's meeting and ended the call.

Seventy-Two.

The following morning Gerry received a call from Foley to say that they had arrived and were sitting in a restaurant in the centre of Pozzallo, and that they were tucking into a delicious breakfast. Gerry and Sam drove into town immediately and found the restaurant, it had several tables outside and Gerry saw that Foley was sitting at one of the tables with two other people.

He and Sam went across and joined them. Before anyone had a chance to speak a waiter came up to the table and took their order. Gerry and Sam ordered coffee. As soon as the waiter had gone, Foley made the introductions.

He kept it all to first names which had been discussed with Carmichael on the flight over. He introduced the other person with him as William.

The coffee arrived, Carmichael kept the conversation light and sociable telling them about the flight over and saying how nice it was to be able to sit outside in the warm sunshine and eat breakfast. He didn't want to discuss anything until they were at the villa.

They settled the bill and left, Foley drove the other two and Gerry was in the lead car. Piero's men had them well covered to make sure that they weren't being followed. In the event all was quiet, their backs were clear, and they arrived at the villa after about ten minutes.

The villa had a large dining table situated on the veranda which overlooked the Mediterranean. Gerry introduced everyone sticking to first names as Carmichael had done.

Carmichael spoke first. "I cannot tell you too much about myself and the organisation that I am part of. But I will tell you what I can, on the basis that you all agree not to ever repeat it to any other person or discuss it with anyone who is not sitting at this table. Right now.

They all agreed to this condition.

"Ok said Carmichael. I am part of an organisation that has existed for several hundred years. Our primary remit is to defend the realm, that is to say we defend the Monarch, her family, and the institution that she represents i.e. The Royal Family. We are also charged with defending our Democracy against any and all those people or organisations who would seek to damage it.

We are not civil servants nor are we politicians, we are simply members of various families whose agenda is, as I have just explained to you.

We are all very wealthy people and do not get paid for doing what we do.

Now, this man, Bob Towers has made a credible threat to our monarchy and democracy. He has stepped over a line, once he did that he came under our remit.

We possess enormous powers, set in stone by statutes laid down in parliament hundreds of years ago, and something called the Royal Warrant. Every incoming government has to agree not to interfere in any way or speak about those statutes and fortunately for us they have been largely forgotten over time.

We all have diplomatic immunity."

"So what do you want us to do? Asked Jenna.

"For now, nothing. DCS Foley tells me that you are on the point of releasing an algorithm that will denude them of the $20 odd trillion that they have accumulated over several years by way of robbing the various health care providers in the UK, US and Europe. This in the UK at the very least means that they are in turn robbing the UK taxpayers.

Also, that you intend to crash Towersoft's system immediately afterwards.

I would ask you to hold fire on that for the time being. Although they have had some sort of warning, hence what happened to Malcolm Villiers? They know no more than that which Villiers told the Minister of Defence, which was just that he had had a possible conspiracy against democracy brought to his attention. Nothing more, but just for this they had him, and Morgan Jones killed. They have been trying to kill you people, but so far you have been very adept, shall we say, at thwarting their intentions."

Gerry interrupted. "Sam, Josh, and I have all had military training, we were all involved in different ways with Special Forces groups so got their training as well."

"Yes I know, don't worry, I read some of your files on the flight over. Very impressive indeed, what I need is time, due to the large number of high-profile people involved, I need that time to get our ducks in a row, before we move against them. If we move before we are ready, some will escape before we have a chance to net them. We need to get them all in order to stop this happening. And I assure you that, move against them we will. So if you can give me that time it will be a great help to all of us.

If you can go to ground or disappear for say, a month. Then we will be able to coordinate our move against them at the same time that you drop your bomb on them."

Sam said, "When we do, they are bound to try and retaliate in some way or other, and remember they seem to be getting a lot of help from the Chinese government."

"I am well aware of that. But if you can stay on the move, I can give you a burst transmitter, it is smaller than a mobile phone, and you just type in your message and press send. It reduces the message to a burst of a Nano second and cannot be tracked or traced. To any listener it sounds just like a bit of interference. By sending a message and giving your location you will get immediate back up, wherever you are in the world. It can receive messages as well. That way we can contact you when and if we need to."

Gerry said "We were discussing getting on the move again. Possibly visiting the Greek Islands as there are plenty of anchorages in that region, which means that we can stay away from marinas and the busy tourist places. But if you are going to need a month then we might decide to visit parts of Croatia as well."

"So long as you stay safe and keep out of the way, it doesn't matter where you are.

I want to assure you that this state of affairs will be dealt with in the severest of fashions. This is not the first time something like this has come up. We are very experienced at dealing with these things and as no one knows that we exist, or who we are, they cannot retaliate against us. Once we have finished with them they will not be in a position to retaliate in any event."

He went on. "What would be most helpful is if you could give us all the information that you can, on either disk or flash drive as this is a far easier way to transport this information."

Norman said, "That's easy, I will give you a couple of flash drives. They will be password protected and to make things more secure, I will send the passwords via the burst transmitter. That way if something were to happen to you on the way back, no one will be able to access the information. I will set them up so that three wrong passwords entered will cause them to be wiped clean and not even the FBI will be able to read them. The information will be lost forever."

The one called William spoke for the first time. "I like the sound of that. But are you sure that no one can access the info even after it has been wiped clean?"

"Absolutely certain. Once the third wrong password is entered the flash drive will be totally corrupted and the info that was on it will no longer exist."

Norman went off to create the flash drives.

Carmichael spoke again, "Just to let you know, my friend William here is the new chief of the security services, he will be carrying on where Villiers left off, he has already been in touch with the people in Hampshire and they will soon be moving their operation to the basement of one of our houses, where they will be far more secure. And guarded by our people. From now on our organisation will cover all your expenses. Just give us details of an account and we will transfer whatever you need."

Mary said, "At some stage I would like to go public with the details of my cure for Cancer. My team all lost their lives as a result of us finding and developing this cure, I don't want them to have died for nothing."

"As soon as we have this situation under control and you guys are safe I will put you in touch with the right people, they will make sure that your cure can be released to the general public, and they will also provide you with the facilities and finance that you may need in order to achieve that."

"Wonderful, we can revolutionise medical care in the case of cancer and save a lot of lives if we do that. For too long the big pharmaceutical companies have ruled medical care the world over. No cures, just treatments, that people have to keep taking for the rest of their lives. They, big pharma have consequently been making fortunes every year from this policy. Particularly from the UK because it is all taxpayers money, which is guaranteed year on year and due to the endemic corruption in the health service, big pharma get to charge what they like. They can produce a medication for as little as 10p per tablet, and then they sell it to the health service for £20.00 or more per tablet. The patient then has to take say 2 per day for literally years all paid for by the British taxpayer. Multiply that by millions every year and you can start to see the extent of the corruption that exists. It's the same with consumables like hypodermic syringes, tubing, masks, swabs, all the stuff that is used by the 10's of thousands every day, they are all made for pennies in China and India. Then sold to the health service for a few quid each. It's a massive fraud which has been going on for decades."

Jenna said, "Just take the British government as an example, they are borrowing billions every year to pay for all of this. No surprises that there are so many people living in poverty, the big boys are literally sucking all the money out of the economy, and into their hands, leaving almost nothing behind. No one in the government cares about this state of affairs, they are all on nice big fat salaries and index linked pensions. Small wonder that the people on the bottom are scraping to get by. Extreme greed, going hand in hand with extreme capitalism.

Don't get me wrong, I see capitalism as the best and most workable system, in the world, but it is always the same, the extremists get involved and hey presto a good system becomes completely onerous, and just becomes a way for the superrich to get richer at the expense of everyday folk. It is all so very wrong, why can't they just get a balance where the guys at the lower end get enough to have a decent life?"

"Make no mistake, once we have dealt with this scenario, medical care will be changed forever. No more treatments to make money for big pharma, if there is a cure for a particular condition, I assure you that it will be released to the public worldwide. The people who are currently running big pharma and perpetrating this crime against humanity will be behind bars. Those that survive that is."

Norman came back with the flash drives and gave them to Carmichael. He repeated that he would send the passwords using the burst transmitter once they were back safely at home.

Carmichael then said, "OK, we had better get going, what do you want us to do with the car?"

Gerry said. "Just leave it in the car park where you found it, put the keys back inside the wheel where they were left, and I will get it collected later."

With that they set off back to the airport and flew back to the UK.

That evening Gerry and the others planned out their next move, it was decided that Gerry, Jenna, Mary and Sam would drive up to the Cantolini estate in the morning. Then go with Piero to Trapani, stock the boat up with essentials with a view to moving her to Marina di Ragusa, and depending on what time they were ready, either leave Trapani the same day or first thing next morning. Piero would send the car back so that Josh and Norman had a vehicle at their disposal whilst the others moved the boat.

Seventy-Three.

From Trapani to Marina di Ragusa was about 155 nm which even if they did only 7.5 knots it would take them about 21 hours, so josh and Norman wouldn't be on their own for long. They were all pretty sure that the Pozzallo villa wasn't known to the Cabal. They had the added comfort that Piero's people were keeping a watch over the villa and its occupants.

The next morning they set off to meet Piero.

Bob Towers had instructed Yong to pull his people out of Italy and Sicily for the time being and close his office on Sicily, to make it look like he was complying. He had then sent a couple of his people from the UK to keep watch on the boat and report back to him the minute there was any movement at all. These guys arrived in Trapani around the time that Gerry and the others arrived at the estate. They were under instructions to watch the boat and no matter what, not to do anything else without first contacting him.

They were in fact ex-military and part of the team who had killed Villiers. These guys were very efficient and had been in combat, so knew the score. They had wiped out Villiers, Jones, and the driver without any compunction whatsoever. That's what they did, kill people and enjoyed it.

Yong, before closing his office down arranged for all the equipment that they would need, including firearms and ammunition. After collecting this equipment they took a room at the same hotel that the Chinese guys had used, which overlooked the harbour. They couldn't see Wind Charmer from their balcony but had a good clear view of the marina entrance. They immediately set up a camera on the balcony so that they could keep a watch on the marina entrance. They also had a view of the marina car park. They set up another camera which could cover the car park.

Having done this, they went to get something to eat and chose the marina cafeteria. They planned to have a walk round the marina and identify the boat that they had been sent to watch.

Gerry and co reached the estate, met up with Piero. They transferred to a people carrier and set off for Trapani. The journey took just over an hour, Gerry, Jenna, Sam and Mary went straight to the boat whilst Piero went to the office to speak with Fellini.

They missed the two guys from London by about 5 minutes, having eaten they had wandered down to the pontoons had a quick walk past Wind Charmer, and returned to their hotel.

Piero spoke with Fellini and asked him if all had been quiet, he said that it had been generally quiet, but that this morning he had spotted a couple of military looking types who had visited the cafeteria and eaten, afterwards they had gone down onto the pontoons, walked past Wind Charmer and then walked back and out of the marina.

One of the marineros had been on the pontoon retying some mooring lines that had worked loose, when they had walked past him. He reported that they had been speaking English. CCTV showed that they had walked in and out, they were on foot as far as he could see. Fellini then called the hotel manager who confirmed that they had two English guests who checked in this morning, who fitted the description.

Piero decided to walk over to the hotel, he too knew the manager well. He would have a look at their CCTV, see if they were the same guys who had visited the marina earlier and get their names.

He spoke with the manager, looked at the CCTV and saw clearly that they were the same two men who had visited the marina earlier. They had checked in as Martin Briggs and George Smith. The manager agreed that they definitely looked like ex-military. He confirmed that at present they were in their rooms on the 6th floor numbers 612 and 614. He also gave their passport numbers to Piero. And gave him a print from the CCTV, taken when they checked in. Piero asked him or a staff member to call him should they make a move. Piero thanked him, returned to the marina and walked down to the boat.

Once on the boat, he related what he had found out to Gerry, Sam and the girls. Gerry and Sam looked at the photos carefully but didn't know either Briggs or Smith but agreed that they looked military. They also felt that as all they had done was take a walk around the marina and turned around once they had, had a look at Wind Charmer, it was highly likely they were there to keep an eye on the boat.

Gerry felt that their best bet was to leave at around 02.00hrs in the morning, with luck these guys would be sleeping at that time and would not realise that the boat had gone until they physically checked the next day. That way they would have at least a few hours start on them.

Sam said. "Make it 03.30 just to be sure. There's a better chance they will be asleep by then."

They carried on with their preparations, getting the boat ready and taking turns to sleep, that way they would be rested for the night's sail down to Marina di Ragusa.

Gerry used the burst transmitter to send a message to Carmichael about the two Brits, giving their names and passport numbers.

An hour later he got a call from William, they had checked the passports and found them to be false. But from the photos they had identified them as Martin Salford and George Ramsey.

They had been dishonourably discharged from No 1 Para for attacking a group of civilians in Afghanistan whilst they were on patrol and had hurt a young girl quite badly. They were known to be nasty pieces of work and very dangerous.

A police report said that they had been suspected of killing a lawyer by using a stolen lorry to smash his car off the road when he was on his way home from an evening out with his wife. She too had been killed. The police got nowhere with the case as they had no real evidence. Just that these two had been spotted walking close to where the lorry had been stolen from.

William's curiosity had been stimulated by this latest info, as this method bore the hallmarks of the Villiers killing. He was going to speak with his contact at army intelligence to see what other information he could get.

He said, "I will call you when I have some more information, but in the meantime, be very careful, as these are very dangerous people who have been trained by the Paras. And they are likely to be formidable opponents. Having said that, I would like to have a word with one or both of them in a quiet place. Just be careful."

"We will, you can be certain about that." They hung up.

Gerry then went and brought the others up to date.

Sam said. "Well we know first-hand what their training will have been like. This gives us an idea of their possible tactics. They obviously like using stolen lorries against unsuspecting drivers, but what are they going to try against us, when we are in a boat?"

Jenna said, "Smash into us with a much bigger boat?"

Seventy-Four.

Piero, who was good at second guessing the enemy said. "It would appear that they like to use overwhelming force, hence the lorries but, they also have a sadistic streak to their nature and my guess is that they will try and take us alive, the women at least so that they can satisfy their sadistic tendencies."

Mary spoke. "So we need to set a trap for them. Our new friend, William, said to give him one live one to talk to. That makes a big difference for us, as I am thinking that it will be easier to kill one and take the other prisoner, than to try and take them both alive."

Piero said, "If they check the marina and ask where the boat has gone, I will talk to Fellini and make sure that one of his people tells them where we have gone. That way we don't have to change the boat's name until after we have dealt with them. What do you think?"

Gerry said. "We will need somewhere close by to take them to, so that we can talk to them, somewhere quiet, and not the villa."

Piero said. "I have a friend who has a farm about five kilometres outside Pozzallo let me talk to him, he has a warehouse on his farm maybe we can use that."

He immediately called his friend who said that it would be ok to use his warehouse, it was only a small building, but he would make sure that all his staff members were kept away from it and that it would be left unlocked.

He then called Federico and arranged for him and Marco to go to the marina and wait for Fellini or the hotel manager to call in the morning with news of the two English guys. Then to follow along the coast road at a good distance behind them, as they would be heading for Marina di Ragusa, there would be no need to stay in visible contact.

He then went to the office, spoke with Fellini and explained that once they had set sail, should these two English guys come looking, that he would like it if, one of his people would point them in the right direction.

Fellini confirmed that this would be done.

With all the preparations done, they had topped up the boat's diesel and water tanks on arrival at Trapani, so she was ready to go.

Seventy-Five.

They left the berth at 03.15 and headed out of the harbour, Gerry set a westerly course to take them straight out to sea, he wanted to clear the land so that the English guys, if they were watching, wouldn't know which direction they had gone and thus would have to ask at the marina to get this information.

The English guys were in fact asleep, but their camera recorded the boat leaving. There was just enough light to identify her. Which they spotted just after they woke up at 06.30, by which time Wind Charmer had gained some sea room, had turned Southwest and was headed for the channel between Favigana and the main Island of Sicily.

With a decent westerly wind they were making a good 9.5 knots. All, including Piero were enjoying the sailing, it was sunny and warm and Gerry and Co. were delighted to be at sea again.

Salford and Ramsey dressed quickly and went down to reception and ordered a hire car, they were told that it would be at the hotel within an hour. After checking that Wind Charmer was no longer on her berth they went to the cafeteria at the Marina and ordered breakfast. Salford went to the marina office and spoke with the girl in reception.

"I was supposed to meet my friends and go sailing with them today, but I am very late and have missed them. You don't happen to know where they are headed so that I can join them at the next port of call. I have tried to contact them by mobile, but they are out of range."

She said. "I am not supposed to give any information about boats coming and going but tell me the name of the boat and I will see what I can do."

He said, "She is called Wind Charmer."

The girl made a pretence of looking at her computer and said, "They are headed to a place called Marina di Ragusa, which is on the Southwest coast." She wrote the name down on a piece of paper and handed it to him.

He smiled and thanked her, then returned to the cafeteria. They ate their breakfast while looking at the map. Saw where Marina di Ragusa was situated, and Salford said. "It will take the boat over 18 hours to get there with the head start that they already have, so we will pick up the car and head straight to Ragusa. We will be there a good few hours before them which will give us time to recce the marina and surrounding area well in advance of their arrival.

Fellini called Piero and relayed to him what had taken place. Piero thanked him and hung up. He turned to Gerry and said. "They have taken the bait."

Salford and Ramsey finished eating and returned to the hotel. Their hire car was waiting. It was a red 2 litre Alfa saloon. Ramsey went to their room and collected the things that they would need, put them all in a black holdall, whilst Salford sorted the paperwork for the car with the guy at the desk.

They went out to the car put the holdall in the rear foot well behind the driver and set off. Marco and Federico watched them go.

The guy at the hotel reception desk went immediately to the hotel manager's office and gave him a copy of the rental agreement. He immediately phoned Piero and told him the make, colour and registration number for the car, Piero in turn called Federico.

"They have left the hotel, and these are the details of the car they are driving."

"It's Ok boss, we saw them leave we have all the details, we will be leaving here in a few minutes to head down that way ourselves."

"Be very careful. I will arrange for a couple of the others to wait just outside of Marina di Ragusa, so that we know when they have arrived."

"Ok boss." Said Federico. And hung up.

They too set off for the drive to Ragusa.

On board Wind Charmer the wind was freshening, still from the West and they were making a good 10 knots. At this rate they would reach their destination by mid to late evening. Soon they would turn Southeast which would put the wind and waves on their starboard aft corner. This would make the going more comfortable and might increase their speed a little, in any event if the wind held they would reach their destination well before Gerry's original prediction.

Once everybody was up and fed, they gathered in the cockpit to discuss and plan their next moves. They needed to lure Salford and Ramsey into a trap.
As long as Salford and Ramsey thought that the others weren't aware of their existence, their task would be much simpler.

Gerry said. "What if Sam and Mary go for a meal at a nearby restaurant. Somewhere within walking distance that has tables outside. That way these two Jokers will have to follow them on foot. With Federico and Marco plotted up en route somewhere that they can observe the restaurant from. Jenna and I can follow on a few minutes later, keeping our distance. They can take a long lunch which will give us time to get everyone in position. Federico, Marco and the other two of your men can move to a quiet street or area away from the restaurant. Sam and Mary can then do the tourist bit, finish their lunch and go for a stroll. Leading the two away from the main area and into the quiet area, we will need a van with a sliding side door.

I will follow on, again at a distance with Jenna, Piero can drive the van. Once we have lured them into the ambush site, with a bit of luck, these two will spot an opportunity to take Sam and Mary, once they reach the quiet area and make their move against them. There will be seven of us to move in and take them. Piero drives up in the van, we bundle them in and take them to your friend's farm. What could be simpler?"

Jenna said. "We need to refine it a bit, but it should work. Anyway we have the rest of the day to think about how we are going to do it."

Sam added. "Once we get there, we will have a chance to recce the local area and form a plan based on the lye of the land. Basically, we are going to need to take these guys in a nice quiet way and be very discrete about how we accomplish it."

Piero spoke. "I know this marina quite well. There is a restaurant at the end of the harbour wall on the landward side. It has a carpark at the front, and it backs on to the beach, we may be able to do something there, but we will need to check it out first." He turned to Gerry. "What's our ETA?"

"We should make it by 17.30 – 18.00hrs this evening."

"Ok, what if we all go for a meal once we get there this evening. I will tell Marco and Federico to watch the boat. Just in case, then we will have a chance to check out the area and finalise our plan?"

"Sounds good. Let's see how the rest of the journey goes. So far the wind has been good to us and looking at the weather forecast, it is set to remain that way for the next 24 hrs or so. We will just have to wait and see, we all know how unreliable these forecasts can be."

Seventy-Six.

Salford and Ramsey were well on their way to Marina di Ragusa. It was a pleasant drive, and they were not in a hurry, they were moving much faster than the boat could go, and were thus confident, that they would reach their destination well in advance of Wind Charmer.

5 kilometres behind them were Federico and Marco, who were taking it easy as well, they were not in a hurry as they knew exactly where Salford and Ramsey were going.

Another pair of Piero's people had arrived at the marina and were on the lookout for Salford and Ramsey to arrive. They were sitting on the terrace of a rather nice bar/restaurant which had a clear view of the marina entrance. The marina was recently built, had around 700 berths and was very well laid out with excellent facilities and could accommodate vessels of up to 50 metres in overall length.

They had been there for about an hour when they spotted the Alfa of the two English guys drive in, and slowly make its way round the perimeter road towards where they were sitting. They pulled up and parked quite close to where Piero's men were, and walked straight to the same bar/restaurant, they walked in and sat at a table close by. Ordered some food and drink and settled down to wait for Wind Charmer to arrive.

One of Piero's men sent a text to Piero letting him know that the two English guys had arrived and were sitting quite close to them in the restaurant. He got a reply saying that Wind Charmer was around 1.5 hours from arrival, they were making very good time.

He texted Federico as well and told him that the two English had arrived and were sitting close to them on the terrace of the restaurant so not to join them. He also told him Wind Charmer's ETA.

Federico carried straight on, drove past the boatyard and parked at the end of the harbour mole. Both he and Marco got out, stretched their legs and leant on the harbour wall looking out to sea. They stayed there for about 15 minutes then got back in their car and drove back around the perimeter road and pulled up in the carpark outside another restaurant which backed onto the beach. They went in and ordered some food and coffee. Now it was a case of just waiting for Wind Charmer to arrive. It is always good to eat when you get a chance, doing something like this, as you never know when your next meal would come along.

The English guys were doing the same thing. What they didn't realise was that they were slowly being surrounded, as unknown to them, they had well and truly stepped into the 'Lion's Den.'

Salford called Bob Towers. He brought him up to date on the current situation, that they were waiting for the boat to arrive and what did Towers want them to do after that.

Towers said, "Just observe and call me with the boat's exact location once she has arrived. Sharon Richards should be arriving soon, keep an eye out for her and give her any assistance that she asks for,"

After disconnecting the call, he made another, a woman answered, he related the latest information to her. She just said, "Thanks" and disconnected the call, she was in a mid-range hotel in Trapani. She packed her bag, spent some time wiping down the room and checked out. Went to her car and put the bag in the trunk and drove off in the direction of Ragusa.

She was in her mid-thirties, very attractive and obviously fit. Her name was Sharon Richards, and she was a very accomplished assassin. American by birth.

The information that Towers had about her said that she had a reputation for completing a mission successfully, and then disappearing into thin air. Towers had used her in the past and she had a 100% success rate. He was paying her two million dollars to dispose of these people who had been a thorn in his side for months. This was nothing compared to the profits he would lose, should Professor Kelso's cure for Cancer, end up being widely used.

Seventy-Seven.

He had taken personal charge of the situation involving Mary Kelso and her accomplices. He was not going to waste any more resources on this matter. He was used to getting his own way in all things. He wanted this sorted and quickly as he had more important things to deal with i.e. the Pandemic and all that followed. This had been 30 years in the making and was now coming to fruition. It was a critical time for him and his accomplices, nothing should be able to interfere with the main plan that he and his friends had spent all this time trying to achieve.

His net worth had increased by over $20 billion since the start of the Pandemic. All of it taxpayers money from the US, UK, and mainland Europe. Taxpayer's money, he thought. The greatest source of funds ever invented. Government contracts, they always accepted massive cost overruns, and no one batted an eyelid.

This new railway that the Brits were building, the original cost estimates were in the region of £30 billion. Which was mightily over the top. It could easily be built for a third of that figure. But now they had managed to push the estimated cost to well over £150 billion. A lot of that would end up in his pocket and those of his friends, he held shares in the majority of companies involved, through a spider's web of blind trusts, offshore companies, and others that he owned via his foundation and the charitable trusts that he controlled.

He was going to be the richest, most powerful man in the world. Taxpayer's money, the greatest gravy train in the world. It never ran out. The best part was, that he was stealing their money, then lending it back to them so that they could pay him even more. And they just kept on giving it to him.

During this Pandemic that Towers, and others had created, the British government had spent £37.5 billion on their ridiculous track and trace system and PPE. Ultimately most of that had been paid to him, it was a wonderful scheme, and they just kept handing it over.

This had all started when his friend Trevor Barton became prime minister of the UK. He had created a business environment whereby the global companies that he, Towers owned, were given a clear field to come in and make huge profits, house prices in the UK were driven ever upwards, which meant that the owners of those properties had more equity that they could use to borrow even more money and spend it on anything they liked. The mantra being, borrow and spend and you would create the illusion that people were doing well. It made the economy look good. And of course the guys at the top of the food chain benefitted the most from all of this.

Barton had opened the floodgates and the global boys went from raking in millions to raking in billions. Barton had changed the way inflation was counted so that the people in the UK, and the rest of the developed world were convinced that it was just a couple of percent. When in fact it was nearer to 25%. Interest rates were kept at an all-time low so that people and companies could borrow ever more money. And so it went on.

And the biggest beneficiary was him, Bob Towers, and some of his fellow multi billionaires. Anyone who stood in their way was dealt with. Either paid off, forced out of business or disposed of. He would be supreme ruler of the Western world. He had his eye on the Royal Palaces in the UK. And the treasure and secrets that they held. It would become his, all of it. Maybe he would have himself crowned king.

He was of course completely mad. This was partially a result of taking the best quality cocaine for decades, this kept him driving forward it was also destroying his brain, slowly. The downside was that every 6 months he would have to spend a few days at a private clinic in Colorado, which he owned. There his blood would be changed, and his arteries cleaned, using drugs that had been developed for just such a purpose. These drugs of course were not available to anyone but him, and his closest allies. The rest of the world just got treatments that only just worked, as long as they kept taking them every day for the rest of their lives. What a fantastic system, he thought.

Wind Charmer was drawing ever closer to Ragusa, they had enjoyed fantastic sailing, in conditions that suited Wind Charmer down to the ground. Gerry and Jenna were even more convinced that, sailing around the world was a much better and healthier way to spend their lives than working flat out in the UK and forever paying a small fortune to the taxman, who in turn was simply giving their money away to the big guys.

Gerry felt that paying taxes was a part of working life and provided that, the money was spent to the benefit of the whole UK population, was something that one ought to do. But it sickened him to see this money being poured into black holes, like the NHS, and government projects like this new railway that the government were hell bent on building and of course the big defence contractors. The beneficiaries of the new railway would be the big engineering companies and various consultants. Not the people who were paying for it to be built and would then pay extortionate prices to use it.

With no benefit to the people at all. They were lucky to have a few crumbs thrown their way. Yet they, the taxpayers were paying for everything. The whole system was rotten to the core and rife with corruption from the top down and the bottom up. Noses in the trough.

He preferred sailing! He and Jenna could sell all their assets in the UK, put it all offshore and just wander the planet on Wind Charmer. The boat was paid for, so all they had to worry about was, insurance, maintenance, the occasional repair, berthing when there was nowhere to anchor, fuel, and supplies.

It was certainly less than he was paying in, corporation tax, income tax, energy bills and council tax every year. Plus of course VAT. Another con he thought. From what had been discussed, Mary and Sam would join them.

Maybe Josh and Norman too, although William had offered Norman a very well-paid job to go and work for him once this was all over. They had to finish off this current situation first.

A couple of hours later they were safely tied up stern to, on the outer harbour wall. It was a fairly recent marina. Very clean, tidy, with efficient staff, who seemed to know Piero very well?

Piero had gone to the marina office to deal with checking the boat in. Nothing was put into the marina's computer system. There would not be an official record of their visit.

Gerry called Josh to let him know that they had arrived at Ragusa, he told them that they were going to a nearby restaurant, the one that Salford, Ramsey, and Piero's two men were sitting in. Gerry told Josh and Norman to meet them at the restaurant.

Seventy-Eight.

Salford and Ramsey had seen Wind Charmer arrive, had watched Piero go to the office and a short while later, watched as Gerry, Jenna, Mary, and Sam walked to the restaurant. Gerry organised a table for seven people as Piero, Norman and Josh were expected to join them in a while.

Once seated they ordered drinks and waited for the others to arrive. They were all sitting on the terrace as the evening was fine and warm. Salford and Ramsey were sat at the other end of the terrace. A short while later Piero joined them, the restaurant manager made a big fuss of him when he came in and led him to the table where the others were sitting.

Mary said. "They all seem to know you quite well round here."

"Yes, I didn't mention it before, but my family own this marina. In fact, we built it. Some five years ago."

"Well, you did a good job of it that's for sure." Sam said.

Their drinks arrived and they ordered food, Piero explained to the waiter that they were waiting for a couple of friends to arrive so not to serve the food until they were here and had also ordered their food.

They all chatted about the sail down from Trapani, ignoring Salford and Ramsey who were too far away from them to hear their conversation, they were also ignoring Piero's two guys who had been there for some time.

Another car pulled into the carpark, it was driven by a very attractive woman, she got out of her car, and immediately made a call from her mobile. Gerry noticed that a few seconds later Salford answered his. After speaking for a few seconds she looked across at Salford and then her gaze moved across to where Gerry and his party were sitting. Then she looked away in the direction of Wind Charmer.

She finished her call and at the same time Salford finished his. She then walked off in the direction of Wind Charmer.

Gerry said. "Ladies and gentlemen, it looks like we have another player," and told the others what he had just observed. No one looked in her direction, but they had all had a quick view of her when she had pulled up. "We may have to modify our plan a little."

Norman and Josh arrived a few minutes later. They, Josh, and Norman ordered some food and settled down to wait for it to arrive.

Gerry, without being obvious, kept his eye on the woman who had walked up to the boat, then carried on to the end of the breakwater and climbed the steps at the end, these led to a level area where there was a bench by the navigation light, she sat down and took a book from her handbag and started to read it.

Gerry kept an eye on her. By this time the sun was starting to go down, so this woman looked a little out of place. The food arrived and they all tucked in. It was superb.

Ramsey and Salford, finished their meal, settled the bill, and walked off to their car and drove away. Piero called Federico and Marco who were still sitting on the terrace of the beach bar, he told them that the two English guys were on the move and to follow them and see where they were going. Which they did.

Once the meal was finished, Gerry noting that the woman had stopped reading and was watching the spectacular sunset, said "Ok, Josh and Norman can go to the boat. "The rest of us will all go for a walk on the beach and watch the sunset." Turning to Josh, he handed him a key for the boat and said. "As soon as you are on board, get one of the guns out of the stash and watch out for this woman, I don't know who she is, but she is definitely one of them. Just be careful."

"Will do." Josh and Norman then set off to walk to the boat. Josh could see the woman sitting on the end of the breakwater, without looking at her directly he kept an eye on her.

The others left the restaurant walked around the back and set off along the beach. The woman could see them, so whilst she was still there, they kept walking. Just an after-dinner stroll.

A little while later the woman got up, walked down the steps and out of site. Gerry and Sam immediately turned and ran towards the steps leading from the beach to the top of the breakwater. Leaving Piero with Jenna and Mary. They had discussed their tactics whilst walking along the beach.

On nearly reaching the top of the steps they stopped. Gerry looked over in time to see the woman who had reached the stern of the boat, she had obviously called out, as he then saw Josh appear from the upper deck saloon walking towards the stern.

Gerry couldn't hear what they were saying but saw the woman produce a handgun, Josh raised his hands and started walking backwards, as she walked up the passerelle and followed him into the saloon with the gun trained on him, they both moved.

As soon as she entered the saloon, Gerry and Sam moved down the steps which took them onto the part of the breakwater that was level with the moored boats.

She following Josh into the saloon spotted Norman sitting in the lower saloon. She ordered Josh to go down and stand next to Norman, then followed them down keeping her gun trained on both of them at all times.

She spoke very quietly, "Who else is on board?"

"No one, the others have all gone for a walk on the beach."

"When are you expecting them back?"

"I am not sure, as I said, they have gone for a walk and will watch the sunset from the beach and then come back."

She ordered Josh to tie Norman's hands and ankles, put her hand in her bag and produced some lengths of cord, she handed the cords to Josh, who slowly and deliberately tied Normans hands and ankles. She kept the gun trained on him without wavering.

Next, she told Josh to turn around and seeing the Glock in his waist band grabbed it and put it on the saloon table. She bound his hands, picked up the Glock and told him to sit down.

She moved around so that she was facing the saloon entrance with her back to the aft companionway which led to the guest and crew cabins. And covering Norman and Josh with her gun whilst not taking her eyes off them said.

"We are going to wait for your friends to come back, if either of you moves or makes a sound, make no mistake, I will kill you both."

Gerry and Sam reached the stern of Wind Charmer, there was a motor yacht berthed on her port side. Gerry said. "If you get on the motor yacht and crawl along her port side you will be able to step across onto Wind Charmer, go through the forward hatch into the crew cabin and then make your way aft to the saloon. I will divert her attention by walking up the passerelle and calling out, if all is ok no problem but if as I suspect she is holding Josh and Norman at gunpoint, you should be able to come up behind her whilst she is concentrating on me and the other two."

Sam nodded and immediately jumped down onto the bathing platform of the motor yacht, climbed the steps leading to the aft deck and started making his way along the port side towards the bow. He couldn't be seen by anyone on board Wind Charmer as he was the other side of the motor yacht's large deck saloon.

Gerry counted to thirty and then walked normally along the passerelle of his boat and called out, "It's only me, I forgot to take my camera and want to get some shots of the sunset."

He stepped off the passerelle onto the aft deck and walked straight ahead to the deck saloon, as soon as he entered the woman said, "Freeze, and then walk down here slowly with your hands where I can see them."

He got to the bottom step just as Sam came up behind her. She hadn't heard him, Sam just put his arms around her pinning them to her side. She immediately leant forward pushing her buttocks back toward him and stamped on his foot, hard. It had no effect on Sam other than he gripped her more tightly. Gerry stepped forward and gave her a gentle dig to the stomach. Which knocked the breath out of her, and she dropped both guns which were pointing at the ground.

Gerry picked them up and untied Josh and Norman, Sam held on to her, she couldn't move and after Gerry had hit her, she was still struggling to breathe. Gerry using the cord that she had used on Josh, tied her hands and ankles.

They searched her, found her mobile phone, they checked last calls and texts. The last text was sent a few minutes before Gerry and Sam had arrived back at the boat. It simply said, "Need back up at boat. Fast."

Seventy-Nine.

Piero, Mary, and Jenna arrived back.

Piero reported that Marco had called to say that the two English guys had gone to a hotel about 5 klicks away. He had just called two minutes ago, and these guys had just left the hotel at the rush and were headed towards the marina, they weren't hanging about and would be here in a few minutes. Marco and Federico were following and would be there shortly as well.

Piero had sent his other two guys to collect a van. They were just arriving, and they parked a little way back from the boat. Sam carried Sharon, trussed up like a chicken with a piece of gaffer tape over her mouth and dumped her in the back of the van. Piero told his guys to wait with her in the back of the van, until the English guys arrived which would be any minute. He said that he would call them, two rings and then hang up which would be the signal to open the sliding door and emerge ready to help take Salford and Ramsey.

Sam and Gerry then waited on board whilst, Norman, Josh, Mary, and Jenna hid amongst the cars parked beside the harbour wall. Piero hid between the van and the harbour wall. They were all armed.

Ramsey and Salford drove up and stopped at the stern of Wind Charmer. Salford was out first being in the passenger seat. He ran along the passerelle, onto the aft deck, through the cockpit and into the deck saloon which was deserted so he then went down the steps into the lower saloon. He was holding his gun in front but unfortunately for him he ran straight into Gerry's right hook. Which broke his nose and cheek bone and stopped him in his tracks, he dropped his gun. He blinked twice and then dropped to the floor like a sack of potatoes.

Ramsey was just charging through the cockpit when he saw Salford go down, he froze pointing his gun forward. Piero, who by this time had emerged from behind the van, shot him in the right leg, he swung round in Piero's direction and then toppled sideways grabbing his leg with both hands and dropping his gun in the process.

Gerry tied Salford's wrists and ankles and put a piece of gaffer tape over his mouth. Sam went up to the cockpit to deal with Ramsey who was bleeding heavily from the bullet wound in his leg. He called out for Mary to come and help. She came running on board took one look at Ramsey and went to get her medical kit.

As she passed Gerry she said, "What's the state of play with that one."

He has a probable broken nose and cheekbone, he'll live. He ran straight into my fist, there was nothing I could do."

Mary grabbed her bag and ran back up to the cockpit, she quickly applied a tourniquet to Ramsey's thigh which slowed the bleeding down considerably. The bullet had passed straight through and must have grazed the femoral artery on its way. Whilst she had the bleeding under control, she would have to stitch the hole in his artery, otherwise he could bleed to death.

She would have to enlarge the hole in his leg to gain access to the artery before she could stitch it. It wasn't going to be easy.
Sam carried Salford around her and Ramsey, and took him to the van, dumped him in the back with Sharon and returned to help Mary. The two Sicilians kept their guns on Sharon and Salford, whilst taking great delight in telling them just where they would shoot them if either moved or made a sound.

Mary very expertly dealt with Ramsey's leg, she managed to get hold of the artery, and stitch it. The bleeding stopped, so she then stitched the holes back and front where the bullet had passed through. And dressed his wound.

Sam then tied his wrists and ankles, lifted him up, took him to the van and dumped him in the back with the others.

The whole thing had taken minutes from start to finish. They had three prisoners who they were sure, William would enjoy talking to.

Piero then said to his men. "I will drive the van, you two stay in the back with the prisoners, Marco can come with me, and Federico can follow in the car and show the others the way, once they have finished cleaning everything up." He turned to his two guys in the back and said in English. If any of these three tries anything at all, just kill them."

They both nodded and smiled, one said. "It will be a pleasure boss."

Piero spoke to Gerry. "I will take them to the farm, Federico will wait with you and show you the way, let's decide what to do with them once we get there."

"I will message William and see what he wants done with them. Also, with the other six that your uncle is looking after for us."

Piero laughed and said, "I'd almost forgotten about them, good idea otherwise my uncle will start charging us for their board and lodging."

He got in the van and drove off. Gerry messaged William and told him they had nine prisoners and what did he want done with them? As the woman had refused to give her name, he had taken a photo of her which with Norman's help he had attached to the message. Norman liked the burst transmitter and told Gerry that he would like to take it apart and examine it. See how it was made and maybe make his own.

Gerry said, "Ok but you will have to wait until this is over."
Gerry and the others set about cleaning up the cockpit after Ramsey had bled all over it with his leg wound.

Once all was done and the boat secure, they followed Federico to the farm which as Piero had said, wasn't very far from the marina.

Whilst on the way to the farm Gerry received a message from William to say that they had identified the woman as Sharon Richards, a well-known assassin who has no allegiances works for the highest bidder, and very dangerous.

As they arrived at the small warehouse Gerry received another message from William. It said "Great news, transport will be with you in 3-4 hours. They will collect your cargo. Please keep the cargo well chilled in the meantime."

Gerry passed this information to Piero, who called his uncle and asked him to deliver his six prisoners to the farm. He said that it would probably take them around three hours.

Piero had driven the van into the warehouse, and they had left the prisoners inside, except for the woman who needed the toilet, urgently. She was escorted to and from the toilet without incident and put back in the van. Again, her mouth was taped over as were Salford and Ramsey, thus they were unable to talk to each other. They were in fact terrified as to what was going to happen to them.

A little over three hours later a dark blue van arrived. It had windows down each side, all of them had bars inside. The six Chinese in the back of the van were handcuffed and had black bags over their heads. They too, on Piero's instructions, had gaffer tape over their mouths.

Piero had them taken from the vehicle and made them sit on the floor next to the van.

Eighty.

Thirty minutes later a Royal Air Force Hercules C130 J landed at Catania airport, it taxied to an area next to the end of the runway. The ramp at the rear of the aircraft was lowered and a black Range Rover emerged with four occupants followed by a green Ford Transit nine-seater minibus.

Both vehicles drove towards a gate in the perimeter fence, which was manned by two Italian soldiers, they opened the gate as the two vehicles approached. Neither vehicle stopped but drove straight through the gate and onto the road, then headed south. The soldiers, closed the gate, locked it and went and sat in a nearby hut. Neither soldier paid any attention to the two vehicles that had driven through the gate.

Refuelling of the Hercules started 10 minutes after the two vehicles had departed.

An hour and fifteen minutes later the same vehicles drove into the farm, Piero, who had been waiting for them, got in the back of the Range Rover and directed the driver to the warehouse. The main door was open and both vehicles drove straight in.

William got out of the Range Rover followed by three very tough looking guys, obviously military and probably Special Forces. The driver of the transit also got out, he too looked just like the others.

One was carrying several sets of handcuffs and black hoods. No one spoke except William who spoke with Gerry.

Then William spoke quietly to one of the four guys, one of them replaced the handcuffs on the Chinese men, and they put them in the Transit, leaving their hoods on, they then used ankle cuffs and secured them to their seats, the others opened the van holding Salford, Ramsey, and Richards, secured them with handcuffs and put the black hoods over their heads. They then moved them to the Transit, secured them to their seats and put seatbelts on all nine.

None of them could move a hand or a leg.

William said. "Thanks very much Ladies and Gentlemen, we will be on our way now. I will be in touch in the next 48 hours. Well done, all of you." Turning to Piero he said. "What you have done is very much appreciated and will not be forgotten." He handed Piero a small card with a UK number printed on it.

He said. "This number is manned 24/7. If you are ever in serious trouble, just call it, identify yourself and give them the nature of your problem. Help will be forthcoming."

Piero thanked him.

William again spoke to Gerry. "Thanks again, Ramsey and Salford are definitely the people who killed Villiers and Jones. We know how and who was responsible for providing the information on Villiers to them, and to Towers who instructed and paid them. I don't need to question them now, as we have all the info that we need."

"What will you do with them?"

"Don't worry about that they will be dealt with accordingly. They won't be coming back."

With that he took his leave of them, climbed into the passenger seat of the Range Rover, two of the Special Forces guys got in the back of the Transit and sat facing the nine prisoners, a third got behind the wheel. The fourth got behind the wheel of the Range Rover, started the engine and drove off, followed by the Transit.

Mary turned to Jena and said with a wink, "I thought that the help looked quite fit and capable."

"Yeah I know what you mean." Jenna said with a grin. Everyone started laughing.

The Range Rover and Transit arrived back at the airport, as they approached the two Italian soldiers opened the gate, they drove in and headed towards the Hercules, again the soldiers didn't take any notice of the two vehicles that had driven in. They just closed and locked the gate and returned to their hut.

The ramp of the Hercules was lowered as they had driven through the gate. The Range Rover drove straight up the ramp and into the interior. The Transit swung round and reversed up the ramp into the aircraft. Both vehicles were lashed down.

The engines started and the aircraft moved onto the runway and took off immediately. The whole process had been carried out without any radio communication with the tower, everything had been arranged in advance of their arrival and carried out with efficiency and precision.

Once at cruising altitude around 30,000 feet, the Hercules turned to the West and set a course that would take them to Gibraltar.
The prisoners had been left secured to their seats in the transit. Two of William's men sat watching them.

Eighty-One.

Two hours later they started to lose height as they were on the approach to Gibraltar and soon after landing, they taxied to a quiet apron next to the runway, where their tanks were topped up with fuel.

Again, there was no radio contact between the plane and the airport authorities. Everything had been arranged in advance of their arrival.

The Hercules then took off, circled the rock and headed West out into the Atlantic. They stayed on a westerly heading for 40 minutes and then turned Southwest. They remained at the plane's cruising altitude for a further hour and twenty minutes.

After an hour, two of William's men opened the side door of the Transit. They removed the hoods from the nine passengers and the tape from their mouths.

The woman, immediately spoke saying that she needed the toilet desperately, the others all said the same thing. One of the soldiers said. "You will just have to go where you sit, those are my orders and there will be no exceptions."

Salford said. "This is against our human rights, I demand to know where we are and where you are taking us."

William stepped into the van, he said. "As far as your human rights go, you don't have any. You murdered two very good friends of mine, without any compunction whatsoever, did you consider their human rights? As for where we are going, you will know soon enough."

Sharon spoke. "What about my human rights? I didn't have anything to do with the deaths of your friends."

"You murdered another friend of ours. He was the owner of a tech company and refused to sell his shares to Bob Towers. He was the father of five children, you killed his wife as well, just because she was with him at the time. Did you consider their human rights? You killed them on orders from Towers and got well paid for it. You people are all the same, you are happy to kill under orders but scream for your rights when you are in trouble. So tough luck."

They could all see through the front windscreen of the van and could see that they were in the belly of a transport aircraft. None could move as apart from the hand and ankle cuffs they were strapped into their seats. The six Chinese remained quiet.

Since leaving Gibraltar the plane had been in the air for two hours and was well out into the Atlantic Ocean, albeit 30,000 feet above the ocean.

William left the van and went and spoke to the pilot. Who checked the radar screen and did a visual check on the surface below. There were no ships in their vicinity. The soldiers quickly removed the number plates from the transit, all other identification markings, such as the VIN number, engine, gearbox numbers, and ID plate had been removed prior to leaving England. The pilot then lost hight down to around 12,000 feet.

The two other soldiers got out, closed the sliding door and one got in the front, he then turned on the ignition, which released the steering lock and proceeded to secure the steering wheel in the central position so that the front wheels were facing exactly forward. Having done this he then released the handbrake and checked that the van was in neutral.

They then removed the straps securing the rear wheels and replaced them with wooden chocks which both had short ropes attached to them. Once the chocks were in place they proceeded to remove the straps securing the front wheels. The vehicle was now held in place by the chocks in front of the rear wheels.

One soldier was squatting each side of the rear wheels holding the ropes attached to the chocks, each gave a thumbs up sign to William who was standing at the door to the flight deck. They were both connected to the aircraft by safety straps.

He gave them a signal to withdraw the chocks and at the same time gave a signal to the pilot to raise the nose of the Hercules 5 degrees. And open the rear ramp of the aircraft.

Once the chocks had been removed the van started to roll towards the open rear door, gathering pace as it went. It went straight out through the door and started to fall towards the sea.

The occupants, realising what was happening started screaming.

The ramp was closed, and the aircraft continued on its course. William and the soldiers watched as the van hurtled towards the sea below. There were no clouds, so they watched for the few minutes it took for the Transit to hit the water 12,000 feet below.

The vans terminal velocity was such that it completely concertinaed when it hit the water. The occupants were crushed to death instantly, the remains of the van sank down to the seabed some 1000 metres below.

The Hercules continued on its course for a further 20 minutes before making a long curving turn and then set a course that would take them back to Brize Norton in the UK.

William said "Well done everybody. Nice tidy job."

One of the soldiers remarked, "That must be the fastest Transit in the world."

"Yeah it went like a rocket." Another said.

With that they all started to laugh.

Eighty-Two.

Meanwhile, back in Sicily, Gerry and the gang were preparing Wind Charmer for her next voyage. Piero had gone back to his estate. He left two of his people to watch over Gerry and the gang, just in case there were others lurking who might want to do them harm.

Norman spent some time checking the boat for any kind of tracking device, he was very thorough and was relieved not to find any.

They set sail the following day.

Gerry set a course for Malta, just in case anyone was watching them. This took them more or less dead south. He maintained this course for a good three hours before turning east and heading for Heraklion.
They had agreed with William that they would delay initiating their algorithm for seven days, this would give William and Carmichael the time that they needed to put their plan into action. William would message Gerry when they were all ready to make their various moves.

Carmichael had not told Gerry that they had a sister organisation in the US. It was as secret as Carmichael's and was charged with defending US democracy against any and all comers. Not even the US president was aware of their existence, but their influence and corresponding power was extraordinary.

Carmichael had been in constant touch with them since he had first heard about the scheme by Towers and his associates. They had all been working on their respective plans non-stop. The US people had agreed to deal with the people on their side of the Atlantic whilst Carmichael's people would deal with the UK and Europe.

The idea was that no one would make a move until they were all ready. Then the algorithm would be launched, Norman would crash all their systems and then both organisations would make their moves contemporaneously.

Gerry understood that they needed to be in a place where Norman had good access to the internet in order to do this. The marina at Heraklion looked like a good bet. As soon as the Algorithm had been launched they would sail off and try and disappear amongst the thousands of good anchorages around the Greek Islands.

In any event he was gambling on the fact that Towers and his cronies would have enough on their plate to deal with, without having to think about them.

Carmichael had impressed upon Mary that once all their various actions had been carried out, and in particular the launch of the algorithm, Gerry and co.'s job will have been done. He, Carmichael would ensure that Mary's cure for cancer would go through all the normal trials and tests, and he would make sure that it reached the right people, who, in turn would ensure that it was manufactured and sold at a very reasonable price relating to its cost. There would be no profiteering allowed at all. He also promised Mary that she and her late team would receive full credit for its discovery.

Eighty-Three.

Yong meanwhile had put together a team of twenty ex Chinese military, men and women. Their mission was to go to Sicily and attack the Cantolini estate with a view to murdering Piero and his entire family. He wanted revenge for having been ignominiously kicked out of Sicily by this man and his friends. He wanted to have them all butchered as a warning to these Sicilian peasants, which was how he viewed them. Once they were all dead he would buy the estate and burn down the house and any other buildings. He would then have the vines destroyed in order to remove any trace of the Cantolini family.

Like Towers he had become delusional as a result of too much cocaine use. He had become massively wealthy by his connections to the CCP. Without which he would be just another Chinaman working in the paddy fields. He didn't see it that way. He saw himself as a self-made businessman and a clever one at that. The reality was, that he was nothing more than a thug.

The soldiers that he had employed were more or less the same, none had seen real combat against battle hardened soldiers, and they were just bullies who were used to taking on unarmed people who were easily frightened.

On the other hand Piero had nearly sixty battle hardened troops who would happily lay their lives down for a boss, who not only paid them well, but treated them and their families as if they were his own. Yong knew nothing of this, and this was a big mistake on his part. A fatal one at that.

Wind Charmer was about halfway to Heraklion when they changed her name. All on board hid their real identity papers and started using the new ones that Norman had arranged for them. This was the first time that they would have to use them, as all the time that they were in Sicily and due to their association with Piero, they hadn't needed to show any papers at all. There was no official trace of them ever having been on Sicily.

Yong's people had been flown into Malta by private plane and were on board a chartered fishing boat whose owner/skipper was sympathetic to the CCP. A fact that no one on board knew, was that one of the crew, who they all thought was from Milan was in fact a Sicilian from Trapani. His name was Francisco Dominelli, who had overheard the Chinese talking about the Cantolini estate.

All the hardware they needed was already on the fishing boat. They set off from Malta and were headed for a bay that was close to the Cantolini estate. The route they were taking would take them near the Sicilian coast close to Ragusa, where they would then follow the coast in a northwest direction, making it look as though they were fishing just off the Sicilian coast.

Francisco quickly realised that these people were not going to the Cantolini estate to taste the wine. As soon as the fishing boat was in range of the Sicilian coast, he sent a text to his brother, telling him to contact the Cantolini estate and tell them what was happening. He also knew the coordinates of the drop off point, which he included in his text. He told his brother not to reply to his text as these people were very dangerous and that once he had sent the text he would drop his phone overboard.

His brother on receiving the text, immediately went online looked up the Cantolini estate's telephone number. He called and gave the receptionist all the information that he had received from his brother. She immediately gave him her mobile number so that he could forward the text to her. She then called Piero, who was in his office and forwarded the text to him.

He in turn called his two right hand men, Federico and Marco. Called them in, and between them they arranged a nice reception committee for the Chinese. They immediately sent a Land Rover with four men armed to the teeth to the area above the beach where these guys were due to land. They were instructed to stay out of site as given the distance from this beach to the estate they would most certainly need transport. As there would be twenty of them, this would be in the form of a small coach or more likely a truck.

Francisco had reckoned that they were due to reach the beach just after dark, which was some eight hours away. Piero's people had plenty of time to put a plan into action.

An hour later the Land Rover turned onto the track leading to the cliffs that overlooked the beach. Just in case someone was already there, the Land Rover stopped and the two guys who were in the back got out, the Land Rover stayed put and the two went on foot moving fast to check out the cliffs, beach and surrounding area.

Fifteen minutes later, they reported that all was clear for now. The Land Rover moved in, and they called Piero to say that all was clear. He had already despatched another vehicle, one of the estate's trucks with another fifteen men in the back to be followed by another with a similar number of men. The guys in the Land Rover carefully hid it in a clump of trees that was back from the cliff edge and there was also a gorge that led away from the beach up towards the dirt track. The clump of trees made a good hiding place for the Land Rover, and once the trucks had arrived the Land Rover would be driven away to a service area about ten kilometres away to be redeployed when the need arose, along with the trucks once unloaded.

Within an hour and a half all the men had been deployed, they had the whole area covered and all were well concealed.

Piero had a plan that was, that whoever was driving the truck or coach which was going to collect the Chinese may not be known to them. There was a good chance therefore if they took the truck before the fishing boat arrived, they could load the Chinese troops into the back, lock them in and take them wherever they wanted to.

The question was, having got them in the truck, what to do with them then?

He changed his mind and called Federico, "Change of plan. Let them board the truck. Four of you stay there, send the others back. I will make some arrangements and call you back."

Then he called his uncle, spoke with him at length, and then called a friend who ran a civil engineering firm. Made arrangements with him and then called Federico again.

"OK, this is what I want you to do. Just watch for now, stay unobserved, once they are all in the truck let them go on their way. We are pretty sure they will be coming this way, so just follow at a distance. I have arranged a diversion for them. There is only one road they can take, if in fact they are coming here. Contact me at once when they leave there and as I say, follow them at a distance. I will update you once they are on route."

With that, Federico called the vehicles back, rounded up his men and got them on their way back to the estate as fast as possible. By all their calculations they still had at least three hours before the fishing boat was due to arrive.

They also made sure that the Land Rover couldn't be seen from any angle. Then settled down to wait for the fishing boat to arrive. The sun went down and a little while later, the fishing boat came into the bay.

The fishing boat dropped anchor about 100 metres from the shore and very quickly launched two large inflatables. Both the inflatables had black tubes and a 40-hp. outboard each. The Chinese soldiers loaded their equipment on to the two inflatables, six men and an Italian crew member got into each boat, and they came ashore. They unloaded the equipment of weapons, ammunition, grenades, several blocks of Semtex a rocket launcher and provisions for at least two days and nights in the open. They were sufficiently equipped to start a small war

The inflatables returned to the fishing boat and ferried the remaining soldiers to the beach.

The inflatables returned to the fishing boat once they had unloaded, driven by the two Italian crew members. The boats were hoisted aboard, and the fishing boat left the bay to continue going about its normal business of fishing. The plan was for the fishing boat to return to the bay each evening after dark and wait for a signal from the Chinese to say that they were ready to be picked up.

The Chinese carried their equipment up the beach to the start of the gulley and a few minutes later a ten-ton panel truck came down the track and stopped at the top, swung round and reversed so that its back doors were facing the top of the gulley.

There were two men in it, a driver and a passenger. The passenger got out, walked to the back and opened the rear doors. The soldiers ferried their equipment up through the gulley, which was fairly hard going due to the rough terrain.

Federico and Marco watched from their secluded position. Once all the kit was loaded, the soldiers climbed aboard, the passenger closed the rear doors and walked around the vehicle and got in next to the driver. The truck moved off, no words had been exchanged between the passenger and the soldiers throughout.

Marco turned to Federico, "It looks as though they are going to start a war with all that equipment."

"Yeah, I saw a fair bit of Semtex amongst it all, they are definitely not going on a fishing holiday."

He called Piero to tell him that the truck was on its way. Gave him the make, colour and registration number. They waited five minutes and followed without using their lights until they reached the main road.

The truck got 30 kilometres down the road and came across a roadblock whereby the main road was closed due to a lorry that had crashed further along the road. The police were diverting all traffic to a minor road which led up into the mountain. In any event traffic was light. The truck turned onto the minor road and headed up the mountain, the road rose quite steadily but was in good condition.

The Land Rover arriving a few minutes later took the same route as the truck had. Once the Land Rover turned onto the mountain road, the police moved the roadblock and the diversion signs, repositioning them so that they now blocked the mountain road. They moved off having cleared the road and the traffic started passing through as normal.

The mountain road wound its way uphill, the truck had to slow down due to the hairpin bends that it was having to negotiate. The Land Rover kept its distance at about a kilometre behind.

Reaching a plateau, the truck had to stop again, there was a low loader blocking the road with a bulldozer reversing off its side. The truck pulled up about 15 metres from the reversing bulldozer. The driver spoke with an engineer who was holding a battery-operated lantern. The engineer told him that there had been a small landslide around the next bend. He said that they were common on this part of the road, but as it was only small, the bulldozer would clear it quickly and they should be on their way again in 15-20 minutes. He told them to stay where they were and remain in the truck whilst the bulldozer manoeuvred off the truck and into a parking area on the left of the road. The engineer said that the low-loader would then reverse into the parking area to enable the bulldozer to go up the road and clear the debris from the landslide.

Once the bulldozer had reversed into the parking area the low loader driver climbed into his cab and started to reverse the vehicle into the same parking area.

As soon as the low loader was blocking the whole road, the bulldozer lurched forward towards the side of the truck with the Chinese soldiers. The truck driver who was watching the low loader manoeuvre didn't see the bulldozer moving until it was too late.

The bulldozer's huge blade hit the truck square on its side and pushed the truck sideways until its right wheels were over the edge of the mountain with a drop of at least 700 ft. Once the truck's right-hand wheels were over the edge the bulldozer driver lifted the blade, which had the effect of lifting the truck's left-hand wheels into the air, and it slid over the edge, tumbled down the mountain bouncing off the rocks and smashing itself to pieces on the way down. Coming to a halt at the bottom of the ravine.

The Land Rover had pulled up in the middle of what was happening. Federico and Marco walked up to the point where the truck had gone over the edge.

Marco said. "I don't think anyone survived that."

One of the engineers walked up and handed Federico a Very pistol, loaded with a distress flare.

Federico said. "I think we should make sure." And carefully aiming the Very pistol he fired it straight at the truck which was on its side. The flare hit next to the diesel tank, which was leaking badly, a fire started immediately and very quickly the whole vehicle was ablaze. Shortly thereafter the fire reached the inside of the truck, causing the Semtex to explode which in turn set off the ammunition as well. There was a huge fireball which consumed the truck quickly.

Federico said. "No one could have survived that."
"You can be sure of that." Said Marco.

Federico threw the Very pistol down into the fire. Turned, thanked the engineer and both he and Marco got back in the Land Rover and continued on their way to the estate. He called Piero and brought him up to date on what had happened.

Piero said. "Well done, nice tidy job. The best part being that we won't have to get rid of the bodies."

Eighty-Four.

In London meanwhile, William, Carmichael, the Attorney General and one very tough looking individual walked into the office of the Secretary of State for defence. The Secretary was Richard Mullins.

He said. "Good morning gentlemen, I wasn't aware that we had an appointment?"

William said. "We don't, but we would like you to come with us now."
"What for?"
"Just come with us, all will be revealed shortly."
"Well I don't want to come with you, I have a job to do."
William said. "Either come with us willingly or I will have to arrest you and you will be led from here in handcuffs, in front of your staff. I am sure that you wouldn't want that to happen."

"What possible reason would you have to arrest me?"

The attorney general spoke. "How about conspiracy to murder Sir Malcolm Villiers, for starters, then we can throw in treason and one or two other serious charges, we have enough evidence to put you away for life. It's entirely your choice. With or without your cooperation?"

The minister got up from behind his desk and said. "Very well, I just have to make a couple of phone calls first."

William said "You will not make any calls whatsoever, nor will you speak to anyone on your way out. Please give me your mobile phone."

With that Carmichael reached over the desk, picked up the minister's mobile phone, switched it off and removed the battery, and put it all in his pocket.

The minister said. "I am sure that you are making a serious error for which you will pay later."

The tough looking guy said. "Yeah sure." And with a nod from William, took the ministers arm and led him out of the office."

Two other men who had been waiting outside the office came in.

William said "Ok, I want this office searched thoroughly and sealed. No one but you two is to come in here. Once you have finished searching I want two guards on this door 24/7, is that clear?" Both nodded and went about their task of searching the office.

What the minister didn't know was that his house was being raided and searched at the same time.

Another two people were in the minister's outer office watching the six staff at their desks. The AG addressed the office staff and said. "You will all hand your mobile phones to these two people. Anyone who even attempts to make a call or mentions today's incident to the press or anyone else will be immediately arrested and held under the prevention of terrorism act. Do I make myself clear?"

The minister was taken down to the rear entrance where a dark blue transit was waiting, he was put in the back, there were no windows inside just another two men from the security services and he was driven away.

Simultaneously, the Chancellor of the Exchequer was being arrested as he walked out of his country home. He too was put in the back of another dark blue transit van and driven away. A squad then entered his house and began a very thorough search. His office was already being searched.

William the AG and Carmichael along with the tough looking guy went to the entrance at the back of 10 Downing Street, the prime minister's office and residence. He was in his study when the four men walked in, they were joined by the head of the 1922 back bench committee.

The Prime minister, James Blackford, looked up and said "Gentlemen, this must be a serious emergency as I had no prior notice of this, how can I help?

The Ag walked up to his desk and laid a file on it. He said. "In that file is all the evidence we need to arrest and prosecute you for treason, conspiracy to murder the head of the intelligence service and others and plotting to overthrow the British government."

Blackford started to protest his innocence, William cut him off and said. "Don't bother Prime minister, the evidence is all there in black and white. We know everything"

The Attorney General then said. "We have booked a press conference which will start in ten minutes. At that press conference, you will resign. Sighting ill health as a result of your recent bout of Covid. You will not speak or communicate with anyone and come with us after the press conference." He handed Blackford a sheet of paper. "At the press conference you will say exactly, word for word what is on that paper. Nothing else, you won't answer any questions and once you have made your statement you will come with us.

You will be interviewed, and then afterward you will be taken to your country home. Your wife and children are already on their way. You will remain there for the rest of your life, and have no contact whatsoever with the outside world, you will not write your memoirs or speak in public again. Ever. Am I clear?"

Blackford said. "And if I refuse?"

The tough guy pulled a loaded hypodermic syringe from his pocket.
The AG then said. "The contents of this syringe will give you an immediate heart attack which will kill you. A trial would not be appropriate under the circumstances. I am sure that you will understand. So what is it to be?"

"Ok, as I don't have a choice in the matter I will comply with your wishes. But you will not get away with this I can assure you." He said.

William took the Prime Minister's mobile phone and did the same as he had done with the Defence secretary's phone. They went to the press briefing room. Blackford made his statement and afterwards was led away through the back of 10 Downing Street into a waiting Jaguar saloon and driven away with his usual escort. His staff were warned in the same way as the staff at the MOD, and agents were left in place so that there were no leaks to the press.

Alexander Morrison, the head of the 1922 committee was left in charge of the country as, the Deputy Prime minister had been relieved of his post as well and had been taken away.

They were all, with the exception of the Prime Minister, taken to a vast country house in Sussex with over a thousand acres of land surrounding it. The house itself was nearly half a mile from the nearest road and was being patrolled and guarded by the SAS. Various alterations had been rushed inside the house. There were no internet facilities, mobile phones or land lines, the latter having been disconnected.

The house was owned by Carmichael's people. It was empty beforehand as it had just been undergoing a very thorough refurbishment. That was now complete.

None of the people taken there knew of this location. They had all been delivered in the back of closed Transit vans. There were no windows in the back of the transits, thus none of those being held had any idea at all of where they were.

The Secretary of State for defence was the first to be taken to the basement room where he was met by Carmichael and William.

There were no windows, only a single florescent light in the middle of the ceiling. And a table with two chairs on one side, a single chair on the other side.

Carmichael and William sat on the two chairs, Mullins was sat opposite.

William spoke first. "I won't beat about the bush. We know that you have a direct line to Bob Towers in the US. We also know that you have been receiving information from your 'Mole' in my service. Who incidentally has been arrested and is being questioned as we speak. He passed you information as to where the tracker on Villiers' car had stopped, the tracker had been disconnected, but you knew that he would return to the same place once his business had been done and would reconnect it for the journey back, as this was a standard procedure. Thus, it would look as though the tracker had stopped working for a time whilst the vehicle was stationary. It was a simple task of waiting for him to return, then your friends just smashed his car off the road, killing him, Morgan Jones, and his driver.

A triple murder, carried out by your friends Ramsey and Salford, they have been dealt with by the way.

What you are going to do now is that you will telephone Bob Towers, you will tell him what is written on this piece of paper." William handed him an A4 typewritten sheet. "You will say nothing more nor less than that which is written on the paper. You will be driven to a call box close to your office and you will call him from there."

He was then escorted from the room to a transit van, put in the back with two guards and driven back to town.

Eighty-Five.

Arriving in Heraklion Wind Charmer, or Jenma as she was now called pulled up to the visitor's berth and was met by an official in uniform who very quickly told them that he was a friend of the Cantolini's, and all the formalities had been taken care of. They paid him his fee and he handed them a document that confirmed that they had been cleared and all the formalities complied with.

Once all had been done Norman connected to the marina's internet and got back to work. He was waiting for a signal from William before launching the algorithm. So, he decided to have a look on Yong Corp's system while he waited.

The others were preparing a meal and discussing the events of the last few weeks.

Mullins was taken to a phone box near the MOD. His minders told him that the box had been prepared and that every word he spoke whilst in it was being recorded, both ends of the conversation. One wrong word and he would suffer the consequences.

He was terrified, a few hours ago he had been looking forward to a very lucrative retirement, the Cartel had been paying him very well for his help and cooperation, he had accumulated over £20 million in his offshore accounts. Plenty for a nice life in the South of France where he liked to take his holidays. He was thinking that at least they didn't know about his numbered accounts.
Wonderful he thought, Taxpayer's money, the gift that kept on giving.

What he didn't know at this time was that Norman had supplied William & Co. with full details of the accounts, including the complete trail of where the money had come from. It was all money stolen from the British taxpayer.

He didn't know that in a few hours' time, that money would disappear and end up back in the hands of the British treasury.

Nor did he know that slowly, various people in influential positions were being quietly spirited away. Including the top three executives at the NHS who had been instrumental in lying about the figures and deaths going on from this Covid pandemic as well as siphoning off billions to the Cabal.

Every day anyone, regardless of what they had actually died from, was being counted as a Covid death. This was achieved by giving them a test which was engineered to give a positive result, whether they had the virus or not. This Pandemic had been in the planning stage for almost thirty years, it was now playing out in front of their eyes. How had he been found out he thought?

And how much did the security people know about the worldwide scheme to take control?

The facts were that they knew just about everything, all over the world, people who had been involved were being spirited away. The security crackdown was absolute. In the boardrooms of all the mainstream media there were directors and editors who had all gone along with the sanitizing of news, skewing everything in favour of Big Tech, Big Pharma etc. in fact most of the global corporations, who in turn were owned and manipulated by the likes of Bob Towers and the owners of the big social media companies.

None of this could have been achieved without the connivance of the mainstream media giants. They had all been happy to take the money and misinform the world's population on a massive scale. Whistle-blowers were sacked and their reputations ruined to the point where they couldn't get another job in the same industry. It was referred to as the NHS system they, the NHS had been doing this for decades, and the worst part was that the authorities knew that it was going on but, it suited them to turn a blind eye.

Mullins called Towers, when Towers answered the call, he repeated verbatim what was on his A4 sheet. Then he hung up. One of the minders alerted William that the call had been made, he in turn messaged Norman to go ahead and launch his algorithm and crash the Cartel's systems. Then they took Mullins back to the house.

Eighty-Six.

Norman upon receiving the message put his plans into action. It didn't take him more than a few minutes as everything had been ready for some time.

Towers put the phone down ashen faced, he couldn't take it in, the FBI were going to raid all his offices and homes, arrest him and take him to a secure location the following morning at 06.00. The next call he got was from his head of IT to say that their systems had just crashed.

He said, gathering a bit of composure. "What has caused the crash?"
"Haven't got a clue at the moment, but everyone is working flat out to find out what it is. At the moment it would appear to be a mystery virus. That's all I know."
"Keep me posted and call me the minute you have some news."

Towers then made several phone calls to his closest allies, some were unavailable which surprised him. The others he told, to meet him at a private airfield close by, where he had a brand-new Boeing 737 ready at all times as a contingency in case of something like this happening. He got hold of Barton. He immediately stopped what he was doing and headed to the airfield. Towers had a walk in safe in his office, he opened it and removed two briefcases and a holdall. Without hesitating, he walked to his private lift and pressed the button for the basement car park. On arrival his car and driver were waiting, he gave instructions to drive directly to the airport where his 737 was waiting in a closed hangar. During the journey, he made several phone calls, one being to his new head of security Major Albright Brand.

He said. "This situation with Professor Kelso and her associates has to be resolved now. I am getting a gut feeling that they are somehow responsible for our current crisis. I don't care what it costs, but I want it resolved, and resolved quickly and once and for all. My instructions to you therefore are to deal with it in any way you see fit, regardless of the cost. I will pay you $10 million personally, plus any costs that you incur, to make sure that this is done.

That money will be transferred to you once I am in the air. But make no mistake, this must be done now. Use whatever resources are available, but get it done. Understood?"

"Understood, completely." Came the reply. They ended the call.
He was driven straight to the hangar and the car drove inside.

He quickly boarded the jet. Others, including Barton and the head of the WHO, were already on board. Roughly half the people that should have been there, were on board. Towers thought that it was tough on those who were late, but he wasn't waiting for anyone, he told the pilot to take off without delay. The plane was towed out to the apron, started its engines, and began to taxi to the end of the runway, it was given immediate clearance for take-off. The controllers in the tower had been well remunerated for just this eventuality.

Reaching the end of the runway, the plane turned, brought its engines up to power and then roared down the runway and took off.

A man who had been posing as a plane spotter, sitting in the carpark with a clear view of the runway picked up his cell phone and said. "They have just taken off." "Thanks" was the reply, and the line went dead. He then drove off.

The plane was heading west. One of the people on board, Dr. Jeremy Goldsworthy, the chief medical officer of the WHO was the first to speak, "So what happens now?" He said to Towers.

"I have an island off the coast of China. It is leased from the CCP and is kept secure by the Chinese military. We can't be touched there. We will sit tight on the island, it has all the facilities that we will need to continue with our project and once we have brought it to its conclusion, we will be able to go anywhere we want in the world. It won't be a problem as we will be running the world by this time. Let's face it we more or less run everything now. So don't panic. No one other than the CCP and I know of the island's existence."

He was wrong, Norman had known about it for months, and had passed the information on to William.

Towers said to everyone on board. "Ladies and gentlemen, somewhere along the line, there has been a leak. At the moment I don't know how or where, but I can assure you all, that I will find out. Within the next 30 minutes we will clear US air space, at the moment we are heading due west in order to be out of US air space as quickly as possible, once clear we will head Northwest and go straight to the island. Later with luck more of our friends will be arriving, I have tried to contact our friends in the UK. Some have simply disappeared, others, the ones that I have been able to contact are completely in the dark as to what has happened to their colleagues."

Barton asked. "How long will the flight to this island take?"

"8 to 9 hours more or less."

Thirty minutes later they were clear of US airspace, Towers said. "OK everybody, we have just left US air space, so we should be in the clear. In another couple of hours, we will have an escort, compliments of the CCP. But in the meantime, it will be very difficult for the USAF to force us to turn back as this aircraft is registered in China."

Barton spoke, "What if they shoot us down?"

"To shoot down a Chinese registered aircraft in international airspace would be an act of war. I can't see the American authorities doing that. They owe China too much money and China has carefully infiltrated every facet of the US, UK and European governments. And I have lots of friends in the US government, who have received copious amounts of money from us over the years. They won't make a move against me. So let's look on the bright side and have some champagne."

He spoke on the internal phone and a little while later two very scantily clad hostesses appeared pushing trolleys which were carrying bottles of Bollinger and glasses, they proceeded to hand them out to the passengers.

What Towers wasn't aware of, was that the people who were now working against him carried far more influence in the US and the rest of the world than he did. As far as these people were concerned, he and his associates had crossed a line. There was no crossing back. And it didn't matter to them one iota who his friends were, no matter how powerful they were. In any event most of his friends would soon be in jail and cooperating fully with the authorities.

The mood on board the plane started to relax a little. The co-pilot appeared from the flight deck and spoke with Towers. "The pilot asks if you can come up to the cockpit for a minute."

Towers went with him forward to the cockpit. Once there the pilot said, "We may have a problem, I am picking up, what looks like two fast moving aircraft coming up astern, judging by their radar signature they look like a pair of F35's. They are a good 25 miles behind us and at their present speed they will catch us in the next few minutes."

Towers looked at the radar screen and said. "When they catch us, they will try and turn us around and escort us back to the US. When they call you on the radio, tell them that we are a Chinese passenger aircraft and that they have no authority to interfere with us, as we are in international airspace. Stick to your course and there is nothing they can do. Have they tried to contact you on the radio?"

The co-pilot said, "No, but what if they open fire on us?"

"They wouldn't dare, hold your course and keep calm, there is nothing they can do except bluff."

The pilot of the first F35 was closing fast on Tower's 737. He had a device on his console which had two switches and a red light. He flicked the first switch to the on position and the red light came on. Checking his distance to the 737 he then flicked the second switch, which activated a receiver on board the 737.

On the 737 they heard a rumbling, cracking sound coming from the rear of the aircraft, Barton looked around in time to see the entire tail section of the aircraft detach itself and fall away. He was not strapped into his seat and as a consequence was sucked straight out of the back of the aircraft. Others too, who didn't have their seat belts on, suffered the same fate.

Falling nearly thirty thousand feet to the sea below, they were all dead long before they hit the water.

The pilot struggling with the controls quickly realised that something had gone horribly wrong. The 737, plummeted earthwards, eventually tumbling out of control into the sea and disintegrating on impact. There were no survivors. A small debris field had been left on the surface, most of which slowly disappeared as it sank to the bottom.

As what was left of the fuselage sank to the bottom, 2 other small devices that had been attached to the aircraft's black boxes exploded simultaneously, completely destroying both black boxes.

The two F35's then turned and headed back to their base in the US.

Whilst the aircraft had been in the hangar two men had removed parts of the inner lining and placed shaped demolition charges around the interior of the fuselage connected to a radio-controlled timer. They had then carefully replaced the lining. When these charges went off, they had the effect of very neatly severing the tail section from the rest of the aircraft. They had also placed smaller charges on the black boxes on the aircraft. These were depth controlled and were set to go off at a depth of 50 metres.

Eighty-Seven.

Yong left his office in Silicon Valley, his usual chauffeur driven Mercedes was waiting for him at the kerb, he was in a hurry, so got straight in the back and ordered the driver to take him to the airfield where his private jet was waiting to take him to China.

Shortly after the car got on the highway which would take it to the airfield the driver turned off the highway into a service area and parked in a bay.

Yong said. "What are you doing? I am in a hurry."

The driver turned in his seat pointing an automatic pistol with silencer directly at Yong.

Yong said. "You aren't my normal driver, where is he? And who are you?"

The driver said. "I have a message for you from Piero Cantolini."

"Yes, what is it? I am in a hurry."

"He sends his regards." And with that, he shot Yong twice in the forehead. Then he calmly got out of the Mercedes and walked to a waiting Audi, that had followed them, he got in the passenger seat, and the Audi drove away. It would be found later, burned out, on waste ground fifty miles away.

Albright Brand grabbed the files that he needed and headed for the airport. He had booked a flight to London and then on to Nairobi. Towers had transferred the money that Brand needed just after he took off and it was done a few moments before Norman had emptied all the Cabal's accounts.

It took nearly 16 hours to get to the airport, wait for his flight, and arrive in London. He had to rush to get to his onward flight to Nairobi and only just made it. At no time did he get a chance to see or read the news.

Otherwise he would have seen the news that an unidentified Boeing passenger jet had disappeared over the Pacific Ocean.

In all it took him over 24 hours to get to Nairobi. He went straight from the airport to the Nairobi Hilton where he met his contact in the hotel's coffee lounge, his name was Jim Edwards, ex major British army and formerly a member of the SAS. Another one who left under a cloud for mistreating civilian prisoners. He was a nasty piece of work who had formed his own security company and didn't mind what the job was as long as it paid well.

Brand still did not know about the flight that had gone down in the Pacific.

Brand showed Edwards the file who, recognising the names of Gerry Dunbar and Sam Jarvis, said, "Well you certainly know how to pick your enemies."

"What do you mean?"

"I have never met these two characters, but from what I know they were both in the Royal Engineers and were transferred to work with the SAS as drivers and mechanics in the desert. Their reputation was that although they were only supposed to drive the SAS guys on their various missions and fix their vehicles should they have a problem, it turned out that they were very good when it came down to a fight. So much so that whenever they went into action these two turned out to be just as deadly as the SAS that they were supposed to be driving around. Half of them were terrified of Sam Jarvis due to the fact that he could lift most blokes off their feet with one hand. They were both totally ruthless when dealing with enemy soldiers but were very careful when dealing with civilians. In short when it came to a punch up with the enemy, they were a deadly force on their own. I would be happy to take the job on, but I will need extra money for this one."

"How much extra?"

"Double my normal fee."

"Which is?"

"Normal fee is $500K per body, but for Jarvis and Dunbar, I will want a million for each of them. Half of the total upfront, the rest on completion of the mission."

Brand said. "I can agree to that, but I must emphasise that failure will not be tolerated, so far we have sent several teams after these people, which have all resulted in complete failure and we have lost a lot of people in the process."

"Be in no doubt, failure is not in our vocabulary. Your big mistake so far has been to underestimate these people, mainly due to whoever has been supplying you with intelligence on these guys didn't do a thorough job. We know exactly who and what these guys are. And we will complete this mission successfully."

"Good, because my boss wants to see this matter resolved once and for all, and quickly."

Then Edwards dropped a bombshell, "Have they found his plane yet?"

"What are you talking about?"

"I saw on the news earlier, apparently his plane disappeared somewhere over the Pacific."

Brand was stunned, he said, "This is the first that I have heard about it, most of the last 24 hours has been spent in the air. I haven't seen any news."

"Well, what I saw was that the plane had gone missing and your boss and about 50 other people were on board and presumed missing."

Brand immediately tried to call Towers, his phone went straight to voicemail. He then tried to call three of Towers' closest aids, the same thing happened. He then called Towers' lawyer, who he knew hadn't been on the plane and got through to him immediately.

He confirmed to Brand that, yes indeed the plane was missing and that a full air and sea search was taking place at the moment and that was the only news that he had so far about the plane. Added to this Towersoft's offices had been raided by the FBI and they were still there, he commented that he wouldn't be surprised if his own office was raided as well. He told Brand that obviously something very serious was going on, but he was in the dark as to what was actually happening. He told Brand to be careful.

Brand said. "Ok I will contact you as soon as I get back to California." And finished the call.

Brand said to Edwards, "Our deal still stands, I have already got the funds, give me details of the account that you want it paid into and I will get the money transferred. With that Edwards wrote down his account number and passed it to Brand.

Brand said. "I will leave you to deal with it. You have got the files and I need to get back to California straight away." He left Edwards and got in a cab to take him back to Nairobi airport. Within 2 hours he was on a flight to London arriving some eight and a half hours later. Before boarding the aircraft he effected the transfer of 2.0 million dollars to Edwards' numbered account.

Eighty-Eight.

Brand decided to spend the night in London and find out further information as to what had happened to his Boss and the other people who seemed to have disappeared. He proceeded through immigration, showed his passport, and was immediately approached by two men wearing suits. One flashed their ID at him, all he saw was that they were from special Branch. He said, "Good evening Sir, would you come with us, please."

"Why? Said Brand.

"Just come with us please, all will be explained to you in due course."

With that they led him through a door marked, No Entry. Which in turn led to a corridor with several rooms off it. They opened one of the doors and directed him into a room, the room was bare except for a mirror on one of the walls and a small metal table with four chairs around it.

One said, "Please take a seat Mr. Brand."

"Look, what the hell is going on? I am a US citizen, you can't do this to me. I want to talk to my Embassy, now."

"Sorry, I can't let you do that. As for being a US citizen, so what? You are being held under the prevention of terrorism act. And as such I can hold you for seven days without charge should I wish to do so. Please sit down, other people will be coming to talk to you. Please give me your mobile phone."

Brand relented and sat down and gave them his phone The two special branch guys then left the room and locked it as they went. He realised that arguing with these guys was pointless and his best bet was to keep his mouth shut, at least until he knew what was happening.

He sat there in the room wondering what the hell had gone wrong. His Boss's plane had disappeared, others that he had tried to contact weren't contactable, he was being held under the British prevention of terrorism act. These guys weren't at all phased by the fact that he was a US citizen and as the minutes ticked by, he was getting more and more worried.

Eighty-Nine.

Meanwhile in Nairobi, Edwards was getting his team together. He had also contacted people he knew in the CIA to see if he could find out where Wind Charmer had gone. The last info he had was that the boat had been in Ragusa, southern Sicily but that She had left there some days ago.

He decided that he would need 6 people, 4 in his main group and 2 back up people. Until they knew where they would be operating, he was unable to make any other arrangements regarding accommodation, weapons, communication equipment and transport. He spent the waiting time briefing his operatives. And organising lists of the equipment that they were going to need.

Back at Heathrow airport, Brand was becoming more frustrated, angry, and worried. The worst part being that he just didn't know what had happened or what in fact was going on. One thing that he was sure about was that something had in fact gone seriously wrong.

He was left with his thoughts for over two hours, whilst being watched by CCTV and through the mirror that took up most of one wall. Then the door was unlocked, and two very hard looking guys walked in, one said "Major Brand, please stand up."

He complied and was immediately handcuffed and led away. He was taken along the corridor but this time to a door that led to an outside parking area where he was put into the back of a white Transit van. They blindfolded him and the vehicle set off.

Back in Sicily, the fishing boat that had dropped off the Chinese was re-entering the bay. It had been dark for about an hour and the fishing boat again anchored 100 or so metres from the beach. A small customs patrol vessel that had been waiting in the shadow of the cliffs overlooking the southern end of the bay moved out of the shadows and drew alongside the fishing boat.

The skipper on the fishing boat was not unduly concerned as it was quite normal to be stopped and boarded by the customs and his vessel searched for any kind of contraband.

Once the customs vessel was secured alongside the fishing boat four armed officers came on-board. They immediately asked for the boats papers and asked the crew to muster on the aft deck.

Whilst the documents including the crew's identity papers were being checked, two of the officers went below to start searching the boat. One was carrying a large black lamp. No one took any notice of this as it was a completely normal item of equipment needed for a thorough search.

They went straight to the engine room and looked around. The one with the lamp noted that the fuel tanks were positioned on either side of the main engine. He went straight to the tank on the starboard side and very carefully slid the lamp under the fuel tank so that it was out of sight.
Returning topsides they joined their colleagues as they were checking the crew's identity documents on their laptop. One turned to Francisco Dominelli and said, "There is a warrant out for your arrest, therefore we are going to have to take you into custody. One of my officers will accompany you whilst you go below to your quarters and collect your belongings."

Escorted by the officer Francisco went below and collected his belongings and returned to the aft deck. With that the officer in charge spoke to the skipper and said. "Everything else seems to be in order so you and your vessel are free to go," with that they returned to their boat taking Francisco with them.

The fishing boat weighed anchor and set off out of the bay and headed out to sea, the skipper's intention was to return to the bay once the patrol boat had moved on.

Francisco, spoke to the chief customs officer, "Why have I been arrested?" At which point the others all started laughing and it was only then that he realised that the guy driving the boat was in fact his brother who said. "It's OK you haven't been arrested, we just had to get you off that fishing boat." They all started to change from their customs uniforms, and then set a course for Ragusa.

After about fifteen minutes one of them took out his mobile phone and pressed the green button.

On board the fishing boat there was an almighty explosion, the bottom was completely blown out from the boat and the fuel in the tanks caught fire consuming most of the rest of the boat fairly quickly' as it was built of wood. What was left sank to the bottom. The crew had all been killed in the original explosion thus there were no survivors.

Ninety.

In Nairobi, Edwards received a call to say that Wind Charmer was thought to be in Heraklion, and that the boat's name had probably been changed to 'Jenma' as an identical looking boat had arrived there recently.

He immediately called his Greek contact, gave him the list of his requirements then got his assistant to book flights for six of them to fly from Nairobi to Heraklion via anywhere but London. Given his current occupation and history in the British armed forces he didn't want to go anywhere near the UK. He also told his Greek contact to travel to Heraklion without delay and keep an eye on the boat and try to photograph any crew members should he be able to do so without revealing his presence.

In the event they flew to Paris, then Athens and a local flight to Heraklion. His contact met them at the airport. He had rented a secluded villa for them about 14 kilometres outside Heraklion which turned out to be ideal for their purposes, as it stood in the middle of its own private grounds and was surrounded by a densely wooded area.

The house was approached by a long driveway and being in an elevated position had a good view of the driveway and surrounding area, so that any vehicles approaching would be seen as soon as they left the road. There was a good distance between the house and the trees which meant that it would be very difficult to approach the house unseen.

Edwards' contact left them to get moved in and went to collect the equipment that Edwards had ordered, explaining that he hadn't wanted to drive into the airport with enough equipment to start a small war. He told Edwards that he would be back in around an hour also that as he had a vehicle for them, he would return with a colleague in order to deliver it. Edwards changed that arrangement and sent one of his people with the contact to drive the other vehicle to the villa.

Edwards then set his people with the task of checking the surrounding area, looking for security weak spots, vantage points and any other routes by which the house could be approached. Having set them their various tasks, he sat back and waited for his man to return with the vehicle and equipment.

The plan forming in his head was to keep the boat under surveillance and to try and isolate one of the targets in order to kidnap them, take them to the house and then lure the others to a remote location under the pretext of swapping that person for all of Prof Mary's research and details of the cure that she had discovered.

Once they had lured the others to this remote location, his team would ambush them and kill them all. His guys would then go to the boat and search it for the information that related to Mary's cure if Gerry's people had not brought it with them. They would then set fire to the boat which hopefully would eliminate any trace of these people completely.

As according to the news, Towers and most of his close associates were very likely to be dead, if he could lay his hands on all the information relating to this cure, he would be in a position to sell it to the highest bidder. Given the lengths to which Towers and his people had been going to, to try and suppress this cure it must be worth tens of millions to someone. He would have to do something about Brand, but that was a situation that he could deal with when the time came.

Just over an hour later his contact arrived with his equipment and one of his guys with another vehicle. It was a small Nissan saloon so he told his contact that it would be better if he kept the people carrier and that he would require two vehicles and not one as there were six in his team and they would not always be travelling together.

He despatched one of his people in the Nissan to drop off his contact and then go to the marina and check on the boat. He was instructed to locate the boat and then return and report that it was in fact the right boat and the people they were looking for, were on board.

When his contact returned with another vehicle, another Nissan, he set him the task of finding a location for the ambush.

Ninety-One.

Back on-board Wind Charmer, William had updated Gerry & Co by telephone on the various moves that had been made against Towers and the rest of his cabal, there was a way to go yet, before they were completely in the clear, but the head had been chopped off along with the other major players.

The British Prime minister had resigned so had some members of his cabinet. Heads had rolled at the various major pharmaceutical companies, Tech giants and the NHS, where a criminal investigation was taking place. Big Oil, Big Energy and Big Agriculture were also on the cards. All the big banks were under investigation and resignations were happening at an alarming rate. The owners of mainstream media and some editors were also coming under the microscope. Some had already been arrested and were making all sorts of threats.

It didn't cut any ice with the people who were holding them, and the guys being held didn't even know where they were. All this was due to the evidence that Norman had supplied. They were in fact, now being held at a disused RAF base near Leeds. It was guarded by troops from No 1 Para who were under instructions to shoot anyone who tried to escape. The detainees were told of this and warned that there would be no exceptions, they were being held for conspiracy to overthrow the government which amounted to treason. In all their cases the Human Rights act, due to the severity of the alleged crimes and the overwhelming weight of the evidence against them, had been suspended by a special meeting of the now reduced and reinvigorated cabinet. All of whom were known to be absolutely loyal in every respect to the Crown and the authority of Parliament.

Both William and Carmichael agreed that Norman should be invited to the UK so that he could work directly for them. They called Gerry and proposed this to him. Gerry told them that he would discuss this with Norman and the others as he felt that Norman would be safer back in the UK under their care, but that a condition would have to be stipulated that under no circumstances whatever would the US authorities be advised of his existence or his capabilities. In any event it would be up to Norman to have the final say on this.

The Bank of England were mightily surprised at the windfall of a few trillion pounds that had started turning up from various tax havens around the world into the bank of England.

All these payments contained the reference, 'Refund of taxpayers money.' As is normal with bankers, no-one was complaining about the receipt of this money, and nobody was talking about giving it back.

Added to this, various people had just disappeared, and the police, including the fraud squad and security services, were being overwhelmed due to the enormity of what had been going on. Personnel from all three of the armed forces had been drafted in to assist as the magnitude of what had been going on for the last 30 years became clearer and the list of people involved grew by the hour. Carmichael remarked to William, "It just goes to show how greed has become a pandemic, never mind the Covid virus."

The same thing was happening in the US. But on a grander scale. Initially it was felt that due to the enormity of this conspiracy that they should cover the whole thing up. The proponents of this course of action were quickly disabused of this and were told in no uncertain terms that anybody who attempted to either cover this thing up or assist the culprits in any way shape or form would be dealt with very severely, without mercy of any kind. Regardless of who they were or who they knew. To quote Ex-President Trump, 'The swamp was being drained.' Whether they liked it or not. The biggest problem was that they were finding that the swamp was deeper than anyone realised, and it had been slowly getting bigger over the best part of thirty years. Once again the big driver was greed for money and power. Unchecked it would ultimately be responsible for wiping out the human race. It was like a cancer that had been growing throughout the world for decades.

The EU as usual were dragging their heals as, some of the people who were running the EU were up to their necks in this conspiracy as well, their number was up, they just hadn't realised it yet.

Ninety-Two.

No one on board Wind Charmer had noticed the guy who had walked past the boat, seemingly just out for a stroll. However William's two operatives who were still keeping an eye on the boat had noticed him. They were plotted up in the back of a van which was parked about 50 metres from the boat. These guys also had a Honda Africa Twin motorbike, parked near the van They had seen him do the same thing about an hour before, and he looked very much like ex-military, so they filmed him on this his second pass.

They got a good shot of his face and sent the picture to William to see if he was on any of their data bases.

The reply came back 10 minutes later, the result was positive. His name was Ambrose Mitchell, ex number one para, dishonourably discharged and now working for a security company called Tzero Security which in turn, was run by James Edwards, again ex paras, Edwards was known to be a very dangerous man who worked for the highest bidder and totally unscrupulous. He too had been dishonourably discharged from the service.

They saw that he drove away in a silver Nissan but were too far away to see its registration number clearly. William's men contacted him and requested back up of at least another two operatives with all the necessary arms and equipment. William said that he would send them in the private jet directly to Heraklion with immediate effect, he instructed his men to try and rent an apartment with a good view of the marina and the boat if possible.

One set off on the Honda to do just that. He had been given the details of an estate agent who should be able to assist them.

A discussion was taking place on board the boat, about the possibility that Mary and Jenna wanted an only girl's day out at the shops in Heraklion. Both Sam and Gerry felt that at least one of them should go as well but the girls said that they would just like to go shopping on their own.

They also discussed the issue that Norman had been asked to return to the UK in order to help Carmichael and William. William had promised that Norman would be furnished with the latest and most powerful computers that money could buy, he would be set up in his own office in the basement of one of their country houses and accommodated where only he and Carmichael would know of his existence.

He would be given a security detail who would keep him safe 24/7 and a significant salary, with a juicy pension and benefits.

This was Valhalla as far as Norman was concerned, his whole life revolved around computers, he thought of little else and the fact that they were going to pay him large sums of money to do so with the most up to date kit was just the icing on the cake.

In the end Jenna and Mary won the argument about the shopping trip, the others reluctantly agreeing to their proposal, and it was decided that they would go shopping the next day.

With Norman's approval they also agreed that this was an opportunity that he simply couldn't miss. He would be able to use his talents for a useful cause and it would be a fantastic career for him.

Gerry contacted William and affirmed their agreement to this plan, but the overriding factor was, that at no time would his very existence be revealed to the Americans or anyone else for that matter.

William then explained to Gerry about his two operatives that had been watching them and what they had seen, i.e. an ex special forces operative who is working for a security company that they knew of, which in turn was run by a very dangerous individual as well. He also said that the jet would be arriving the next day to bring two more of his people and that this would be a good opportunity to get Norman back in the UK, as he could join the aircraft on its return journey.

This new information was then discussed as to how it would affect the girl's trip to the shops the next day. Gerry and Sam were in a favour of cancelling the trip until they knew more about what these people were up to.

The girls both wanted to stick to their plan as they felt that they couldn't hide away forever, it might also bring these people out of the woodwork so that they could be dealt with. With Josh Sam and Gerry, plus four of William's men they felt that they were pretty safe.

Gerry said. "Before finalising our decision we should talk to William's men."

He sent an immediate message to William. He received the reply a few minutes later. "Don Metcalf and Warren Briggs will be with you in a few minutes."

He had just finished reading the message when someone was calling to him from the quayside at the stern of the boat.

There were two guys standing there. Obviously very military looking. Introducing themselves as Don and Warren. Gerry invited them on board and said. "You got here fast."

Don said with a smile. "We weren't far away."

They went below to the lower saloon and Gerry introduced them to the others. Don explained to them about the guy that they had seen and that they had identified the guy as being someone who worked for a security company called Tzero, who were known to be a very nasty lot indeed. The fact that they were hanging around meant that the danger was still there. So the question was, how do they deal with this latest set of circumstances?

They discussed the following day's shopping trip, the plane, which would be arriving sometime in the late evening, and getting Norman to the airport so that he could catch the flight back.

Don and Warren tended to agree with Mary and Jenna, that as they now knew of the existence of these guys, maybe it was a good idea to try and draw them out. Don wanted to let the girls go and he and his three men would follow them and keep them covered, should these guys try anything other than watching the girls, they would move in with a vengeance. Don was convinced that they might try to kidnap them, but wouldn't, at this stage try any violence, because Gerry, Sam and Josh weren't there, Tzero would want to get them all plus Mary's research and findings.

He related to them William's findings after interrogating Albright Brand, who, when he realised the depth and scope of what William and his people knew, had decided to talk and had told William's people exactly what Tzero's instructions were.

Those were to get hold of all Mary's research and findings and then, and only then to dispose of them all. Don had arranged for two vehicles to be delivered in a couple of hours, one for him, one for the other two of his people, Warren would have the Africa Twin, he was an expert rider and was very experienced at following people without being seen.

He wanted Gerry, Sam and Josh to remain on the boat for two reasons, one to guard it should Tzero's people try and search the boat looking for Mary's information and two they would be recognised by the other side and then they might end up having a shootout in a public place, which wouldn't be a good idea.

Much better to let them try something, Jenna and Mary would be safe with Don's guys watching over them and if he thought at any time that the girls were in serious danger they would immediately move in and take the Tzero guys out. In which case William would have to smooth things over with the Greek authorities, who rightly, would be very angry.

They might even be able to take one of them alive, in which case they would be able to question them as to where the rest of their people were, especially Edwards, who they would like to deal with.

Jenna spoke, "So the bottom line is that you want to use us as bait."

"Well you could put it that way, but I can't think of a better way to draw them into the open, that way we can follow them and find out where their lair is. The people who engaged them have been taken out. Edwards has had half his fee upfront he will know by now that Brand has been arrested, thus he could just walk away with a couple of million in the bank and no one could do anything about it. However, we now believe that Edwards has another agenda and that is to get his hands on Mary's research and findings in order to sell them to the highest bidder. It would be typical of him to pull a stroke like that."

Warren said, "William has stressed to us that we must safeguard Professor Kelso's interest in this and if anyone is to gain from this invention it must be her."

Gerry said, "Ok we will go along with your plan, but the moment any of this lot go anywhere near Mary and Jenna you must call us in. We don't know how many of them there are, but seven of us are better than four, so as long as we are agreed on that, let's proceed on that basis."

Don said, "I have some small tracking devices, they are the size of a large pin that Mary and Jenna can pin to their jackets, I can activate them remotely so that should they grab them and test for any electronic signals, we can give them time to do that before activating the devices. They have a range of five miles.

Also warren will be on the bike, he will be able to follow them wherever they go. They won't be able to outrun him on or off road. I promise you all, that we will have both girls covered."

Sam said, "We will go along with it as long as the girls are happy with this scenario."

He turned to Jenna and Mary and said, "Well what do you guys think?

Jenna was first to speak, "I'm ok with it but maybe we should take one of the Glocks with us, just in case."

Mary cut in, "Yeah and an M16 or two. Seriously though I think we should take the chance and finish this thing once and for all."

Jenna said, "Ok then let's go for it." Mary agreed.

Gerry said, "That just leaves, how do we get Norman to the airport for the flight back?"

Josh cut in, "I will take him in the hire car, Warren can follow on the bike, I will take the direct route so he will know which way I am going, so that anyone trying to follow us will be spotted quickly. The airport isn't far away."

Don said, "In that case we had better get a move on, we will have a quick check and see if that Nissan is around again. The plane should be here in a couple of hours, we have just rented an apartment that overlooks the marina so we will move our stuff in there and call you when Warren is ready with the bike to escort Josh and Norman to the airport."

Don returned to the boat quickly with the pin trackers for Mary and Jenna.

A while later they were having an emotional time saying goodbye to Norman, as a group of people they had been through an awful time together. Norman's input had been an enormous contribution, he had unearthed the Cabal's plans and those of both China and Russia to take control of a large proportion of the world and the greater majority of its vital resources.

Ninety-Three.

Through the unleashing of this Virus and the general misinformation coming from the WHO, the NHS, the EU, mainstream media and a large part of the worldwide scientific community, they had come very close to imposing a state of affairs similar to that which exists in China. I.e. an authoritarian state that would be run by the elites. There would be an underclass, who would become nothing more than slaves.

Now that the various organisations within the US and the UK had acted, this state of affairs would hopefully not now happen.

There was a lot of hugging and a few tears as Norman left, being driven by Josh to the airport. There was someone watching, he had been fishing off the harbour wall for some time, as they drove away, he was reporting to Edwards via his mobile phone. Unknown to him Don and Warren were in their apartment watching him and listening to every word that he was saying.

He was reporting to Edwards that it looked like two of the crew of Wind Charmer were leaving, judging by the bags that had been loaded into the hire car and all the hugs and waves that had been going on. Edwards told him to follow if he could but most likely they were going to the airport and it being so close gave them no time to get there and grab one or both of them.

The guy fishing packed up his stuff and walked to the Nissan. By the time he got going, it was too late as Josh and Norman were well out of site. He drove off, took the road to the airport and kept a keen eye out for the car being driven by Josh. He didn't notice Warren on the Africa Twin following at a distance.

Josh and Norman on reaching the airport were directed straight to where William's plane was waiting in a hangar just off the main apron. Shortly after, Edwards' guy arrived but he couldn't see them or the hire car. Warren watched as he toured the car park and then left his car and went to the flight departures area. Again nothing. Warren wanted to put a tracker on the Nissan, but he couldn't risk them finding it, as then they would know that they were being watched.

Warren waited until he saw Josh drive out in the VW Golf that they had hired, he waited and then saw the Nissan guy come running out of the departure hall, get in his car and roar off in pursuit of Josh. The Nissan guy reported to Edwards that one had been dropped off and the other looked like he was returning to the marina.

Edwards told him to follow at a safe distance and report when he got back to the marina.

Edwards spoke to his men. "Right, we have seen that one has left, there isn't much that we can do about it. What we must now do, is to be prepared to move at a moment's notice so that the next time they make a move we are ready to act." They set about getting everything ready, it was getting late and figured that nothing more would happen that day.

Warren watched the Nissan pull into the marina and turning into a side road, he parked his bike, took off his crash helmet, put it into the pannier on the back of the bike and wandered slowly across the road into the marina. He watched as the Nissan turned and headed back to the road without giving him a second glance.

The following morning Mary and Jenna decided to walk into town as it wasn't far and not worth getting a cab. Jenna told Gerry to hand over his debit card, which he did without arguing and she and Mary set off to walk into town.

The Nissan driver had just pulled into the car park and on seeing the girls, left his car in the car park and followed them on foot. Don seeing that Nissan man was following the girls, left the apartment and followed him on foot. Warren left on the bike and overtook all of them and rode into the town centre, parked and waited.

Don left instructions for his two new guys to take the car and follow on but to go slowly and stop before overtaking him and to proceed slowly so as to stay behind him. They had to stop regularly in order to do this. In the car they had the receiver for the tracking devices that Mary and Jenna were wearing, they were getting a good quality signal which meant that they knew where the girls were at all times. Being in constant touch with Don via radio they kept him up to speed on where the girls were.

Jenna and Mary took their time walking to the town centre, taking in the fantastic architecture of the buildings that they passed on the way. Reaching a pedestrianised shopping area they visited a very nice shoe shop, had a look round and left, wandering along and chatting but at the same time keeping an eye out for anyone paying attention to them. They visited a few more shops and couldn't believe the prices, then they went to one of the numerous coffee bars around the square. Ordered coffee & some pastries. They sat outside and watched people walking around and tried to spot if they had picked up a tail or not. They looked out for Don and Warren, they couldn't spot them either.

Don was watching them, and Warren was waiting in a side street with his bike, he in turn was keeping his eye on Nissan man, who was continually on the phone reporting to Edwards.

Finishing their coffees and pastries, the girls continued on down the road taking in the architecture and doing some window shopping. Neither of them really felt like buying anything they were both more intent on looking out for the enemy. Nor had they been able to spot either Don or Warren, but they were sure that they wouldn't be far away. They also had the comfort of the trackers.

They walked around town for another hour, deciding that they were both starving, they looked for somewhere nice to eat, so that they could have some lunch. Further down the road they found a nice-looking place which was busy with a lot of tables on the terrace, they walked in, and a waiter led them to a table for two on the terrace one row back from the pavement. A few minutes later, a couple in their early forties came in and were led to a table on the edge of the pavement. Mary and Jenna saw them arrive but took no notice as the waiter led them to their table, they looked like a couple of tourists nothing more, and didn't register with Mary and Jenna as being anything more than two people out to lunch.

Mary and Jenna ordered their food and when it came they realised that they had made a good choice with this particular restaurant. The food was superb, and the service was second to none. They ate heartily and enjoyed a bottle of the local wine. As the meal went on they both became more relaxed.

Jenna said, "I'm glad we came, I haven't felt this relaxed in months."
"I feel the same, I'm glad we came too, we haven't done much shopping, mainly due to the prices, but it has been a very stressful time for all of us."

They paid the bill and got ready to leave, not noticing that the couple who had entered the restaurant shortly after them, settled their bill at the same time and the woman was on the phone.
Don was watching them from a bar across the road as Mary and Jenna started to walk off the terrace, he saw the couple get up behind Mary and Jenna just as a blue Renault van pulled up outside the restaurant completely blocking his view.

The side door of the van slid open and at the same time the couple who by this time were right behind Mary and Jenna, pushed them into the van, others in the van grabbed them and pulled them in, the couple got in the back, the door slid shut and the van drove away. It was a very neat, professional move carried out in seconds.

Don was already on the move and crossed the road at a run. He was too late as the van drove down the road and turned right at the first corner. He called his two guys in the car, they drove up and collected him, meanwhile, Warren who had seen it all go down moved from where he was sitting on the bike and followed in the direction that the van had taken.

Ninety-Four.

The car with Don and the other two started to follow, they had the receiver for the trackers and could see clearly the route that the van was taking. Don told Warren, who was in radio contact, to fall back as they could see where they were, and they were getting a clear signal.

He then called Gerry, told him what had happened, gave him the route and Gerry said they would follow on. Don said he would keep them informed but they had the situation well covered and to stay back until they knew where the van was going. Then he would vector them in. Their advantage, as it was at the moment being, the guys in the van would think that they had got away clean.

Don's plan was that once the van stopped moving he would turn the trackers off for 10 minutes just in case Edwards' people checked for a signal once they arrived at their destination. They might check in the van, but it was just a chance that he would have to take.

In the back of the van, they had put black bags over the Girl's heads and searched them looking for weapons and tracking devices, but they were relying on what they could see, the small pin devices once inserted into a seam on a jacket, were more or less invisible. It took less than twenty minutes to reach the house.

The girls were then led into the house still with the black bags over their heads and their hands tied behind their backs. They were made to sit in two upright chairs no one spoke.

Don having seen that the van had stopped shut the trackers down, he could see that the van had turned off the main road then turned left along what looked on the map, like a track and come to a halt about 500 metres along this track.

He called Warren, gave him directions to where the track met the road. Warren rode to the entrance to the track. He found a clump of trees where he could hide his bike. He hid the bike so that it couldn't be seen unless you were right on top of it. From the rear pannier he removed a black rucksack, a pair of binoculars, a compact silenced Uzi with two mags, and a pair of hand grenades also 4 sets of plasticuffs. He put everything other than the Uzi and magazines into the rucksack. He already had a Glock 9 mm in his waistband and spare mags in the pocket of his black leather jacket.

Following the directions that Don had given him, he proceeded on foot through the trees until he could see the house, he could also see the blue van that had been used to kidnap the girls. He then stopped after finding a completely secluded spot in the trees, just back from the clear area that surrounded the house. From here he could keep the front of the house under observation. He called Don and told him that he was in position and described the house and its surrounding area to him. Leaving his rucksack behind and taking the Uzi, his Glock, and two hand grenades, and keeping amongst the trees, he proceeded to very carefully circle the house.

Don had found a parking area about a kilometre from the turnoff and called Gerry giving him precise directions to the parking area. Gerry was with Sam and Josh in their hire car. They had brought with them, Glocks, sub machine guns, spare mags and binoculars. It didn't take them long to meet up with Don and his people.

Back at the house, Edwards had pulled the bags off the Girls heads and said. "We are interested in one thing only, Professor Kelso's cancer cure, if you hand it over you will be let go unhurt. In the morning you will phone Dunbar and tell him to bring all your information to a location of my choosing. Should you refuse to do this you will both be killed."

Mary said, "It won't do you any good. The medical establishment don't want this cure or any others. As we have found out to our cost, they are only interested in producing treatments that people have to take for the rest of their lives. Cures are simply bad for business and the pharmaceutical companies would lose a fortune if they cured cancer. The medical profession likewise would lose fortunes, Cancer surgeons would be out of a job over night, you must remember services like the NHS are run entirely for the benefit of the staff. They couldn't care less about people. It is a worldwide problem. The medical profession, worldwide, but particularly in the developed countries, acts like a mini communist state."

Edwards said. "Be that as it may, if you want to stay alive you will do as I say. The room next door has two beds, we will put you both in there, you had better get some sleep, tomorrow is going to be a busy day. Don't try and escape, the window has bars on it and if you try to escape I will shoot you in both legs."

They moved the girls to the bedroom, it had two beds, each bed had a length of chain attached to it. The other end of each chain had an ankle cuff which was used to secure Jenna and Mary. The chain was long enough for them to move about but not long enough to reach the door or window. Like most villas in and around the Mediterranean the windows had bars on the outside.

Warren had gone full circle around the house, keeping inside the cover of the trees he could not be seen from the house, but he could see the house and noted that there were three guards watching the outside. Warren was an expert at this type of surveillance, his nickname was the Phantom and reckoned that he could creep up on anyone without being seen.

Once he was back at his original hide he reported to Don that he had now circled around the house, that there were three guards and doors at the front and back. At the back the house had an extension that protruded from the main building around 10 metres. On the side of this extension adjacent to the main building was a back door.

The guards were all armed with what looked like Uzis and looked professional in their manner and alert to their surroundings. Moving in against the house was going to be difficult due to the open lawned area surrounding it. TZero had chosen their location well.

Ninety-Five.

The sun was going down, and their only chance was to wait until it was fully dark. One of Don's people, Jed had a Sako TRG42 sniper rifle, it had a silencer, and he was a crack shot. It was felt that the best approach would be to wait until 04.00 hrs. then take out one or more of the guards, then approach the house at the run, take out any guards that were left and then assault the house. They had confirmed that including Edwards there were six of them including at least one woman. If they took out all three guards that would leave three still in the house. Ideally if they could cause some sort of diversion after taking out the guards, and once they were close enough to the house, with a bit of luck at least one of the remaining three would come out to investigate, they would dispose of him/her and then move into the house and take out the other two. They didn't know the layout of the inside of the house so they would have to play it by ear once inside.

Gerry spoke. "We brought some distress flares with us, if we let one off in the trees at the northern end of the house, the house faces west, and there are three guards on the outside, their natural reaction will be to investigate which means that they will move to the northern side."

Don spoke. "Then three of our people could move out of the trees on the western side and go directly towards the front of the house. Jed can climb one of the trees and position himself facing the northwest corner, he will be perfectly placed to take out anyone on the northern and western sides with his sniper rifle. Another two can approach from the east, if any of the guards are on the western side they can be taken out by Jed, who will remain in the trees with a silenced rifle, he is the best marksman.

Gerry and Sam will be part of the team who will attack the eastern side and head straight for the back door, The rest of us will attack the front of the house and hopefully draw those in there to the front and away from Gerry and Sam who will be coming through the back door."

They all settled in their various positions to wait until 04.00 hrs. The signal to move would be the flare going off in the trees. This would be set off by Josh who, after setting the flare off would move to the trees at the front of the house and would be available as back up to the guys going into the front.

Fortunately there was no moon so by 04.00 it was as dark as it was going to get.
Josh let off the flare in the trees, it lit up the area on the northern side and the guards, as predicted, ran to that side to see what was happening. Jed took out two of them immediately the third who had been watching the eastern side ran back to his post, he ran straight across Gerry's path, who immediately dived to the floor, the guard seeing movement to his left let loose with the Uzi, he missed as by the time he had swung round and fired Gerry was on the floor. Gerry then shot him three times and he fell to the ground dead.

Sam reached the back door at the same time and shouldered it open, this door led straight into the kitchen where the female member of Edwards' team was making herself a cup of coffee. The door suddenly opening knocked her to the floor, but she was fast and came to her feet grabbing a carving knife from a block that was on the work surface close to her. She came straight at Sam with the knife in her hand, unluckily for her Gerry was next through the door. Quickly spotting the knife in her hand he hit her in the side of the head which knocked her unconscious to the floor.

The force of his punch had in fact broken her neck and she was dead. Meanwhile on hearing all the commotion Edwards ran into the room where the girls were being held. He went straight to Mary, as he intended to use her as a shield and hostage to enable his escape, he had realised very quickly that his people were being overwhelmed and typically his first thought was self-preservation. He couldn't understand how Dunbar and Jarvis had found them so quickly. As he went to grab Mary who was sitting on her bed he made the mistake of turning his back on Jenna, who in one swift movement got the slack part of her chain around his neck and pulled hard which jerked his head back. He reached up to his neck and tried to grab the chain. As he did this, Mary stood up and kicked him as hard as she could between his legs. This had the effect of him lowering his arms to protect his crotch with his hands and he sank to his knees.

Jenna exerted all the force she could muster and twisted the chain against itself whilst putting her knee in his back pulled even harder and was stopping him breathing and at the same time the chain was cutting of the blood supply to his brain, weakening him. Mary immediately pinched his nose with her left hand which forced him to open his mouth in order to breathe. Mary started pushing the corner of a pillowcase into his mouth, his eyes were bulging, and his face was turning from red to blue, he went limp, and Jenna increased the pressure on the chain around his neck. Mary stuffed the pillowcase further down his throat and then after sixty seconds, checked his pulse. He was dead.

The door burst open, and Gerry ran in, taking in the scene before his eyes, he said to Jenna and Mary, "Are you guys Ok?"

"Yeah," and with a smile Mary said, "What took you so long, did you stop for tea on the way?"

Sam had entered the room by this time, he went straight to Mary and gave her a hug lifting her feet off the ground. Gerry was doing the same to Jenna and she said. "How about getting these chains off us."

Gerry said. "I don't know about that, I think it might be a good idea to keep you both in chains for a while," and pointing at Edwards said. "Look what you've done to this poor fellow." At which point they all burst into nervous laughter.

As Don had reached the front of the house the remaining TZero operative had come running out Uzi in hand, Don was faster and shot him in the head.

Gerry searched Edwards for the key to unlock the chains holding the girls whilst Don and the others gathered the bodies that were outside the house and took them indoors.

Don called William, brought him up to date and William said that he would arrange a clean-up operation at the house, they didn't want to leave any evidence as to what had taken place, he told Don and his people to stay at the house until the clean-up squad arrived.

Sam, Gerry, Josh and the girls all piled into the Golf and set off back to the boat, it was a bit of a crush, but no one minded after the night's events. All were mightily relieved with the thought that with luck, this whole nightmare was finally over for them.

Sam said to Mary and Jenna, "You guys did well, that was quick thinking dealing with Edwards like that."

Jenna said, "We planned it whilst we were waiting for the cavalry to arrive. We realised that once the fireworks began that, it was highly likely one of them would come into the room where we were being held and that if that person approached one of us he or she would have to turn their back on the other one, whichever that was they would wrap their chain around his neck and the one facing him would kick him hard between the legs and once he went down onto his knees that person would then pinch his nose and stuff a pillowcase into the back of his throat thereby cutting off his air supply completely. It worked a treat as you saw."

"It certainly did." Said Gerry. "Well done both of you."

"It only worked that well because Mary told me how to position the chain to have the greatest effect, once the chain was in the correct place, the restriction in the blood flow to his brain meant that his cognitive powers diminished rapidly, and he could no longer control his limbs to good effect."

Ninety-Six.

They were soon back on-board Wind charmer, all was well, and they were all mightily relieved that they could now get back to some semblance of normal.

Their intention was to sail back to Ragusa, leave the boat there where it could be kept an eye on by Piero's people. Then they would all return to the UK, sort out their affairs, Gerry and Jenna would sell the garage, Sam would put his farm and other holdings up for sale, they would then return to the boat and continue their cruise around the Eastern Med.

Before doing that, with William and Carmichael's help Mary would put her cure for Cancer up for final approval with the health service and oversee it being put into full production and rolled out at cost to the cancer sufferers worldwide. There was no one left to stop her as anyone who could have done was either dead or in custody. Those in custody wouldn't be seeing the light of day for years to come, if ever. Unknown to them at this time was the fact that Norman had siphoned off a billion dollars into a Swiss numbered account to fund getting Mary's cure out into the public domain where it could be used to help cancer sufferers worldwide.

The big pharmaceutical companies would for now be taken into state ownership, until the extent of the corruption and theft of taxpayers money on both sides of the Atlantic was known, and all the perpetrators had been taken out of the picture. No one was under any illusion that the uncontrolled greed that had led to this state of affairs in the first place wouldn't rear its ugly head again, but with luck and some clever legislation it could be stopped from getting out of control again. The same would be done to the Tech giants, they would be broken up and sold with legislation brought in to ensure that no single person could become so rich and powerful as to be able to even attempt to try to do this kind of thing again.

Mainstream media would be legislated in order that no one single individual or company would be allowed to own more than one periodical or TV news outlet. And laws would be introduced that would stop any owner having editorial control, they could own it and reap the benefit of the profits generated but they could not exert editorial control to further their own personal agenda.

It was all going to take some time, and some very grown up and well thought out legislation. Those with vested interests would not be allowed to lobby or influence law makers. It was a big call but with older and wiser heads leading the changes, it stood some chance of success. Only time would tell.

The NHS was being overhauled from the top down and bottom up, the bureaucracy that had done so much damage was stripped out with a new system in place that not only admitted mistakes but crucially learned from them and put those lessons into action. Whistle blowers were encouraged, and it became a criminal offence to engage in a cover up. In short the NHS would no longer be able to kill or maim people with impunity as it had been doing for decades and getting away with it. Forensic accountants were trawling through their accounts going back over decades and with the information that Norman had supplied they were quickly able to see where the various frauds had been taking place.

Ninety-Seven.

In another part of the world, Putin and his Chinese counterpart were engaged in what they thought was a highly secure and encrypted telephone conversation. They were both speaking English.

Putin said. "We almost got away with it this time, someone managed to crack Towersoft's system and bring the whole thing crashing down."

Xi said, "We have lost most of the 'useful idiots' that we have spent the best part of thirty years recruiting and bending to our will. It looks like we will have to start again."

Putin said, "We have also lost a huge amount of money that again has taken thirty years to amass. That is a major blow to our plans."

Xi said, "We will soon be able to make that money back, by robbing the West of even more. Do any of your people know to who or where that money went?"

"No but we are working on it."

Then another voice cut into the conversation, it was a very English voice, "I wouldn't recommend that course of action gentlemen."

Both were stunned, they were speaking on what they thought was the most secure telephone line in the world.

Putin was the first to speak, "Who are you and how did you cut into this line?"

"Neither of those things are relevant, all you need to know is that I can hack into your conversations any time I want. At the moment I have control of all your satellite controls and your defence systems."

He turned in his chair and gave Norman a nod, who in turn pressed a half dozen keys on his keyboard and nodded back to Carmichael with a smile.

He went on, "I suggest you check, whilst I stay on the line."

They didn't have to, phones were ringing on both leader's desks. On answering both were told the same thing, that they had lost control of their respective defence and satellite systems.

Both told their operatives to trace whoever had hacked their telephone line. They were wasting their time.

Carmichael continued, "I can do this anytime that I choose, therefore I have a suggestion to make."

Xi said, "And what is that. Bear in mind that we will find out who you are and then you will be dealt with."

"I very much doubt that, but you are welcome to try."

Putin said. "What is your suggestion?"

"That is quite simple, you both stop this nonsense now. Should you continue I will take over your systems again, without warning and fire a nuclear missile from each of your countries at the other. Neither of you will be able to stop this happening as I will have control of both your respective missile and defence systems. The rest of the world will believe that you have gone to war with each other, and you will both bear the blame. Consider the ramifications of this and you will see that personally you will both be finished, and your respective countries will become pariah states. It will set you back decades. No one will want to do business with either of your countries for many years to come. Do I make myself clear? You will also drastically reduce the number of your countrymen who are attending universities in the west, starting today, I will be monitoring this and if you fail to comply, retribution will be swift and without any kind of warning."

Both were fuming and making all sorts of threats about it but knew in their heart of hearts that given the ease with which their systems had been taken over, there was absolutely nothing either of them could do about it. They had no choice but to comply.

They both agreed and Putin said, "We will find you."

Carmichael said, "Good luck with that gentlemen. There is however one more thing. There are certain individuals, I won't name them as you know exactly who I am talking about. You have tried several times to kill them. Should anything happen to any of these people I will take control of your systems again and then launch a missile at each one of you. In short you will both be killed, wherever you are." And with that he severed the connection.

Both Putin and Xi charged their respective intelligence services to trace where the interruption had come from, to no avail. They would spend years trying to identify the Englishman but were destined to fail.

They both realised that they were powerless in these circumstances and resolved that they would just have to live with it.

Ninety-Eight.

After taking the boat to Ragusa, Gerry and the others all returned to the UK. Sam and Mary were married and with the others, and all those who had been involved, threw a massive party.

Piero rewarded Francisco and his brother by purchasing for them a brand new 75-foot fishing boat.

Gerry, Jenna, Sam and Mary having disposed of their assets returned to Ragusa to continue their travels with a promise from Josh that he would join them the moment that he had settled all his affairs in the UK.

Gerry standing on the aft deck of Wind Charmer put his arm around Jenna and said, "I wonder how long it will be before another lunatic comes along who wants to rule the world?

Jenna said. "One things for sure, it will happen again."

Printed in Dunstable, United Kingdom